Ghost Light

Ghost Light

LeeAnne Hansen

SANDI x,
I LOOK FORWARD TO
MEETING YOU!

xox,

Special thanks to Marissa, for dancing out of my life and into my book, my director Stuart for inspiring me to always look deeper, and to Karin and Stephanie for always being there.

And a very extra special thanks to my lovely editors Samantha Bolton and Carolyn Grogan—wine and martinis soon coming your way!

ACT I

'Love looks not with the eyes, but with the mind.
And therefore is winged cupid painted blind.'

—William Shakespeare

Devon slammed his glass down onto the wooden desk, sloshing whiskey onto his hand.

His demeanor changed from anger to pain so suddenly that Katherine caught her breath. He kept his back to her–causing her a brief moment of concern–his words almost lost as he spoke softly. "You've come here only to tell me that you are marrying Jeffery?"

She needed him to turn around. On cue, he did.

His dark brown hair, combed back so elegantly earlier, had since broken free and fallen over his even darker, ravenous eyes. He was her definition of handsome. Katherine felt she was losing herself, perhaps as he just had. This was turning out to be a most unusual night.

"Was there no other reason?" he continued, his eyes pleading now, almost begging.

Katherine broke her gaze from his, knowing that she could not speak while looking at him. "No, my lord, none of importance. I should have sent word. I am sorry; I should never have come."

Feeling the need to escape, Katherine walked toward the door, for how else would he follow?

"I love you!" Devon commanded.

She stopped dead.

"Does that not mean anything to you?" he challenged.

Katherine turned to face him as he approached. Her words struggled over a pounding heart and a shortness of breath. "Yes, it does. It means the world to me."

"Then why in hell would you agree to marry Jeffrey?" The force of his words caused her to take a step back.

"I have been promised to him since I was a little girl." She lowered her head meekly. "I would have to be foolish to believe I could ever have something more."

"Be foolish. Believe."

She looked up at him, her eyes filled with pain. "I would surrender my family, my dowry, my title. To live with you would be a bittersweet bliss, a subtle misery that would always be there. I don't want that; you don't want me like—"

"I will be damned if you are going to tell me what I do or do not want!" He cut her off, grabbing her roughly by the arms. She could feel the heat emanating from him. "I want you! To hell with everything else!"

She smelled the sour whiskey on his breath.

"Damn the engagement, damn your family, damn the dowry!" he shouted. "*My family* has thrived for decades, and as for your name, you will be sharing mine!" He shouted so convincingly that she very nearly believed him.

Katherine opened her mouth to speak, but he was so close she could think of nothing else but her ache for him.

He spoke for her.

"You are mine!" He pulled her tighter. "I have owned you since the first time I saw you."

There was always a warm rush when she knew she was about to be kissed. Her body tingled as his scent fogged her mind.

His eyes sparkled with a hint of mischief as his breath slowed. "I will make it so that you never utter another man's name again."

Katherine smiled, knowing he had won, like he did every night. But then, so had she.

"Try," she challenged, seductively.

The word was barely out of her mouth when he drew her into a passionate kiss. Her hand wandered up to run through his hair, as his slowly drifted down her back.

I love this, she thought, as the magic of the moment flowed through her body. Time seemed to stand still as it did every night at this time. She cherished this moment, this kiss, this intimacy. For her, nothing else mattered.

If only it were real.

Then the lights fell to black.

And the curtain dropped.

Fiona blushed as she broke free from the entanglement, stumbling away from Patrick in the darkness of the stage. She had hardly caught her breath when the roar of applause shattered what was left of their moment.

The audience stood in an ovation as the house lights rose to reveal the two actors trying to restore their true identities.

Patrick grabbed Fiona's hand and swept her into a bow.

"You played well tonight, Lady Katherine," he whispered as he let go of her hand.

Fiona bowed again. "I tasted *real* whiskey on your lips, a tasty surprise."

Straightening, Patrick leaned over and kissed her on her cheek.

"I'm full of surprises," he whispered.

"So I'm beginning to understand, Mister Berenger," Fiona grinned. As the curtain fell, her cheeks burned once more.

"Until we meet again, Miss Corrigan," Patrick whispered from the darkness.

* * *

Fiona stopped just outside of the Madog Pub—one of many the quaint Welsh town of Llandrindod had to offer—to catch a glimpse of her reflection in the window. Her long, light brown, curly hair was perfectly in place, falling down her back with just a few rebellious strands to frame her face and, combined with just a touch of freshly-applied make-up, she thought with a wry grin, that her reflection looked younger than her twenty-six years. Although normally modest, she was quite pleased with her appearance.

She had remained behind to prepare for this evening. The dress she chose fit tight, highlighting her figure, and was cut low enough to reveal just the right amount of mystery.

Patrick would be sure to notice.

Patrick did notice. He was chatting with the other actors when he spotted Fiona just outside the pub, looking in at them. He waved to her, but she didn't wave back. She appeared transfixed. Then he realized that she was not looking in, she was looking at her own reflection. He smiled. Well, if she was going to stand there staring at herself, he might as well too.

Patrick found Fiona to be quite a contradiction: fragile of beauty, yet tenacious of spirit. On stage she could be either a wildcat or house cat, whatever the scene called for, but in private she maintained a quiet reserve, although lately even a blind man could see that she was romantically interested in him. Normally he would have no problem taking her to his bed. He had had no shortage of women in any fashion of beds, but there was something about Fiona that kept him from moving forward.

She had an intangible quality that elicited something in Patrick that he had never felt from a woman before. Lately, he was finding it harder to break from their staged grasps. He had held himself back so many nights from going to her, for reasons he couldn't even fathom. Fiona could easily be seduced, he was sure of that. She advertised it in many ways; the blithe way she moved, the perfumed breath of her lilting voice, the truth in her smile. She would easily fall to him, fall for him, and that terrified him. He had some unusual yearning to confess his life and motivations to her, before he could seduce her. And that would send him down a path he did not want to follow. Perhaps it was not Fiona at all that frightened him, but himself.

"Check out little Alice at the looking glass," Gavin Shepard laughed, interrupting Patrick's thoughts.

Patrick nodded. "She is beautiful."

Fiona was startled to find her own eyes staring back at her. How long had she been looking at her reflection in the window? She stifled an embarrassed laugh at her vanity, but none-the-less glanced one more time at her reflection before reaching for the door and pulling it open.

Stepping inside, Fiona was greeted by a warm fire and the aroma of beer, whiskey and cigarettes. It was a small, comforting pub, with an ancient wooden horseshoe bar where normally a dozen people sat, but tonight, it was nearly empty. There were five or six tables scattered about the room. Despite the dim light, there was no mistaking that the raucous laughter coming from the far corner was her acting troupe. They had pushed two tables together with the only open seat next to Patrick.

Perfect.

As she approached, Fiona realized that the laughter seemed to be directed at her. Fiona checked herself, frantically. She found nothing off with her appearance, but the cause of the laughter was soon apparent.

"Ah! Young Alice! Our beloved actress of the looking glass," roared Gavin. Fiona had known the young actor who played Jeffery tonight for over six years and was no longer surprised by his natural talent to blurt out whatever he was thinking.

"Looking glass?" Fiona glanced about the room to discover that the window in which she had been checking her reflection was directly across from them! She had unknowingly captured herself an audience.

"Oh lord! I–I had no idea ... " she stammered, embarrassed. This was not the kind of entrance she had planned.

"Come now, Fiona," Patrick said, his eyes twinkling in the candlelight, "for the briefest moment we learned what it would be like to possess your mirror. I, for one, am envious." His gaze lingered over her dress.

Fiona blushed slightly, whether it was the embarrassment of what had just happened or the way Patrick was looking at her, she wasn't sure. She made her way to the empty chair next to him, pleased with his compliment. Unlike Gavin, Patrick had a knack for saying precisely the right thing at the right moment.

Samuel smiled over at her as she sat. "Aye lass! Everyone appreciates a pretty face in a window. I know of no man worth his salt that would tell you different." Samuel McDermott was the ultimate Scotsman. A bear of a man, he had unkempt red curls, an enormous bushy beard, brilliant blue eyes, and a face littered with freckles. He always wore his tartan kilt, regardless of the weather.

Fiona always thought of Samuel as a Viking who had lost his place in time. While his appearance could be quite intimidating, Fiona knew of no one that could build sets, hang lights, pull ropes, and play the villain as he did. Since he was too late to by centuries to rape and pillage, raising and razing sets, combined with occasional moments of villainy, seemed to quell his Viking urges nicely.

"Skol!" Samuel called out in toast.

Samuel and Gavin slammed their glasses together and downed the contents.

"Oy! Why are you leaving me out?" demanded Abigail, as she held up her empty glass, pouting like a three-year-old.

Abigail McGauligh was a simple kind of pretty in an overflowing package. She enjoyed life and men to the fullest, but was modest in her acting talents. Abigail was content to make costumes and perform the occasional small role with the fewest lines possible. She and Fiona were thick as thieves with no jealousy between them at all. Although Abigail was a few years younger than Fiona, Fiona was pleased to have a female ear to talk to and Abigail was always happy to listen.

"Not so, Abby," said Gavin. "We were just trying to catch up to you is all."

"Oh, were you?" Abigail said with a hint of mischief. "Then I better go and get another round for everyone." And with that she made her way to the bar.

"There's a good girl!" Patrick called out after her.

He looks so handsome tonight, Fiona thought. The gel in his hair had been washed away and his black curls were spilling out in such a way that his dark eyes flashed in the light. His voice was lower than usual, casting a beckoning tone that hinted to any listener that a most amazing story could fall from his lips at any moment.

"You caught me tonight, Fiona," Patrick said, leaning over conspiratorially. "I thought maybe a wee dram of the peat to ward off the winter chill might also enhance my performance," he grinned. "It certainly brought something out in you."

"You are always most talented once whiskey is in play, my lord," Fiona teased.

Patrick laughed. "All joking aside, I do believe that this was our best performance yet."

"The last performance in a town is generally the best," Gavin butted in.

Fiona nodded in agreement. "Especially when it's *the* final curtain." Over her years of acting she had discovered that the first show was plagued with rockiness, the second to last cursed with minor things going wrong, and the last was always the best.

"It's a shame that we are ending this run," Gavin said. Suddenly, his voice dropped in register, his face darkened as a creepy version of Jeffery's persona declared: "I grew rather fond of Jeffery and his cowardly, despicable, evil ways."

Unnerved, the table went silent for a moment.

"I, for one, am relieved to see the end of that bastard," Patrick announced jollily. "Although I did best him every night and always won the lady's heart."

He grabbed Fiona's hand in his and squeezed it.

"I, too, am ready for the next one," growled Samuel, the flickering flames from the hearth made his hair look as if it were on fire. "Hopefully a villain will be needed and perhaps a clashing of swords! I'm tired of moving lights and pulling curtains. I want to be evil!"

"What? No desire to play the love interest to a buxom bar wench?" Abigail asked, arriving with pints of ale for the whole table. She threw her shoulders back, emphasizing her swelling bosom. "You'd rather play with swords than with these?"

She was the only one who could redden Samuel's face. She was also the only one who dared tease him mercilessly and come away from it unscathed.

"Aye, Abby, you do have quite a pair," stuttered Samuel. "I just miss playing me self is all."

Samuel didn't realize his faux pas until the entire table erupted in laughter. He ignored them and sheepishly passed around the drinks. Abigail patted his shoulder as she squeezed by to take her seat.

"What should we toast to?" asked Gavin.

"Surely the show and how wonderful it was?" suggested Fiona.

"No, we drink to that every night," Gavin shook his head.

"How about to the pretty face in the window," Patrick nodded to Fiona.

"To a pretty face in the window," they said in unison. Fiona found herself blushing as they clanked glasses all around.

Soon they fell to stories of various plays done before they found each other. Abigail described an embarrassing costume malfunction before she had mastered the art of proper pinning; Samuel told of an overly enthusiastic sword fight that scarred his upper right arm; Patrick's story involved falling off the stage in Dublin and into the waiting arms of a rather large and very happy woman; and Gavin reminisced of performing *Trojan Women* with Fiona, the first play they had performed together.

"Was Fiona a good Helen?" Patrick asked.

"'And Cypris if he deemed her loveliest beyond all heavens, made dreams about my face. And for her grace gave me. Indeed she was. And lo! Her face was judged the fairest and she stood above those twain,'" Gavin quoted.

"And I'd still judge her the fairest," Patrick interrupted.

Gavin appeared a bit peeved as he added, "Fiona stepped into that role as if it had been waiting for her."

"I thought I played her rather well," Fiona replied modestly, pleased with Patrick's compliment while also surprised that Gavin could recite *her* lines from so long ago. Helen's powerful strength of character was something Fiona hoped she had somehow managed to instill in herself these past three years. It had been the last play her father had seen her in before he passed. He had been so proud of her.

"I would like to have seen you in that role," Patrick slurred. He had continued to pound down whiskey and was now quite drunk. "Not a good show for me, no strong male leads, but you must have taken the audience's breath away."

Gavin bristled at the obvious jab, but said nothing.

"I tried my best," Fiona said.

"I am sure you did," Patrick said, as he leaned in closer. "Pretty Fiona, you do make the male audience crave you nightly," Patrick grinned wickedly, as his left hand, hidden under the table, slid to her leg.

Fiona's intake of breath was surely a give-away that something was going on, but the others couldn't see and besides, they were too drunk to notice or care.

Fiona's excitement grew. Patrick was about to say what she'd been longing to hear, she was sure of it. His breath tickled her ear as he whispered, "Lady Katherine, I have an urgent matter that concerns only you."

"And what might that be?" Fiona whispered back, her voice unsteady with desire, remembering how he had grabbed her in his arms on stage.

He leaned in closer, his lips brushed her ear, his breath unsteady as he asked, "What did you think of me tonight? I tried to play it much bigger. Was it too much?"

Fiona's heart sank. Surely he was he kidding! How did it even matter? This was the last night and then they were off to a new town and a new show.

She turned to face him in disbelief. He gazed back, waiting for her reply, totally sincere, no hint of mischief.

"You were wonderful, as always. I did notice your changes and I thought it added more depth," she sighed, defeated.

Patrick lit up. "You honestly think so?"

"I do," Fiona nodded. And with that his hand fell from her leg taking Fiona's hopes for the night with it.

Just then, as if they had known to come to the rescue, the director, Nicholas Ashbury, and their playwright, Andrew Wade, entered the pub.

"'Elo, gang," said Andrew, flashing a boyish grin at them. Although slightly over twenty-two-years old, his appearance was that of a young bespectacled child with clear blue eyes, unruly blond hair and no sense of fashion. Andrew made up for his boyish looks in his writing; his depth of wisdom spoke of an ancient soul. He looked at the same world as everyone else, yet he'd see something inspiring in people and places and could jot it down in the most amazing words. The audience fell in love with his characters, and Fiona was grateful to have the honor of portraying them.

"'Elo, Andrew," Abigail purred. "Why don't you sit beside me?"

"There's not a chair there, Abby," he replied.

Abigail rose, undaunted. "Why don't you lads go and pull up another table and chairs. Samuel, would you be a love and grab some pints?"

Samuel gladly complied and made his way to the bar. Patrick and Gavin went to find a table and some more chairs. Abigail winked at Andrew and urged him into the newly vacant seat beside her.

Nicholas took Gavin's seat directly across from Fiona.

"You really shone tonight, Fiona," said Nicholas.

"Thank you. It's your words that inspire me," she replied.

"You give me way too much credit; it is you actors that make *me* look good," countered Nicholas.

Nicholas had long been a hero to Fiona. He was, indeed, the best director she had ever had the privilege of working for. His method of direction and innovative staging was a complete rarity. She believed him to be in his early forties. His brown hair and beard was sprinkled with gray, but she thought it portrayed wisdom, and his demeanor was that of a pure gentleman, even if he was an American. Nicholas fought in England during the

Great War and decided to stay on. He talked little of the experience but hinted he was involved in intelligence of some kind. Everyone was entitled to his or her mysteries.

Soon they were all settled in with pints in hand and drinking to a fine closing night. Gavin called out, "To a pretty face in a window," but the joke was lost on the two new arrivals.

"So, what kept you two?" asked Abigail.

"We were going over the particulars for the next play in Edinburgh," Nicholas replied.

"It's my latest one," announced Andrew, a look of triumph on his face.

"Is there a villain?" asked Samuel, hopefully.

"Aye, that there is, a real beast of a man. There is also a dangerous love triangle for our lovely Fiona, Patrick and Gavin to take on."

"And what of me?" asked Abigail.

Andrew turned to her with a slight grin. "Actually, the love triangle is more of a square. Abigail you're to play Patrick's wife who dies tragically at the beginning, leaving him believing he will never love again. Thus begins his journey for vengeance for your death."

"I get to die!" squealed Abigail with delight. "I've always wanted to die! I hope the audience cries!"

"Do I achieve my vengeance?" asked Patrick. His eyes had begun to gleam with the promise of a new character.

Fiona hoped there was a lot of kissing in the script. She was almost resigned to believe it would be the only intimacy she was going to get from Patrick. *Almost*. She was not quite ready to give up completely.

"Forget about the script." Andrew waved off any more inquiries. "Tonight we drink!"

Although they were used to this, the actors murmured their half-hearted disappointment. Andrew never liked to reveal too much of a story, preferring to witness the cast reading it cold, while making final notes.

A sudden chill swept over Fiona. Shivering, she instinctively leaned into Patrick. Patrick put his arm around her and drew her closer to him, without thought or hesitation. She enjoyed the warmth of his body, feeling hope rise again. Hearing footsteps she looked up to discover a man approaching the table.

He was a tall, gaunt, balding man dressed in black. His face was pale and unattractive. He wore a long coat that swept about him as he walked. He carried a small dark envelope, which he opened as he arrived at the front of the table. He withdrew two parchment letters from inside the envelope, each with a blood red wax seal.

He looked the group over then asked wearily, "Which of you is Patrick Berenger?"

"Aye, that would be me," replied Patrick with a wave of his hand.

The stranger scrutinized him for a long moment, before allowing his gaze to move to Fiona. The stranger studied her as if memorizing her face or trying to recall where he had seen her. She snuggled deeper into Patrick's arms.

The stranger abruptly returned his attention to Patrick and held out one of the letters. Patrick pulled away from her to take the parchment.

"Nicholas Ashbury?" the stranger asked the group.

"Right in front of you," Nicholas replied, taking the second parchment.

"What's this all about?" asked Andrew.

The mysterious messenger ignored Andrew. He turned and strode away, his coat sweeping behind him like a black wing.

Fiona felt the chill once more as the door opened. She glanced at Patrick, seeking his warmth. Patrick had gone almost completely white as he stared at the parchment.

The explosive cough of an automobile starting up outside broke the silence.

"Did someone die?" asked Gavin, bluntly. They all had begun to think the same thing but were too afraid to ask. Patrick didn't answer.

"No," replied Nicholas, "it seems we have just received an invitation."

"An invitation?" repeated Gavin.

"*We?*" Abigail asked. "Who? All of us?"

"To a céilidh?" asked Samuel, hopefully.

"I don't know. It doesn't actually say." Nicholas passed the parchment to Andrew. "See what you can make of it."

Andrew took the parchment and after glancing it over, began to read it aloud: "'Nicholas Ashbury and troupe are hereby invited to Loglinmooth on the thirteenth of this month to attend to a matter of great importance and mutual benefit. All travel and lodging has been paid in full, and you will find train tickets under your names at the train station. The train will leave at seven-thirty in the AM, tomorrow. Make sure to be on it.'" Andrew moved the parchment closer to his face and squinted. "It's not signed."

Fiona again glanced at Patrick; he was still staring at his parchment.

"Does yours say the same thing?" she asked.

Patrick came out of his trance and stared up at them. He had sobered up quickly, and his eyes had lost the sparkle they had earlier.

"No. I have been summoned to be in attendance at some legal matter," he replied, vaguely.

"Do you know of this town, *Loganmouth*?" Nicholas asked, butchering the pronunciation with his American tongue.

"*Loglinmooth*," Patrick corrected him. "Yes. I grew up there, but I left many years ago," he replied darkly.

Fiona glanced over at the letter.

"Who is Sean?" she asked.

Patrick snatched the letter away from her sight and rose angrily.

"He's nobody," Patrick growled, then stormed off.

Fiona had seen him angry many times before, but that was always on stage. This sudden real darkness frightened and worried her.

"What do we do?" Andrew asked, breaking the silence.

"We go," Nicholas said. "I have no idea what this is about, but since we aren't needed in Edinburgh until the twentieth, and everything is paid for, we can have a nice little holiday."

* * *

In another town, in another theater far away, the ghost light's flame went out as if by a soft whisper. The theater was now pitch black. Restlessness awakened the quelled.

She shuddered awake.

The darkness unnerved her. It made her feel uneasy and alone.

Disoriented, she glided out from behind the curtain over to the sleeping body of a man, a bottle of Laphroaig whiskey clasped close to his chest.

She stood over him,.

Who was this intruder?

She studied him, searching her memory. He was handsome, tall and wiry, with dark unruly hair and a well-kept beard. She leaned in closer; his soft breathing warmed her coldness.

She stared into his closed eyes ...

They opened.

"AHHH!" Both equally startled.

Sean Berenger backed up hard against the wall he was propped against, his whiskey bottle tumbling to the floor. She faded back into the darkness. He looked around. No trace of anyone or anything.

"A dream," he laughed softly, unconvinced. "I'm such a child I spook myself with nightmares." Then he noticed that the glass-enclosed candle perched on the tall, metal stand in the center of the stage had gone out.

"The light, shite." He tried to push himself up, but his hand slipped on the spilled whiskey. "Arggg," he swore sadly. "No cause for this kind of tragedy." He reached around and found the bottle. He could tell by its weight that it was now nearly empty. "Damn."

A sudden crash from behind the curtain caused him to jump again.

"Who's there?" he cried, standing up. No answer. He held the bottle out like a weapon as he made his way to the curtain. He paused, his hand on the heavy satin cloth, his breathing fast and nervous. He pulled aside the curtain, and could barely make out a still, pale shape, several feet in front of him.

"Who are you? What do you want?" His voice did not betray the nervousness he felt. The shape remained silent and motionless.

"Speak!"

No response. Sean fumbled in his pocket for a match. He struck it against the wooden floor. It sparked into life. He held it out in a shaking hand to reveal ... a dressmaker's dummy standing mutely in front of him.

"Jesus, Mary, and Joseph, you frightened the piss out of me." He breathed a sigh of relief. His match went out just as the dummy fell forward and crashed to the floor.

"Christ!" he scrambled back and out through the curtain. He stumbled to the center of the stage and struck another match. He lit the candle. The ghost light sent the shadows scrambling back into the darkness.

All was calm and quiet.

He bowed and left the stage.

A soft sigh from the darkness could barely be discerned.

Sean made his way to the lobby. He did not believe in spirits or superstitions or other such bunk, unlike many of the foolish theater folk he despised. He especially did not believe in the ghost light; a single light meant to keep the theater ghosts at bay. *Superstitious idiots!* No, not him, although it did seem practical to keep a light burning so as not to trip around on the stage in the dark. Which is why, and only why, he had decided it was best to keep this one burning.

Sean pulled the heavy rope that lowered a trap door from the ceiling. A casing of wooden stairs unfolded and dropped down leading to his room above. He stared up into the blackness, hesitating for a moment before climbing unsteadily to his bed.

* * *

The acting troupe stood alone at the Llandrindod train station at that cold, early morning hour. Their bags were piled on the empty platform; there wasn't a train in sight. They stomped feet and huddled arms, miserable with too little sleep and hangovers. Fiona stood alone, longing to share Patrick's warmth, but he remained as distant as when he left the pub.

Nicholas was talking to an ancient man in the cramped ticket agent's booth. He looked as cold and miserable as the lot of them. And true to the gaunt stranger's word, a packet of tickets was waiting for them in Nicholas's name.

"Where's the train?" Nicholas asked.

"Aye, she'll be here. *The Luna Express* don't run often, but she always runs on time," the ticket-taker said. Nicholas quelled the need to point out that 'she' was late now, and asked instead, "*The Luna Express*? That's an odd name for a train."

"Not so odd," the man countered. "She's numbered sixteen forty-nine."

The man's logic made no sense to Nicholas. Perhaps it was a Welsh thing?

"Aye, and she's the only train that will make this run," the old man continued. "Not many trains will chance the highlands this time of year. Especially not to Loglinmooth."

"Why not?"

"Loglinmooth is a queer place."

"How so?" asked Nicholas, but he was drowned out by the chugging of a steam engine coming around the bend. It was a quaint old train; number '1649' painted brightly on the polished black steam engine pulling five cars. She pulled into the station and exhaled a billow of white steam across the platform.

"All aboard!" McElroy, a taciturn, ruddy Irish conductor called out even before the train had come to a complete halt. He was on the station in a wink, grabbing bags and hurrying everyone aboard.

"Don't we have to wait for the others?" Fiona asked, as McElroy grabbed her bags and led her to the first car.

"Ain't be no others wanting to go to Loglinmooth," McElroy explained with little patience. "And we need to hurry, to keep on schedule."

Nicholas stepped up alongside them. "Oh, do you have a lot of stops to make?"

"No stops," McElroy said, practically pushing Nicholas on board. "This is an express."

When they were all aboard, McElroy signaled the engineer. *The Luna Express* took off in a cloud of steam.

The troupe settled in for the long journey. Thankfully the train was well heated, and the rhythmic chugging sent most of them to sleep almost immediately.

* * *

Sunlight streaming in through his window warmed his face and made his head ache.

"Ach. Go away," Sean grumbled, covering his head with a blanket.

He was in a sour mood and no amount of brilliant sunlight was going to change that. Early winter in the Highlands meant a late rising sun and an early falling night. The days were very short, sometimes with only six or seven hours of daylight. For the sun to be this high in the sky meant it was late morning already. Sean knew he had to face the day and his hangover and get up.

He flung the sheets off with a vengeance and lay on his back blinking painfully at the ceiling, trying to recall what had happened last night. His memory was fuzzy. He had had a strange dream but couldn't recall it completely. There was something to do with the stage and the ghost light and a woman ...

Sean climbed out of bed, pulling his half removed trousers back on. He searched the cupboards and found an old tin of coffee. Opening it he found a handful of stale coffee grounds and poured those into a battered kettle, added some water, and turned the stove on underneath it. He dropped onto the wooden kitchen chair and stared at the dull, metal finish of the pot and the bluish flame beneath it.

Sean didn't believe in living in the past; as a matter of fact he had done his best to erase it, yet, the bony-faced stranger in black had somehow found him, even after he had gone to such pains to stay undiscovered.

The stranger had said very little; he had just handed him the summons and walked away, humming some dreadful tune. Sean had left for Loglinmooth immediately. He soon discovered that it was not an easy journey to make. Few seemed inclined to offer passage, regardless of the fee. He wasn't sure why he had been summoned, but he did know that there was one last painful mystery waiting to be solved and that he would never be free until it was. It was a mystery he dreaded facing.

"I have a very bad feeling about this," he said to the flickering blue flame.

The coffee was beginning to boil. He rubbed his eyes and stared balefully around. He let out a low, extended sigh. He rose, went to the cupboard, found a chipped cup and poured the coffee into it. He took a sip and grimaced.

"God awful!" He looked around for something to kill the taste. One of the bottles of scotch from last night lay on the floor. He poured what little remained of it into his cup and tried the coffee. Again he grimaced.

"Ach. Not good, but a wee bit better."

* * *

Trains fascinated Andrew, which was why he had climbed his way over the coal car into the noisy steam engine cab to speak with the engineer.

They had left Llandrindod far behind, and were chugging through the bleak darkness of barren Scottish landscape by the light of a three-quarter moon.

The engineer made an adjustment to slow the train for an upcoming curve that preceded a steep climb up a narrow passage through the hills.

"More heat!" he yelled to the fireman. "We got a hill to climb!"

"Aye," the fireman growled, as he shoveled coal into the furnace.

"Now, what were you saying, lad?"

"Loglinmooth. What's so strange about it?" Andrew repeated.

"I take it you never been?" he asked, squinting ahead through the smoke.

"No. Never even heard of it," Andrew nodded. "Should I have?"

"Nah. No reason ever to talk about it." Then added, as a chilling warning, "It's a dangerous place."

"Dangerous? How?" Andrew pried.

"Aaah ... " The engineer spat out the window. "Forget it. Just old lady gossip is all." He grew angry. "I just don't like making this trip is all. Bad things happen on this line."

"Why?" asked Andrew.

"It's a private line, for one," the engineer began.

"Private line? What's that mean?"

"That means it's off our normal route. Someone's paying a fair amount of quid to run your little gang up into the far highlands. That's why you're the only passengers."

"Who's paying for it?" asked Andrew.

"Don't know," the engineer shook his head. "A queer looking gent showed up with an envelope and instructions to take the lot of you up to Loglinmooth. Plenty of bob inside the envelope to keep me from asking any questions." He spat again.

"You said this was a private line?"

"Aye. Some rich lord installed these rails for his own amusement quite a time back. It's a detour from any normal route and a dead-end. There's no switching, we got to back down the steep hillsides for a good three miles before we can get on a main line and turn around."

Andrew nodded. "So it's a lot of work?"

"Aye, and it's a dangerous ride this time of year."

"How so?" Andrew asked. As a writer he was always looking for inspiration, and he was getting an earful from this character and from the train ride in general.

Perhaps a mystery play next? Maybe, even, aboard a train?

Andrew had just read Agatha Christie's 'The Mysterious Affair at Styles' and thoroughly enjoyed it. He was looking forward to reading more of her work, and hoped she would continue writing. He was so into his own thoughts he missed some of what the engineer was saying.

" ... tracks not maintained, with this storm coming in we're going to have to be very cautious. This trip will take a while. You best take some rest."

"How about you? There's only the three of you aboard the train. Do you get a break?"

"There's no rest for the wicked," the engineer blasted the lonesome steam whistle out over the moors. "I'll rest once we get the hell out of Loglinmooth."

* * *

Sean stalked up the barren hillside toward Thornbury Castle. The tiny village of Loglinmooth lay spread out below him like so many huddled birds. The only three distinctive buildings from this distance were the theater, the pub, and the church. He despised them all, well perhaps not the pub so much, he acquiesced.

Sean completed the climb and was surprised to find himself winded. As a boy, he and his brother would challenge race up to the castle, while their father made his slow and steady pace way below them.

The castle walls still stood strong, although the surrounding walls enclosing the overgrown, tangled garden were knocked down in places.

"I'm a crumbled ruin me' self," he said aloud, taking a seat on a pile of rocks that was once the retaining wall around the garden.

"Aye, you're not so old," came a voice from somewhere behind him. "And this place is far from ruined."

An ancient man, weathered and torn by wind and sorrow, appeared from behind the garden wall. He held a handful of ratty looking, yellow flowers.

"Tormentils," he said, misinterpreting Sean's stare. The old man smelled the flowers. "Amazing to find them so late in the year. A brilliant bit of life still kicking in the decaying season. Much like me, I should say," he laughed.

"I'm sorry. Who are you?" Sean asked.

"I know who I am!" The man was insulted by the question, but his anger disappeared as quickly as it appeared. He sat down on the broken wall beside Sean. He seemed fascinated by the flowers he carried. His wrinkled fingers caressed and brushed them delicately as he spoke.

"The 'Hammer of the Scots' he was called back then. King Edward the First, always scheming with the Knights Templar, always attacking the Welch ... not well loved, I can tell you, still he fought with Robert the Bruce against us Scots until his death at Burgh-By-Sands. King Edward requested his bones be carried on into Scotland to continue the fight. No one knows where they ended up, but it makes a great tale, eh?"

Sean stared at the old man.

The man rose and started walking toward the castle.

"My granddad used to tell me those stories. I'd hunt all over the castle looking for the Hammer of the Scots' bones," he chuckled. "Skeletons in closets aplenty, but no bones."

"Where are you going?" Sean called out to the retreating figure.

"Home," the old man called back. "Come, if you like. I'll put the kettle on." He continued talking as he walked off. "Speaking of skeletons, the great Lord Richard of Thornbury is buried just beneath your muddy feet."

Sean looked down to discover he was in fact walking on a faded headstone, now lying flat on the ground. He noticed that there were scores of semi-buried rocks around them, some leaning upright, others fallen flat, most of the engravings long since rubbed away by wind and rain. They must be walking through the Thornbury family burial ground.

"Careful not to step on my grave," the old man chuckled, unperturbed, as he continued on his way. "I'll be needing it soon enough."

He was quite nimble for his age, and Sean strained to keep up with him as he followed, gingerly avoiding the resting bodies beneath his feet.

"They say Lord Richard was a profound lover of all theatrics, both from the royal family and the stage. Of course this was a good three hundred years before Shakespeare put quill to paper. This area was once quite famous for its theater. Yes. Yes. Quite famous indeed ... "

They arrived at the castle entrance.

It was a towering, grand stone entrance sealed by a huge, ancient, wooden door. Over the door was carved an ornate bas-relief of a royal figure in profile surrounded by laurel leaves. The inscription read simply: *Edward I.*

The old man creaked open the heavy door.

"You live here?" asked Sean, incredulous.

"Of course I do," snapped the old man. "Where else would I live?"

"Sorry, it's just that I thought this place was long since abandoned."

"Given up to the ghosts? Is that what you thought?" He laughed. "You may well be right, soon enough."

They entered the castle.

Sean had never been inside before and was astounded by The Great Hall's enormity. While somewhat sparse of furniture, it was surprisingly clean and well lit. Thornbury Castle must have been the height of elegance in its prime. The old man noticed his interest.

"Many a great ball was held here," he said. "Thornbury Castle was built in the thirteenth century, a sprawling maze of countless rooms, walled-in gardens, secret passages and a hedge labyrinth of massive acreage. I often lose my way. Even this morning I awoke to find myself in a strange room I'd never seen before ... " Thornbury trailed off, confused.

"Lord Thornbury must have had a large family then?" Sean prodded.

"Eh? Oh yes. Lord Richard spawned a huge family, sowing his seed into every room of the estate. He was a gregarious man full of life and love. Especially love. He had two great loves: the theater and his mistress, the famed actress Teva."

"Are you the caretaker?" Sean asked.

"Caretaker! You insult me thrice now, sir. I know who I am! I am a Thornbury!" The old man's anger flashed. "Carlisle Thornbury the Third!"

"I meant no insult ... " Sean tried to apologize. "Wait a minute! There was a Thornbury living here when I was just a boy."

"Aye, that be me. The last of the Thornbury's, I'm afraid." Carlisle's mercurial anger once again quickly dissolved, this time into poignancy.

He suddenly brightened.

"Ah, the tea!" and scurried off to the kitchen.

"My father may have been a friend of yours." Sean explained, as Carlisle dropped the bright yellow flowers into the boiling kettle of water and stirred.

"Oh?" Carlisle answered, only mildly interested.

"Angus Berenger?" Sean prodded.

Carlisle thought about it as he brought the steaming pot to the table where Sean sat. He poured two cups. He handed one to Sean. He put the pot back on the stove and sat down to sip his tea. Finally he nodded and said: "Aye. Berenger, the *actor.*"

"Yes," Sean conceded with barely disguised disdain. "My father the *actor.*"

"How is he? Still acting?"

"No. Actually, I don't know. I haven't spoken to him in years. I hoped he was dead and that was why I was sent for. Have you not heard any news? Is he not dead?"

Carlisle stared off into space, recalling some distant, private memory. "Perhaps. I may have heard something to that effect. He is around here somewhere, though."

"What? Where? In this castle?" Sean felt unaccustomed fear and anger rising.

"No. No. Drink your tea."

Sean tried the tea. It was too bitter and too hot.

"And you claim to be his son?" Carlisle queried.

"Yes, of course. One of two."

"Aye," Carlisle scratched his ear, puzzled, "there's the rub."

"What's the rub?" Sean asked, beginning to lose patience with the old man's roundabout way of conversing.

"Angus Berenger claimed he had no sons."

* * *

The Luna Passage screamed through the desolate Scottish moors like a wounded banshee racing down gleaming silver ribbons lain upon black velvet.

The actors were gathered in the dining car, drinking, as was their wont. Their glasses threatened to spill as they rode over a rough patch of track. Fiona snagged her glass of red wine before it toppled onto her lap.

"Quick hands there, Fiona," Nicholas remarked, sitting across from her. "And a quick wit as well, eh? Patrick?"

"What do you mean by that?" Patrick snapped icily. He was still solemn and brooding, and it appeared he might stay that way the entire passage. He had insisted on sitting next to Fiona, which now was becoming a mixed blessing.

"Just her cunning ability to improvise on stage," Nicholas replied calmly. Before anything else could be said, Andrew, covered in coal dust, made his way down the swaying car like a drunken sailor, calling out: "Oy, gang! You'll never guess what I learned."

He plopped down in an empty seat beside Abigail, his boyish grin threatening to split his face.

"What happened to you?" Abigail asked, brushing some of the coal from his face with a napkin.

"I had to climb over the coal car to get to the engine."

Samuel handed his pint to Andrew. "Aye, take a drink there me boy. You look a fine mess."

Andrew thankfully quaffed the beer in huge gulps. He wiped the residue off with his sleeve, smearing more coal dust onto his face, but his grin remained.

"Well," began Andrew, making sure he had the attention of all those at the table, "this town we're heading for, Loglinmooth, as I'm sure Patrick can attest, has quite the sordid history. Mystery surrounds it."

"Well, spill it, lad," Samuel implored. "What mystery?"

"Hold on a minute." The conductor was happening by and Andrew grabbed his sleeve. "Another 'round, please. And a pint of cider for myself."

"Aye." The conductor went off to fill the order.

"Well?" Samuel insisted.

"I don't actually know. The engineer was too frightened to say."

Everyone groaned in disappointment.

"That's no way to tell a tale, Andrew," Abigail scolded.

Andrew turned to Patrick. "True, the intrigue's there but not the details. Perhaps Patrick can fill in the rest?"

Patrick met every eye turned to him with a steely gaze.

"You sure you want to know?"

Fiona slipped her hand into his and squeezed it for encouragement.

"Yes, please," she begged softly.

The others all joined in raucous agreement. By now the conductor had returned with fresh drinks. He handed them out, then remained just within earshot, listening.

"The *mystery*?" Patrick began, softly, utilizing all his acting techniques to draw his audience in. "The *mystery* of Loglinmooth? You wish to hear of the scurrilous legend of the town in which I was born? The ancient tale of ghosts and ghoulies and banshees that scream bloody murder throughout the castle walls? Of the wraiths and shades that roam the streets? Of the *curse*?"

"Yes, damn it!' Gavin blurted out. "Tell us about the bloody mystery, already!"

"THERE IS NO BLOODY MYSTERY!" Patrick shouted, standing suddenly. "Now, I'm going to bed and suggest all you gullible, superstitious children do likewise!"

With that he stormed out in the direction of the sleeper car.

The others stared at each other in shocked disbelief. Finally, Samuel burst out with gales of roaring laughter. "What a performance!" he cried.

The ice broken, the others joined in. Soon they were all laughing and toasting Patrick's performance. Only Fiona occasionally looked down the way Patrick had left, her brow wrinkled with concern.

The conductor went to a window and pulled it open. He stuck his head out into the freezing wind. Outside, snow had started to fall. He pulled his head back inside.

"Aye, this is not good," he said, pulling his head back inside and making a quick sign of the cross. "Not good at all."

Only Abigail heard him. A look of fear crossed her face.

"I'll tell you a grand ghost story," Gavin began, "I was playing Hamlet's father in a small theater in London when—"

"Excuse me," Fiona rose.

"Oh, have you heard this one?" Gavin asked.

"*I* have!" laughed Samuel. "A million times!"

Fiona shook her head. "No, I am just tired. Please, excuse me." The gentlemen rose.

"Would you like an escort to your chambers?" Nicolas asked.

"No. Thank you. I am sure I can find my way. Goodnight."

"Goodnight. Sweet dreams," the crowd chorused. "Now I will tell you a *true* ghost story, "Andrew roared, already well into his cups," one about a gent who went by the name of Deacon Brodie. Infamous was he, for he was the only man to be hanged thrice by a device he himself invented ... "

Andrew's voice was drowned out by the roar of the train and finally shut out completely by the closing coach door as Fiona made her way toward the sleeper car.

* * *

Sean left the castle feeling strangely sad. It was one thing to disown your parent, but quite another to find yourself disowned. He felt alone.

The skies had darkened ominously. Although it was early afternoon, nightfall was going to come very quickly. He began to make his way down the steep hillside while he could still see.

His thoughts returned to his situation. If not his father's death, then why *had* he been summoned here? And, although he had gone to great pains to remain a reclusive stranger, hidden to all, especially his family, in the end he wasn't really that difficult to find. Now he was wondering just how hard anyone had been looking, if at all. Patrick's name was also on the summons. The thought of seeing him again (assuming he was still alive after all these years) brought bile to Sean's throat. Sean had lost contact with him, by choice, many years ago ...

It was May Day, an ironic omen if there ever was one, a cool morning in Nineteen Fifteen when he boarded the *RMS Lusitania* in New York, sailing for Liverpool. He was an unofficial passenger, having worked in the Clyde Shipyards; and he had pulled some strings to slip aboard anonymously. She was 'Clydebuilt' the standard for quality synonymous with reliability. She was one of the many fine ships of standard built from the steely shipyards lining the banks of the River Clyde from Greenock to Glasgow, like silver mushrooms. And he was proud of her, as he had helped build her.

It only took seven days to cross the Atlantic, and when she broke through the fog around eleven hundred hours, she was within view of the Irish coastline. No other ships were in sight.

She sailed on toward Queenstown harbor. U-boats had been sighted in the area, but the captain had felt assured they were too far off to be of any danger. He sailed his ship onward, unmolested, for two hours when the German submarine, *U20*, slipped in close, undetected, and launched a single torpedo.

Sean was making love to a dining hostess named Lisa when it happened. They had met the night before. He stayed at the bar, drinking, waiting for her shift to end. When three o'clock finally rolled around, she appeared in his blurry vision. They had made their way to his cabin and Sean had managed to help her out of her clothes before passing out. Miraculously, she had stayed the night, and some seven hours later he was making it up to her.

Although his head was pounding, he was able (much to his amazement) to still be effectively seductive.

"You move like no other woman," he whispered into her ear. "A tigress *and* a kitten."

"You'll have to hurry," she gasped, in response to a change in his position. "My shift starts in an hour."

"I'll do what I can," he said making no promises. Even though he was tiring, he thought he could still make her at least ten minutes late.

Then came the explosion that rocked the ship.

Lisa screamed. "What was that?"

"I don't know." Sean rolled off her and scrambled to the porthole. The ship was already listing. There was smoke and flames coming from further up the bow.

"We've got to get above decks, now!" he screamed, scrambling into a pair of pants. She had barely managed to slip on her petticoat when he grabbed her hand and dragged her outside into the hall.

The hallway was in pandemonium, crowded with confused, scared passengers screaming in panic.

The ship was already tilting drastically to starboard, causing the passengers and crew to have to struggle to stay on their feet. Sean held tightly to Lisa's hand. He yelled over the din: "Come on!"

They squeezed and shoved their way to the upper deck.

On the port side, the crew was gallantly trying to free one of the five-ton lifeboats, even as passengers attempted to scramble inside.

Sean held the trembling Lisa in his arms as he quickly assessed the situation. He knew the list of the ship was going to make dropping those lifeboats into the sea nearly impossible.

"The port side lifeboats will be useless! We've got to get you to the starboard side!"

But before they could act, the ship took a violent lurch and one of the lifeboats filled with passengers broke free. Instead of falling in the water, it slid down the deck, a wooden battering ram, smashing and crushing any unfortunate passengers that got in its way.

And then it was heading straight toward Sean and Lisa!

Sean shoved Lisa hard out of the way, and almost made it himself, but was clipped by an oarlock that sent him smashing into a cabin wall and then into darkness.

Terror, screams, desperation . . .

It was only a nightmare, or so he thought when he awoke in a hospital bed, dazed and bandaged. But no, it was all too real. He knew from the cast on his arm and the burns and bruises on his body.

A nurse came in, happy to see him awake at last.

"How did I get here?" he croaked, his lungs still raspy from the smoke.

"From what I understand," the nurse explained kindly as she dressed his bandages, "you were knocked unconscious and someone pulled you aboard a lifeboat."

"Who? Who saved me?"

"I don't know."

"How ... how many?" he whispered.

"The newspaper said nearly twelve hundred. They are still tallying," she said gently. "The Yanks are up in arms. I think they will finally join us."

"What about Lisa?"

"Lisa who, dear?"

Sean realized he even didn't know her last name.

"I shouldn't be here. I should have stayed aboard."

"Then you would have drowned," the nurse said sensibly. "What good would that have been to anyone?"

Later, Sean searched through the papers for news of the sinking. He found the official passenger manifest, first. He was not surprised to see that he wasn't listed. There were no Lisa's, but a few Elizabeth's and a Liza. Then he checked the survivor's list. There were no Lisa's although the paper warned the list was still being updated and confirmed.

Sean felt survivor's guilt and dishonor for 'his' ship being so easily destroyed. His brother had no idea of his whereabouts, but if he tracked him down to the Clyde Shipyards enough people there knew he had planned to board the *Lusitania*. If he never went back, he, and everyone else, would most likely presume him dead.

Sean decided to keep it that way.

He slipped out of the hospital in the dead of night and had been living in shadows ever since, that was until that strange man had somehow managed to locate him and summoned him here to Loglinmooth.

A sudden, icy gust of wind woke him from his revelry. Dark clouds were rolling in fast. *It's blowing from the North Sea,* he thought. *Gon'na be a bad one. I'd hate to be caught in that.*

Far to the south he thought he could make out the faint plume of a steam train chugging north, heading this way.

* * *

Fiona was not prepared for the freezing temperature and sudden, heavy falling snow as she stepped outside of the dining car. In order to pass between the carriages, she had to step outside onto the gangway then step across the coupler to the next car's carriage. This had to be done between every car.

She was not sure which it was: the darkness, the scream of the speeding train, or the freezing snow that made her shudder more. She had drunk too much and her stance was a bit unsteady as she contemplated crossing between the couplings. The fast moving ground below made her dizzy.

She summoned up her courage and quickly stepped across, noticing that ice was already building on the platforms. She pulled open the smoking coach door and hurried inside. The sudden quiet was unnerving.

There were only five carriages on the train, not counting the engine. The dining car was the first car, then the smoking car, followed by two seating cars then the sleeping car. Since the actors were the only passengers, the train felt very empty. Adding to this emptiness, the other cars were kept mostly dark.

"There is nothing to be afraid of," Fiona whispered to herself. "It is only an empty train."

The train whistle blew its mournful blast, (as if to deny her solace.)

Fiona moved through the dark, empty car, dreading the thought of having to go into the freezing cold again, no matter how briefly.

She made it safely across the coupling, into the first riding coach. One more coach, then she would be in her warm bunk. She made it into the next carriage, again without incident. Now she only had to cross to the sleeping coach.

She opened the door and stepped out into the gangway. The ice had built up and she held onto the handrails for support. She hurried across and was about to enter when she saw Patrick through the glass coach window. He was returning from the washroom, bare-chested, toweling his hair, wearing only long underwear. Fiona had never noticed how powerfully built he was. She couldn't help herself; she remained transfixed at the sight of him.

"I should wait until he is in bed. I don't want to embarrass him," she convinced herself, shivering on the icy gangway. "But I'll catch my death out here."

Patrick was still coming towards her, his berth being the closest to the front of the coach. She decided she could wait no longer. She went to open the door. It was stuck!

She tried harder and harder, but it would not open. Panicking, she pounded on the glass to get Patrick's attention. He looked up and was surprised to see her when suddenly her face dropped out from his view.

The Luna Passage had lurched violently, and Fiona was knocked to her knees, holding on to the railing for dear life!

Below her, the speeding ground threatened as the frozen wind pulled at her grip.

"Help!" she screamed, her voice lost in the roar of the night.

The coach door was yanked open and Patrick was quickly at her side. He picked her up in his arms and carried her inside.

"What were you doing out there? You could have been killed!"

Fiona could only nod, shivering violently, as he held her close to his bare chest. He brought her to his berth, a very small room with a fold down bed, already lowered. He set her on the bunk, grabbed a heavy woolen blanket and wrapped it around her. She continued to shiver.

"Let me ring the conductor and get you some hot tea," Patrick insisted.

"No," she finally managed to speak. "I'll be fine, just let me warm up here for a bit."

"Are you sure?"

She stared into Patrick's dark brown eyes and nodded. Of course she was sure, where else in the world would she rather be? She brought her knees right below her chin and pulled the blanket tighter.

Patrick dropped to his knees to be eye level with her. "Fiona, what were you doing out there alone?"

Still shivering she looked towards the small window and the landscape rushing by. "I was looking for you. You ran off so fast. The way you have been acting lately, you just haven't been yourself. I just wanted to check on you."

"Of course you did," Patrick eased a bit and moved to sit on the end of the bed. Fiona's gaze moved to his chest again. *God he looks so alluring.*

"Fiona, you know me too well." He moved closer to her on the bed. "I'm just sorry that my actions led you to follow me. But I am thankful I was here to rescue you," he smiled. "At least I got to be some kind of a hero."

"That you did," Fiona agreed.

They sat in silence for a few moments. The train lurched and moved beneath them.

"I'm just ... " Patrick began. "I never thought I would be coming back home. I left years ago and I thought that was it, the end of the story." His gaze shifted to the window, Fiona could see she was losing him to his past.

"What happened?"

He kept his gaze on the window. "Loss, I lost ... and my brother, if that bastard is still alive ... " he trailed off.

There was such a chill in his voice that Fiona found herself shivering all over again. He must have been hurt terribly. She wrapped her arms around him.

"Everything will be all right. It's never as bad as it may seem."

"Sweet Fee, you would think that." Touched by her words, he kissed her on her forehead. She shivered again, but not from the cold.

"Fiona, you're freezing! You should have let me get you some tea."

"I am fine, really," she protested. Of course she was, she was in his room, wrapped in his blanket with the image of him half-naked racing to her rescue firmly imbedded in her mind.

"Come here," he insisted. He laid her down on the bed and wrapped her in his arms.

He pulled the blanket around the two of them and she was in heaven. She lay still, afraid that any movement or words would cause the moment to shatter.

"I fear I am too tired, shaken and cold to move," Fiona murmured.

"Then please don't, Fee," he responded as he pulled her in to his chest. "I could use your company tonight."

"Do you mean that?" Fiona asked, intensely aware of his breath on her neck.

"Of course."

She rolled over to face him. "You really want me here tonight?"

Patrick reached to slip his fingers through the hair framing her face. "I won't have you anywhere else."

She leaned in and their lips met in a small, gentle kiss.

She gazed up at him; her breath slowed almost to a stop. She had surprised herself with being the first one to act, but since she had started it and he hadn't stopped her ...

She leaned in hitting his lips again with a desperate force as her hands found his bare chest. He welcomed her lips this time, drawing her closer. She could sense such desire in him, such need.

It only took a few strokes from Fiona across his chest to fully spark Patrick. Abandoning all hesitation, he sought her breasts under the blanket. He quickly tired of the feel of her dress shielding her flesh from him, so he found the bottom of her dress and caressed his way up the inside of her clothing until he could cup her breasts while nuzzling her neck.

"Hmm . . . " Fiona sighed, finding his lips again. She drew him closer, hoping to slide beneath him.

Patrick moaned and pulled at her dress, anxious to see her out of the pesky garment, but Fiona was making it difficult. She had left his lips and was nibbling on his ear while she slid her hands down his sheer build.

Patrick got the hint. He shifted intently and rolled atop her, resulting in an exquisite moan from Fiona who ran her nails down his back in reciprocity.

She eased her fingers into lazy circles as she whispered her need for him. He continued tugging at her dress as he brought his mouth back to hers. Filled with fire, Fiona's nails again dug deep encouraging him to pick up the pace.

It was that deep scratch that jolted him back to reality. He backed off from her as if stung.

"No. No. I can't do this," he stammered, pushing away, against the wall, eyes wide with shock. "I'm sorry, I am so sorry, Fee."

Fiona looked at him confused. "Patrick, it's okay. Don't worry about me, I've been wanting to—"

"No!" he cried, cutting her off. "It's not okay." He rushed from the bed and paced the small room in quick steps. He took a deep breath and then kneeled down in front of her.

"Listen, Fee. It's not that I don't want to, it's that I can't." He leaned closer to her face, resolute to get his message across. "You must believe me. There are a thousand things I want to do with you ... " He rose and turned to open the door, letting cold air rush in. "Just not tonight."

"But, I don't understand," Fiona insisted, the blast of frigid air mocking Patrick's sudden mood shift.

Patrick stood in the doorway, oblivious to the cold, refusing to reply.

Stunned and hurt at his silence, Fiona grabbed for the blanket that had fallen to the floor and pulled it around her as she stood.

"Fiona ... "

"What?" she snapped with more force than intended. All she wanted now was to rush to her bed, to forget he had just rejected her. She needed to replay these events over and over until she figured out what had gone wrong.

She moved to leave but he slammed the door, stopping her. "Don't leave!"

"Why?" she asked. "You just asked me to!"

"No, I didn't. I just needed to ... cool off," he said, trying to meet her eyes. "I'm in a very dark place, Fee. I am not sure of what I'm even say—"

"Well, I'm saying good night!" She pushed past him to the door.

He stopped her by wrapping his arms around her.

"Let me go!" she insisted, squirming in his grip.

"Wait. Please," he pleaded. "Listen, I don't know what is coming tomorrow and I can't bring you into that. I just can't and I won't." He paused to see if she would respond but she didn't. "Stay with me tonight? Not as a lover but as a friend. I *really* need a friend tonight."

Fiona stopped resisting and took a deep breath. She contemplated what he was asking when she finally met his eyes and saw the struggle of a confused, hurt man in them.

"Just for the time being, be my friend tonight, Fiona," he pleaded.

She nodded her head slowly, not sure of what she was answering.

Patrick sighed and hugged her. "Thank you, Fee. I just can't bear the thought of going through this night alone." He released her and flipped the light off. "Come," he extended his hand.

She took it lightly and he led her back to the bed and left her wrapped up in the blanket as he lay behind her again, spooning, but this time the only warmth Fiona could feel came from the blanket.

"I'm sorry," he whispered. "Goodnight, sweet Fee." He squeezed her one last time "Thank you."

Fiona nodded, tears beginning to well in the corner of her eyes. She stared out the window and prayed.

Tomorrow it will all be different. He will awaken to find me in his arms and will find his heart ... Everything will be different from then on ...

After a few minutes Patrick's breathing shifted to one of sleep. Fiona closed her eyes and felt a small tear trickle down her cheek – sleep a distant hope. At least she had finally shared a bed with him, she conceded, at least she had that.

The train rocked like a cradle into the night, lulling the travelers into a deep sleep. Except for one, whose sleep was troubled and uneasy, who in her semi-dream state noticed the train slowing down, slower and slower until it came to a complete stop.

Then an odd thing happened. The rumble of the train resumed its journey, but now somehow the constant crick-snick of the wheels along the tracks, the back and forth swaying of the cars was gone. Even the huffing exhalation of released steam faded into silence.

But how? How could the train move off and be silent at the same time?

That's what finally woke Fiona. Not the sound, but the silence. The stillness.

Confused, she looked down to remember that she was in Patrick's bed, with his arm holding her safe.

She slipped out from his hold and rose quietly. She went out into the dark hall. The cold air instantly chilled away any residual drowsiness. She noticed a light on under Abigail's door and was tempted to knock but decided to remain with her own thoughts a while longer.

She made her way to the front of the car and peered out the window. It was opaque with frost. She felt the need for some fresh wintry air to clear her head. They had stopped and she wondered why. Surely someone from the train crew was up and could tell her.

She pulled open the door and stared out into emptiness. Only the sleeper car remained, alone on the tracks. The rest of the train was gone.

The troupe was wrapped in heavy blankets and jackets (except Samuel, who stood defiant in his winter kilt) as they stood on the carriage platform. The snow was falling and daylight was beginning to break.

"Where the devil did they go?" Gavin asked for the fifth time.

"We don't know," Samuel growled. By now ice particles had crystallized on his red beard, so every time he mumbled, they shook and fell down his chin. Fiona watched them fall as she stood silent, wrapped safe in Patrick's arms. Patrick remained stoic, a quiet storm raging inside him, saying little.

"Maybe this car just broke loose and they haven't noticed?" suggested Abigail.

"Aye," Andrew considered, not sure he believed that. "I suppose it's a possibility."

"Sure," Abigail said, trying to convince herself. "They should be backing up any minute. Listen! I think I hear them!"

They all listened for a moment. Only the soft howl of the wind was heard.

"I don't hear a blasted thing," Nicholas replied disheartened. He couldn't believe what was happening. They were just an acting troupe, damn it! Why all this drama?

"They are *not* coming back," Patrick said darkly.

"How do you know?" Gavin snapped.

"Because most people are afraid to come even this close to Loglinmooth. And those were cowardly, superstitious men."

"You're joking," Gavin laughed.

"No. I'm not." Patrick met his eyes. He was definitely not joking.

"What's there? What's so frightening about that place?" Abigail asked, fright growing inside her.

Patrick didn't answer her question. "We'll have to walk," he said instead.

"How far is Loglinmooth?" Nicholas asked.

"Probably take a couple of hours," Patrick figured.

"This is madness!" Gavin cried. "I'm not walking through this snowstorm to some God forsaken cursed town!"

"Then stay here," Patrick shrugged.

"I'm not sure the women can make it," Andrew said, taking Abigail's hand in his.

"I'm not afraid," Fiona said, speaking for the first time since they had gathered. "I'll go."

"I can make it too!" Abigail declared defiantly.

Nicholas attempted to take charge of his troupe. "Perhaps we should go back inside and discuss this. Work out a plan of action."

"Fine," said Samuel. "So long as it includes me having a bit of a row with those train gents once we catch up with them!"

"Definitely," Nicholas agreed. "And I'll join you. But for now let's all go inside where it's warm and figure this thing out."

They all shuffled inside, except Patrick who lingered, his gaze fixed towards Loglinmooth. Fiona gently took his hand. He allowed her to lead him inside.

Nicholas's cabin was cramped. The mood was dire. "Suggestions?" Nicholas began.

"I say we wait it out here," Gavin jumped in. "It's warm enough, and surely they'll be back."

"They won't be back," Patrick said with certainty. "And there's no food. The dining car's gone in case you haven't noticed."

"Then you go!" Gavin challenged. "And bring back help."

"What kind of help you be thinking of boy?" Patrick asked darkly.

"Surely the townspeople can rig up—" Gavin sputtered.

"Loglinmooth ain't likely to be happy to see me as it is," Patrick insisted,

"Why? What have you–" Abigail started to prod.

"Nobody's coming!" Nicholas cut them all off, irritated. "I have no idea why we were cut loose. But I can wager that no one is in any kind of hurry to come out here and pull this railroad car into town just so we don't have to walk a few miles!"

His outburst silenced the room.

"As I see it, there's really no choice," Patrick stated, flatly. "Those that want to live, walk into Loglinmooth with me. Those that don't can stay here and freeze or starve to death."

The others looked around. Gavin seemed about to speak up but held his tongue.

"Patrick's right," Nicholas said, relinquishing his leadership. "You lead the way."

Patrick met the eyes of each.

"Do any of you have any weapons?"

Samuel pulled out a menacing looking dagger. "Aye. I always carry me blade."

"I have a gun," Gavin announced, surprising everyone. "I fancy a bit of hunting, now and again," he explained.

"Why do we need weapons?" Andrew asked. "We're just walking a few miles into town."

Patrick said nothing

"If it's wolves you're worried about, I can handle wolves, no worries," Samuel said confidently. "It's them things I can't see what bothers me."

"What about our luggage?" Abigail piped in. "Do we leave it?"

"Carry what you want to keep, take only what you want to carry." Patrick headed for the door. "I have no idea what will still be here if and when we return. We leave in ten minutes."

Patrick walked out of the room.

The others all glanced at each other, astonished. Nicholas rose. "You heard the man. Grab your things."

Fiona stood alone on the tracks, letting the snow fall upon her. She had one small valise.

"Is that all you're taking?" Patrick asked, startling her, as he appeared beside her.

"Oh! Yes. It's all I need."

Patrick wore a medium weight jacket and no hat nor gloves. The cold didn't seem to affect him at all. He carried a small suitcase. He stared straight ahead into the whiteness.

"Can you find your way in all this snow?" she asked, her words coming out in frost clouds.

"We'll follow the tracks," he stated matter-of-factly. Before she could say anything else, Samuel joined them. He carried a large duffle bag, which seemed to weigh nothing to the huge man.

"I'm ready," he declared.

Gavin stomped up, trying to get some circulation in his feet. His thin leather shoes were not made for tramping in the snow.

"Let's get a move on already," he complained. "Who are we waiting for?"

Nicholas, Andrew and Abigail arrived together.

"That would be us, I presume," said Nicholas. "I locked up the car the best I could. Not that it would keep out any scoundrels."

"Let's go," said Patrick, moving down the tracks.

Fiona followed close behind, followed by Gavin, Abigail, Andrew, and Nicholas with Samuel bringing up the rear.

They followed the tracks, north, through the falling snow. They had walked for over three hours when Nicholas quickened his step to come alongside Patrick.

"How much farther?" he asked, panting.

Patrick took a moment to reply, reflecting on the past. "I used to make this journey in about two hours when I was a kid. I would run down here to see *The Luna Passage* when it was scheduled to roll past. Any hope to leave this place. But back then I didn't have this snow and cold and you others to slow me down."

"Even so, we must be close?" Nicholas asked hopefully.

"Aye."

"Can we take a break then?"

Patrick looked back at the tired faces of the others. He nodded. "Yes. Fifteen minutes. But I don't want to be caught out here once darkness falls. It's hard enough to see the tracks and it'll get a lot colder."

Nicholas agreed. "Yes. Fifteen minutes everyone." Groans of relief arose from the group as they found boulders to sit on and rest their weary feet. Gavin flopped right onto his back in the snow.

"You okay there?" Patrick asked Fiona, who was looking wearily about for a place to sit.

Fiona nodded. She sat down and let out a sigh. "I'm okay, but my feet are angry." She started to take off her shoes when Patrick stopped her.

"Don't. They'll swell more than they are already and you won't be able to put your shoes back on."

Fiona stopped. "Okay. Thanks for the advice."

Andrew and Abigail plopped down beside them. Abigail exchanged a look with Fiona that she knew meant 'we have to talk, and soon.' Fiona acknowledged it.

"What can we expect to find in Loglinmooth?" Andrew asked Patrick. "Is there a place to put us up?"

"Aye," replied Patrick. "There's a wee pub, The Broken Piper. Used to be run by a queer miss by the name of McStargle. Might be she's still there. She has a few rooms. There's also a handful of farms, a general store, Thornbury Castle up on the hill, an old church, and ... a theater."

"How strange that such a small town has a theater," Abigail commented.

"The pub's sounding mighty fine right now. I hope they have a blazing fire!" called up Gavin.

"Aye!" Samuel piped in. "And a wickedly warm serving wrench with a steaming leg of lamb and a warm lap."

"Where did you live Patrick?" asked Fiona.

"We had a place connected to the theater."

"Had? Is it not still there?"

"No. I heard it burned down." Patrick rose suddenly. "It'll be getting dark soon. We need to move on."

Patrick grew silent as they walked. It was getting colder, and Fiona longed for his warm embrace though she knew it was not coming. She allowed herself to fall to the back of the group and surveyed them as they trudged along through the snow. No one spoke; all seemed lost in their own thoughts. This bizarre journey seemed to have affected them all, except perhaps Samuel.

Samuel appeared right at home in the Scottish wilderness. His thick, tartan kilt was apparently warm enough for him, as he was the only one who hadn't complained about the cold. His expression was one of complete acceptance of the situation. Neither worry, fear nor doubt appeared on his brow. Fiona admired his spirit.

They walked on. The snowfall lessened. Fiona thought that they must be nearing the town, because she noticed a hunkering of rocks surrounding what appeared to be a decrepit cemetery, visible over a small hill.

As they passed, she saw that it was indeed a very old cemetery. Overgrown with dead or dying trees, many of the weathered headstones had sunk into the soil, others leaned precariously as if waiting to fall. Tired and longing for rest, their epitaphs were faded or washed away.

What an amazing place, thought Fiona. *Here's where it all ends, soil and stone, dust and dirt* ... A sudden rush of cold wind blew snow over the whole scene erasing it like a dream.

They moved on.

It was just dark when the troupe followed a sweeping turn in the track and came upon Loglinmooth.

They stopped, relief in most, trepidation in some.

A few lights burned through the snowfall: warm beckoning pub lights, flickering fireplaces from homes, and a cold blue light from the room above the theater.

"Welcome to Loglinmooth," Patrick announced joylessly.

They walked the narrow streets, a somber, silent parade. The yellow light of The Broken Piper was their beacon. The comforting smell of an occasional wood fire wafting from the chimneys only reminded them of how icy cold they were and hurried them onward.

Like a distant star on the horizon a single light burned high in the hill. Fiona asked what it was.

"Thornbury Castle," Patrick replied. "You don't want to go there; it's haunted."

"Ha!" Gavin laughed. "All of Scotland is haunted. That church probably has a haunted belfry, and that old theater right over there," he pointed to the Berenger Playhouse, "is most certainly haunted."

"There is a light on upstairs ... " Fiona started towards the theater. "Does someone live there?"

"No. No one lives there. Come! The Broken Piper is just ahead," Patrick insisted.

Samuel laughed heartily. "Now those are the kind of spirits I take kindly to."

Fiona stopped to peer in the window of the theater. She could make out a single, faint flickering light far inside the darkened theater. Abigail paused besides her, noticing the light as well.

"The ghost light is lit," Fiona whispered.

"Someone must be around," Abigail observed. Fiona nodded. "What a forlorn place." Abigail shivered.

"I don't know. I think it may be quite lovely inside," Fiona, replied.

The others had already moved on. Patrick was pulling open the door to the Broken Piper, as the group cheered their arrival.

Abigail grabbed Fiona's hand and pulled her toward the pub. "Come! I can't wait to meet McStargle!"

The two girls scurried to the pub.

The Broken Piper was small and inviting, made extra cozy by the warmth of a roaring fire. The bar area was up front and had a few stools and a bronze footrest running the length. The bar itself appeared to be made of a single plank of ancient wood, hand polished and elbow worn to a glossy smoothness. A connected room featured tables and chairs, a dartboard and some faded travel posters of Jersey Island.

The pub was empty, except for Miss McStargle, a pleasant enough older woman, who seemed happy for the intrusion standing guard behind the bar over a small cache of whiskeys, vodkas and cider. There was a room in the back where she slept and another small kitchen where she cooked for the pub.

"I was expecting you," was her odd acknowledgment as they entered.

"Really?" Nicholas shook the snow off his jacket.

"Aye. Been waiting all day," she replied. "I take it you're all peckish?"

"Yes, indeed, if that means hungry," Nicholas answered for all of them. "Thank you, madam. We'll have whatever you are kind enough to provide. And shots all around, when you have the moment."

"You're a Yank," she said. It wasn't a question.

"Yes." Nicholas replied with a smile.

She nodded and started to go into the kitchen when she turned and pointed at Patrick. "You," she stared hard at him. "I remember you."

Patrick returned her icy glare unflinching. Finally, she broke it off.

"Have a seat." She disappeared into the kitchen.

"That was odd," noted Gavin, but everyone else was too tired and hungry to care.

Dinner was a hearty, traditional Scottish feast, quickly served, eaten, and cleared. They were well into their nightcap drams of whiskey and coffee when Abigail finally asked the question that had been bothering her all evening.

"She said she was *expecting* us?"

"Obviously whoever hired the train, hired her," Samuel replied.

The group went silent upon Miss McStargle's re-appearance, arms full of clean glasses. She eyed them all suspiciously, as if she knew they had been talking about her, as she replaced the glasses behind the bar.

The conversation picked up again once she left the room.

Andrew turned to Samuel. "So who might that be?"

"Might be what?" Samuel asked, confused.

"Who might it be that hired us and her?" Andrew insisted.

"How should I know?" Samuel replied indignantly.

"I imagine we'll find out soon enough," Gavin said.

Fiona stayed out of the conversation. She leaned back in her chair to see Patrick still brooding in his corner. She wondered if he had sought out that dark corner or if it became dark and gloomy after he sat there. He had chosen a seat as far away from everyone as he could. He was staring into his chops and gravy as if they were the cause of his life gone wrong.

Now that everyone had eaten, regained their energy, and thawed out, they began to laugh about the whole adventure and the tales began.

"Aye, and did I tell ya of my skirmish when I went off exploring for a shorter trail this morning–" Samuel began.

"You mean to relieve yourself?" Gavin laughed.

Samuel glared at him then continued. "And I encountered an entire family of stalking, disease ridden, snarling wolves?"

Abigail gasped. "What did you do?"

"I took 'em on one-by-one with my trusty blade–" he pulled his knife out and slammed it on the table. "Killed the lot of them, I did."

"No blood?" Gavin asked coyly, examining it.

Samuel reddened slightly as he yanked it back from Gavin's hand. "Nah, 'cus I wiped it off on their carcasses."

"I seem to remember reading that wolves have been hunted to extinction in Scotland since the late seventeen hundreds," Andrew pointed out, with a slight grin.

Samuel grew even redder. He challenged everyone at the table with his baleful glare then said simply. "Must've been werewolves then, eh?"

"Perhaps," Nicholas agreed, drinking to hide his grin.

"Perhaps they were rabbits," offered Andrew, courting danger.

"What? Bloody snarling rabbits?" Samuel roared.

"Were-rabbits then," Andrew offered as a compromise.

"Aye. That they may have been," Samuel took his way out graciously. "There was a lot of snow falling and blurring me eyes." They listened to the rest of Samuel's tale of were-rabbit attacks, hanging on his every word.

"He's a gifted storyteller, none can deny that," Fiona said, leaning into Gavin with a laugh.

"Aye, and he even tells them in his sleep," Gavin grinned. "Between snores, that is. Sleeping on the train with him was like sleeping in the same room as a wounded bear. Any chance I might join in on you two?" His eyes shifted hopefully from Fiona to Abigail.

"No," Abigail said. "Fiona and I will share a room ... alone."

"How can you share a room alone when there are two of you in it?"

"Alone from you," Abigail quipped.

Fiona glanced over at Patrick as Abigail and Gavin continued to josh back and forth. He looked as sad as she'd ever seen him.

"I just don't understand him," she said aloud.

"No need to," came Nicholas' loud, fatherly baritone, as he sat beside her. "If he wishes to walk the Earth all grave and sad, let him! A man has a right to his darkness."

Andrew raised his beer and shouted out a toast. "Tonight, we drink and be merry! And we give thanks to Samuel, without whom we would not live safe, in his relentless defense against were-rabbits or moor bunnies or whatever!"

"Thank God for Scottish tongues!" Abigail added. "They wag so well!"

"Cheers! Sláinte!"

They drifted back into the familiar drinking, laughing and storytelling. Fiona was happy for the comfort of it after the strange day in this very strange and foreign town. No one mentioned how they would leave or where they would be going two days from now; they were all just happy to be together.

Andrew talked passionately about his new script and the gruesome details of Abigail's character's death, much to Abigail's delight.

"Instead of just being run through by one sword," Abigail suggested, "how about if I am found hanging from a noose, after being run through by *three* swords, holding an empty vial of poison that I just drank?"

"That is a bit much," Andrew hedged, his eyes roving over her. "But we'll see." Fiona had noticed that he had been eyeing Abigail most of the evening.

"Shall see what?" Abigail pouted, as she leaned forward, her ample bosom just inches from Andrew's widening gaze. "You must admit that it would add such depth to my death!"

"Whatever you want, you shall have!" Andrew cried, surrendering. Everyone roared with laughter.

"I know!" said Gavin. "Fiona, you should sing! You used to do that all the time when we first met."

All eyes turned toward Fiona. "Oh! No. No. I couldn't," she protested. But Gavin was already stepping on top of the table and pulling at her to join him. Fiona normally hated this type of attention; like many actors she was shy in public, but as she was being pulled atop the table, she glanced at Patrick. He was looking at her, intrigued.

This is just what he needs, Fiona thought, to see us all being silly and carefree. Maybe then he will join us.

So, with newfound motivation, she grasped Gavin's hand and cleared her throat.

"What should I sing?" Fiona asked.

"Something light," he replied.

And then it came to her. A simple melody her father taught her.

"To dance like an Irishman is really quite simple ... " she began, cheerily. "Just drink four pints and try to walk to the door."

Samuel and Abigail burst into fits of laughter. Fiona noticed Patrick grinning from his dark corner. Gavin squeezed her hand and pulled her closer. "No, Fiona, sing something pretty. You have such a lovely voice."

"Alright," she called out. "And now something pretty, per Gavin's wishes."

They cheered.

She pulled Gavin roughly to her and began to dance across the table with him.

"You made me love you ... " she began. The troupe cheered loudly, recognizing the recent Al Jolson hit tune.

"I didn't want to do it ... " She looked away from Gavin, her face a look of mock disgust. "I didn't want to do it."

"Damn right you didn't!" yelled Andrew, laughing. Fiona turned back to Gavin.

"You made me want you," she continued.

"*Gavin?* Really?" teased Abigail.

"Oy!" Gavin protested, as he tried to keep in toe with Fiona.

"And all the time you knew it, I guess you always knew it. You made me happy sometimes, you made me glad."

"She must have been blind drunk!" roared Nicholas.

"But there were times," Fiona continued; pouting like a sad child. "You made me feel so bad."

"Gavin, you bastard!" cried Andrew.

"I'm sorry! Never again, I promise" cajoled Gavin. He tried to wrap Fiona in his arms, but she deftly spun away.

"You made me cry for I didn't want to tell you. I didn't want to tell you."

"So why ya telling him now?" Samuel slammed his drink on the table as he rose up. "Forget him. He's a jakey arse! I'm the one you want!"

Fiona winked at Samuel slyly as she pushed him back down into his seat with a waving finger, never losing her beat.

"I want some *love*." This line brought renewed cheering and catcalling.

"That's true, yes I do." Fiona slid across to Nicholas, bent down and mussed his salt and pepper hair.

"Indeed I do," Fiona rose, spun to Samuel and pinched his cheeks, reddening his face. He tried to rise again, and again she pushed him down, this time with her foot. "You know I do."

Fiona went back to Gavin, who was waiting dumbstruck at the other end of the table. She reached out for him. "Gimmie, gimmie, gimmie what I cry for."

"Give it to her, Gavin!" yelled Abigail.

"I will!" Gavin smiled, and suddenly took Fiona in his arms and dipped her.

When he pulled her back up, Fiona found herself face-to-face with him. A sudden hush filled the room.

They exchanged a look that only actors know. They silently agreed to play the hopelessly in love characters to the hilt and go over the top. Fiona put her hands on either side of Gavin's face and swung his head in beat with the next line, dripping with sensuality. "You know you got the brand of kisses that I die for!"

There were no catcalls from the table this time. The scene playing out hushed them all, not quite sure how much was real and how much fantasy. Gavin felt the rush, and swung his arm behind her back to prepare for the final dip. Fiona smiled to let him know she was ready.

"You know you made me love you." Fiona leaned back, with total trust and abandon. As she was letting herself fall, she glanced at Gavin. He was staring past her, confused, at someone behind her. *Patrick!* He must be signaling to Gavin to let him catch her. What a perfect ending to the song, to fall into Patrick's waiting arms and sing the last line to him!

Fiona became thrilled, her heart pounded.

"You know you made me ... "

Closing her eyes, she pushed at Gavin, until she felt his arm give way, and then a glorious second of free-fall into nothing, before another pair of strong arms caught her.

Completely beside herself, she blindly reached up and brought Patrick's lips to hers. After all, the troupe was expecting a show. He returned her kiss deeply, openly, his tongue searching hers. She was surprised by the harshness of his kiss mixed with his lack of modesty. She no longer wished to finish the song; she wished only to remain suspended in this moment for the rest of her life. She kept her eyes tightly shut, savoring this dream come true.

She pulled herself closer into his hold, her hands leaving his hair and finding his face.

Something was wrong.

She was startled to feel his hands on her rear, caressing it roughly, exploring further ...

She pushed back on his chest, conflicted, as much as she wanted it, this was not the time nor place! As she opened her eyes to scold him, her gaze unfogged as a different face, bearded, brighter-eyed, came into view.

A stranger looked down at her, intimately holding her, a wry smirk on his lips.

"You all right there, lassie?" his low, husky voice asked. He tried to pull her close again. Astonished, Fiona opened her mouth to scream, but all that came out was a small feeble cry: "Patrick!"

The stranger flinched and unceremoniously let her go.

Before Fiona could grasp anything of what was going on, she hit the dusty wooden floor hard, knocking the breath out of her.

Gavin was at her side in an instant, holding her, overly concerned.

"Fiona, are you okay?"

Fiona shook her head, gathered herself, and finally replied, "It's okay, Gavin. I'm all right."

Sean stared down at the two of them a bemused look on his face. Gavin's anger flared at the callous stranger. He jumped to his feet and stood in Sean's face.

"Oy! What's your problem? You have no right touching her like that!" He shoved Sean hard.

"Easy mate, she slipped is all. The rest was her doing," Sean replied calmly, with a slight but obvious undertone of danger in his voice.

Fiona felt her face redden, unsure if it was anger, fear, or embarrassment.

Meanwhile the rest of the troupe was on their feet, silently backing Gavin should a fight break out.

"Always the troublemaker, eh, Sean?" came Patrick's voice from the top of the stairs.

"Well, good to see you too, brother," came Sean's curt reply.

Brother! Fiona looked from Patrick to Sean. Yes! She could see it now. They did share a lot of the same features but it was their eyes that set them apart. Sean's were of the darkest blue, almost black – and Patrick's were a warm brown that perfectly matched his hair. Patrick appeared younger. They shared the same build. Sean's obviously earned from being a member of Scotland's working class. He was rougher at the edges. His hands more worked, were now held casually at his side, with only a slight twitch in his left little finger betraying his otherwise completely calm exterior. His thick beard hid almost all emotion from his face, and Fiona now realized why she had found the kiss so harsh. She imagined that if he was clean-shaven they could almost pass as twins.

Seeing he no longer had a fight, Gavin took two steps back, but continued to stand between Sean and Fiona. He was trying to guard her, and Fiona felt she had entered some weird passion play where her honor was at stake. There was complete stillness.

No one in the troupe spoke. Fiona caught Abigail's eyes and she appeared just as rattled as she was.

"What the hell are you doing here?" Patrick broke the silence, as he took one hesitant step down the stairs.

Sean smirked again, "Just came in for a pint, Paddy."

"You know what I mean, Sean!" he yelled.

"Aye, that I do," Sean agreed. "I assume it's the same reason that you are here. Got me a summons I did, but unlike you, I came alone." He allowed his gaze to encompass the troupe.

"You should not have come!" Patrick took another several steps down the stairs, his eyes wildly alive.

"Easy there, brother, I could say the same thing to you," Sean's fists tensed.

"What's all this then?" burst in Miss McStargle. "I'll have no more of this dancing on tables and rabble rousing tomfoolery!"

Nicholas intercepted her. "Aye, you're quite right Miss McStargle. I can guarantee you that there will be no more such unruly behavior. Our spirits are a bit high after our long and arduous journey. Perhaps I can buy you a wee dram to settle your nerves?"

"At least there's one gentlemen amongst the lot of you." Miss McStargle grudgingly allowed herself to be led back to the bar. She glared at the brothers.

"I knew there'd be trouble the moment those Berenger lads came back into town; they were no good, the lot of them, no good I tell you."

"Please do tell," Nicholas insisted as he found a half-empty bottle of single malt on the bar. Apparently, Miss McStargle had been busy. He poured the both of them two very large glasses of the whiskey. "I have all night."

After Nicholas and Miss McStargle made their exit, Sean felt it was time he left as well. He turned to face the troupe, bowing theatrically to them.

"My apologies. I dinna mean to cause a scene. I merely came in from out of the cold, searching for a pint to warm me bones, but I can see now I best retire to my bed."

Abigail caught his eye. He winked at her, eliciting in her an unexpected blush, before he returned his attention to his glaring brother.

"Patrick," he smiled and nodded. "We'll continue our discussion tomorrow, I trust?" Then, back to the others.

"Gentlemen ... " his gaze lingered lustily over Fiona's body, "and ladies." His eyes burned uncomfortably into Fiona's, obvious to everyone in the room. "Until next time."

Gavin had had enough; he started to rush forward, his face a fiery red, his fists clenched. Fiona grabbed his arm and held him back. "Gavin, no! Let him go," she implored.

Sean burst into a low and unsettling laugh, turned and left.

No one reacted for a moment. Samuel walked over to Gavin, fists still clenched. "Come on Gavy. I got me some cigars. Let's grab some air."

Gavin relaxed and turned to Fiona. "Sorry, Fiona, I ... "

"It's alright, Gavin," she said. "Go with Samuel. But take your knife in case those were-rabbits come back."

Gavin finally smiled. "I will." He and Samuel headed out the front door.

When Fiona finally turned back to look at the stairs, Patrick had vanished. This time she wasn't at all surprised.

"Well," Andrew said, breaking the tension. "I have the strangest urge to go upstairs and write."

* * *

"He *read* his script to you all night on the train?" Fiona asked, not sure she had heard Abigail correctly.

Abigail giggled and leaned back against the bed. "Pretty sure of it. It's still a bit hazy really," she began pulling her right shoe off.

"Does he usually do that?" Fiona asked. Although she couldn't imagine that he had been doing it often, otherwise she would have heard about it by now.

Abigail shook her head.

"First time," she said, throwing her shoe towards the wall and turning her focus to her remaining shoe. "Maybe it was the train. He likes trains."

Fiona stifled a laugh.

"Andrew said that since I seemed so interested, he had something exciting to share with me." She threw her remaining shoe towards the wall. "I didn't realize that was what he meant or I would have just gone to bed."

They had all been talking about how tired they were, but upon reaching their room they somehow found themselves not in bed but leaning up against it on the floor. The room left much to be desired. There was one lumpy queen-sized mattress captive within a chunky wooden carved frame and headboard, oddly placed right in the middle of the room. The walls were lined by peeling, dated wallpaper–a hunting motif of dogs and ducks. There was one window, heavily shaded and a wooden table that held their only source of light, a lonely oil lantern.

They had tried the light switch when they entered, but nothing happened. Apparently Miss McStargle didn't see the need to keep these rooms with live electricity, even though the bar had it.

The room was also chillingly cold. There was a fireplace, but Miss McStargle was as stingy with the firewood as she was with electricity. Little heat was emanating from the embers.

Abigail pulled the bed covers off the bed and wrapped them around her and Fiona. "I don't think I dare sleep on that lumpy monstrosity of a bed." She turned to find Fiona smiling at her. "What's so funny?"

"Nothing. I just think it's cute is all. Was Andrew's new script any good?" Fiona asked.

"Honestly," Abigail leaned in close to her, "I can barely remember. I so was afraid he was going to ask me about it during the walk into town," she giggled.

"Abby, he probably thinks you hated it!" Fiona scolded her.

"I know! He probably thinks I hate him as well! Fiona, we can't have that! He's so adorable."

"Well, he'll never know you think that way if you keep forgetting all his conversations," Fiona said.

"I don't forget all his conversations!" Abigail looked like a scolded child. "Oy! And what makes you so clever? Was it your *one big night* with Patrick? I went to your room first you know." Abigail's pout turned into a playful smile. "I have been dying all day to ask you about what happened."

Fiona felt a wave of relief. She had wanted to talk to her friend about the events of the previous night, but just didn't know how to bring it up after all the strange events. Fiona took in a deep breath and proceeded to tell her about her night with Patrick. When she finished, Fiona leaned back against the bed and waited for Abigail to speak.

"But he kissed you?" Abigail asked.

"Yes." Fiona replied.

"And then he stopped?" Abigail asked.

"Yes. He said there were a thousand things he wanted to do with me but couldn't."

"It just doesn't make any sense!"

"I know!" Fiona replied, desperately. Of course she knew that, she had been thinking about it constantly and could not find any reason behind what happened.

Abigail reached out her hand and held Fiona's. "Men are strange to begin with, and Patrick is going through something, I'm sure has nothing to do with you."

"It's just so strange! Everything: the train, this town, Patrick's attitude, and now his brother. I doubt Patrick will be back to normal anytime soon." She felt as miserable as Patrick had looked.

"We'll be gone from here soon enough," Abigail said. "And then maybe he can relax."

Fiona nodded. She hoped Abigail was right. She decided to change the subject.

"Did you see how mad Patrick got at his brother? I wonder what happened there?"

"He was probably mad because you kissed his brother and not him," Abigail suggested.

"That I did." She could not believe that she had done that. *But, what a complete bastard!* She had fallen into the arms of a man who may have destroyed her chances with Patrick; to add insult to humiliation, he dropped her! She unconsciously rubbed her bruised behind and felt where he had inappropriately put his hands.

"He looked a lot like Patrick, he did. Just with a beard," Abigail said wistfully, breaking Fiona's reverie. "He's a fine looking one, that dark stranger."

"I hate beards!" Fiona replied. "Beatrice had it right in Much Ado About Nothing."

"You wish to dress Patrick's brother in your apparel and make him your waiting-gentlewoman?" Abigail asked, knowing the play well.

"That might actually make Patrick smile again," Fiona laughed.

"Makes me smile as well," Abigail teased.

The night was bitterly cold, but Gavin barely noticed. His thoughts were inflamed by the recent past.

"I should have killed that cocky son-of-a-bitch," he said. To anyone looking, the two men would have been mere blended dark shadows against the tree across from the Broken Piper were it not for the two glowing tips of their cigars.

Samuel grunted, neither in agreement or disagreement. He was enjoying his cigar and preferred the night's stillness to rehashing what was to him, an inconsequential evening. He drew deeply on his cigar, rounded his lips and let float out a perfect smoke halo. It seemed to hover indecisively in the frigid night air before dissolving into mist.

Gavin didn't notice. His eyes were locked on the Berenger Playhouse where the single light still burned.

"They're even better when you actually smoke them."

"What?" Gavin was yanked back to the moment.

"That cigar." Samuel indicated the cigar in Gavin's hand that was burning away untasted. "Cost me half a quid."

"Oh, sorry." He took a deep draw.

"Beautiful night." Samuel puffed away, as he examined the starry sky, visible in patches between the scattered clouds and soft snowfall.

"No it isn't," Gavin answered, bitterly, having had enough of this night. He stubbed his cigar out against the tree trunk. "I'll smoke this later. I'm going to bed."

"Good idea," Samuel agreed.

Gavin took a few steps toward the pub.

Samuel sighed, took a final puff then put his cigar out as well. He quickened his pace to join Gavin.

As they entered the pub they heard Miss McStargle's voice, slurred by alcohol.

" ... If the Vicar's not drunk I says, then Bob's your uncle." She giggled like a naughty schoolgirl telling tales.

They found Nicholas and Miss McStargle still at the bar. McStargle stared up at them with bleary eyes. It wasn't clear if she even recognized them.

"You coming up, Nick?" asked Samuel.

"In a bit," Nicholas grinned. "Miss McStargle's just finishing up a fascinating tale."

"Aye." Samuel grunted. "Be seeing you later, then." Gavin had already moved on, trudging up the stairs.

Gavin reached for the knob to the door on the right of the landing when Samuel caught up with him.

"Not that one. That's the girl's room," Samuel informed him as he crossed the hall to the other room.

"Oh, my mistake." His hand lingered a moment longer than necessary before finally turning and following Samuel into their room.

Ducks and dogs. The men's room was lined with the same peeling wallpaper as the women's. Their room was quite a bit bigger: two double beds and a cot, a writing table and chair and a fireplace with a fire blazing.

Patrick was on the cot, his back to them, apparently asleep. Andrew was busy writing away at the desk. He finished with a flourish of his pen then turned to the two men.

"You two take that bed," he pointed. "Nicholas and I will take the other. Patrick has claimed the cot, as you can see."

Samuel nodded, plopping down on the lumpy bed. Gavin warmed his hands. "Nice fire."

"I had to scrounge around to find some wood." Andrew leaned back in his chair. "Where's Nicholas?"

"Talking to the old lady."

Andrew grinned. "He'll come back with a story for sure, trust me."

As if on cue they heard footsteps climbing the creaky stairway. The door opened and Nicholas entered, a wide grin on his face.

"What did I say?" Andrew beamed. "Go on Nick, spill it."

Nicholas sat heavily on the bed.

"Oh there's much to tell that's for sure, but not tonight. The hour's late." Nicholas said, removing his shoes.

A low rumbled snore issued from Samuel who had fallen asleep on his back, fully clothed.

"Point made," Nicholas laughed.

Patrick tossed and turned over on his tiny cot, trying desperately to find a comfortable position. He pulled his pillow over his head.

Andrew extinguished the lantern and crawled into bed as Samuel snored on.

* * *

Sean sat on the edge of the stage of the theater drinking from a bottle of scotch. The ghost light flickered behind him, almost going out.

"Damn light," he muttered. "Got to find a better candle." He took another drink. "Tomorrow," he decided.

He sat and stared into the muted shadows, thinking.

"Patrick ... " he murmured. "It *has* been a long time."

He was surprised at how intense his emotions were on the subject. He had managed to block out most thoughts about his brother–hell his whole family for that matter–but these last few days, especially coming back *here*, had been like a memory avalanche.

"If I wasn't so fookin' broke, I'd never have come!" he swore aloud. However, there was one bright light on the horizon; that pretty lass in the pub that fell into his arms. Divine providence, if ever he saw it. "Aye, she was a feisty one, for sure."

Sean knew her type well. She was the kind that preferred to hide her fire behind a veil of respectability; the type you had to charm, seduce and even trick into your bed. And while she would definitely be a firecracker between the sheets, (the kiss had hinted that!) you'd want to take your time with her, to slow the sparks.

When was the last time her fuse had been properly lit?

That rustic lad was ready to fight for her honor, but it was Patrick she looked to for support.

Interesting that. I wonder if he'd ever tried to tame her?

Patrick did always know how to pick them, but then again he also always knew how to steal them. Sean's mood darkened. This was not a memory he wished to visit tonight.

He drank a bit more. Then a lot more.

He thought he heard something behind him. He turned, but there was nothing there. Then the heavy back curtain billowed slightly in the dead air.

"Who's there?"

No one answered.

He rose on shaky feet, staggering across the stage, toward the now still curtain. The bottle dropped unnoticed, as he ran his hands down the thick red velvet.

He spun to face the empty seats. He took a step or two forward and glared out at the non-existent audience. Without preamble he burst out in a deep, majestic, baritone that rang across the wings of the building:

"To-morrow, and to-morrow, and to-morrow,

Creeps in this petty pace from day to day,

To the last syllable of recorded time ... "

He held the stage for a moment longer, then slumped to the floor. He lay there for a moment before spying the bottle just out of reach. He crawled to it. There was still plenty left. He took another swig. His thoughts returned to women, as his thoughts tended to do whenever he allowed them free reign.

It was too bad he dropped her–she was quite warm and supple, but hearing himself called by his brother's name was just too much. Insult was added and thus injury was received. Still, she had a nice rounded bottom to cushion her fall. He mused over that for a moment.

"Here's to slippery women and stickier hands!"

He took another swig as he stared up at the ceiling.

"'And all our yesterdays have lighted fools ...
The way to dusty death. Out, out, brief candle!
Life's but a walking shadow, a poor player
That struts and frets his hour upon the stage
And then is heard no more. It is a tale
Told by an idiot, full of sound and fury,
Signifying nothing ... '

The ghost light flickered and went out.

"Ah, the curse of Macbeth," he whispered to the darkness.

* * *

Fiona trudged through the snow, heading back to the abandoned train car. She had to get back! Yet, she couldn't remember why. She slogged through the deep snow banks making slow progress.

She paused to catch her breath when she sensed something following her. She searched the countryside still bathed in moonlight that made the falling snow look like tiny cascading blue diamonds.

She shook her head. *What am I doing?*

All she knew was that she had to keep moving! The cold was chilling her bones, climbing up her spine with icy fingers. She began walking again, faster now, the only sound was her frozen feet crunching in the snow.

She kept glancing behind her, but all she could see was the cloud her nervous breath made. She sensed that whatever it was was also circling her, staying just out of her vision, gliding through the snow like a ghost.

What was that sound?

She stopped to listen. Confused, Fiona became aware of a strange growling sound behind her, growing louder.

Turning, she thought she saw a shadow dart between the trees.

There it was again!

Suddenly the shadow was running full speed at her!

The growling thing was almost upon her!

"It's one of Samuel's werewolves!" she screamed. Her eyes flew open and she gasped for air.

"Fiona?" Abigail whispered.

Fiona, gasping, was surprised to see Abigail's face right in front of hers, also terrified.

"Wh-what? Where?" Fiona asked, confused, still half in her dream.

"Shhhh! Don't you hear it?" Abigail hugged her tight in fright, almost crushing Fiona. They were still on the floor, never having made it to the bed.

"Hear what?" Fiona started, and then she heard it. The terrifying noise she heard in her dream. It was *real* and it was right outside their door!

"I hear it too," Fiona choked back her fear. The embers had died completely, the lantern was extinguished, and there was a different chill in the room. Only a sliver of moonlight gave off any illumination.

SCRAAAAAP! GROWWWWWWL. The muffled sound came again, just outside their door.

Fiona began searching the room for a weapon. All she could see within arm's reach was Abigail's shoes with their large, hard heels. Yes, she thought, that will have to do.

Fiona fought her way out of the covers and grabbed the shoe.

"Fiona! What are you doing?" Abigail gasped. "Don't go out there!" But Fiona was already rising.

"Fiona! No!" Abigail hissed, pulling at her arm, trying to drag her back.

Fiona pulled free. "It's alright," she whispered. "Besides, the boys are right across the hall."

"What if it's a ghost?" Abigail asked, softly.

"It's probably just Miss McStargle," Fiona tried to assure her.

"McStargle? Maybe if someone's strangling her."

"Shhhh!" Fiona warned.

Her hand shaking slightly, Fiona reached out and grabbed the doorknob. It was icy cold.

Outside the dragging sound grew louder.

Fiona turned the knob very slowly, very quietly, barely pulling open the door when the sound suddenly stopped.

The door creaked open abnormally loud, surely alarming whatever was outside of her presence.

Silence.

Fiona raised the shoe above her head as she peered around the door into the dark hallway.

Someone or some *thing* called out, "Fiona?"

"EEE!" she yelled, throwing the shoe at the shadowy form in the hallway. Almost as an echo she heard Abigail scream from inside the room.

"Ow!" the voice cried.

"Go away!" Fiona screamed. As her sight began to adjust to the dim light seeping in from the only window, it was not a monster she saw, but Patrick sitting on his cot in the middle of the hallway.

"Fiona?" Abigail called out from inside the room, her voice panicky.

Patrick scrambled to his feet and searched around behind him. "What is it? Are you and Abigail okay?"

"No! Damn it, Patrick! You nearly scared the life out of us!" Fiona turned to see Abigail completely hidden under the bed sheets, one hand reaching blindly for her remaining shoe.

"Abby, it's okay," she called out. "It's just Patrick dragging his stupid cot out into the hall is all."

"Oh," came Abigail's muffled voice from under the covers.

"I'll be back in just a minute. Go back to sleep," Fiona insisted as she closed the door.

She turned on Patrick. "What in the hell?" she began, "you better have a damn good reason for trying to frighten us. Oh, and don't you start talking about being all sad and alone, we all already know that! And, by the way, it's all your own fault!"

"Whoa, slow down there, Fee!" Patrick sank back onto his cot, pulling the covers up to his neck in mock fright.

Fiona glared at him.

Patrick couldn't hold it in any longer. He burst into laughter. Fiona tried to remain mad, but couldn't. Suddenly she was laughing with him, overjoyed to see his change in mood.

"Was that supposed to kill me?" he gasped, between laughs, pointing at Abigail's thrown shoe on the floor.

"What? Yes. It's all I could find," admitted Fiona, giggling.

"God forbid I was a monster. Although, you nearly poked out my eye." He rubbed the bruise above his eye where the shoe hit him. "Damn your ferocity, Fiona!"

"Yes, yes, I get it. Next time I'll find a cricket bat or something," Fiona smirked, hugging her arms from the cold.

He noticed her shivering and lifted the blanket inviting her in. "Come now, Fiona. There is room enough for two in here."

Fiona's heart leapt.

"Just a couple of minutes, then I have to go back to Abigail."

"Agreed."

Fiona dove to his side, burying herself under the covers. Patrick wrapped his arms around her.

"Two nights in a row, lucky me." Patrick said, as he rubbed her arms, trying to still her shivers. "And to answer your question, the reason I am out here is because Samuel's snoring got so bad I actually feared he was turning into one of his werewolves. Not to mention that five guys in that tiny room is four too many."

"And now here I am crowding your little bed." Fiona nuzzled in closer to him. "Perhaps I should leave," she joked, making no effort to move.

"You'd better not; I have no idea where that shoe went. I'm completely defenseless."

"That sounds like my line," she purred into his chest.

A few moments of soft, comfortable silence followed.

"This feels so right, Fee," he whispered as he brought his head down to meet her lips. She didn't shy away. Their lips met ever so slightly. They kissed once.

Fiona waited for the rush of deeper kisses to follow, but instead Patrick pulled away.

"Abigail will be wondering about you. And rest assured, we'll be out of this cursed town soon enough," he added.

Fiona, shocked, simply stared at him, her lips still slightly pursed and wanting.

* * *

"I do so wonder what that summons is about," stated Abigail for the tenth time.

They had found out that morning that the mysterious summons was not going to be explained until later that evening at the castle looming just ahead.

So, the two girls had decided to wander off together in the early afternoon, to explore the small town, desiring to get some fresh air during a break in the storm and to discuss all the strange happenings. By the time they returned to the pub they found a note instructing them to meet the others at the castle. The others had gone ahead, and they were making the spooky walk alone.

"I imagine it has something to do with the estate. It usually does," Abigail continued, not bothering to wait for Fiona's reply. Abigail chatted incessantly when she was nervous.

"I don't know. Patrick has been reluctant to talk much about his family," said Fiona. "It's an area that seems to harbor dark secrets."

"Ooooh how wonderfully debauched. But how do we fit in? Why was our entire troupe invited? Why not just call for Patrick and Sean?"

"I'm sure I don't know," Fiona sighed. Why speculate? They would know soon enough. Yes, there was definitely something mysterious about the whole affair.

They continued their climb up the hill. It was now pitch dark, and their lanterns did little to light up anything other than their own faces. They had bundled up against the cold, but it still seemed to bite through. Fiona had the eerie feeling that they were being followed, but every time she turned around, there was nothing there.

"God, I wish Andrew was here!" said Abigail, through chattering teeth. "No offense, Fiona, but he is much better at keeping the cold away."

"I am sure he is," replied Fiona.

"I told him, you know," Abigail said with a note of triumph in her voice.

"Told him what?" Fiona asked.

"That I didn't really remember much about his script, and do you know what he said?"

"No. What did he say?"

"That he would gladly read it to me again!" said Abigail, beaming.

"That is really sweet of him," Fiona said, feeling a slight twinge of jealousy. She was happy for Abigail but wished that some Andrew would rub off on Patrick.

They walked on in silence.

"Do you think Andrew will save me a chair? I hope he does. Right beside him!" Abigail speculated.

"We will soon enough find out," Fiona replied, tiring of her chatter.

"Do you think him asking to read me his script again was a bold move?"

Fiona did not reply. She chose to walk on as if she had not heard.

"Well, I think it was. I really think he likes me a lot, Fiona. Don't you?"

"Yes. I do." Her voice hopefully gave away her displeasure with the subject.

"What's ruffling you now? Don't tell me Patrick's mood has rubbed off on you?" Abigail queried, frustrated that Fiona was not sharing in her joy.

"No, it's just hard for me, Abby. You have this great guy who takes complete interest in you and I have nothing even remotely like that."

"Fiona, stop it! He likes you," Abigail insisted. "It's just this town has put a queer way about him. Give him time."

Fiona spun unexpectedly on her shivering friend and exploded. "Really? More time? Patrick's only feelings for me are on the stage or as a mate. He had me in his bed on the train and in his arms and then ... nothing. And last night his cot, again nothing! I feel like his sister! If I hear 'sweet Fee' from him one more time, I'll punch him!"

"Didn't he say he wanted to do a thousand things with you, *to* you? I've seen the way he looks at you. It's not like a mate or a sister," Abigail insisted, her voice sounding unusually mature.

"Then he's not seeing me at all," Fiona sighed.

"Oh, poor Fiona, I know what's wrong with you," Abigail said in an all-knowing way. "You have been struck down with the itch."

"The itch?"

"The itch is the itch that only a man can scratch," Abigail said with a sly grin.

"Oh, *that* itch!" Fiona smirked. "I guess I might have that."

"You *guess*?" Abigail exclaimed, bursting into laughter.

Abigail was right. Fiona had been left unfulfilled ever since that night on the train. And it seemed like Patrick was content to leave her that way.

"Oh Abby, I'm sick of complaining about Patrick. It feels like it's all I have ever done. Let's talk of something else."

"Okay," Abigail agreed. They kept walking in silence until Abigail added, "Just promise me you won't sing tonight, okay?"

"Are you implying my singing was horrible?" Fiona asked, feigning hurt.

"Nay. You know that's not what I mean. We don't want a repeat of last night. Another grab from Sean and Gavin might start a row to end all rows."

Fiona laughed. "I didn't realize my singing had that kind of effect."

"He really is handsome," Abigail mused.

"Who? Gavin?" Fiona asked, surprised that anyone could find sweet, annoying, overly protective Gavin attractive.

"No! Are you daft? Patrick's brother! But, I forgot, you hate beards."

"Beards *and* pompous asses," Fiona corrected.

"Honestly though, don't you think he's handsome? He does look a lot like Patrick, and I know you like how he looks." Abigail goaded her for details. "Besides, it looked like you were enjoying your time in his arms."

"I thought he was Patrick! And he had no right to touch me as if we were husband and wife! That man has no respect for a lady. He acted like some kind of highwayman!"

"And exactly where did he touch you?" Abigail prodded.

"Nowhere you need to think about," Fiona quipped, embarrassed.

"He winked at me you know, when Patrick was yelling at him," Abigail's smile glowed in the moonlight.

"Good for you," Fiona said sarcastically.

"Was it a great kiss?"

"I don't remember," Fiona lied, reliving it as she spoke. She also remembered how Sean's eyes had landed on her right before he left. Blue black light illuminated from them with the strangest intent deep inside. He stared at her as if the rest of the world had vanished. She felt extremely uncomfortable, violated even, but she had held her ground never breaking eye contact. She did not like being fondled like a common whore and wanted to show her distaste for his actions. Luckily, Gavin's overreaction had brought Sean's penetrating stare to an end.

They turned a corner and the castle came into full view for the first time. The crescent moon, half-hidden by clouds, looked like a sinister, winking eye.

Abigail and Fiona froze in their tracks.

"It looks simply haunted," Abigail gasped.

"Don't tell me you believe in ghosts?"

"Don't you? I thought everyone did."

"I suppose you also believe in fairies and leprechauns?"

Abigail looked around, nervously. "Of course, and they can hear us you know."

Fiona laughed. "I'd watch my step Abby, or you'll step on one in the dark."

"It's bad luck to mock the fairies," Abigail bemoaned. She called out to their surroundings. "She didn't mean it, fairies. We are both quite fond of you and respect you. We would never disparage your kind. Amen." She crossed herself.

Fiona started to laugh but had to swallow it when she heard a distant chuckle rumbling from the darkness. *What the hell was that?*

The sky darkened. The moon vanished, and the air took on the electric feel of an imminent storm: the kind of storm that snatches the last of fall and rips it apart introducing the icy grip of winter.

Fiona and Abigail looked at each other.

"We'd better make haste!" Fiona insisted.

"Aye!" Abigail agreed.

They hurried up the road.

They arrived at the foreboding castle relieved and quite out of breath. Although parts were obviously in ruins, lights shone from several windows. Fiona and Abigail's apprehension was significantly reduced by the promise of a cozy fire and a meal with friends.

Abigail was about to lift the heavy, dragon's head doorknocker when Fiona stopped her.

"Look," she pushed lightly on the door and it swung open. "I'd say we're expected."

Abigail giggled nervously. "That's a bit spooky, don't you think?"

Fiona smiled wickedly. "Come now, Abby. It really is *just* a castle. And we really *are* expected."

"If you say so."

The entrance hall was warm and well lit by candles. They could hear murmuring voices and tinkling glasses down the hall. Abigail headed in the direction of the noise when once again Fiona stopped her.

"How hungry are you?" Fiona asked.

"I'm quite peckish, now that you mention it," Abigail replied, noticing the mischievous gleam in Fiona's eyes. "Why?"

"Because we may never have another opportunity to explore a haunted castle."

"I thought you said it wasn't haunted?" Abigail implored.

"I thought you said it was?" Fiona retorted.

"Either way, I'm not interested." Abigail turned toward the comforting sounds of eating and conversation.

"Oh, come. Don't be such a baby," Fiona said grabbing her arm again.

"Andrew will be worried about me," Abigail insisted.

"It's good for men to worry. He'll appreciate you all the more when you finally arrive," Fiona explained as she walked over to a nearby door. "I wonder what's in here?" She tried the handle. "It's locked," Fiona said, disappointed.

"Good." Abigail said with relief. "Let's eat."

"After we try one or two more doors."

Abigail considered this. "Okay. But just the ground floor, no musty attics and no dark basements."

"Fine," Fiona agreed. "No musty attics and no dark basements."

Unlike most of the castle, the dining room was well lit, warm and cozy–as were most of the guests. Miss McStargle had out-done herself. The table was littered with the remnants of a feast: roast turkey, meat pies, peas and carrots, mash, and a great number of bottles of wine and crackers. Coffee and deserts were now being served.

Carlisle sat at the head of the table wearing the full kilt regalia of his family's tartan topped off with a child's paper crown. Overjoyed at having company, he was the consummate host, telling stories, encouraging his guests to imbibe and feast (not that much encouragement was needed) and laughing in a most contagious way.

"You could mark their movements by the circular tracks in the sand," Carlisle was saying.

To his left sat Patrick, looking dour again, barely tolerating the constant slaps on the back and laughter in his face. Andrew was next to Patrick, watching the door as he held vigil over the empty seat saved for Abigail.

"Where the devil is Abigail?" Andrew asked Patrick, as Carlisle continued with a tale about the Seven Sisters, an ancient circle of standing stones once visited as a child, that he had swore moved.

"Probably the same place she was the last four times you asked," Patrick replied.

"She missed dinner," Andrew worried as he downed the rest of his wine. He reached for another bottle and re-filled his glass. "I'd at least think you might be worried about Fiona."

"Fiona can take care of herself," came Patrick's succinct reply.

To Carlisle's right sat an empty seat reserved for Sean. Nicholas, just to the right of that, was having a grand time. He couldn't remember the last time he found someone as charming and eccentric as Carlisle.

Samuel, diagonally across the table from Nicholas (also in kilt and jacket), couldn't agree more. He constantly rose to toast one of Carlisle's *bon mots* or join together in a spontaneous, rowdy drinking song, which the others gallantly attempted to join.

Next to Nicholas sat Gavin, becoming more and more outraged as Carlisle's wild tale spun on. He too held a seat, this one for Fiona. He made sure it was as far from Patrick and, assuming he was coming, Sean's as the table would allow.

"I remember sitting atop one for hours, waiting for it to take off and gallop to the sea with me upon it," Carlisle laughed.

Gavin raised his hand like an overly exuberant schoolboy as he rose up in his seat to challenge Carlisle. "You *are* talking about stones? Giant stones that *move?*"

The table erupted in a chorus of laughter, playful debate, and general shouting over one another regarding the veracity of the tale.

All conversation stopped dead as Sean made his sudden entrance.

"Did someone mention the Seven Sisters? I've been there and they do most certainly move."

"I said no dark basements," Abigail complained, clutching Fiona's arm as they descended the cobwebbed laced stairway.

"It's not a dark basement, it's a wine cellar," Fiona explained, "and look, there's a wee light at the very end."

"I don't care; it's still spooky and I'm still hungry," Abigail whined.

"We'll go right after—wait! Do you hear that?"

"No ... yes. What the hell is it? It sounds like a sick animal." Abigail peered into the darkened cellar.

"The plooman ladies. They come 'round for the plooman's handle ... "

"My God, that's someone singing," Fiona realized.

"It's 'orrible," Abigail grimaced.

"Hush, let's go see who it is."

Abigail allowed Fiona to drag her deeper into the cellar. The singer raised his deep baritone voice in painful gusto as the song climaxed into a verbally obscene chorus that graphically depicted the plowman's plans for the virginal milk maiden.

"That's obscene!" Fiona cried as they came upon the perpetrator of the Terpsichorean torment, a tall, gaunt, balding man dressed in black, his face in shadows. He was holding a dusty bottle of port up to the feeble light, attempting to read the label. The last verse of his tune died on a startled, strangled note at Fiona and Abigail's sudden appearance. He stumbled back into a wine rack and dropped the bottle of port. It exploded with a sticky crash.

"Banshees!" he screamed, frantically making the sign of the cross. "Be gone wid ye!"

"No. No. We're not banshees." Fiona approached cautiously. "We're invited guests. I'm Fiona; she's Abby."

The gaunt man eyed them warily for a moment. "Aye, the Master said there would be several ladies for dinner."

"That's us," Abigail exhaled, equally relieved to find him to be a flesh-and-blood human. "Two hungry ladies, foolishly wandering a spooky old castle instead of eating."

"It's not a safe place to be a' wandering," he warned. "There's parts that be crumbling and others where the wraith's like to dwell ... "

"Fine, we're done," Fiona said. "Just lead us to the dining room, Mister ...?"

As the man stepped out fully from the shadows, he ignited a spark of recognition in Fiona.

"Jeppsen Galbraith's the name, Miss. I'm caretaker of Thornbury Castle, and for this evening I'll also be your wine steward. If you'd forgive me, I must select a port for afters."

"Please do," Fiona insisted. Jeppsen moved off to a far rack searching for another bottle of port.

Abigail pulled Fiona aside and whispered, "Let's leave right now! Did you hear what he said?"

"You mean about the wraiths?"

"No! Afters. He said *afters*. We've already missed the main course!"

Fiona laughed. "Don't worry, there's bound to be enough food." Then she added, her voice lowered, "but what about that Jeppsen? Haven't you seen him before? I swear I have."

Abigail shuddered. "Only in my nightmares."

"Aha! Found it!" Jeppsen cried. He appeared holding a twenty-year-old bottle of port. He blew the dust off the label. He held it up for Fiona and Abigail's approval. "If the madams approve?"

Fiona and Abigail regarded the bottle without a clue to its quality. They both nodded.

"Very good. It's the last bottle of port we have anyway. Now if you would walk this way ... "

"Wait a minute," Fiona cried, finally placing his face. "You were the man at the pub in Llandrindod! The one who brought the letter to Patrick!"

Jeppsen turned and bowed. "Indeed I was."

Sean sized up the situation in the dining room. Neither of the ladies were yet present, and two of the gentlemen regarded him with undiluted disdain. His brother's hate he expected, but the challenging glare he received from the man from the pub last night–*Garvin* wasn't it?–was interesting.

"Young man! I remember you! Please come, join us, take a seat," Carlisle yelled at Sean, practically jumping out of his seat in his excitement. This was certainly a grand evening for him.

There were three empty chairs to choose from. One beside Carlisle, one next to a very young, studious looking chap in glasses–but a bit too close to his brother for his tastes–and finally the one beside the scrapper, Garvin. His decision was made for him as Jeppsen entered the room, followed by the two beautiful, young ladies.

"Miss Fiona and Miss Abigail, sir," Jeppsen announced. The two ladies were surprised to find Sean standing next to them. They ignored his casual leer as they surveyed the situation, refusing to acknowledge him. Abigail spotted the empty seat beside Andrew. She whispered excitedly to Fiona. "See, I told you." She practically skipped to it, 'accidentally' bumping Sean on her way past.

"Ever so sorry, sir," she apologized, through heavily lidded eyes, that blinked very slowly. "I'm so clumsy."

Sean merely bowed, accepting her apology, a slight smile on his lips. Andrew rose and pulled the chair out for her, and as she sat she glanced one last time to Sean before burning Andrew's ears with all that had just happened.

Fiona remained in the entryway, standing very close to Sean seemingly transfixed.

"I saved you a seat," Gavin said to Fiona, his eyes throwing pointed daggers at Sean. He pulled out the chair beside him.

"That's very kind of you, old chap," Sean said gallantly, dropping into the seat before either Fiona or the shocked Gavin could react.

"Over here, my dear!" Carlisle called out to Fiona, indicating the seat beside him. "It's about time we met, don't you think?"

Fiona took the seat next to Carlisle, sneaking a glance at Sean who was doing his best to ignore Gavin's seething glare and barely contained rage. She smiled secretly before turning to face her host.

"You must be Carlisle Thornbury," she offered her hand. He took it and brought it to his lips. "The Third, and perhaps the last, Lady Fiona."

"*Perhaps* the last?" Fiona asked.

"One never knows does one?" Carlisle replied, slyly.

"No, I suppose one can never be sure what good fortune fate has to offer."

Fiona wasn't sure if she hadn't just been the victim of a coy seduction by an eccentric old man in a paper crown, but she found that she wasn't really offended. He had a wild, carefree look in his eyes, eyes that held many dancing secrets and promises of much mischief before his candle was finally snuffed. She felt an instant and immediate kinship to him.

Jeppsen appeared next to her, pouring the port into her glass. He also had some cold cuts, salmon slices, bread, and several, steaming steak and kidney pies on a serving cart.

"Would madam care for some cold meats or pies?" he inquired.

"No, thanks, Jeppsen. This will be fine, but Miss Abigail may wish some."

"Very good," Jeppsen replied.

"So what kept you girls?" Nicholas asked. "We were beginning to worry."

"Just a late start," Fiona replied. Abigail giggled over something Andrew said, lost in her own world.

"My brother was late as well," Patrick announced curtly, scrutinizing her.

"Oh?" Fiona glanced over at Sean, who was engaged in a lively conversation with Samuel on the efficiency of ancient Celtic weaponry, apparently oblivious to all else. "I wasn't aware that he just arrived."

Was she lying? Patrick considered her reply with some doubt. *She and Sean had arrived at practically the same moment. How could she have not seen him on her way up to the castle?*

He hadn't seen his brother since the incident with Bethany, when their kinship–already a fragile skein–was ripped apart for what he assumed was permanent. He had never planned to see his brother again–a feeling he knew was mutual. He also knew that now they were together again, his brother would surely plan to inflict some revenge on him. Patrick understood his culpability, but Bethany had to take the lion's share, whether Sean cared to believe that or not. *I did him one huge favor yet I doubt he will ever see that.*

Patrick stole a glance at Fiona. *Sean will destroy her completely.*

Andrew wiped his glasses with his napkin. They always seemed to steam up when Abigail was near. "So, Abby, what kept you and Fiona?"

Abigail was digging hungrily into a steak and kidney pie. She washed it down with a gulp of wine before answering. "Fiona insisted on wandering through this spooky old castle, heaven knows why!" she giggled. "Have you seen this place? A good strong blow and whoosh! Down it'll come. I'd hate to spend a night here!"

Andrew had actually thought differently. As a writer, new environments intrigued and inspired him. This place–hell this entire trip so far–had ignited his senses. He was practically imploding with new plots and scenarios and was impatient to write them down.

Even Abigail seemed more alive and adventurous. He was anxious to see how this newfound energy and confidence would translate on stage. He felt he could now write her some deeper, more challenging roles. He knew she would like that. She seemed more eager to hear his writings than ever, and he was more eager to share them with her. Their relationship was definitely blossoming. And she seemed more than fine with it. He regarded her as she ate with enthusiasm.

"I don't know," he said, glancing around the ancient dining hall. "It might be fun to spend the night here."

Abigail stopped eating to stare at him.

"Are you daft? You would spend a night here? I could never sleep a wink in this god forsaken place."

"With the right person," he concluded, locking eyes with Abigail. "But I agree, I doubt I'd sleep a wink."

Abigail blushed. She shifted in her seat, trying to disguise her happy confusion.

Samuel downed another dram of scotch; a fine, peaty, single malt from the Isle of Skye. This castle, the lonesome atmosphere, the clean frigid air, heavy with the fragrance of peat, took him back to his childhood in the Outer Hebrides. Aye, he felt right at home here. He had never taken to the big city life and was always glad when the troupe played the smaller towns. He was a pragmatic man, always taking things as they came, so he hadn't given much thought as to why they were now here in this spectacular ruin, nor what to expect from the future. For Samuel the moment was all that mattered, and all that mattered at the moment was more scotch for his glass.

He signaled Jeppsen for a refill, who was immediately by his side.

"Leave the bottle. It'll be easier on the both of us."

Jeppsen nodded.

Sean held his empty glass to Samuel. "Would you mind, mate? I'm sorry, but I haven't properly introduced myself. I'm Sean Berenger, infamous brother of Patrick."

"Samuel McDermott," Samuel nodded as he poured. "Always pleased to meet a fellow Scotsman."

Samuel and Sean raised their glasses and gave a toast to their motherland. Sean excused himself to return to his talk with Gavin, while Samuel took time to consider their host.

He found the old man fascinating. He was all too familiar with the air of faded royalty these Lords maintained, but for some reason wasn't bothered at all by Carlisle Thornbury the Third. Perhaps it was the paper crown that he wore in self-mockery, or his overt generosity, or even the shared wearing of traditional kilts for auspicious occasions—whatever the case, Samuel felt very much welcomed here and by him.

There was, however, much more going on here than met the eye. Carlisle, Patrick and this brother Sean were tied together in some odd way. The faint, ancient aroma of battle was certainly in the air, awakening an instinct that lay dormant in Samuel's ancestral blood. Not that it mattered much to Samuel, but it might be worth keeping a wary eye. He drank to the notion.

Sean sipped from his glass, turning away from the huge, kilt-wearing man sitting next to him.

Nice chap, this Samuel. But I certainly wouldn't like to meet him a dark alley if he had it in for me. Can't really tell how closely aligned to Patrick he is, but I'd better watch my step around him.

Sean took a moment to regard Patrick. Patrick continued to glare at him.

This should be an interesting evening. I doubt it will end well. I'm certainly not making friends with this Garvin character either. Another typically over-strung actor wearing his emotions on his sleeve like a war badge. To top it off, he has burning eyes for Fiona, which, unfortunately for Garvin, she refuses to see.

He almost felt sorry for Garvin, but some instinct inside him would not allow it. Was it because he was dangerous? Nah? Garvin could barely contain himself. He could be manipulated to fly off the handle at any moment. The only truly dangerous man was one that controlled and quelled his hatred until just the right moment.

Still, he could ill afford another enemy–his brother was certainly more than enough for any man to deal with. Perhaps now was the time to try to mend the fence with Garvin.

"So, Garvin, how are you enjoying the evening so far?"

"It's *Gavin*," Gavin replied, through clenched teeth. "It's too bad you missed the main course. The pheasant was exquisite."

"I can well imagine," Sean smiled benignly.

What an ass this Sean is, Gavin seethed. *No wonder Patrick had disowned him. And now he's trying to make small talk? Well two can play at this game.*

"What kept you?" Gavin prodded.

"Oh, this and that, " Sean replied nonchalantly.

"You had no trouble finding the place in the dark?"

"No. I've been here before, many times."

"You didn't come across Fiona and Abigail then?" Gavin asked pointedly.

Sean hesitated for the briefest of seconds before smiling. "No, unfortunately not, but I can think of no two lovelier companions to have escorted in."

He's lying, Gavin fumed, *the bastard! He intentionally took the seat I was offering to Fiona. He'd better stay away from her!*

"Yes, Fiona in particular is quite lovely," Gavin replied, intently. "We go way back, together. We are quite close."

"Yes, I noticed," Sean nodded. Then added, pointedly, "like brother and sister."

Gavin's eyes narrowed. *I do not like this man at all.*

"Well, you three missed a delicious dinner," Nicholas announced to Fiona, as he leaned back in his chair with a satisfied grin, sipping his port. "Not to mention some very entertaining tales from our host."

Nicholas had certainly been entertained by Carlisle's tall-tales, but he had also been intrigued by his careful avoidance to answer any questions about the summons. Carlisle always managed to steer the questions onto a different subject, usually something concerning theater, which effectively piqued

Nicholas's interest. The old man had an amazing knowledge of theater, poetry, and literature.

Nicholas had been moved to poetry upon entering this slumbering ruin: "'Dear God! The very houses seem asleep; and all that mighty heart is lying still!'"

To which their host suddenly appeared and called out, "'Asleep, perhaps, but my heart is not lying still.' It bursts with joy at seeing you all. And you sir, a fellow Wordsworthian man is most welcomed. Most welcomed indeed!'"

And it would almost seem he had witness the original staging of Othello at the globe, so intricate was his knowledge and appreciation of the Bard's words.

In fact, when Fiona and Abigail had finally entered the dining room, so astute was the old man's eye that he had nudged Nicholas and pointed at Gavin's gaze upon Fiona and muttered: 'the green-eyed monster which doth mock the meat it feeds on.'

Nicholas had to stifle his laughter.

But there was also a strangeness that Nicholas couldn't quite put his finger upon. It was as if the old man was testing him. Nicholas couldn't help but feel he was being manipulated for some unknown reason as the old man coaxed and prodded him into revealing his knowledge of the intricacies of the theater, until like a fish being slowly reeled in, he was suddenly left dangling, staring into the eyes of the one who held his fate in his hand. He shuddered involuntarily at the thought. It was almost as if Carlisle needed to know the true depth of his passion before revealing anything about the reason for this bizarre journey. And somehow that reason also held certain lives in balance.

Nicholas shook off the dark mood that had come over him. The old man was surely just an eccentric lover of the arts and nothing more. And whether or not he had passed the test–if indeed there was one–he assumed he would soon find out. In the meantime, he had the lovely Fiona beside him to warm his eyes and heart and an excellent port to warm his belly.

What more could one ask?

Fiona sensed different tensions around the table tightening. Did she and Abigail arrive too late? Was everyone else already clued in to what this evening all about?

Fiona turned to Carlisle. "Surely I didn't miss the explanation behind our invitation?"

A shadow darkened Carlisle's face for a fleeting moment and then was gone.

"Surely not! All must be present, and now all are. Perhaps it is time. Yes, it most certainly is." Carlisle rose suddenly. "But one thing first. If you will all rise, I propose a final toast."

The others rose and raised their glasses.

"To Angus Berenger: my good friend and confidant, easy may he rest."

The toast was greeted with a confused silence from across the table.

Angus Berenger? Was this the father? Fiona wondered. It seemed likely, based on the uneasy sour looks on Patrick and Sean's faces. They both refused the toast, slamming their drinks down on the table, un-sipped.

The others remained frozen, unsure what to do. Finally Samuel broke the stalemate. "To King and Country!" he roared, and the others toasted.

Unfazed, Carlisle finished his drink and turned to Jeppsen.

"Jeppsen, we shall take our tea and afters in the library. I trust it is prepared as requested?"

"Yes sir," Jeppsen bowed.

"Grand. Then off we should all go. Come everyone. Grab your cups and wits, the moment has arrived!"

Carlisle led the somewhat staggering troupe with Patrick and Sean maneuvering to remain as far apart from each other as possible out of the dining room and across the hall to the library, which was the locked door Fiona and Abigail had tried when they first arrived. It was unlocked now and Jeppsen stood prepared to open it.

Carlisle announced regally, "Jeppsen, the door!"

The door swung open to reveal a comfortable, heavily oaken library with wall-to-ceiling books, a blazing fireplace, an imposing wooden desk, a few comfortable-looking leather couches, some overstuffed chairs, a serving dish piled high with fresh baked cookies and cakes, and pots of steaming tea. An open coffin rested on a pedestal.

Patrick turned on Carlisle in open rage. "Am I to assume that this is your idea of announcing my father's death?"

"That is the body of the man you called 'father' and who called you 'son', yes," Carlisle said calmly.

Patrick was apoplectic. "I have no intention of honoring that ... that man! How dare you trick me into a wake!"

Carlisle remained unconcerned. "This is not a wake. If you will take a seat, I shall explain."

Patrick looked at Sean to see his reaction. Sean, nonplused, made his way to the cakes and casually chose one.

"I don't believe you can take this so casually, brother. You hated him worse than I!"

Sean looked up. "True." He walked over to the open coffin, peered inside, munching on a piece of cake. "And now that I've seen him and this proof-positive evidence of his death, I'm quite delighted."

He casually nudged the coffin lid. It closed with a crash. Abigail jumped. "Oy! You'll wake the dead you will!"

Nicholas approached Carlisle who had taken a seat behind his large desk and was shuffling through some paperwork. "Perhaps we should leave this to family. I see no reason for the rest of us to be here."

Carlisle looked up at him startled. "Oh no, you are all deeply involved in this, you must be here. Please take a seat."

Fiona reached out and took Patrick's hand. "Come Patrick. Let's take a seat and get this behind you as quickly as possible."

Patrick resisted, wrestling internally and shrugging off her grip. "No! I will not be a part of any of this! I despise this house!" He jabbed a finger in the direction of the coffin, "I despise that poor excuse of a man! And I despise all of you! Damn you all!" And with that Patrick stormed out.

Fiona started to follow him when Gavin grabbed her arm.

"No, let him go," Gavin insisted quietly.

Fiona allowed Gavin to lead her to a seat. He sat next to her, holding her hand in his, but she barely noticed. Her thoughts were only of Patrick. *I really should go after him; he needs me.*

She started to rise, but as if reading her thoughts, Gavin's hand tightened on hers and held it firm.

The others had taken seats around the room, equally staggered by the events of the evening as intrigued by the revelations yet to be imparted.

Carlisle cleared his throat.

"As this is a most unusual circumstance, unorthodox procedures had to be taken to assure that all of you would come. If it has instilled any discomfort in any of you in any way, I apologize. You will soon see that it was necessary."

Silence.

"I, Carlisle Thornbury the Third, am sole executor of the will and provisions therein in regard to the final estate of Angus William Berenger."

Sean leaned back in his chair. "I was under the impression he had nothing to bequeath except the tarnish on our good name."

Carlisle eyed Sean narrowly. "Do not speak harshly of the dead. There is plenty that you do not know."

Sean held his gaze, then his tongue.

Carlisle rose and walked the room as he gathered his thoughts finally speaking.

"Now, for those of you who did not know Angus Berenger, which is apparently all of you," he said pointedly to Sean, "he was a man with a singular love: the theater. Which is not to say that he didn't love his wife and two sons. He did. However, the Berenger PlayHouse was his lifeblood. And it pulsates with him to this day, even after his passing."

Fiona and Abigail exchanged a glance. Abigail whispered, "What the hell is he babbling about?" Fiona shrugged.

"His will, Sean, as you seemed to have guessed, bequeaths nothing to you and Patrick unless ... "

He paused here, as if lost in thought.

"Unless what?" Nicholas prodded. Carlisle appeared to come back into the present. He licked his lips.

"'I brought not here to read, it seems, but hold and freshen in this air of withering sweetness; but on the memory of one absent most, for whom these lines when they shall greet her eye.'"

Nicholas was incredulous. *Now he's quoting from Frost? I'm afraid he's gone around the bend, short trip that it may have been.*

"Just a random thought that wormed its way in," Carlisle apologized, as if this were nothing new. "As I was saying, there are provisions in the will, rather unusual I must agree, that would allow a rather large sum of money and property to be bequeathed to the estate of Patrick and Sean Berenger equally should they decide to accept these terms."

Sean, who seemed to be the least interested one in the room, had gone over to decide on another cake. He looked over at Carlisle in surprise. "Terms? Really? How mysterious, do continue."

Before Carlisle could answer, Jeppsen entered with a letter on a silver tray.

"Telegram, sir. It appears to be very important."

"Oh?" Carlisle took the telegram and read it, then nodded. "Yes. This is most significant indeed. It changes everything. Thank you, Jeppsen." He placed the note on his desk. "Now, where was I?"

Nicholas rose up in frustration.

"Come now, sir. You cannot interrupt this proceeding with a note of such significance and then carry on as if nothing happened. What does it say? You claimed that this affected us all!"

Gavin jumped to his feet.

"I agree! Stop stalling! What is this all about?"

Andrew, Abigail, and Fiona rose as one. Only Samuel remained seated, studying the Scotch in his glass, either unaware or uninterested in the proceedings.

Fiona noticed Sean smiling wryly, munching on another piece of cake, totally unconcerned. She could not figure him out at all.

"Aye, you're right," Carlisle agreed, as he looked across the eager faces. He retrieved the telegram and he handed it to Nicholas.

"Read it aloud, if you will," he insisted.

Nicholas took the telegram and read it as instructed. "To Nicholas Ashbury and company, care of Carlisle Thornbury the Third, from the Royal Theater of Scotland, Edinburgh. I regret to inform you that due to circumstances beyond our control we must postpone your performances until March of this coming year. We are sorry for the inconvenience and hope that you will be able to adjust your schedules accordingly. Stephan Redmond Carlisi–Prescott, Proprietor."

Nicholas sat down heavily, the telegram limp in his hand.

Abigail and Fiona rushed to his side.

"What does this mean?" Abigail asked.

"It means we are all now officially out of work until spring, and I for one, am officially broke," Andrew answered for him, also collapsing in his chair, his head in his hands.

Nicholas sighed, equally devastated. "I was guaranteed a six month run, with a two month advance. It took everything I had to take us this far. I can't afford to live on what's left, much less pay you all to wait around for six months."

"I don't understand. Why can't we just find another theater? There's always Glasgow or Inverness?" Gavin demanded.

"For one thing, we can't leave here, can we Mister Thornbury?" Samuel spoke up suddenly, staring at the old man knowingly.

Carlisle matched Samuel's stare unabashed. "That is correct, good, sir. Once winter sets in nothing moves from here for many months. Not by beast, rail, or foot. And winter is scheduled to arrive in full force tonight, if I'm not mistaken."

As if on cue the wind howled outside, rattling the shutters loudly.

"But, if I may continue?" Carlisle asked. He started in with a litany of legal jargon from the will. The others were in too much shock to care one way or another.

Fiona listened to him speak as if from very far away. She felt lost and lonely, trapped and afraid. Once again Gavin took her hand, but hers lay limply in his. She had no desire for his warmth or companionship, but neither had she the awareness to pull away. She wished Patrick were here. She desperately needed his comforting arms, his strength, and his smile. *He should be here.* She looked across the room at Sean. Their eyes met and locked for a second before she looked away. *Is this hard for him as well?*

Carlisle continued to read on, what was to her just legal mumbo-jumbo, until he finally came to the point. She sat up quickly, abruptly pulling her hand away from Gavin.

"Patrick and Sean Berenger shall both agree to perform one final play in the Berenger Playhouse on December thirty-one, of this year 1923. Both men shall be required to perform in major roles. Upon completing this task, they will be given the deed to the playhouse and all property surrounding it and the cash sum of twenty thousand royal pounds silver to split evenly and to do with as they wish.

"An additional sum of fifteen hundred pounds is available for the writing, acting, and staging of said play, an outline of which has been left in the care of Carlisle Thornbury the Third, who shall see to it that all conditions of this bequeathment are carried out to the letter. Additional provisions are listed separately and also in Mister Thornbury's custody. Should they decide not to perform this task or fail trying, all property and money shall be turned over to Carlisle Thornbury the Third. So sayeth I and so shall it be done. In proper mind, spirit, and body, signed and dated Angus William Berenger. Witnessed by Carlisle Thornbury the Third."

Carlisle put down the paper.

The room was silent.

The stillness was broken by the uproarious laughter of Sean Berenger. He stumbled to his father's coffin and clapped a hand upon it.

"Brilliant! Well done, father! You will make fools of us all yet." He began to laugh. "We'll perform all right, or die trying!"

The rest of the troupe sat in stunned silence, the joke too bizarre, too complicated to even resonate with them.

"What? Wait. I don't get it. We're putting on a play?" Abigail queried.

Andrew raised his head from his hands. His sad confusion gave way to a twinkle of hope from behind his lenses.

He whispered to Nicholas, "And if this were indeed just some perplexing play, thus would end Act One."

ACT II

'Thou art to me a delicious torment'

–Ralph Waldo Emerson

The silence that replaced Sean's echoing laugh was unsettling. The troupe remained transfixed.

The room felt more crowded, Fiona was aware now of the fact that they were sharing the space with a dead man.

Carlisle seemed unchanged by all that had transpired. He still wore a foolish grin matching his paper crown.

"We need to have a brief conversation alone," Nicholas said quietly to Carlisle. "There are some details I'd like to go over with you before I talk to my actors."

"Of course," Carlisle agreed. "Let's go into my study."

"The rest of you can wait for me in the entrance hall," Nicholas said, heading out. "I won't be long."

As they filed out, Sean remained standing beside the coffin, hand upon it as if he thought it might slink away.

As Carlisle walked by Sean, he paused, placing a hand on his shoulder. "'My words fly up, my thoughts remain below. Words without thoughts never to Heaven go,'" he said in a tender voice. Then Carlisle nodded, making his crown shift about his head, appearing startled by his own words as if he had just said the most magical, completely astounding thing. Then he turned and walked out.

The rest of the troupe gathered in the entryway. Abigail sought protection in Andrew's arms; Samuel searched about for a decanter or bottle to refill his glass; Gavin searched for Fiona, who had broken her hold on his hand and remained in the doorway.

She waited until the wobbly Carlisle, who smiled at her as he creaked past, had vacated the library before boldly stepping back inside and closing the door behind her.

She and Sean were alone. He seemed unaware of her presence. Fiona took a couple of tentative steps towards him.

"Being Patrick's brother, how would *you* approach him with all of this?" she asked.

Sean's back remained to her. He stood still, no indication if he had heard her at all.

"I wouldn't," he finally replied.

Fiona realized she had indeed interrupted a very private moment. She had selfishly been looking for her own peace of mind, but she was too much a fool to see that Sean was seeking the same.

She started to leave when he spoke again.

"Do just what you said, approach Patrick. He can't resist a good passion play, especially if he is the center of attention. If that doesn't work, try telling him about the money, and if that is still not enough ... " he turned to face her, "lure him into your bed. A lusty lass with your infidelities, who kisses like you, should be able to convince a man into doing any foul deed." He turned back to his father.

Fiona was stunned. She should just leave this insufferable ass alone. She was about to do just that when she thought about how broken she was after her father's passing. When her father died she had needed that, just someone there.

"My father passed a couple of years ago and I took it–"

"Save your breath," he cut her off, not bothering to turn to face her, "until you know what you are talking about. I do not need your pity!"

There was harshness in his voice that nearly masked his pain.

"I was just trying to help," she replied in a weak voice.

"Help my brother, then!" he bellowed. "You obviously seek someone who is weak to nurse. Now leave!"

Not knowing how to react, Fiona nodded.

"As you wish," she whispered and crossed to the door. She caught one more glance of him as she left, his back still to her, as he stared down at the coffin.

She opened the door to reveal Gavin waiting on the other side.

"What do you think you are you doing?" he asked, sternly.

"I thought I had left my coat inside," she lied.

"Here, you can wear mine," Gavin offered as he began to remove it. She stopped him. "That's okay. I think I would rather feel the cold tonight."

She shut the door on Sean.

The troupe was half frozen by the time they returned to the Broken Piper. The wind was so harsh and the night so dark with heavy falling snow that they were forced into a huddled mass to safely make it down the slippery path.

Fiona's eyes stung with cold-induced tears as she entered the pub. It was obvious that everyone had wanted to talk about what had happened, but Nicholas suggested that they should all reconvene in the morning after a good night's rest.

By the tired looks on everyone's faces, Fiona saw that Nicholas was right. The troupe bid their goodnights when Fiona spied Patrick sitting in his dark corner.

She moved toward Patrick. Gavin stopped her.

"Leave him. You need your rest," he insisted.

"I'm fine, Gavin," she said, twisting away. His familiar manner was starting to annoy to her. "Goodnight."

Gavin stood still for a moment, contemplating a stronger response. He decided instead to hold his tongue, turned and left.

Patrick looked a complete mess. His hair was wild and his eyes dark. Fiona sought traces of the kind and gentle features she loved, but they had vanished.

Not knowing what to say, she sat down across from him. They sat in silence for a long time. The wind continued to yell outside, rattling the front door.

"I didn't mean it ... what I said," Patrick finally said.

"Nobody thought you did," she replied.

Patrick shook his head and leaned back in his chair.

"What did it say?" he asked.

"I'm not sure now is the right time to talk about it."

"Please," he said, his eyes fixed to hers. "Just tell me."

"It said that you and your brother will each be given twenty-thousand pounds, the theater, and all the surrounding land if you agree to perform one last show together, along with the help of our troupe."

Patrick looked stunned.

"What? That makes no sense. What did Nicholas say? What about our show—"

"It's been postponed; there was a telegram."

"Of course it was." He exhaled slowly. "And what of my brother? What did he do?"

"He laughed. It scared us all silly," Fiona said.

"Sounds like him." His gaze dropped to the table. "So what's the decision then? Are we going or staying?" He sounded as if he could care less either way.

Fiona grasped his hand. *He's so cold.*

"None has been made. We are all to meet in the morning, but I believe the choice is up to you."

He looked at her, his eyes dark and haunted. "How can I decide for all of you when I don't even know what's best for me?"

Fiona touched the side of his face. Patrick seemed to relax.

His gaze moved to the window's frosted glass. "He shouldn't have done that," he stated. "Put my father in the room like that. He should have told me in the letter that he was dead."

"I know. He meant no harm. He's just a silly old man who can no longer think straight."

His eyes remained on the window.

"I never thought I'd see him again. All those times he raised his hand to us. Now to see him lying there ... so helpless."

He took the smallest bit of joy in that last thought. His gaze shifted to Fiona, "I'm sorry Fee. You look so tired. Don't worry about me, I'll be fine."

* * *

Sean remained in the castle, leaning on his father's casket, lost in his own thoughts long after all the others had left. A nearly empty bottle of Scotch was balanced precariously on the coffin within hand's reach.

Carlisle finally came back around. He looked exhausted from the long night's events. He took the bottle away before it had a chance to fall.

"You can stay here tonight, son, if you'd like. There's plenty of room and the night's turned bitterly cold."

Sean regarded the old man; there was genuine concern and even a spark of compassion shining through. He really didn't know what to make of this character, but the evening was too late and he was too drunk to bother trying to figure it out now.

Sean straightened, and with the exaggerated dignity of one who is well into his cups, adjusted his clothing and smoothed his hair ineffectively into place. He stood face-to-face with the old man, trying hard to focus, stroking his beard absently as he cleared his throat.

"Do you like my beard?" he finally asked Carlisle.

Carlisle expected almost anything but that question. "Err, aye, it makes you look quite regal."

Sean nodded. "I thought so, too," he agreed. He suddenly reached out and snatched the paper crown off Carlisle's head and placed it crookedly upon his own.

"Goodnight, sweet Prince," he slurred, patting the old man on the shoulder. He turned and staggered away.

Outside, the wind snatched the crown off his head. It tumbled and flew off into the night. Sean had no light, so he elected to take the longer, less steep path. It was bitterly cold and his hands and feet were nearly numb when he arrived at the theater.

"I'm home!" he called out, as he collapsed onto the stage. The theater was nearly as cold as the outside, but he was too tired to light the furnace. The ghost light was again burning. He fell back and stared up at it.

"What a bloody turn of events, eh?"

There was a rustle in the darkness as shadows shifted.

He slept troubled, in starts and fits, with cloudy dreams that assailed him with confused images: his father in the coffin, a paper crown upon his head, gold coins upon his eyes, muttering Shakespeare through pale lips. Sean lying in the coffin, feverish and weak. A ghostly woman appeared, reaching down and lifting him up easily, carrying him to bed, and brushing his feverish brow with her cool hands and singing him a sweet lullaby in a familiar voice. He looked up into her eyes and saw his own hovering, bloated face reflected back—as if in a dusty fun house mirror; he fell into the reflection, and found himself standing before another mirror, a shiny, glimmering straight razor pressed dangerously to his throat. His voice, (although his lips never moved), whispered, "Sweet Fee ... " As the razor flashed ...

He awoke in his own bed. He didn't remember climbing the difficult ladder up to the loft, but his head pounded too much, his eyes too nearly glued shut with sleep and his body too aching from cold to give it more thought.

He ran his hands through his matted hair, dragged them down over his eyes and cheeks then stopped. *This is bloody strange,* he thought, as he allowed his hand to rub his suddenly smoothened cheeks, lips and chin. *Where the hell is my beard?*

There was a pounding on the front door of the theater.

"Who the bloody hell is that?" He climbed down the precarious ladder as the pounding continued. "I hear you!" he shouted.

He pulled open the door to find Nicholas standing there, stamping his feet in the cold. Behind him stood the others, Patrick at the very rear.

"Yes?" asked Sean, sweetly.

"We need to talk," Nicholas said, not unkindly.

Behind Nicholas, Sean heard the two girls gasp. Abigail whispered loudly to Fiona. "He shaved his beard!"

"So?" Fiona hissed back, although she couldn't take her eyes off him.

"He looks just like Patrick!"

"Hush!" Fiona threatened.

"Would you like to come in then?" Sean asked Nicholas, pretending not to hear the commotion the two girls were making.

"Please. It's colder than a coal miner's ... elbow," he amended in reference to the girls. Sean bowed as they began to file in.

Abigail stopped in front of him and held her face close to his. "You shaved your beard!" she accused.

"Apparently," he replied congenially. Fiona shoved Abigail inside. "Good morning," Fiona said as she hurried past him.

"It is now."

Gavin bumped past him roughly, causing Sean to take a step back. Sean took it in stride. Samuel noted Gavin's rude behavior. He slapped Sean heartily on the back.

"How you holding up there, laddie?" he growled, his voice thick from last night's drinking.

"Fine. Fine. Thank you."

Samuel grunted something and slipped inside, followed by Andrew who passed with a congenial nod. That left only Patrick.

Patrick stood in the doorway, snow falling heavily on him. He didn't move.

"Don't you still have your key?" Sean finally asked.

"I threw it into the Thames," Patrick responded.

"Are you inviting me in? Or do you plan on becoming a snowman?"

"Is that an invitation?" Patrick asked.

Sean cocked his head. *Was it?*

"Aye, I suppose it is."

"I don't need your permission. It's my place too." Patrick pushed in past his brother, then thought better of his behavior. He stopped and turned.

"Are we going to be able to do this? You and I?" Patrick asked.

"I don't know," Sean answered.

"I don't either," Patrick agreed. "You can be a bit of a bastard at times."

"Aye, as can you," Sean nodded.

Patrick had to smile at that.

"It's just about the money with you, is it?"

"Of course. What else could it be?"

"Nothing. Then we should have no problems," Patrick turned and entered the theater.

"I doubt that," he said to himself with a slight smile, then joined the others.

"Make yourselves at home, ah ... I see you already have." The troupe had scattered about the theater, inspecting, prodding, and walking the stage getting a feel for the place.

"I see you have a ghost light lit," Fiona said to Sean.

"Aye. I'm a very superstitious one. No whistling on stage, no mentioning Macbeth, respect for the fairies ... " he quipped.

Abigail and Fiona shared a quick look. Abigail urged Fiona away. "Let's check the costume room!" The two girls went off, whispering.

"Sean, when was the last time you checked this leg rigging?" Samuel asked, inspecting the aged ropes and pulleys that operated the curtains.

"I've only been here a couple of days, and I hadn't planned on staying, much less putting on a play." Sean replied, coming over to where Samuel pulled gingerly on the ropes. The thick curtains pulled closed slightly. A fine snowfall of dust rained down on them.

"How do they look?" Sean asked.

Samuel grunted a non-committal reply. He eyed the rigging with a squinted eye. He shook his head. He didn't look happy.

"Can't see for sure, but they look a little worn to me. Like to climb out on the catwalk and check the knots."

Sean looked up into the dark upper stage area where a creaky wooden walkway without a railing, ran the breadth of the stage. Here was where the curtains were hung and scaffolding and braces assembled in order to add lights or lower props.

"Are you sure you want to walk around up there? Perhaps we should send up a less weighty man?"

"Aye, but if it can't hold me, then it ain't safe for no one, I be figuring," Samuel said sternly.

"Okay then. Have at it. I'll go below and start the generator. If you're going to fall, we may as well be able to watch."

"Good lad. Some light will make it much easier," he slapped Sean heartily on the back, taking no offense.

Sean walked over to the trapdoor in the stage floor and was bending down to pull it open when suddenly Andrew popped his head up through it.

"I love a good trapdoor. I'll try and write a use for this."

Sean jumped back in surprise. "Whoa, didn't expect that!"

"Sorry if I startled you," Andrew apologized as Sean helped raise him up. Andrew was covered in dust and held a dripping candle.

"No worries," Sean said congenially. "I found plenty of similar uses for that as a young boy," Sean reflected.

Andrew dusted himself off. "The lowering mechanism needed oil," he said as he wiped some smudges off his glasses. "I found some grease and it's working fine."

"Great," Sean said, climbing down. "I'm heading into the cellar to start the generator."

"Here you'll need this," Andrew said offering Sean his candle.

Sean took the candle and prepared to lower himself down the trapdoor.

"Need any help?" Andrew asked.

"No thanks," Sean said, disappearing.

Even with the candle Sean found himself fumbling in the near darkness. He made his way to the back of the building toward a thick wooden door. He unlocked the padlock and placed it to the side. He was about to open the door when he heard a shuffling sound coming from the darkness behind him. He turned quickly. No one was there.

"Hello?" he called out. No answer. "Feel free to join me, if you'd like." No answer. "There's plenty of wine down here ... "

Nothing.

"Oh well, your loss." He pulled open the door and descended the creaking stairs to the basement room that served as a wine cellar and storage as well as housing the diesel generator.

"There you are," he said approaching the generator. He pulled the fuel stick out. It was nearly full. "I guess now's as good a time as any to see if you still work, eh?" He pulled out the choke and yanked the starter cord.

Samuel didn't wait for Sean to get the generator working before starting up the ladder to the catwalk at stage right. He figured he'd had enough light to make it to the landing, at which point he could at least see if the catwalk was going to hold him.

He had no fear of heights. After a quick climb he found himself sitting high in the rafters on a shaky but sturdy enough catwalk.

He let his feet dangle free in the air as he surveyed the stage from a sight not witnessed by many. Down below Nicholas wandered and mumbled, lost in thought. No one else was in sight.

Aye, now this is a bit of pleasance; I know where I'll be coming when I need a moment's peace. Samuel reached into his vest pocket and pulled out his ever-present silver flask. He took a sip. Down below, Nicholas had vanished from sight. Samuel took another sip and looked around.

The rigging at hand seemed fine, the main curtain supports appeared sufficient, however the lighter inner curtain ... *What's that?*

On the extreme far end of the catwalk, stage left, Samuel thought he could make out the form of a person. In the dim light, its outline was shadowy and indistinct, tinged in blue catching some distant light source.

Which one of our loonies be daft enough to be up here?

"Hello!" Samuel called. "Are you mad? Go back down! T'ain't safe!"

The figure stayed in place, moaning softly. The hairs rose up on Samuel's arms and neck. "Are ye scared? Do you need help?"

No answer. Then another moan. It sounded like a woman's.

Foolish git. Probably one of the lasses deciding to be brave and now lost all her courage.

"Wait right there, I be coming."

I wish Sean would hurry with the damn lights. Samuel rose to his feet. The catwalk was a good three feet wide, but there was no railing to hold on to. Samuel took a tentative step. It held. He looked across the way. The woman waited.

He started across the creaky wooden support. He looked down. The stage was still empty below.

Which one was it? Fiona or Abigail? Fiona was braver, but Abigail more foolish. Aye, it's a coin toss.

But whichever, he was going to give her a piece of his mind.

He was about half way across when he nearly lost his footing. A loose board had cracked when he stepped on it; a small piece of wood fell silently to the stage below. He crouched down to inspect it. From what he could see, it was just a small slice, broken around a knothole. It should be fine. He rose up and she was standing right in front of him.

"Sweet Mary!" He stumbled a few steps backwards, again nearly losing his footing. The woman's features were oddly blurred in the dim light. It was no one he had seen before.

"Who the blazes are you?" Samuel asked. She stood perfectly still. Elegantly attired, she wore a dark blue, velvety dress. She *seemed* to be watching something happening just beyond him.

When she spoke, it was a calm pleading.

"She's in danger," her voice was like a faint breeze.

"Who?" Samuel asked.

"Don't let her drink."

"Who? Drink what?"

"The sweet one," she exhaled.

"What do you mean?" Samuel's nerve was threatening to vanish. He wavered dangerously on the catwalk. "Who are you?"

The woman reached her hand toward him, as if to graze his cheek. It took all the courage he had to not shy away.

"Someone will die." Her hand was very close to his cheek. He could feel the coldness emanating from it. "I'm so sorry," she added sadly.

Suddenly, sparks ignited around the theater as long disused lights sputtered to life. Samuel was momentarily blinded as a light very near him blazed on. For the third time he stumbled and nearly lost his footing in what could have been a deadly fall if it were not for the icy grip of a steadying hand on his arm. He regained his footing and went to thank the woman but she had vanished.

Nicholas was back on stage below him looking up. "You all right there, Samuel?"

"Aye!" Samuel called down weakly. "We're all fine up here."

Abigail and Fiona wandered down a dark hallway behind the stage. They peered into an even darker room. A broken mirror peered back.

"Must be a dressing room," Fiona suggested.

"I can't believe Sean can sleep in this spooky place," Abigail said, reaching for Fiona's hand in the darkness. "Doesn't it have any lights?"

As if on cue, several overhead lights sputtered on.

"The Fairies must be listening," giggled Fiona.

"Don't mock the wee folk!" Abigail hissed. Then with sudden realization: "Do you think Sean was following us?"

"What? When?" Fiona asked.

"Last night! When we were walking up to the castle!" Abigail exclaimed. "Why else would he mention the fair—wee folks," she corrected.

"Don't be silly," Fiona replied. "Look here's the costume room!"

The girls ducked inside, delighted to see all the elaborate old costumes. They each pulled a dusty dress off the rack and held it up. Fiona chose an exquisitely detailed renaissance dress, while Abigail went for a glamorous red satin ball gown.

"Who do you think made all these?" Abigail wondered. "They're beautiful!'

Fiona was lost, staring at her image in the mirror. "Patrick would be so taken by me in this," she said wistfully.

"Look! Hats!" Abigail buried herself in a box of hats on the floor.

Nicholas paced, making mental notes. He stopped and looked out into the empty seats in the audience. He counted the rows. He looked puzzled.

Sean came up beside him.

"The generator's working fine. Might need some more diesel soon though."

"Okay," came Nicholas' distracted reply.

"You look confused," Sean said.

Nicholas turned to him. "This house seats over a hundred," he stated.

"Yes. That's true. So?"

"Was this town bigger when this was built?"

"I doubt it, why?"

"Then how did they ever expect to fill the house?" Nicholas asked.

"Don't know," Sean admitted, "Can't imagine how we're going to fill—"

"They came by train from all over England," Patrick interrupted, walking up to Sean and Nicholas. "Father used to tell me stories of meeting royalty on the train when he was a boy ... "

"I never heard those stories," Sean remarked flatly.

"Maybe he didn't think you liked trains," Patrick stated.

"Or he didn't like me," Sean replied.

Sean and Patrick stared at each other during a long uncomfortable silence.

"Speaking of trains–" Nicholas broke in.

"Sounds like you had a most peculiar journey," Sean said. "It's probably why I don't like trains."

"Or ships either, I imagine," Patrick suggested, pointedly.

"Touché," Sean smiled tightly. *So Patrick did know about my fateful voyage.* "You always did have a rapier wit."

"Still sharp with a rapier, as well," Patrick jabbed back.

"Maybe we'll have a chance to test that."

"I'll look forward to it," Patrick nodded.

"Speaking of trains–" Nicholas repeated, loudly. "Has anyone heard about ours? Our grips are still on that car. I, for one, could really use my kit."

"Oh yes," answered Patrick, his gaze remained locked onto his brother. "I talked to Jeppsen this morning. He said he'd arrange for a few of us to go to the railroad car to gather everyone's belongings."

"I'll go," Gavin volunteered, suddenly appearing, covered in dust, with sword in hand.

"Where'd you come from?" asked Sean.

"I was checking the weapons props." He waved the sword professionally, just under Sean's nose. Sean didn't flinch.

"Just wondered," was Sean's enigmatic reply as he grabbed the sword from Gavin's startled grip and instantly had it reversed with the tip pressed upon Gavin's Adam's apple.

Nicholas ignored their childish antics. "Fine. Gavin, go round up the others. We still have a few issues to sort out, so we may as well do it now."

Gavin, his face beet red, turned to find the girls.

Sean waved the sword in a mock salute at his retreating figure.

Patrick grabbed the sword from Sean. "Are you planning on constantly being such an ass?"

"Probably," Sean grinned.

"Did Jeppsen happen to mention whatever became of the Luna Passage?" Nicholas asked Patrick, once again interrupting before their emotions could escalate. *This play was not going to be easy.*

"No, he said he hasn't heard a word. Bit strange, that. Then again, he says the telegraph lines have been down for over a month. Can't get a message in or out. Bleeding ice on the lines I suppose."

"Down for over a month?" Nicholas quizzed.

"That's what he said," Patrick replied.

"But we got a telegram last night," Nicholas pointed out.

"That we did," Sean agreed. "Curious, eh?"

"Obviously, someone's lines were crossed," Patrick said.

Gavin swore under his breath as he scoured the passage behind the stage. "Fookin' Sean. Thinks he's God's gift to the world, he does!"

He peered into an empty dressing room. He called out for the girls. "Fiona! Abby! Where are you?"

He thought he heard giggling coming from down the hall. He approached quietly.

"Come on Fiona," Abigail pleaded. "Just try it on."

Fiona was now holding up a dark blue silk dress, very sheer and very sexy. "I don't know. It's pretty risqué."

"Well I don't care. I'm going to see how I look in this," Abigail said, indicating a white, Victorian era bustier. Abigail removed her thick, wool sweater.

"Hey! I just had a great idea," Abigail exclaimed, as she undid the buttons on her shirt, "Isn't Nicholas' birthday in a few days?"

"Yes. Why?"

Abigail took off her shirt, and now, bare breasted, picked up a bustier. Abby had bigger breasts, which fit her more substantial figure, Fiona noted, although, she thought perhaps her own were a bit more attractive. Meanwhile, Abigail had tried to pull the bustier on over her head. She couldn't get the tight fitting garment completely past her head.

"I'm stuck!" came the panicked, muffled reply.

Fiona laughed. She helped her off with it.

"It unbuttons in the front silly. Here let me help you," Fiona offered. Abigail giggled. "No! You put your own dress on! I don't want to be the only one dressing up."

Fiona thought about how Patrick might find her if she were wearing this gown. "Okay. You win." She pulled off her sweater.

In the shadowy doorway, Gavin hovered. His breath came in short quick steps as he watched Fiona strip down to her sheer camisole and underwear, her firm breasts and pointed nipples obviously visible through the thin cotton top. Almost as if aware she was being watched, she quickly pulled on the dark blue dress, which was a size too big, but none-the-less very striking.

"It's beautiful," Abigail gasped.

Fiona spun around in it. "Do you think so?"

"Absolutely, it's a wee big, but it could be taken in," Abigail said, coming over and tugging here and there at it.

"I would love to wear it out," Fiona said wistfully.

"That's just what I was going to say," Abigail exclaimed. "Nicholas' birthday. Let's make it a surprise costume party!"

"That's brilliant, Abby. Let's do it." Fiona spun around one more time in the dress. "I guess we'd better change before someone comes looking for us."

"What if it's Patrick?" Abigail teased, batting her eyelashes, her index finger beckoned enticingly. "Come here, my sweet Fee!" she whispered in her best Patrick voice, which in fact sounded nothing like him.

Fiona leaned in close, as if to kiss Abigail, her hand lingered teasingly on her silk covered breast, mocking Abigail's overtly flirtatious style.

"Oh Andrew! My dearest, Drewy bespectacled one," Fiona teased back. They giggled uncontrollably.

Then Abigail sighed, "Maybe some day ... "

She began to pull the bustier over her head again, when Fiona stopped her with another laugh. "Wait! Let me help you."

She unbuttoned the garment for Abigail. Fiona slipped the silk dress off her, pausing to rub the soft silk wistfully against her cheek, before reaching for her skirt.

Gavin took one last look at the two girls before he slowly released his breath, unaware that he was even holding it. He backed away from the door, adjusted his suddenly tightened trousers and took a few silent steps backward into the hall. He took another breath. Then he called out, "Fiona? Abigail?"

He heard the two girls squeal. "Don't come in. Stay out! We're not decent!"

"Okay, sorry. It's just me, Gavin. Nicholas wants us all on the stage for a meeting as soon as possible."

"Okay, thanks," Fiona called out. "We'll be just a few minutes."

Gavin turned, and with a smile, headed for the stage.

The troupe gathered around Nicholas, sitting on the hard wooden stage, except for Sean who chose to sit in one of the plush seats.

"First, I need a volunteer to go with Gavin and Jeppsen to the train car to collect our baggage."

"I'll go," Fiona volunteered quickly. "I need some fresh air." Gavin looked very happy.

"Okay fine. Now, as for sleeping arrangements, last night, Mister Thornbury, offered rooms in the castle for any who wish to stay there. By the way, our contract includes free room and board either there or at the Broken Piper."

Sean spoke up. "If any of the ladies would wish to sleep here with me they are more than welcomed. I can't speak much for the room, but I guarantee you'll never be bored."

Abigail blushed. Fiona gave him a disgusted look. "No thank you, Mister Berenger. Abby and I will be staying at the Piper."

"I'll stay at the Piper too," Gavin insisted.

"Okay," Nicholas agreed. "That's fine."

Abigail turned to Andrew. "I assume you'll be staying across the hall," she suggested hopefully.

"Actually, no Abby. I'm going to stay up in the castle with Nicholas." Andrew's glasses slid down his nose as he nodded. "We haven't much time to write this script, so I'll be working day and night."

"Oh." Abigail's disappointment was palpable.

"Besides," Andrew said excitedly, pushing his glasses back up his nose. "It's such a creepy place, I'm sure I'll be inspired to write some spooky scenes should the play call for it, of course."

"I'll take the other bed beside Gavin, unless you want it Patrick?" Samuel offered.

"I'll stay up in the castle," Patrick replied. Now it was Fiona's turn to be disappointed.

"Okay, then, that's all settled," Nicholas mentally checked it off his list. He paced the stage, making eye contact with each of the troupe as he continued. "Now while Gavin, Fiona, and Jeppsen bring our belongings from the train to our new residences, the rest of us need to catalogue the props, costumes, and set pieces here. Samuel, you continue inspecting the rigging. Andrew and I will have our first story meeting tonight with Thornbury, after which I hope we'll have a better idea what manner of play we will be performing. Now I know that this situation is most peculiar, and I wish to thank you all in advance for being the professionals I know you are and the understanding and patience you will surely exhibit. We will perform this play on schedule and in fine manner. This I promise."

* * *

Fiona stood just outside the Broken Piper shivering and making small talk with Gavin. They had finished a very warm and hearty stew, and while the others went their separate ways, they were told to wait outside for Jeppsen. Luckily the snowfall had eased, but it was still very cold and the sun was already halfway in the sky, which meant they would have to walk fast to beat the freezing night.

"We might have to leave without him," said Gavin.

Gavin seemed to be losing his patience more and more these days. Maybe this town had an effect on people. The Patrick she knew only flickered in at random times and Abigail, albeit well enough for her, was flirting more openly, which also did not seem like her. Her open sexuality did seem to be infectious, Fiona mused, remembering the fun they had trying on clothes. She would never have been so brazen in front of anyone, even a week ago. Now all she could think of was which outfit Patrick would most like to see her in? Was she, too, being infected by the town?

Suddenly there was a CLANG followed by a BANG and then some kind of a stutter. Fiona glanced behind her to see Jeppsen driving an automobile in their direction.

He brought the car to a noisy stop right in front of them and without turning off the engine yelled: "Hop in! Sorry I was late, couldn't get the damn top on and I had to put ropes around the wheels. Snow driving can be quite tricky."

Gavin rushed towards the small door behind Jeppsen and held it open for Fiona.

"Come on girl, it's not everyday you get to ride in one of these."

Fiona took Gavin's hand for support and climbed into the backseat. Gavin followed. It was a snug fit as the back seat was quite small.

"There's a blanket back there should you need it," called Jeppsen. "Sorry about the top. Never could figure out how it fit."

Fiona grabbed at the blanket as they slowly began to move.

"This is a model T, right?" called Gavin excitedly to Jeppsen.

"Aye, my lad, it is at that. Isn't she a beaut?" he called back.

"She's brilliant! It must have cost a small fortune to get this brought over from America." Gavin was impressed.

Jeppsen spun his head around, to talk to Gavin. He smiled, which did not help his appearance in the least. "That is where you are wrong. They've been making them in Manchester for sometime now. Master sent me there to fetch this one. Third one off the assembly line she was!"

"Jeppsen, the road!" Fiona called out.

Jeppsen turned to find them veering off to the right, nearly completely off the road.

"Right" Jeppsen called, "Sorry. The steering is a bit tricky as well!"

"Maybe you shouldn't ask him anymore questions until we have stopped," Fiona whispered into Gavin's ear, not wanting to offend Jeppsen.

"Sorry."

They rode in silence for a ways, bouncing and inadvertently grabbing onto each other each time the car took a skid or hit a deep rut. Gavin looked forward to every bump, although Fiona did not seem to notice. She was in love with the town that slowly passed by. She wasn't sure why. The town wasn't much different from the small ones they had traveled to or the one she had grown up in. To her the idea of complete isolation out in this remote part of Scotland was most romantic.

As they rumbled past the theater, she wondered: what if Patrick decided to remain here after the play? He would own the theater with Sean. Of course, those two would never agree to stay together. Certainly Sean couldn't wait to move on. So that would mean Patrick could stay and continue the family tradition. And he would need a wife to be by his side ...

Fiona's imagination ran wild. She pictured winter days with a fire in the hearth and huddled under a blanket with Patrick, drinking tea and laughing. Then she saw their two young, children, a boy and a girl dressed like a prince and princess, putting on a mock play, yelling nonsense from their theater stage, swooning, swaggering, chasing, and giggling. She saw Patrick chopping wood then stopping suddenly to take her in his arms and swing her around. She saw how he would make love to her on a long winter night beneath the flannel sheets, his tender eyes sparkling with passion ...

"Isn't it nice?" asked Gavin, breaking into her thoughts. "Like fate, all of us being here."

"Aye," she replied, keeping the smile she gained from her daydream. "It is as if the whole world doesn't exist but this moment, this time."

"Oh, but Fiona, it doesn't," he agreed.

They were out beyond the town's limits now. Fiona caught sight of the cemetery in the distance. She shivered.

"You want me to ask Jeppsen to slow down? Might help with the cold," Gavin asked, misinterpreting her shivers.

"No, I'll be fine." But Gavin was already leaning forward in his seat.

"Could you slow down? The lady is a bit chilly," he asked.

"I'm only going six miles per hour," he argued, but Fiona felt the car slow right as they came upon the cemetery. It looked eerily beautiful in the glittery snow. She tried to look away, but her eyes were drawn to its desolate beauty.

They bounced on; the car having slowed down only seeming to make the persistent bounces more noticeable. She barely registered Gavin's constant embraces.

Fiona closed her eyes trying to recapture her daydream of Patrick but sudden thoughts of Sean infiltrated. She was pretty sure that Sean had been hinting to her and Abigail that he had overheard them last night. What had they talked about? There was the fairies, Andrew saving the seat, Fiona's dislike of being called 'Sweet Fee', that's about it. No, she had talked about her hatred for beards and then this morning his was gone.

Pompous ass! She had said she hated beards and pompous asses! Fiona smiled. He still retained that trait. However, Fiona could not deny that when Sean emerged clean-shaven this morning he had looked incredibly handsome, but then he would, seeing as he shared a lot of the same features as Patrick.

The bouncing had stopped and Fiona opened her eyes to see the train car right in front of them. It looked lost and abandoned–a thick layer of snow adorned the top, all the windows frosted over and dark.

"It looks so out of place," she remarked.

"I imagine we all do," Gavin replied.

The sleeper car was quiet as Gavin and Fiona made their way through it, pulling out the suitcases and tossing them out the open door to Jeppsen, who seemed content to stay outside and load up the wooden trunk that had been fitted to the back of the Model T.

It was freezing inside and when they talked their words came out in frosty clouds. Something about the stifling atmosphere inside made them instinctively whisper. Fiona tried desperately to avoid being alone inside one of the rooms, as the stillness really unsettled her, but discovered herself alone outside Patrick's room. Gavin had grabbed an armful of Abigail's clothes and was heading down the far end of the train car.

Fiona paused in the doorway. Patrick had almost taken her to bed here, but at least she had spent the night in his arms. She felt a tremendous heat rising as she gazed at the small berth. Fiona entered the room, eyes locked on the berth and the promise it had held.

Then she heard something stir behind it. She froze. She held her breath for a long moment.

Silence.

She sensed something in the room. The soft hairs on the back of her neck rose as if tickled by a slight breeze. She took one cautious step toward the bed. She thought she could make something out behind it, a dark shape cowering. Summoning up all her courage, she took another step forward.

She leaned on the bed, not daring to breathe, as she peered over the edge.

The dark shape whirled around and rose up hissing, red gleaming eyes flashing at her!

She screamed, and in a whirlwind, turned to run out the door, colliding into Gavin. She buried her face into his chest. "Help me!"

"Easy there, lass, it's just a raccoon," he laughed.

"A-a-what?" she refused to turn around.

"Turn around. Trust me," Gavin urged.

The raccoon, just a baby, cowered in the corner of the berth, as scared as she was. It backed against the wall until it found the broken window it had slipped in and vanished. Gavin kept his arms wrapped around Fiona.

"A bit spooked are we?" he asked.

Fiona stepped back, prying her way out of his arms. "Sorry, just got startled is all," her cheeks reddened with embarrassment. "This place is a bit spooky," she admitted.

"You all right there?" called Jeppsen from down the hall. "I thought maybe I heard a scream?"

"We're fine, Jeppsen!" Fiona called back.

"Why don't you wait in the car? I can handle what's left in here," Gavin insisted.

"Thank you," Fiona said. She hurried outside.

* * *

The sun had almost dipped behind the horizon when Andrew arrived back at the theater. He had promised Nicholas that he would let the others know of the auditions tomorrow and gather the available props and costume lists before he started on the new script. Andrew couldn't help but smile, thinking of how he dumped Carlisle's 'script' into Nicholas' lap.

The conversation with Carlisle had been maddeningly obtuse. He had talked about everything from kittens to kettles before finally getting around to the point of the meeting–the plot of the play. Still unclear if it was a ghost story, (or for that matter a story at all) Andrew and Nicholas had watched in amazement as Carlisle pulled out a stack of what must have three or four hundred pages of tight calligraphy, hand-written on both sides of the paper. He carried this stack over to Andrew and handed it to him. "It's all in here," he announced proudly.

Andrew had looked through the papers. It was a random mish-mash of scribbles, recipes, what appeared to be parts of a diary or journal, drawings (the old man was not a bad artist), along with a lot of dialogue and stage directions.

"We should begin casting tomorrow," Carlisle had said excitedly. "I'll choose the main characters. I think I know best.

This young lad here can begin writing the script. The ghosts can sort themselves out as they please. They tend to do that anyway, don't you agree?"

He continued to ramble on about ghosts and Scotland while Nicholas noted the look of horror on Andrew's face at trying to decipher a plot from this deluge. Being a magnanimous director, and a fair writer in his own right, Nicholas offered to look through the massive pile to see if he could find some ghost of a story that Andrew could develop.

Now, that would be a miracle, Andrew thought. Nicholas was probably cursing the fates out loudly this very moment.

Andrew was more than happy to be given this task, as it meant he would get to seek out Abigail for the costume list.

Abigail.

Lately she had seemed more than open to him, she giggled frequently when he was around, often held his eyes with her lovely green ones, and found ways to cling to him at increasingly random moments. Yes, he was more than happy to be returning to the theater.

Arriving inside he saw almost no trace of the troupe. The lights were on but all was still. He thought he heard a distant groan. He assumed Samuel was pushing something about behind the stage, but he could not see anyone.

Andrew climbed up and walked the stage, mapping in his mind the number of steps he took and soaking in the feeling that the theater emanated. He really enjoyed this, the quiet bare stage that, like a blank canvas to a painter, cried out to him, begged him to bring a story to life. *And I will,* he promised.

He stopped halfway through his walk across the stage to examine a costume dummy that had fallen on its side. After returning the dummy to its feet, he continued to the other side of the stage.

Carlisle had seemed to be really adamant on what he wanted, although for the life of him Andrew had no idea at this time even if it was to be a comedy or tragedy.

"Ghosts or no ghost, that is the question!" he cried out dramatically in a deep baritone, not at all like his own natural tenor. Not unlike most people who happen to find themselves alone on a theater stage, he briefly fancied himself an actor. But he certainly wasn't. However he was a writer, and a damn good one. And what a challenge he had been given! To transform the odd thoughts and twisted plots of a crafty–possibly insane–old man into a coherent passion play. It was a challenge he looked forward to, even if Nicholas most likely didn't.

It was then that he heard humming, a sweetly soft, off-key sound that floated around the stage. Following the sound Andrew discovered Abigail standing in the far wing.

What he did not catch was that Abigail had noticed *him* just a moment prior. She held papers in her hand that she set down on a chair, all the while still humming; pretending not to know Andrew was watching her.

She danced out onto the stage, humming her song. She did a clumsy pirouette at the center of the stage then froze to gaze out across the empty seats, much as Andrew just had. She danced toward him as if oblivious of his presence.

Andrew was mesmerized. She was beautiful. As she danced nearer, Andrew battled with when and how to announce his presence.

Abigail stopped about thirty feet from him, beside the blood red secondary curtain. Still not acknowledging Andrew's presence, she continued to hum as she coyly ran her hands along the silky curtain fabric, teasing it across her body, when suddenly she looked straight up and said, "Shite!"

The curtain came crashing down upon her. Andrew watched her disappear beneath a mountain of red. He rushed over, grinning, at the lump that appeared in the middle of the fabric mound.

"Abigail?"

"Yes?" came from the muffled lump.

"You alright in there?"

"No. Quite embarrassed, actually."

"Really, I can't imagine why," he laughed.

"Leave me, so I can find my way out with dignity please."

"A little too late for that, my dear."

The lump laughed. *Well, it's now or never.* Andrew picked up the edge of the fabric and crawled beneath.

Underneath the curtain, Abigail was mortified. *Why had I thought it would be cute to prance around in front of him! All I did was bring the bloody curtain down! More fool me!* She lifted the curtain about her head but saw nothing but deep red. Thankfully the fabric was sheer enough to allow some light to filter through. If it had been the heavy main curtain, she would be in serious trouble.

She lay for a moment trying to figure out the most elegant way to get out from beneath this disaster, when she heard rustling and breathing coming from behind her.

"Abby? You okay?" Andrew asked. He had made his way through the folded maze of fabric.

"I'm fine. A bit stifled, but fine."

"I am here to save the lady who lies beneath the crimson curtain," said Andrew in a very gallant voice.

"What if the lady wishes not to be saved? What if the lady is too mortified to be saved by the handsome prince?"

Handsome? She called me handsome! Andrew exhaled. He slid closer to her.

"Then, I guess we shall have to live out our lives right here," his voice was both playful and anxious. She giggled again but was stopped by the sudden presence of Andrew's mouth on hers in a sweet, soft kiss.

He started to pull away only to have Abigail throw herself with such force to his lips that she knocked them both over in the process. She no longer cared what he thought of her openness, she only cared that his arms continued to fold about her and his mouth never left hers. They tumbled and rolled beneath the curtain, pent desires finally realized.

* * *

Gavin and Fiona rode back in silence. It was Jeppsen who finally broke it with what was supposed to be a song—sung loudly and off-key, competing with the noise of the car's engine. Gavin grabbed Fiona's hand and held a finger up to his mouth to signal her not to laugh, although she had already started.

They made the rest of the ride smiling as they were serenaded by the worst music one could imagine. Jeppsen pulled the car up in front of the theater.

"I'll drop off the kits and grips that belong at the Piper next then head up to the castle. Mr. Thornbury be expecting me in a wee bit."

"Fine, Jeppsen," Fiona said as she climbed down from the car. "Perhaps we will see you later. Thanks for the ride. And the entertainment."

'Dona' mention it." He blushed as he tipped his hat, his unruly thinning hair falling in his face. He quickly smashed his hat back on his head then hit the gas. The car exploded with a backfire and cloud of smoke and roared off at four miles an hour.

Fiona and Gavin waved 'goodbye' to the strange man in his strange car. Neither of them noticed a thin trail of cigar smoke that wafted out from behind a nearby tree.

Gavin turned to Fiona. *"Thanks for the entertainment?"* Gavin asked incredulously. "Do you really want to encourage the man?"

Fiona laughed. "I suppose not." She turned to enter the theater when Gavin grabbed her arm and spun her back around to face him.

"Fiona, wait." He had an odd look in his eyes.

"What is it, Gavin?" Fiona asked, impatient to escape the chill.

"Oh, Fiona, I have been waiting to do this for what seems like a lifetime!" Gavin pulled her to him suddenly, his lips smashing into hers, his embrace overpowering, squeezing the breath from her chest.

Fiona was completely taken by surprise. She tried to pull her lips away, but he only pushed harder. She tried to pound on his chest, to thrust him away, but his grip was too intense.

He stopped abruptly, releasing her. She shoved him away as she stumbled quickly back, wiping her mouth roughly with her gloved hand.

"Gavin!" she cried. "What in the hell do you think you are doing?"

Gavin was abashed by her response. His face twisted through a series of emotions. "I thought ... thought you were fond of me," he said, his voice a pained whisper.

"What? How could you possibly?"

Gavin was obviously in pain.

"Gavin, I am so sorry. I have always loved you as a brother. I've never looked any further than that. I wish I could say I had," she added with tenderness.

"A *brother*? That's how you see me?" His eyes sifted to the ground and no sooner had they looked down but they swung right back up, anger leaking from them.

"Well, no wonder! When your whole world is PATRICK how could you ever see anyone else?" he shouted.

"Patrick has nothing to do with this," she said evenly, trying to hold her ground.

"He has EVERYTHING to do with this! You have been falling all over him ever since he joined the troupe! And Patrick, the selfish bastard that he is, revels in it, while he dismisses you again and again!" In his rage his hands slowly became fists.

"Gavin, please. I don't want to talk about this."

"Of course *you* don't! You don't even see it do you? All the women he takes to his bed night after night, town after town, after he kisses you good night. Then the next morning he charms you again and you honestly believe that you're his 'sweet Fee', don't you?"

"You're lying."

Gavin chuckled. "Ask him yourself. Ask your sweet, charming Patrick if he has been anything but faithful."

Seeing the expression on Fiona's face caused Gavin to soften. He took a tentative step towards her. "I, on the other hand, have seen only you since the beginning. I wait day by day, night by night hoping that someday you will see how much of a boy he is and how much of a man I am."

Gavin was closer and suddenly he had her in his arms. "Then today, we were so close and you were so warm ... it felt so right ... "

"Gavin. Stop it!"

Gavin persisted. "Fiona, it's your choice. You can have me or you can be one of Patrick's many whores."

"Stop!" Fiona shoved him away with all of her strength, sending Gavin stumbling onto a snow bank. He landed hard on his backside, but the sinking snow cushioned his fall.

"You bastard! You're mad to think I could ever want you, especially after you call me a whore!" she screamed.

It was then that Fiona heard clapping. She whirled around to see Sean smiling and standing about a foot behind her, a cigar hanging casually from his lips.

"Well done," he laughed. "I was coming over to help save the very beautiful damsel in distress, but as it turns out, she can take care of herself."

"You! Get the hell out of here! This does not concern you!" roared Gavin as he scrambled up, snow falling off him in white cakes. His fists were clenched in rage, his eyes wild.

"What? Am I to allow you to disparage the good name of my beloved brother?" Sean looked insulted.

"You hate him as much as I do!" retorted Gavin.

"True, but that's beside the point. I think the lady no longer wishes you to remain in her company. Isn't that right, Fiona?" Sean asked.

Fiona glanced at Gavin. "Gavin, it would do us both good if you were to leave."

Gavin took one step towards her, but Sean stepped, in blocking him. "I believe that way would suit you better," Sean said, pointing. Gavin was completely beside himself. His raging eyes swung from Sean and then to Fiona, where they lingered. She thought she saw the faintest glimmer of desperation in them before they turned black and he spun away and stomping off towards the Broken Piper.

Fiona didn't breathe until she saw the front door of the Broken Piper slam shut behind him.

"I'll see to it that he sleeps in the castle tonight," Sean said.

"That won't be necessary," Fiona said quietly. "I'll talk to him once he calms down. We have been through a lot together. This was just a little misunderstanding."

"As the lady wishes, " Sean said gallantly. "However, I will ask Samuel to keep an eye on Gavin in the event he sleepwalks."

Fiona looked over at Sean in surprise, not willing to believe that he was seriously concerned about her. She found no clue in his eyes. She wrapped her arms around herself, seeking comfort.

"You okay?" he asked.

"Yes, I just– "

"T'was nothing. I had a feeling about him," Sean grinned. "Ever since he dropped you."

"That was not his fault," she snapped.

"Easy. I'm not too proud of how I dropped you as well," he said, as he moved closer, still keeping his distance. "Although I was enjoying myself while I had you."

"I was too," she admitted, a bit savagely, "until I found out that you weren't Patrick."

Sean cocked his head not taking the bait. "Oh, and at what part exactly did you stop enjoying yourself?"

"That's not what I was trying ... " Fiona answered flustered. "I meant I *thought* I was–" He was suddenly beside her.

"Want another go then? I did just rescue you. That should be worth something. I can make sure that this time you enjoy yourself thoroughly and never once think of Patrick."

Her anger arose instantly. "No, I do not want another go! And you did not rescue me, I rescued myself!"

Sean smiled at her. "Aye. Then what say we try it again? This time we'll pretend you're rescuing me from big, bad Gavin."

"I will do no such thing! Thank you for your complete lack of help! Good day!" She whirled around and stomped into the theater.

From the front window of The Broken Piper, Gavin watched Fiona storm into the theater as Sean chuckled. Gavin's breath fogged the glass and he could see no more.

Fiona barged into Samuel who was leaving the theater just as she slammed through the front door. He caught her in his bear arms and held her for a moment.

"Whoa, Fee. What devil's after you?" he asked.

Fiona took a deep breath. "Sorry, Samuel. No devil, at least not one for certain. Just need to be alone."

"Well, we are alone," he said indicated the vacant lobby. "Did you need to be *alone* alone, or would you like to talk a bit?"

Fiona saw the sincere concern in his eyes and realized just how much she liked this man. She was about to say something when a faint and eerie moan floated up from inside the theater.

"Did you hear that?" She asked in a hushed whisper. She was surprised to see Samuel go very pale.

"No. I didn't hear anything. It was probably just the wind. Let's go to the Piper and have some pints, eh?" Samuel looked around anxiously.

There was no mistaking the moan this time. It was louder and more mournful. It was definitely coming from inside the theater.

"We have to see what that is," Fiona insisted, feeling very brave with Samuel beside her.

"Do we now?" he asked with a gulp.

She nodded. "Yes we do."

* * *

Andrew had no idea how long they were underneath the curtain entwined in each other's arms and lips and legs when he heard the sound of approaching footsteps.

"Wait, stop!" he whispered.

"What? Why?" moaned Abigail.

They sat up as best as they could under the curtain.

"Do you hear that?" Andrew asked.

"No. I don't hear shite," Abigail replied.

"Abigail?" came Fiona's voice.

Abigail giggled a reply.

Suddenly the curtain was yanked off. Abigail and Andrew blinked up into the staring faces of Samuel and a wide-eyed Fiona.

"Andrew? Abby? What are you doing here?" Samuel asked.

Andrew tried to sputter some clever rejoinder, while Abigail smiled crookedly up at them, her hair in all directions.

* * *

Abigail sighed heavily then pulled the covers up closer to her chin. "It was just wonderful!"

"I am sure it was." Fiona replied, resignedly. "Sure looked like fun," she added under her breath.

Fiona tried to get the fire to catch. She had pleaded with Miss McStargle about the lack of heat and now had more firewood than she knew what to do with. She watched the kindling catch beneath the lone log, waiting until it was fully ablaze before adding another.

She turned to look at Abigail, who had a far away look. *She's going to start talking about Andrew again.*

"I could have gone on forever," Abigail said, wistfully.

"You have been," muttered Fiona as she added a third log to the growing fire.

Why was it so easy for her? she wondered. *Abigail pranced around, casually flaunting her sexuality and Andrew ran right for her! I dance on a table and sing a love song to Patrick and he could care less. Instead, I get Gavin!*

"He didn't even ask! He just kissed me! I hate it when they ask. Don't you, Fiona?" Abigail cut through her thoughts.

"Not always," Fiona said, thinking of Gavin.

Fiona opened her suitcase. She pulled out a few different dresses and skirts, trying to decide which ones she wanted to hang in the small closet she and Abigail shared. She was happy to do any small task that would distract her from Abigail's irrepressible joy. She *was* happy for her friend but felt lost and miserable in her own desperation. Had she been kissing Patrick under the curtain, Fiona knew she would have wanted to talk about nothing else and Abigail would have been overjoyed to listen. Fiona had been aching to tell Abigail about what Gavin did and what he had said about Patrick, but now wasn't the time. Abigail could only think of one thing at the moment.

"Was he a good kisser?" Fiona asked.

"The very best!" Abigail exclaimed. She crawled across the bed to be beside Fiona. "I just wished he wasn't staying all the way in that spooky castle. Who knows when we will get a chance to do that again?"

A knock came at the door and Abigail was on her feet instantly. "That's him!" She smoothed her skirt and spun around to Fiona.

"How do I look?" she asked.

"You look fine. Go and open the door."

Abigail ran to the door, opening it very slowly as she plumped her lips big and pouty in anticipation.

"Did you want to come in?" she asked seductively.

Gavin's face appeared in the doorway. "Sure."

"Oh. It's you," she said despondently, blocking his entrance. "Is Andrew with you?" she peered around him.

"No, sorry. It's just me. Can I speak with Fiona? Privately?"

Fiona tensed hearing his voice. She relaxed a little once she saw that Gavin now appeared calm.

"I'll be right there, Gavin," she called from inside the room. "I'll be just a couple of minutes," she said to Abigail as she made her way past her to Gavin. She shut the door behind her.

Gavin stood in silence, his eyes lowered, searching for the right words to say.

"Yes?" she asked, her voice tight.

"Fiona ... I am so sorry. I was just so taken with you today, I never meant to say or do what I did," his gaze remained fixed on the floor.

"And I am sorry I pushed you," she said gently.

"No. I deserved that, deserved much worse really." He finally met her gaze. "I should have made sure of your feelings before ever doing that. I promise, I can deal with my feelings, and would rather be a brother to you than to not be with you at all. I just hope we can remain friends?"

"Gavin, we could never not be friends. We have been through too much together," she reassured him with a smile.

He smiled back at her and exhaled. "Thank you."

They stood for a moment before Fiona leaned over and punched him in the arm. "Just don't ever do that again," she warned, jokingly.

He punched her arm back, "I won't."

Fiona was relieved to see the Gavin she had always known shining through. She hugged him. He tensed at first, and then gave in.

"Tell me one thing?" Fiona whispered.

"Sure," Gavin replied.

"What you said about Patrick? Was that true?"

Gavin started to answer but was cut off by his door opening and Samuel stepping out into the hallway.

"Everything alright out here?" he asked.

"Yes, thank you, Samuel," Fiona replied.

Samuel appraised the situation. "Gavin, I could use your help. McStargle wants us to go and fetch some more firewood for her. I think she must be planning on burning a witch for all the firewood I've brought up lately."

"I'll meet you downstairs," Gavin replied.

"Or you can come with me now, if you'd like?" Samuel's request was a trifle intimidating.

"Go ahead, Gavin. I think we're done here," Fiona said.

Gavin nodded. Samuel allowed him to go first, then fixing Fiona with a watchful eye, nodded to her and followed Gavin.

Fiona opened her door only to find a very startled Abigail standing directly behind it.

"What was that about?" she asked, not even trying to hide the fact that she had been listening.

"Nothing, just a small misunderstanding is all," Fiona said, plopping down on the bed. "Now tell me more about Andrew."

* * *

Fiona tossed and turned. Every time she closed her eyes she was confronted with images of Gavin yelling at her or a snarling, hissing baby raccoon or Jeppsen's caterwauling he called singing, and worse yet, Sean taunting her while she watched Patrick tumble with one woman after another.

Fiona sat up in bed.

The fire had died down. A chill hung in the room. She found herself shivering as she rose from the warmth of her covers. She crossed to the fireplace and added another couple of logs before going to the door. She glanced at Abigail, her gentle snores assured she was sound asleep. On soft, slippered soles, she tiptoed out into the hallway and pulled on her heavy jacket.

Arriving at the pub downstairs, she was disappointed to find it empty. A few lights had been left on for any late night-cappers, but her hopes of sharing a drink with one of her friends, to better help her sleep, had vanished.

She walked the length of the bar, running her hand along the polished wood. She had been told that the liquor was free for all, as part of their compensation, but she felt wrong in taking anything without telling Miss McStargle, and she didn't like to drink alone.

Her gaze moved to the frosted window where she caught sight of a hazy image through the glass. It was Samuel, standing by a tree smoking a cigar. Smiling, Fiona realized that maybe she wouldn't have to drink alone after all.

Fiona let the door of the Broken Piper close with enough noise to announce her presence as she made her way through the snow to Samuel. He was not caught off guard in the least bit.

"Would you care for one, lassie?" Samuel asked in his deep Viking voice.

"I would love one," she replied, taking the proffered cigar from him. She took a bite out of the end and spit it out onto the snow.

Samuel smiled. " I usually use my knife, but that was probably the most beautiful thing I have ever seen you do."

Fiona grinned back. "Thanks. Light?"

He struck a match and held it near Fiona. She moved closer, pushing the mutilated cigar into the flames. It caught and after several deep draws.

"What are you doing up so late? We have auditions tomorrow you know?"

"Aye. Just keeping me eye out for werewolves," he said, "And you?" He took a drink from his flask.

"Just looking for a nightcap," she replied, eyeing his shiny flask. "What have you got in there, Samuel?"

"Nothing. Just a wee nip o' scotch." He started to offer it to her then remembered the ghostly warning and pocketed it quickly. "Probably not a good idea. Like you said, we have an audition tomorrow."

"Yes, you are probably right." Fiona drew on her cigar as she scrutinized him, puzzled. It was very unlike him to not share in his drinking. "How are you doing Sam? You haven't really said much since we arrived. Do you like being here?"

Samuel shifted, looking towards the theater. His eyes betrayed a nervousness rarely seen. "Alright, you know, takes a little getting use to."

Fiona nodded. "I love it! I'm not really sure why either."

Samuel did not reply. His eyes lingered on the theater.

Silence settled around them as they continued puffing out heavy smoke.

Samuel leaned down and touched his cigar to the snow causing a small hissing sound as it went out. He straightened and stamped his feet in the snow, as he pocketed the remainder of his cigar.

"Should be going to bed, lass."

"Sounds good," Fiona yawned. "Looks like I didn't need that nightcap after all."

"Aye. Maybe you should hold off on the drinking for a while. We got a bit of work ahead of us." His eyes were suddenly serious, so much so that Fiona no longer even questioned his comment, or the fact that he didn't seem to include himself in that statement.

"You are always the voice of reason," she replied.

* * *

"Okay, everyone listen up," Nicholas announced to the troupe gathered on stage. "Mister Thornbury has some very unusual methods of deciding the casting. Although I am the director, he is technically the producer and will have his say in the casting and final script decisions. So for today, only," he emphasized, "you will be taking your directions from him. Mister Thornbury," he gestured to Carlisle to take command.

Carlisle stood up and inspected the somewhat baffled actors.

"Aye. Good morning all," he said, as he walked along the front of the stage, craning his head to look up at them. "You are a tall bunch, eh? Anyway, that should not be a problem. As you all know this is a love story ... "

The actors exchanged glances. They knew nothing of the sort.

"And there are many exciting roles, complicated emotions, dangerous liaison's—as the French say—and what not," Carlisle explained.

"You!" he pointed suddenly at Patrick. "Step forward."

Patrick did. "Yes?"

"I wish to see you act," Carlisle said.

"Certainly. Do you have a script?" Patrick asked. "Or a scene you'd like to see?"

"No," the old man said, taking a seat in the front row. He peered up at Patrick intently. "You are in love. You have to leave, you have to break *her* ... " he pointed to Fiona, "heart. Now, take her hand. The rest of you move aside."

The others shuffled off. Patrick walked to Fiona and offered his hand.

"This is the strangest thing I've ever encountered," Patrick whispered.

"I know, me too," Fiona agreed, as she took Patrick's hand in hers.

Patrick and Fiona stood in silence for a moment, not sure where to begin. Patrick suddenly pulled her close. She looked deep into his eyes.

"Darling, you know I cannot linger here much longer ... " he began.

She placed her finger to his lips. "No," she whispered. "I only want you to hold me a moment longer."

"I love you," he said softly.

"And I love you," she replied. "Please come back to me, I fear I can no longer breathe if you do not."

"Shh ... do not worry." He ran his hand down her back. "I will come back. I promise." He pulled her to his mouth, kissing her, passionately, his hands sweeping about her hair and waist. He started to pull away, but Fiona pulled him back, trying to draw him nearer, needing him to be nearer.

Patrick managed to break away from her.

"No more, my love. I must leave you now."

"You are always leaving," she complained.

"I have my duty," he reluctantly turned to leave.

"Promise me one thing."

He stopped and turned around. "Anything."

"Do not lie with anyone else but me. I can be quite vengeful."

Patrick's eyebrows raised.

"What?" he asked, thrown off by her remark. "You know I only have eyes for you."

"That is not what I have been hearing."

"Okay! That's enough. Thank you!" The old man jumped up from his seat.

"What was that last bit there?" Patrick whispered to her.

"Nothing."

Patrick took a bow and walked to the side of the stage, leaving Fiona alone, as usual. Abigail clapped enthusiastically. Fiona noticed Sean staring at her, totally amused by the whole scenario. She silently cursed him as she stomped back to the line.

"That was quite something," Carlisle said, once again walking in front of the stage. "Quite something indeed. But now I need to see something comedic."

He pointed to Abigail. "You, I think you are of the spirit of a sprite. You shall be the lady. And you ... " Gavin started to walk forward eagerly, but instead Carlisle pointed to Sean. "Shall be the gentleman."

Gavin froze, confused. Sean patted him on the back. "Better luck next time old boy."

Sean stepped pass him and up to Abigail. He took her hand. She curtsied, coyly. She looked into the audience and saw that Andrew was watching her, suddenly intent. Gavin backed off to the side stage, glaring.

"What are our instructions?" Sean asked.

"Just have at it," Carlisle said indifferently.

"As you wish," Sean said. He whispered to Abigail. "Just follow my lead."

"Okay," she whispered back. Then he grabbed her suddenly and kissed her full on the lips, hard. Then, just as suddenly, he pushed away.

"Oh! Finnoula, I have been waiting to do this for what seems like a lifetime, well, at least since the car ride home."

Abigail staggered back, surprised. "You have? Er ... Robert?"

Sean pulled her to him again suddenly, his lips smashing into hers, his embrace overpowering, squeezing the breath from her chest. Andrew sat up in his chair, disturbed.

This time Sean shoved her away as he stumbled quickly back, wiping his mouth roughly with his hand.

"Finnoula!" he cried. "What in the hell do you think you are doing?"

Abigail was properly perplexed.

Fiona suddenly realized what was going on.

"Oh you wouldn't dare! You bastard!" Fiona whispered loudly.

Samuel, standing beside her, looked confused.

Gavin had also caught on. His glare sent daggers at Sean.

"Robert, I'm a wee bit confused, " Abigail struggled. "Don't you want me?"

"I thought you wanted me," Sean said, his voice a loud whisper.

"What? I mean, I do, dearest, Sean ... er, Robert," Abigail moved toward him uncertainly. "Really. Really I do."

"Finnoula, I am so sorry. I have always loved you as a sister. I've never looked any further then that. I wish I could say I had."

"A sister! Robert that's sick!" Abigail slapped him. Then thought better of it. "Or, did you mean as in a nun?"

Carlisle exploded in laughter. "Very good! Very good indeed! I have made my decision. You four all shall play the parts I have in mind. And for you ... " he pointed to Samuel, "I have a very special role indeed."

With a spry ability few thought he'd be capable of, Carlisle leapt to the stage and strode over to take both of Samuel's massive hands in his. He spoke with reverence to the kilted giant.

"You shall be the soul and breath of our Motherland."

Samuel shook his head, "I don't quite get ya, sir."

"Location personified. Scotland, lad. *Scotland!* You will be, you *are*, Scotland."

Samuel considered the idea and, although he wasn't sure exactly how he was supposed to portray Scotland, he rather liked it.

"Aye. I'll give it me best, sir," Samuel said proudly.

"I know you will, my boy," Carlisle agreed. "Now gather around actors, gather around all."

Carlisle signaled for Nicholas and Andrew to join them on stage. The troupe gathered around the old man. Fiona, arms crossed, stayed near the back, glaring defiantly at Sean. Sean appeared not to care.

"Now about the story. It's very simple. We have three lovers, two couples ... you, Sean!" he said gaily, pointing at Sean, "and Fiona are madly in love."

Fiona's mouth dropped open, but she was too stunned to protest.

"But Patrick here is in love with Fiona as well. And Fiona knows whom she loves most, although circumstances will decide whom she shall marry. Will she end up with her true love or an eternally broken heart? That is the question. And you my sweet Abigail, the faithful wife, shall be the grand ghost, although you are not dead yet, and you are sadly in love with love itself, but not loved. Until, you're dead. Of course, from then on your heart will ache lonely from the grave. Or something like that. I mean parts to be funny, so we shall see."

The actors were all stunned silent.

"Oh yes. And like I said, Samuel is Scotland. And a lovely Scotland he will be. All scabbard, kilt, and king, with craggy bluffs and moors, don't forget the moors! Make no mistake about that. They must not be overlooked."

Samuel nodded solemnly.

"Now that all the parts have been cast ... " Carlisle continued.

"Wait a minute!" Gavin interrupted, stepping full into Carlisle face. "What about me?" he demanded.

Carlisle met his steely, challenging glare.

"Aye. I have not forgot you. Someone must pull curtains and run lights."

"What?" Gavin exclaimed. "No! I will not. I am an ACTOR!"

The old man stared at him. "Then you will be an ACTOR who pulls curtains and runs lights."

Gavin was apoplectic. "Bollocks!" He stormed off.

Carlisle smiled, undisturbed.

"This is all working out so marvelously."

* * *

Sean couldn't help but notice the icy reception he received from Fiona, Patrick, and Andrew—so when the others announced they were going to lunch he decided to remain behind. Samuel, quite taken with his role, also waved off the others to begin building his character. Or so he said. Sean believed something was bothering the big guy, but he was not sufficiently invested in any kind of personal connection to him to instigate an enquiry, so he waited for him to broach the subject should he decide to. It didn't take long.

Sean sat in a seat in the front row, thinking about what to drink for lunch and musing over the 'audition' as Samuel stalked the stage. Sean enjoyed kissing Abigail, but he had enjoyed the look on Fiona's face even more.

Every few minutes, Samuel would stop and peer up into the rafters, eyes squinting, trying to pierce the darkness. Sufficiently distracted, Sean was just about to ask him what he was looking for when Samuel, head tilted back, eyes locked on the darkness above, suddenly called out: "So do ya mind if I ask ya something?"

"Go right ahead," Sean called back.

"You live here, do ya?" Samuel asked. "All *alone?*"

Sean wasn't quite sure what Samuel was intimating. "Well, I've only been here for a few days. Do you fancy one of the girls? Because, if you do, you need not worry, I haven't brought either of them—"

"No. No. Nothing like that," Samuel finally dropped his gaze to Sean. "I just mean, is there anyone else *living* here?"

"*Living* here?" Sean replied, confused at the emphasis.

"*Living* here," Samuel repeated.

"No." Sean nodded. "Just me and the ghosties," he joked. Samuel's eyes grew very wide. "What?" Sean asked.

"So you've seen her too?" Samuel whispered.

"Who? What are you talking about?" The fact that this mountain of a man could look so suddenly vulnerable made Sean ill at ease.

"Nothing," Samuel said. He shook off whatever appeared to be spooking him. "I've been wondering, where's your kip? You don't just sleep here on the stage, do ya?"

"What? No. Well, only when I can't get up to the loft. Come, I'll show you."

Sean led him to the lobby and showed him the hidden release that dropped the folding stairs to the loft.

"It's difficult to notice by design. The loft occupies the space on the backside of the balcony, designed by Thornbury the First as a boudoir for an actress named Teva. A secret rendezvous, if you will. Come on up."

Sean climbed up. Samuel followed.

* * *

"Utter crap!" Nicholas exclaimed, throwing the heap of mismatched pages Carlisle called a 'script' down to the floor. The pages splayed across the carpet. "Have you seen this shit?"

Andrew nodded as he bent down to collect the sheaf of papers. "It is a bit confusing," he admitted.

"*A bit?* You English and your penchant for the understatement. No it's not *a bit* confusing, it's *a bloody pile of bloody confusing* with no hint or semblance of any storytelling!" Nicholas growled a few more choice epithets then rose to go to the bar.

They were in Nicholas's room, a large homey affair with a roaring fireplace, thick curtains and stout shutters, which kept the howling storm at bay. The king-sized bed occupied a good third of the room. However there were two comfortable chairs by the fire and a writing desk with a third more utilitarian chair behind it. One wall had a well-stocked bookcase built of heavy oak. A trolley of scotches and whiskeys had been brought in along with several cut crystal glasses and decanters. It was here that Nicholas was seeking solace.

"And what the hell was that audition about?" Nicholas asked as he poured himself a stiff tumbler of whiskey. "Who casts a play based on such absurd scenarios? What were their motivations? Who in the hell were they even talking about? Is this a damn comedy or drama? That's what I'd like to kno– oh! Sorry, would you like some, Andrew?" he asked, holding up the decanter.

Andrew didn't answer or even hear him. He was too engrossed in some hand-written pages he found scattered amongst the miscellany.

"Andrew?" Nicholas repeated.

"'I fear I may explode without you by my side and as I slowly descend into nothing but jealously ... '" Andrew read aloud. "'It tears my heart to ribbons! I almost cannot explain the divine hatred I hold for your wife. She's awarded your name while I am left with no claim on you. It haunts me all the while I walk these stonewalls, but vanishes the very moment I see you. Even this constant fear of being discovered will not keep me from you. Come to me. I wait on you endlessly, my love that is mine and yet not.'"

The room fell silent. Andrew looked up at Nicholas who, now frozen, stared down at him.

"What was that?" Nicholas whispered.

Andrew held up a hand written sheet of paper, aged older than most of the others.

"It appears to be a page from a diary of some sort. There are a few more pages scattered amongst these drawings. They seemed to have been torn out of a book or journal."

Nicholas walked over and gently took the aged page. He held it to the firelight and read it. He took a deep breath and exhaled it slowly. "There are more?"

Andrew nodded. "Yes," he began pulling more pages out. "Perhaps twenty, or thirty pages total, all written in the same feminine hand."

He handed them up to Nicholas as he found them.

Nicholas scanned them, reading quickly. He seized the last page Andrew found and read it aloud. "'The pain of my silence is in not being able to shout to the world what is ours. And to this treasured secret I am forever bound. This secret, I promise, never to break. This secret I take to my grave ... '"

Nicholas placed it carefully down on the table. He bit his lower lip as he scratched the stubble of a day's growth on his chin. He gazed over at Andrew.

"The old lunatic was right," he stated, flatly.

"How so?"

"There is *certainly* a story here. One worth telling."

Just then there was a knock on their door.

Carlisle Thornbury was in his drawing room, as he referred to it in the non-traditional sense. It was in a part of the castle in much disrepair. The north wall had crumbled in parts, and Jeppsen had patched it haphazardly with a few well-placed stones and a smattering of mortar. Consequently it was cold, windy, and not that pleasant in the summer and murderous in the winter. Small flurries of snow would blow in and remain as icy puddles in the northwest corner of the stone floor.

There was an inadequate fireplace that issued only a semblance of warmth. Carlisle was bundled up in his finest Harris tweeds–jackets, socks, knickers, and wooly scarf. Atop his head sat a fur hat of black sable, looking for all the world like a curled kitten. His hands were bare, but they needed to be, as he was painting.

"Jeppsen said you might be here," Patrick announced as he cautiously entered the room. "Do you mind if I join you?"

Startled, Carlisle turned happily, his paintbrush accidentally streaking a blue line across the canvas. He didn't appear to notice.

"Yes! Yes! Please come in young Patrick."

"About the play ... " Patrick stepped inside, rubbing his hands and arms together at the chill of the room.

"Yes. You were fine! Don't worry, it will all turn out fine!" Carlisle grinned.

"But my brother? I don't think I can act with him," Patrick began.

"Nonsense. You are both fine actors. It is in your blood. I should know. I've seen you both bleed enough."

"I can think of nothing worse than being on the same stage as him."

"I can," Carlisle replied.

Patrick pulled his hands through his hair in frustration. "Look. Why not cast Gavin in his role and let Sean go and get drunk and forget to raise the curtains or whatever cock up he'll surely achieve?"

"No. There is a reason for all things. Trust me." Carlisle hummed a little nonsensical tune and continued to paint. Patrick gave up.

"So, you're a painter as well as an author?" he asked, regarding Carlisle as he continually attacked the canvas with paint and paintbrush.

"A mere dabbler," Carlisle corrected him.

"May I?" Patrick asked, wishing to look at the work in progress.

"Please," insisted Carlisle. He stood aside to give Patrick a better look.

It was definitely an attempt to capture the face of what Patrick could only assume was a beautiful, young woman, now with a blue streak across her cheek. The seemingly random blaze of colors and thick clumps of paint, made it difficult to be sure.

"It is a woman?" Patrick asked.

"Yes." Carlisle continued to randomly add color and shade. "She's meant to be viewed from a distance."

"How far?" asked Patrick, sincerely.

"Not space," Carlisle explained, "Time."

Patrick didn't know how to interpret that.

"Who is she?" he asked instead.

"No one," Carlisle answered. "She no longer exists."

It was then that Patrick noticed that the far wall was filled with paintings of every size and color, all of the same abstract woman, at different ages, in different styles, but all with the same haunted eyes, pursed red lips, and single mole on her cheek.

Just like my mother's.

Carlisle made one last stroke then satisfied, laid down his brush. He wiped his messy stained hands on a towel then turned to Patrick. "You didn't come here to discuss art, my son. Or did you?"

Patrick turned back to the old man. "No. I didn't. I wanted to ask you ... " Patrick fell into unease, unable to complete his sentence.

Carlisle stared at him with unflinching eyes. He seemed to have no inclination to offer Patrick a seat or a warmer location or any comfort.

"How did my father die?" Patrick finally asked.

"Oh, that," Carlisle seemed relieved. "There was a fire."

"Yes. I saw the remnants. Luckily the theater wasn't burned."

"Yes. Good fortune that," Carlisle replied.

"Was anyone with him when he died?" Patrick pursued.

"No. He died alone." Carlisle took the painting he just finished and went to the gallery wall. He picked up a large mallet and a nail and pounded the nail into the stone wall.

"He was never the same after your mother left," he yelled over his pounding. "Neither was I, to tell the truth."

Patrick seized his hand to stop the hammering.

"Did he kill her?" Patrick asked seriously.

Carlisle met his stony gaze. This was obviously a question that had been haunting Patrick for some time.

"I need to know."

A sudden rage came over Carlisle.

"No, your father did not kill her! He would never hurt her or you!" he screamed, yanking his hand free from Patrick's grip. He turned and swung the hammer viscously at the nail, driving it completely into the wall.

"Then *what*? What happened to her? You were here! What happened to her?" Patrick yelled back at the old man.

Carlisle's voice suddenly dropped to a whisper. "I don't know." He turned, dropped the hammer, and walked out of the room.

Patrick stood there stunned. He picked up the dropped painting and stared through the mess of colors. It resolved itself. He saw it now. It *was* his mother's face. He looked up. A wall of his mother's faces stared back.

More snow drifted into the room, chilling it even further.

* * *

Samuel stared down the ladder to the landing and realized that there was no way he was going to climb down those steps. He swayed drunkenly in place, trying to decide what to do. Sean and he had drunk fistfuls of scotch, and he'd be damned but the skinny lad could hold his liquor better than he.

"Another?" Sean offered, slurring a bit himself now, Samuel was pleased to hear.

"Aye, just until the stairs quit their wiggling."

Samuel joined Sean back at the small kitchen table. He sat heavily onto a protesting wooden chair. They had been sitting there for hours, drinking and telling tales. Samuel had learned a lot about Sean's missing years, his intentional distancing from his brother, even a bit about early life in Loglinmooth.

Then the conversation turned to Scottish history, drama, and shipbuilding and the night slipped past on lighter notes. Sean poured again. They raised their glasses.

"To Scottish lasses, who drink with glasses," Samuel toasted.

"Aye," Sean nodded. They drank, both satisfied to saying nothing for the moment. Outside the wind howled.

Samuel listened to the wind. "Banshees," he said.

"Eh?" Sean asked.

"Do ya believe in the spirit world, lad?"

"I'm of an open mind, I'm not afraid to say," he admitted.

Samuel nodded, content. They sat in silence a while longer.

"The sweet lass ... " Samuel started.

"Aye?" Sean prodded. "The one I dropped? I still regret letting her slip through me fingers."

"You fancy her, do ya?" Samuel leaned in, conspiratorially. "I only ask because she needs looking after, you know?"

"What do you mean?" Sean leaned in as well. "Isn't she Patrick's lass?"

"Forget Patrick," Samuel slurred. "She needs looking after." Samuel started to nod off. "Don't let her drink ... " his head hit the table with a thud and he immediately began snoring.

Sean finished his drink, wondering just what the hell Samuel was trying to say.

* * *

"Did you see Andrew's face when Sean kissed me?" Abigail asked excitedly as they made their climb towards Thornbury Castle.

"That I did," Fiona lied. She had been too mad at the time to even think of looking at Andrew. They had agreed to walk up to the castle, despite the freezing temperature, to inform Andrew and Patrick about Nicholas's surprise party, although both had alterative motives neither of them were discussing. Neither wished to make the cold journey back, nor be sleeping in their lonely bed tonight.

"He looked like he might jump from his chair and punch Sean!" Abigail said.

"That doesn't sound like Andrew at all," Fiona stated flatly.

"I know!" Abigail smiled, misinterpreting Fiona's disbelief. "His blood was boiling. He must really have it bad for me, don't you think?"

Fiona's was aware that Abigail was still talking but she tuned her out. Fiona's thoughts, mood, and body grew colder the closer they came to the castle, so much so, that she was beginning to find that she was afraid to even face Patrick. She wished she could go back, before they arrived here. Everything was fine then. Patrick was still a devoted, charming man, Gavin was nothing more than a brother, and she had never met Sean!

Fiona sighed. *If only I could go back ...*

Fiona's thoughts went back even further than she intended, many years back to the last time she had been with a man, a man she loved and who loved her. *David.*

David had been Fiona's first and only love. Fiona and David were inseparable growing up. They lived on adjacent farms in a small town in county Kildare, where there were few others to compete for attention. They became best friends, partners in crime, and eventually as adolescence struck, young lovers.

Their sexual relationship had been brief, but it had been intense and sweet all at once. They had foolishly talked about marriage and what names they would choose for their children, but Fiona had grown increasingly restless. As much as she loved David, she knew she could not be contained in their tiny world.

At first she turned to books. She became a voracious reader, thinking she could at least travel in her imagination. Then she came across a book of short plays. She began reading them aloud. Soon she was practicing her monologues and dialects every chance she got in front of an attentive gathering of cows and pigs in the barn. Finally, she got up the nerve to perform a scene from Chekhov's *A Marriage Proposal* for David and he was overwhelmed.

He didn't realize that it was the beginning of the end.

Soon, she began traveling miles to Dublin to audition for plays. She finally landed a small part, just a two week run.

Later, when she was asked to try out for a part in a musical, it was discovered that she had a natural, lilting voice and a real talent for singing. By now, she was completely in-fevered by the rush of performing in front of a live audience – the applause; the laughter; the heat of the spotlight.

She tried to explain all this to David, but he never really understood. He couldn't imagine a life more enticing than having Fiona in his arms every night and living the simple, quiet life of the farm. Fiona couldn't be contained. She needed to travel and she needed to experience new worlds – in reality and through the fantasy of theater. He begged her to stay. She begged him to move to Dublin with her. Hurt that he could not understand, she had left, never looking back.

She saw him one last time. She returned to attend the funeral of her father. David was still there, still alone. After the funeral, she spent one last night in his arms. She had needed to both remember and forget for a night, needed to feel something other than the blinding grief that was consuming her and the sudden, rising, complicated emotions she felt seeing David again. In the morning she was gone. And this time there was nothing left to bring her back home.

Looking back on it now, Fiona was convinced that she and David had just been too young to understand what was happening between them, how their love evolved as much from simple convenience as necessity. It felt right and it made sense. It was the love to which all others would have to compare, and Fiona was hesitant to spoil that idyllic memory with just anyone. And no one had ever come close to tempting her. Until now, until Patrick ...

"Sean is a great kisser, but not as good as Andrew," Abigail said, jolting Fiona out of her thoughts.

"What?" Fiona asked.

"I just hope Andrew's not mad at me, I'm sure he knew it was just a scene and Sean really gave me no choice." Abigail seemed worried that she had gone too far. She grew silent, apparently musing on this last revelation, as they reached the castle.

They paused at the huge front door. Abigail reached for the handle.

"Here goes," she said and they walked inside. The foyer was quiet and deserted.

"This place always gives me the creepies. I don't know how Andrew can stand it," Abigail whispered.

Fiona thought she could hear the muffled very excitable voices of Nicholas and Andrew, coming down the stairs from one of the upper bedrooms.

"They're all probably upstairs." She grabbed Abigail's hand and led her through the foyer toward the staircase. They had to pass by the library that had once held the very deceased body of Angus Berenger. The door was open and it revealed a much more charming book-lined room minus one coffin. They peered inside.

"I wonder where the body went?" Fiona asked.

"Maybe they buried him?"

"But then why weren't any of us invited? Surely if Patrick went he would have mentioned it. Besides, when would he have had time?"

"Maybe Ol' man Berenger just got tired of waiting and up and walked away," Abigail giggled nervously. "Can we please go now?"

"The ground's too frozen. Can't dig," a voice beside them suddenly announced.

Both girls jumped and squealed in fright.

"Moved him to the cellar, no one ever bothered to ask, 'til now that is," said Jeppsen, who had just arrived from the drawing room.

"Jeppsen, don't ever do that! You gave us such a fright!" Abigail cried.

"My apologies. Just grabbing me self a little something to read before I retire. What are you lasses doing here?" He made the question sound vaguely threatening.

"I need to talk to Andrew," Abigail said quickly.

"And I need to speak with Patrick," Fiona replied.

"Andrew is upstairs with Nicholas. Patrick spoke with me earlier about having a word with Carlisle. I sent him to the drawing room. I suspect he is still there."

"And where is that?" Fiona asked.

"It's in the North Tower. I'll walk you there if you like."

"That's okay, Jeppsen. If you could just point me in the right direction."

"Certainly, just go north," he said without a trace of sarcasm. "Now if you'd excuse me," he entered the library and began perusing titles.

Abigail giggled, then whispered, "You do know which way is north?"

"I'll follow the stars. You go talk to Andrew, I'll be fine."

"Aren't you the brave one? This place is really spooky and so's 'e." She nodded toward Jeppsen who was climbing a stepstool to reach a book from a high shelf.

"He's mostly harmless, I suspect. Just looks the part. If need be, I'll sic the fairies–"

Abigail shot her a dirty look.

"Sorry, the *wee folk* after him."

"They will protect you. They always protect me!" Abigail skipped away down the hall towards the staircase. Fiona headed north.

Patrick had stayed long after Carlisle had stormed out. He stared into the countless faces of his mother. He was consumed with the relentless weight of her loss. He walked from painting to painting, taking his time to scrutinize, studying them like an obsessed art critic. Some he gently touched, others he took down and held up to the light. He noticed that each one was titled the same: *Delia.*

Why? Why paint his mother over and over again?

He began looking at them each again, with a new eye, searching for some kind of clue. He thought he saw a pattern: here in her eyes, in this one her hesitant smile, in that one her furrowed brow. As bad as each painting was, Carlisle had managed to capture some part of his mother in every one. Perhaps, by seeing them all as a whole Patrick could somehow piece together the explanation he was looking for.

He held up a painting that was an extreme close-up of her face. Done in a mess of blues, yellows, and purples her bright green eyes shone out particularly lively.

"Where are you?" he asked, pleading for her crudely painted yellow lips to answer one last time.

These were questions he had blocked out since he learned that she had disappeared. He sought an escape and found it in two places: theater and women. He abused them both, shoving his ego down everyone's throat. As long as he could be desired, as long as everyone was looking at him, he didn't have to face the past that kept haunting him.

Did I run out just when she needed me most?

Coming back here, his escapist lifestyle crumbled to pieces, he could no longer pretend to be some other character, playing a role day in and day out. That façade was dead, lying in the coffin beside his rotting father.

Father. He hated the word. That man did not deserve the title. What does one call a man who loved to drink and raise his hand to those he supposedly loved? Who could have saved her but was too blind drunk to notice? There was no word. Now that he was dead, perhaps his black memories would die too and Patrick could stop searching.

But *Delia* ...

His mother had been an amazing beacon in his life. Always caring, always loving, always there for him. Much like Fiona, he realized. Fiona loved him beyond reason, almost as if she had no choice, and her entire happiness seemed to depend on it. Perhaps she saw something in him that he thought he had lost?

Suddenly he knew why he was here. It was to clear his mother's name. His gaze went back to the views of his mother's soft, loving face. She looked like a saint one would pray to.

"Forgive me," he whispered.

Fiona grew colder the further she walked toward the North Tower. She was astonished by the disrepair of this part of the castle. Through a hole in the roof she could see a single star shining through a break in the clouds.

The North Star; it must be a sign.

She smiled, wishing Abby were here to see this; she'd be convinced the fairies had placed it there to guide her to Patrick.

A light from an open doorway was visible down the hall and Fiona picked up her pace.

As she entered the doorway she found Patrick standing in the middle of the room, holding a painting, his back to her. The room was filled with portraits. All the paintings, although amateur at the kindest, were quite obviously meant to be the same person. She walked quietly to Patrick, trying not to startle him.

"Carlisle painted all of these?" she asked.

Patrick showed no surprise at her sudden appearance as he turned to greet her. "Yes. They are all of my mother."

"Really?" She looked deeper, recognizing the beauty among the chaos. "She's lovely."

"Aye," he replied, turning back to the paintings. "She was quite beautiful."

"Why did he–?"

"I have no idea," Patrick cut her off. "Sorry, it's just been awhile since I've seen her face, and to see so many ... "

"No need to apologize. I understand."

"Should we sit?" He indicated the small fireplace and motioned to Fiona to come and join him. They sat on the stone floor close to the warming fire.

"So, Fee, what brings you to this spooky tower without even a spare shoe to protect you?" he asked.

Fiona paused. She *wanted* to ask him about the women Gavin had said he had; she *wanted* to know if he had any intention of ever being with her; she *wanted* him to assure her she wasn't a fool for wanting him. She drew in a sharp breath.

"Abigail and I are planning a surprise birthday party for Nicholas in a few days. It's here at the castle so I hoped you would come. Oh, and you have to wear a costume."

Patrick nodded. "Sounds like fun, Fee."

"I thought maybe we could all use a little frivolity after all that's been going on here recently. Carlisle even agreed not to hold rehearsals the next day."

"Oh, don't remind me about that God-forsaken show! I keep hoping maybe something will happen and we won't have to do the play at all. Foolish wishes I suppose."

"Really? I think it's kind of an adventure. True we are out of our usual element, and it will most likely be a very strange performance, but after the audition today, I think it will be a challenge that will season us as actors."

He laughed. "Fee, of course you would see it that way."

He paused, musing over his next question before finally asking.

"The auditions today were indeed strange, I'll give you that. Fee, what happened in our scene today?"

"Nothing, I was just a little flustered."

Patrick seemed to accept her answer. Then he asked, "Was my brother, was he trying to make fun of you about something?"

"No, I think he was just trying to be an ass."

"Aye, he is brilliant at that. I'm sure it was all directed at me anyway, whatever his muddled point was. He'll hate me 'til the day he drinks himself to death."

"Why would you say that? Were you two really competitive when you were younger?" she asked.

Patrick's gaze went back to the fire. "Aye, not for acting roles, but for women. When I stole Bethany, he no longer wanted anything to do with me."

"Who is Bethany?" she asked, although she wasn't sure she wanted to know.

Now was not the time to confront this. Soon, but not now. Not here.

"Someone from the past," he finally said. "It doesn't matter."

It was obvious to Fiona that there was much more to tell.

"He might come after you Fiona. Be careful, don't believe anything he says."

"Why would he do that?"

His hand went to her cheek before moving to her hair and stroking it. "Because of me, Fee. He knows we have feelings for each other." He continued to stroke her hair.

A log in the fireplace crackled and hissed, drawing their attention to the fire. Fiona watched a curl of green flame lick along one of the logs before fading out.

Patrick spoke softly, almost inaudibly.

"I'm not the man you want me to be, Fiona. I believe I'm not even the man that you see me as. You ... you deserve so much and that night on the train was a cruel thing to put you through."

Fiona wanted to tell him that there was nothing cruel about that night on the train, that he couldn't know how she saw him, but she was too afraid to speak.

"But I don't want to be that man, Fiona," he added a little louder. "I can't ask you to wait, I am just asking you to understand."

The heat Fiona had been feeling rushed out and was replaced by the worst chill she has ever felt. She looked away from him, tears rolling down her cheeks as he continued to stroke her hair and stare into the fire.

"But I warn you," he added. "Sean is not that man either."

Fiona didn't trust herself to reply. She just wanted to run away from Patrick's words and this audience of paintings, all staring at her and all sharing in her quiet desperation.

$* * *$

Darkness was moving all around the loft. It felt unease, and in its unease it managed to penetrate, without trying, without even realizing what it was doing ...

Fiona was falling.

Sean caught her and tried desperately to hold onto her this time. She was dressed entirely in black ribbons that unraveled in his hands, spinning her loose, like silk ribbon sliding off a spool, no purchase for him to hold. He had no grip; his hands filled with slithering, black ribbons, and so she fell, naked to the floor with a heavy thud. She glared up at him.

"I'm sorry," he tried to apologize. "I couldn't hold on."

She rose, silent, turned and walked away. He followed. "Fiona wait."

She turned and spoke, her lips moved but not quite in sync with her words, as if there were a slight delay between them. "I need a drink."

Sean hesitated. *Wasn't there something about her not drinking?* She stepped toward him, lustily, her skin shimmering. She stopped just a handbreadth away from him. Her eyes burned. Her breath smelled of jasmine and wine.

She reached her hand through his hair, playfully, before lightly kissing him on his cheek.

"Get me a drink, Sean," she sang at him.

Sean stared, fighting the urge to take her right then and there on the dirty wooden floor of the loft. *But something wasn't quite right—*

"Now!"

Sean was startled into action, desperately searching the loft for a drink. He looked everywhere slamming open cupboards and sweeping glasses and dishes onto the sink and floor, not finding even a single drop of alcohol.

He stopped. Right before him on the dining room table, how he missed it he couldn't fathom, stood an open bottle of wine and two glasses.

He snatched the bottle with shaking hands and poured. He turned to offer her one. She had moved across the room and was now standing just inches from him. He could feel the heat radiating off her body. She was vibrating. He was hardening.

She took the glass and leaned in to him, her lips lightly falling on his.

"'Wine is bottled poetry.'" She drank the entire glass in one long swallow, her eyes never leaving his. She licked a bit of the blood red residue off her lips. "Slipped through your fingers again," she said, wanly. "How could you, I warned you."

Something was wrong.

She paled, shivered, and appeared ready to faint. Suddenly her hands leapt for his throat. Her eyes grew wild and feral.

"You killed me!" she screamed, through bleeding lips. "You bastard! You killed me!"

He was as shocked by her words as her sudden strength. She forced him back, back, back ...

"Fiona," he pleaded, croaking out the words. He was having trouble breathing. His knees caught against a low table and he fell to the floor with a spine-crushing thud. She landed on top of him, her hands never leaving his throat, her weight crushing the breath out of his chest.

"Bastard! Bastard! Bastard!" she screamed.

"No," was all he could manage to gasp. He was starting to black out. He reached up and closed his hands around her throat. As strong as she was, he was stronger. Just as the last of his consciousness was ebbing, he managed to force her to loosen her grip. Suddenly he rolled to his left side, twisting her underneath him. Now he was on top and his hands tightened around her throat.

Her eyes rolled up into her head. He stared into her eerie white orbs blank as anonymous tombstones; a shiver of terror ran down his spine.

She growled a chilling, beastly howl that grew louder and louder.

Whatever this was, it wasn't Fiona.

He squeezed tighter and tighter.

"What are you? WHAT ARE YOU?" he screamed, trying desperately to kill it.

"WHAT THE FOOK!" Samuel cried, awakening from a deep slumber to find his head still smashed into the tabletop while someone leaned over him, hands clenched around his throat, trying their best to strangle him.

Samuel instinctively shoved his head backward, head butting the assailant away, nearly breaking his nose. Quick as a snake, Samuel was on his feet and shoved the man as hard as he could. His strength being what is was, it sent the man flying across the room, crashing into his bed and shattering it.

He took a few seconds to catch his breath. He grabbed a candle and cautiously walked over to the groaning man on the bed. He held the light down to his face.

"*Sean?* What the bloody hell's wrong with you?" he cried.

Sean shook his head to try and clear it. His nose was bleeding profusely and staining his shirt. Still half in the dream, he looked around panicky. "*Fiona?*"

Samuel held the candle up to his whiskered face. "*Fiona?* Do I look like bleeding *Fiona* to you?"

"No, she tried to ... I need ... kill her ... " Sean started, confused.

"Hush. No one's killing no one," Samuel easily lifted him up. He upturned two chairs and placed Sean in one and took the other. Sean eyed the darkness suspiciously.

"Sorry about the toss, mate, and the bed. Maybe it can be fixed." Samuel lowered the candle to examine the broken legs. "Or, perhaps not."

"No matters," Sean managed to mumble.

"Here, you're bleeding a bit," Samuel handed him a cloth to clot his bleeding nose.

"Thanks," Sean gingerly dabbed it.

Samuel noticed a bottle of scotch on the floor under the bed, miraculously unbroken. He retrieved it, opened it and took a long swig. He handed it to Sean.

"Do you want to tell me about it?"

Sean took a deeper swig and handed it back. He exhaled the tension out. "Must've been a dream. I have had a lot of strange ones lately."

"Aye. Figured that one out me-self when I found you on me back," Samuel drank. Then added, "Didn't think I was your type."

Sean still un-nerved, managed to grin.

"Aye. Though it's not that you're not a fine looking gent—" Sean stopped suddenly, cocking his head toward the floor. "What's that?"

"What's what?"

"Shhh! Listen!" They listened. They heard a very faint singing.

"Do you hear that?" Sean whispered. Samuel nodded. Sean put his finger to his lips to signal Samuel to remain silent. Then he beckoned him to follow. He walked as quietly as possible over to the trap door in the floor. He lowered it. The singing was louder now. Sean could make out the words.

"Oh he was a lord of high degree and she was a lass from the low country
But she loved his lordship so tenderly
Oh sorrow, sing sorrow
Now she sleeps in the valley where the wild flowers nod
And no one knows she loved him but herself and God"

Sean carefully descended the ladder to the lobby. Samuel, thinking quickly, grabbed the candle and followed.

The lobby was dark and deserted. Sean led them to the nearest theater entrance. The voice drifted out.

> *"One morn when the sun was on the mead*
> *He passed by her door on a milk white steed*
> *She smiled and she spoke, but he paid no heed."*

They followed the delicate, haunting voice through the lobby, into the theater. Sean noticed the ghost light had gone out. The stage was dark, but a glimmering, indistinct shape appeared, standing center stage. The song seemed to shimmer and float out from it. They crept nearer.

> *"If you be a lass from the low country*
> *Don't love of no lord of high degree*
> *They haint for a heart for sympathy."*

At the edge of the stage, in the feeble light of his candle, Samuel could determine that it was the same woman he had seen before, wearing the dark blue, velvety dress. Her face was still a blur, but perhaps less so now.

"You again," Samuel whispered.

Sean looked over at Samuel confused. "Who is that?"

Samuel didn't answer.

"Who are you?" called out Sean to the apparition. Her only reply was the sad refrain of her song.

> *"Oh sorrow, sing sorrow,*
> *Now she sleeps in the valley where the wild flowers nod*
> *And no one knows she loved him but herself and God."*

Then she vanished.

"Are we still asleep?" Sean asked.

"Nay," Samuel replied.

"Fook," Sean swore.

"Aye." Samuel agreed.

"What was that, then?" Sean asked.

"Can't say for certain. A haunt?" Samuel ventured.

"Don't know that I believe in ghosts."

"Maybe you better start," Samuel suggested.

Sean thought about it. "I don't know that I can." He paused. "Maybe we best not mention this to the others."

"Aye." Samuel nodded. "I'll be getting back to the Piper for some breakfast. You coming?"

"Nah. I think I'll stay here for bit."

"Suit yourself." Samuel considered then added. "Would it help if I mentioned that I've seen her once before. That she warned me about the sweet one? That she was in danger?"

"Fiona?" Sean looked up sharply.

"Aye, I suppose that's whom she be meaning," Samuel met his eyes. "She's not supposed to drink. Don't know why."

Sean's face lost what color it had left. He nodded. "Have a nice breakfast."

Samuel nodded back and left.

* * *

"Fiona! If you don't stop moving, God help me, I am going to stab you with a pin!" Abigail warned.

"Sorry," Fiona replied. "I am just so nervous about the rehearsal! I've never worked without a script before."

Abigail stuck another pin through the dress's blue silk fabric. It was the same dress Fiona had tried on the first time she and Abigail had discovered the costume room. Fiona had instantly decided on that dress for the costume party. She liked the way it hung down to hint at cleavage while covering her arms but also showing her figure. It gave Fiona the feeling of elegance with just the right hint of exposure, which is exactly what she wanted.

Abigail took a step backwards, viewing the dress in full and looking over her work.

"Fiona, you look so beautiful! Patrick will not be able to take his eyes off you!"

Fiona hoped that was true. She was still confused by what he had said last night. *'I want to be that man Fiona, I do.'* She wanted to tell herself that he was already that man, but the way he had been acting lately, she was beginning to doubt if she knew whom he really was.

Fiona decided she would not think about Patrick until the costume party. *Maybe once he sees me in this dress it will make him realize that he desires nothing in this world more than me.* Perhaps it was a foolish wish, but she could dream.

Fiona sighed. She was not likely to see him today. Nicholas had only called for her, Samuel, and Sean for rehearsal and as far as she knew, none of them had received a script. She was also dreading rehearsing with Sean with or without a script.

"I can have the dress finished by tomorrow. Should be quite easy, really. You can take it off now Fee."

Fiona pulled the dress over her head and handed it to Abigail.

"Thank you so much!"

"Please, it's my job," Abigail smiled, then added slyly, "I would recommend a nice corset with this dress, it'll push up your breasts, giving the men a lot more to stare at."

"You think so?" Fiona blushed.

"It always worked for me!" Abigail giggled.

Fiona wasn't used to such immodesty, but she suddenly found the idea emboldening.

"Actually," she confessed, "I did buy a very risqué corset in London, but I never had a reason to wear it."

"Oh, how positively, sinful," Abigail teased. "Then it's settled, you'll wear it to the party."

"I don't know ... " Fiona was already having second thoughts.

"Aye, but I do!" Abigail insisted. "And so does Patrick!" as she slipped Fiona's dress over a costume dummy. Abigail had a sudden thought. "What do you think of the white Victorian dress I tried on?"

"I think you will look ravishing in it," Fiona assured.

"Really? I want ... I just want to look perfect." Abigail's doubts were beginning to surface.

"Oh honey, you will!" Fiona said as she wrapped her arms around her in a hug. Neither she nor Abigail had discussed what had happened last night as they walked home together, although it was clear that both had failed and had not wanted to talk about why. Abigail had remarked little about Andrew today and discouraged Fiona from any conversation in that direction, which was very much unlike her, to say the least. It was obvious that something about her visit last night was troubling her. It also seemed that Abigail had the same sense about her, since she had not asked her about Patrick.

Abigail burst into tears. "Oh Fiona, I didn't want to say anything! Andrew was so standoffish last night. I think I really hurt his feelings by kissing Sean the way I did. He appeared so jealous and–"

"It's okay. Don't worry, Abby." Fiona soothed her. "If he seemed jealous it's because he really likes you."

She pulled Abigail's tear soaked face to hers.

"You wear that dress with nothing underneath it and Andrew will never be jealous again, I promise."

Abigail smiled through her tears. "Sorry, I just didn't know what to think. It's been driving me mad all day."

Then a thought occurred to her.

"A gift!"

"What?" Fiona asked.

"A gift! Fiona we haven't thought of a gift for Nicholas!"

Fiona sighed in relief. She could only handle one catastrophe at a time from Abigail.

"Don't worry, we have a few days to think of something. Perhaps we can find something in one of the local shops. We haven't even looked around this town since we've been here."

"But do you think three days is enough time to see all the wonderful goods Loglinmooth has to offer?" Abigail laughed.

"We'll have to do our best. Perhaps if we stick to the main street only," Fiona joked back. They both laughed, and the tension finally dissipated.

Abigail rushed to a nearby garment rack. She searched feverishly through the many costumes before pulling out her white dress.

"Help me try it on again?"

* * *

Andrew glanced down at the hastily written pages in a jumbled heap in his hands. *I can barely make head or tails of this; I don't know how the actors are going to.* Andrew looked every bit the mess he felt. He had been up all night writing and re-writing, consulting with Nicholas about characters and plot lines, trying desperately to weave a tale from the fragments and tidbits of suggestions from Carlisle and generally pulling his hair out. Not to mention Abigail's poorly timed visit. Asking her to leave did not sit well with her; he would have to make amends soon, but right now he had more pressing problems.

He wiped his brow, knocking his glasses askew. He had never encountered such an arduous, insane task as this. Now the actors, Sean, Fiona, and Samuel waited for his pages with Nicholas on stage, while he sat in the front row, still clueless. Nicholas had bought Andrew some time by discussing motivation with the actors. What he managed to come up with, considering the paper-thin plot, Andrew had no idea.

His pen scratched quickly across the papers adding some words, crossing out others, trying to be sure he made the same changes on all the script copies.

Sitting beside him, Carlisle looked on pleased, as punch. "Be sure to mention the haggis, young man."

Andrew stared up at him. "*Haggis?*"

"Aye. It's our national dish, it's made from the heart, liver, and lungs of a sheep, chopped and—"

"I know what haggis is, I just don't know what it has to do with the play."

"Tsk. Tsk," the old man shook his head, disappointed. "It has everything to do with the play. Perhaps I should write it myself?"

"That won't be necessary," Nicholas announced, stepping up to them. "Andrew has a firm grasp on the story. May I have the scripts please, Andrew?"

He reluctantly handed up the pages.

Nicholas took them and handed them out. The actors read through them, puzzled looks on their faces.

"Naturally these are preliminary drafts. They are more to give you the feel for the characters and the basic storyline. Don't memorize them, merely use them as a guide." Nicholas strode back and forth across the stage as he talked. Andrew slumped down in his seat, while Carlisle leaned forward in anticipation, his wool blanket across his lap. In the very last row sat Jeppsen, also keenly interested.

"Okay, the setting is Scotland, a small village very much like this one. The location is a castle. Very much like our producer's. The year is the late sixteen hundred's. Fiona, you are, of course, playing the part of Iona. You are a simple farm girl from the local village who has fallen in love with the Lord of the Manor, Sir Keir Maclaren, played by Sean."

"I'm supposed to be in love with *him?*" Fiona asked with barely disguised disgust.

"Shouldn't take too much acting on your part," Sean chided her. "Think how hard I have it. I'm supposed to be keen for you as well."

"Why you pompous—" she began, before Nicholas cut her off.

"Quiet, you two," Nicholas scolded. "This is difficult enough without bickering."

Sean smiled his most innocent smile. Fiona glared at him. Nicholas ignored them both as he checked his script. He continued.

"Iona you have just stolen into the grand costume ball at Maclaren's Manor and have caught the eye of Maclaren, who has no idea you are of peasant stock. You must keep the charade going as long as possible, hoping you will win his heart and he'll fall in love with you. Let's just try this. Andrew, you take notes."

Nicholas started to leave the stage when Samuel stopped him.

"And what about me, sir?"

"Ah yes. Scotland. When I point to you, step forward and say something about your country." Nicholas shot Carlisle a short look. "We'll try and work it in somehow."

"Aye," Samuel said confidently.

Nicholas returned to his seat. "Okay everyone, begin."

Sean and Fiona slowly circled each other like prize cocks in a fighting ring, each waiting for the other to make the first move.

"Will someone please read a line!" Nicholas cried, exasperated already. Sean nodded. He reached out and took Fiona's hand and kissed it gently, shocking her.

"My eyes' have never vacationed on such a lovely vista as you," he began. "And disguised no less. May I have this dance, mysterious Madam?"

"Certainly, my Lord." Fiona replied with a curtsey.

"Ah, I see you have penetrated my guise. Perhaps I can penetrate yours before the night is over?" Sean pulled her close.

"A woman can be many things," Fiona teased. "It is wrong to assume we are all alike."

"One dance then, I imagine you are quite skilled." He escorted her to center stage, and held out his hands. Grinding her jaw, Fiona took his hands. They glided across the stage in perfect form to a silent orchestra.

"Have we met?" Sean asked as they continued to dance silently. "Or is that too bold a clue to your secret identity?"

"I have seen you, but you have never seen me," Fiona whispered into his ear. A deep sadness filled her voice. "You look right through me as if I were–"

"A ghost?" he finished her sentence for her.

"As well as," she agreed. "You pass right through my heart every night like vapor."

"Were that true, I cannot believe that I would not have lingered."

She stopped the dance and started to pull away.

Sean grabbed her arm, forcing her to stay put. "It might take more than one dance. I fear I am too taken with you to give you up so easily."

"I am not yours to give."

"The others have all departed," Sean announced, glancing around. "We are quite alone."

"That we are," Fiona agreed. Sean suddenly pulled her close, very close. She gasped.

"Perhaps it is time to reveal yourself?" he suggested, his lips very close to hers. "I am desperate to know your name, whose bed you share."

"Desperation is not becoming to a Lord," she snapped.

He smirked. "You speak so freely."

"I speak my mind."

"I am gathering that. Let me speak mine." His reply was a low deep voice. "Your actions betray what you say. You do not feel safe when I am around you. I challenge you and you like that because you fear me. You crave my touch; my hands upon you, my lips." He inched forward. "Oh, how you crave ... my lips."

His lips touched hers gently at first, before he kissed her passionately, a kiss that was held for a very long time. She did not resist. She couldn't.

Sean suddenly stopped. "I believe I have just penetrated your guise." He walked away from her, leaving Fiona flustered and furious.

The gathered audience was stunned silent.

Samuel chose this moment to step forward.

"Gretna Green is a village in Scotland. It's a wee bit famous for the many runaway marriages performed there every year. If ye be seeking a quick marriage, you should elope to Gretna Green, where your vows need only be performed before witnesses, it's quite simple and thrifty."

Nicholas turned to Andrew, who appeared equally baffled. "Did you write that?"

Andrew shook his head. "Some of it."

Jeppsen began clapping from the back. "Bravo!"

Carlisle stood up suddenly. "I like it. Ye forgot the haggis, but next time. Keep up the good work. Jeppsen! Bring the auto around!"

"It seems we have a play forming," Nicholas announced. "Good work everyone. Fiona, remember your character is trying to seduce him, not degrade him. Sean, that was fantastic. Now do it again."

* * *

When Fiona stormed into the Broken Piper she found McStargle in a cheery mood, lost in her own thoughts, humming to herself as she wiped down the bar. She didn't seem aware of her new arrival.

Fiona took a seat at the bar and impatiently waited to be noticed. She was still steaming over the rehearsal, and being ignored was not helping matters at all. She was about to say something, when McStargle finally looked up and smiled at her.

"And what can I do for you?"

"Are you still serving lunch?" Fiona asked, doubtful.

McStargle reached beneath the bar and pulled out a very full plate of haggis and slid it over to her.

Fiona couldn't help but laugh. "How did you do that?"

"Always be prepared. That is what me mother always said to me. Actually it was to be my lunch, but there's plenty more in the kitchen. The old man loves his Haggis on Thursdays, don't you know, so I always make an army's worth."

"Well, I thank you, your mother, and the old man," she began to eat.

Twenty minutes later, Fiona was completely stuffed and more content. She had been so consumed with her delicious food that she had not thought any more of the rehearsal.

When McStargle arrived to take her empty plate, Fiona couldn't help praising the cook. "Brilliant dish. It does wonders for forgetting."

"Why, thank you lass, but what makes a pretty thing like you want to be forgetting anything?" She leaned in conspiratorially. "Those Berenger lads aren't causing you any trouble are they?"

Fiona moved to respond but McStargle was already continuing.

"I said to me self, '*self* here comes terrible trouble', the moment I saw the likes of the two of them again. It was like a bad omen it was. They were always inseparable back in the day, you know. Like the Katzenjammers kids, those two growing up were. If you saw one, you saw the other. Until that pretty thing walked in and split them up for sure."

Fiona blinked back her surprise. "What pretty thing?"

"Why Bethany, of course. I'm sure you have heard of her by now? You can't go too far in this town without hearing of her, what with all the trouble she caused."

"No," she lied.

"Well, she was a catch, she was–if you could catch her. Trouble was both Berenger lads wanted her, along with every other man jack in this town. She teased them all, you see, leading on anyone who was sorry enough to lay eyes on her. She was a wee thing, like yourself, so dainty and pretty as a fairy."

"Wee folk," Fiona corrected her, but there was no stopping McStargle when she was on a roll.

"You see, Sean, poor thing, fancied himself hers, but so did Patrick." She paused reflecting on her memories. "They fought each other like the devil themselves when they were alone but were always on their best behavior around that girl. I had never seen Patrick, the wee troublemaker, the brutal heartbreaker, work so hard at stealing Bethany right from under Sean's nose. She never had a chance, did she? While Sean, no saint himself, mind you, would do all he could to expose Patrick to be what he really was. But a wolf in a sheep's blanket is still a wolf, eh? So try as they may, neither could keep their true spirits locked away. Have I ever told you about the time those two locked me in me own basement for three hours just to see if they could drink my entire bar? No? Oh, so anyway, when Sean finally proposed to Bethany, Patrick was fit to be tied ... "

"Wait a minute," Fiona insisted. "Sean proposed to her?" She couldn't believe a cad like Sean who chased every woman moving would ever think of marrying. "Then what happened?"

A dark cloud crossed McStargle's face.

"Not really sure what happened at the end there, but one day all three were here and the next all had vanished. No one knows for certain; everyone assumed that she ran away with one of the lads, but now that they're here, neither with her ... well, one can only guess. She's probably somebody's mistress now; that suits her, but those poor boys, to run off after her and lose their mother around the same time. My heart just aches for them, poor souls."

Fiona was upset that the story apparently ended there. It was obvious that McStargle loved her gossip and she probably never realized that she both vilified and pitied the two brothers in practically the same sentence. Still Fiona was not going to allow her to leave her hanging like this.

"What happened to their mother?"

"Don't you be asking me to spread evil gossip! I have nothing to say about a woman who disappears from a drunken and terrible husband. I would have run away a thousand times as well. If you ask me, he deserved a lot worse than to die in a fire. I just hope that she has found joy wherever she escaped to."

McStargle ended there and took a deep breath. She began viciously wiping down the bar. She was out of gossip, and she didn't like being out of gossip.

"Has Mister Thornbury spoken to you about the little party for our director in a few days?" Fiona asked, hoping to bring McStargle back around.

It worked. McStargle's mood changed as quickly as Scottish weather. She brightened instantly.

"Aye, that he did. He wants every type of food and desert imaginable for the damn thing. He likes to get carried away with these things. God bless him, he is really lonely."

"I've seen that, the carried away bit. The night of the summons was the most lavish meal I had ever seen."

Now it was McStargle who blushed. "It was nothing, just something I came up with on short notice. Had I'd been given more time, I could have managed a proper meal."

"By the way, do you know of a shop where I can buy a gift? I would like to get something for Nicholas's birthday," Fiona asked.

"Well, there is a shop that Karin Hannah runs down the way, just past the church. They have a little of everything in there. Found me some amazing lace once, not that your fine director would want that or anything, unless he is married ... " McStargle hinted.

Fiona nodded, 'no'.

McStargle beamed. "Aye, it's a fine shop, they carry a little of all things."

Fiona smiled; she was becoming more and more fond of Miss McStargle by the second.

"Do you have any idea what I should serve that night? I mean what Mister Nicholas enjoys?" McStargle asked, innocently.

"He has always talked fondly of meatloaf, not sure what that is, but he seems to miss it," Fiona was happy to suggest.

McStargle nodded. "Whatever it is, I am sure I can make it."

"I'm sure you can. Are you equally as skilled with a needle and thread, Miss McStargle?"

"Aye," she boasted. "Why do you ask? Do you need some mending? Or does Mister Nicholas?" she added hopefully.

"No, but I'm sure Abigail is overwhelmed with all the costumes she has to work on at the theater. It's just so much work for one person and Abigail would love the company. I'm sure we can pay you."

McStargle's face drained of color as she took a step backwards. "I would be glad to help miss, but as God is my witness, I will not place one foot inside that damned theater."

"Why is that?" Fiona asked concerned.

"Not even Satan himself would enter that damned place," she whispered. "With the way Angus died, I am sure he is roaming those halls angry as hell." She crossed herself. "Bless you, child. I pray nothing bad happens to you and yours, but you will not be seeing the likes of me in that place. Ever!"

Fiona felt a chill run down her spine and then reminded herself that out in the country people were more superstitious, believing in salt rings, fairy mounds, and the devil running around at night.

The only evil she knew of was across the street and probably drinking.

* * *

"What do you think of a tweed scarf?" asked Fiona, holding it up above her head to show Abigail. She immediately changed her mind. "No, Nicholas is more refined. Isn't that a cashmere one over there?"

Abigail barely looked around before nodding her head no. She was impatient to get back to the subject at hand. "Forget the scarf. You said Sean was *engaged?*"

Abigail and Fiona were in Hannah's store. It was a lovely shop, very bright and airy. The shop seemed like a bit of a secret. From the outside no one would assume it was such a large store, filled to the brim with a little of this and a little of that, so crowded that it was hard for both girls to walk its aisles. Fiona was overjoyed to be distracted with the mission of finding something for Nicholas, anything not to think about Patrick and his dark past and Sean with his asinine ways.

"Seems that way. Although I think Patrick may have stolen her away."

Of course he would have. Who in their right mind would want Sean over Patrick? Fiona had to admit, she had been cut to the quick by Sean and did not like it in the least bit.

"You ladies need some help?" asked a short, stout man who appeared suddenly from behind a corner. He sported a heavy red beard and lengthy, untamed red hair which made him appear like some sort of a goblin that had somehow lucked his way into running a shop.

"I don't suppose you're Karin?" Fiona said. "Miss McStargle told me that this shop was the place to go."

"Aye, it is, but I'm Wade. Karin would be me wife," he grinned. "And if you ever be meeting her, you'd not be mistaking us." He laughed heartily at his own joke.

"It's a pleasure to meet you, Wade. I'm Abigail and my friend here is Fiona. We're looking for a birthday gift for our director."

"Was wondering when you lot would make it in here. The town has been talking about the likes of you for some time now," he winked and scratched his beard.

"Really?" Fiona asked. Now that she thought of it, she realized that she hadn't really seen anyone else since they had arrived in town. Perhaps she had been too busy to notice anyone else, that and the dreadful storm. Still, it was a little strange that the pub was always empty.

"Aye, you are the stuff of legend. Showing up with the Berenger Boys, working secretly in that rotting theater on some kind of a show. You've got a lot of tongues waging."

"Haven't heard a peep," Abigail smiled, obviously thinking the same as Fiona. "They must all be whispering. How many people are in this town?"

"Ah, let me see ... since the McGregor's had twins and Seamus up and died, I reckon close to forty-five. And most are all excited to see this new play, especially me wife. She used to go to every show that Sean and Patrick were in, when they were just wee lads. She has a soft spot for those two, being what happened to their mom and all."

"What did happen to her?" Fiona asked on impulse.

"Can't say." Wade looked suddenly uncomfortable. "T'was a tragedy."

"Likewise with their dad," Abigail added

Wade said nothing.

"How come no one from town came to the wake?" Fiona asked, bluntly.

Wade looked down at his shoes, as if seeing them for the first time.

"Well, it's like this Miss, old Angus wasn't so well liked, least not since Delia vanished. So not too many tears were shed when news got out that he was gone. Some believe she ran away, some believe he killed her."

The room became uncomfortably silent.

Wade broke the silence at last. "You lasses care for tea? I have a kettle on in the back."

"No, thanks," Fiona said.

Once again, an uncomfortable silence filled the shop.

"You know, I'd like some tea after all," Abigail spoke up. "If it's no trouble?"

"No trouble at all," Wade insisted. "I was planning on one for meself anyway. Be back in a wink." He winked then disappeared down the same aisle he appeared.

"Hey!" Abigail spotted a collection of cut crystal brandy glasses. She rushed over to it.

"How about this glass?" She held up a thick glass with gold trim around the rim. It was simple; it was perfect.

"Yes. I love it, it's a really nice and proper gift for Nicholas," Fiona said. "It looks like something a director would enjoy drinking from. How about adding a vintage bottle of single malt or port to go along with it? He can break them both in at the party."

"Great idea, Fiona. No wonder Nicholas dotes on you. I wonder where Wade keeps his liquor?" she asked.

"In his belly, by the looks of him," Fiona joked. They both laughed. "Actually I thought I saw a bottle over there," she pointed to the front of the store. They went over to find it was a twenty-year-old bottle of Speyside. Fiona was just reaching for it when the little bell over the door tinkled, announcing a new customer.

"Oy! We're not alone in this town after all," Abigail said, craning her neck to see over the aisle. "Maybe it'll be a handsome young, single farm lad, eh?"

A giant, kilted figure covered in snow stomped in, and shook himself free of the white stuff.

"Oh. Never mind. It's just Samuel," Abigail said, disappointedly.

Wade re-entered holding two steaming cups of tea. He looked up at the giant before him and smiled. "Hello there lad, anything I can get for you?"

"Hello." Samuel glanced over to Fiona and Abigail. "Hello ladies," he bellowed.

"Hey, Sam!" they called back.

Samuel turned back to Wade. "I was hoping you might have some fine cigars for sell, good sir."

"You're in luck, lad. Got me some fresh ones in the back. Wait here." Wade put down his teacups and then disappeared again into his backroom.

Samuel walked over to where Fiona was examining the bottle of scotch. "What's that you got there, Fiona?"

"Scotch. Nice bottle huh? Abigail and I thought ... "

"Aye, you're right, I've been looking for such a bottle. You lasses are so sweet thinking of me like that, only I can buy it me-self," he pulled the bottle out of Fiona's hands.

Shocked Fiona glanced at Abigail who simply shrugged her shoulders.

"Do you think Nicholas will like this glass?" she asked.

"Aye, he will love that, and with the castle being fully stocked in spirits he will have plenty of fun with that, although I hope *one* of you girls can keep a *sober* eye on him to make sure he doesn't drink too much," he said, deliberately to Fiona.

"I haven't known Nicholas to take advantage of his liquor before," she replied.

Samuel ignored her, glancing instead to Abigail. "I imagine you will be with your gent that night? He was just talking with me about the party, seems he is really looking forward to it."

Abigail beamed, suddenly anxious to leave in hopes of catching Andrew at the theater, she shoved the glass in Samuel's free hand.

"Would you mind picking this up for us to? Here's a few quid, should be enough. I have got to get back to the theater and finish some costumes."

Abigail gently shoved Fiona towards the door.

"Sure. Nice job today, Fiona, you and Sean are certain to steal the show if you keep that up," Samuel called out.

"Thanks, Samuel." She was not sure if he meant it as a compliment. "You were wonderful, too," Fiona called back as Abigail pulled her outside before Samuel could reply. Abigail immediately began leading them towards the theater.

"Slow down Abigail. When I left, Andrew was talking about going to the castle and writing," Fiona cried, already out of breath.

Abigail slowed. "Sorry, just got excited. I really do need to work on some costumes too, but possibly seeing him did light a little fire there."

"Relax, you'll see him tomorrow night for sure," Fiona assured her.

"Did he say anything at the rehearsal about me? I mean the character he is writing for me?"

"He really didn't say much," Fiona replied.

Abigail, although disappointed, asked, "Was the scene he wrote for you wonderful?"

"It was more of a work in progress, but yes, Abby, it has the signs of a great play I believe."

"And how is Sean as an actor? Does he take after Patrick?"

"No. He was terrible." Fiona lied. She did not want to admit to Abby that he was almost charming and that she hated him for that. She didn't want to talk about the kiss that stopped her heart, or that for the first time Nicholas had scolded her performance while praising Sean. No, there was nothing else to say.

Fiona spied Samuel across the road, following them discretely as he smoked his cigar, the bottle of scotch and glass in his hands.

Once he was spotted, he ducked behind a tree.

How curious.

* * *

"In this scene, Sean, you, or rather, Lord Keir Maclaren, are in the village with your betrothed, Lady Lilias, as played by Abigail. She is shopping for a wedding dress."

Nicholas handed out sheets of script pages as he spoke. He was suffering from a massive hangover but was determined to work through it.

On stage, contained tension could be felt between Sean and Patrick. They isolated themselves at either end of the troupe: Patrick, stage left, stood next to Fiona, then Abigail, Samuel, and finally Sean on the far right. Neither brother had said much to each other, although they did manage to 'accidentally' bump into each other in the lobby.

Fiona felt the tension the strongest. Patrick was being over-protective of her. Every time she turned around, he was right there, shielding her from Sean. She didn't understand this sudden change in him, and was uncertain if she liked it, as she was unclear of his motivation. What made it especially awkward was that she was desperate to talk to Sean alone, which didn't seem possible, at least until after the rehearsal was through. She glanced at Sean. He sensed her looking his way and turned to meet her gaze. Patrick, noticing the two of them, grabbed her hand in his and squeezed it. Sean looked away in disgust. She sighed.

Brothers. Little boys pretending to be men.

"What?" Abigail whispered, irritated that Samuel was nudging her insistently.

Samuel didn't notice the edge in her voice as he whispered back, "I came up with a most clever interpretation of my scene."

"Really?" She scanned through the pages and found it. It was handwritten in Carlisle's wispy scrawl. "This scene? *Really?* This scene?"

She indicated the page and read it aloud.

"Scotland. *Bean-Shidhe.* The plaintive wail foreshadows the appearance of the Banshee. She, as the spirit of the land in the form of a stunningly beautiful woman, will rise from the moors, wailing and moaning, signaling that someone is going to die."

"Aye, that's the one." Samuel grinned a Cheshire grin. "Wait and see. It's a real show stopper, that is."

Nicholas stopped his scene explanation, nearly as confused as the actors, and raised his head at the sound of distant whistling from backstage, coming closer. This was not his usual way to direct a play, but then again this was not a normal play, and with opening night only a few weeks away, there was simply no time to do things in the conventional manner. His head throbbed painfully. The stress of making this script work, combined with the sets that still needed to be built, the costumes that still needed to be tailored, and the props that needed to be assembled were what Nicholas attributed his headache to, and not the large amount of scotch he had consumed last night or that infernal whistling ...

"WHO THE HELL IS WHISTLING?" he screamed, startling the actors.

"Sorry!" Jeppsen called out, appearing from behind the left curtain. "That would be me. 'I dreamt that I dwelled in marble halls' it was, sir. From the opera, 'The Bohemian Girl', composed by Michael—"

"I don't give a shit who composed it. Just stop the damn noise!" Nicholas yelled, exasperated.

Abigail whispered to Samuel. "Doesn't Jeppsen know it's bad luck to whistle on stage?"

Samuel nodded. "Aye, one of us will be out of work, they say, or the sets will fall on us."

Abigail looked around nervously. "Is he trying to doom us all? What's wrong with him?"

"He's just not sensible theater folk like us," Samuel remarked, proudly.

"What are you doing back there, anyway?" Nicholas demanded as Gavin appeared beside Jeppsen. "He's helping me move some backdrops," Gavin called out.

"Well do it quietly!" Nicholas rubbed his temples. "You're giving me a terrific headache!"

"No problem," Gavin replied. "Everything's in place now."

"Fine." Nicholas sighed. "Now where was I?"

Gavin disappeared backstage.

Andrew leaned in to Carlisle. "Nick's headache wouldn't be of the *Scotch-ish* variety, would it?"

Carlisle grinned back in acknowledgment. "Aye, he's been going through my stores faster than William Wallace downing the Brits at Stirling Bridge!"

Andrew laughed. Then he had another thought. "You didn't wish him happy birthday this morning, did you? We want him to be completely surprised."

"Nay." Carlisle shook his head. "Nary a word escaped me lips. I can hold a secret, ye can be sure of that." He eyed Andrew with a penetrating stare that seemed to add additional weight to his words.

"Quiet! *Everyone!*" Nicholas yelled, glancing pointedly at the two in the front row. "Alright. Fiona, you are, of course, Iona, the shopkeeper. You're afraid that Lord Maclaren will recognize you from the costume gala the night before—"

"Excuse me for asking," Fiona interrupted, as she scanned through her script. "If I'm a common shopkeeper, then why was I invited to the gala at the Lord's castle?"

"Good question," Nicholas agreed. He turned to Andrew. "Andrew you want to answer that?"

Andrew stood up. "Yes. I haven't written that scene yet, but actually you were not invited, the hoi polloi were never invited. Iona snuck up there hoping to experience how the other half lived. She was recently married, to Rory Lachlan, a brutish scoundrel and owner of the shop where you work, played by Patrick. Although he is handsome and wealthy, and loves you, it's a marriage of convenience for you, as your family is indebted to him. You hope one day to find a way to love him but—"

"Thanks, Andrew," Nicholas interrupted. "I prefer not to give away too much at this time, seeing as the script is not yet completely determined." He turned back to Fiona. "Does that help, Fee?"

She nodded yes, but her mind was elsewhere. *So Patrick and I are mismatched lovers?* Even though it was only a play, the thought somehow bothered her.

"Okay, so is everyone clear on their roles? Good. Let's do a run through, starting on page fifteen. This is where Lord Maclaren and the future Lady Lilias enter the shop. Patrick you are backstage for the moment, Fee you are in the back room of the shop."

The actors took their places; this being the first run through, Nicholas wasn't too concerned about the blocking.

> SCENE: Lachlan's – *a fashionable dress shop oddly situated in a remote town in northern Scotland.*

> TIME: *Midday.*

> *The scene opens as* LADY LILAIS *leads* LORD MACLAREN *enter the dress shop.*

> LILAIS: I saw the loveliest fabric in here and I knew I must have it for my wedding dress.

> MACLAREN: I thought it was a misfortune for the groom to see the wedding dress before the nuptials?

> LILAIS: Don't be silly. You won't see it. I'll try it on in the back and keep it well under wraps until you get to unwrap me.

> (MACLAREN *takes her hand and kisses it.*)

> MACLAREN: An appetizing thought.

> (LILAIS *swoons under his spell.*)

> LILAIS: Yes, I feel your hunger. Now, where is that clerk? Miss!

(IONA *shyly steps in from offstage.*)

IONA: Yes, My Lady? May I help you?

(MACLAREN *starts at the sound of her voice. He looks deeply at* IONA. IONA *averts his stare. She looks exclusively at* LILAIS.)

LILAIS: You were going to make some alterations on my wedding dress. Is it ready?

IONA: Aye. It is in the back. Would you like to try it on now?

LILAIS: Yes. Excuse me, My Lord.

MACLAREN: Of course.

(LILAIS *and* IONA *exit.* MACLAREN *whistles as he waits for* IONA *to return. She returns, quickly.*)

IONA: The Lady Lilais is most lovely, My Lord.

(MACLAREN *stares blatantly at* IONA. *She is unnerved by his stare.*)

MACLAREN: Your voice is familiar as well your look. Have I seen you before?

IONA: I have seen you, but you have never seen me.

MACLAREN: You look right through me as if I were–

IONA: A ghost."

MACLAREN: It was you last night! I scoured the halls for you all night long! I feigned insomnia so Lady Lilais would not wonder why I roamed.

IONA: I am so sorry to trespass, My Lord. It was unforgivable of me for so many reasons.

MACLAREN: No need to apologize. It was a lovely dance. Perhaps we can do it again?

IONA: Are you not still engaged to Lady Lilais? Perhaps I should stop her trying on the dress?

MACLAREN: Such a sharp wit on one so young. Aye. Sadly, 'tis true. Not totally by choice, if I may be so honest. Now, if only the stars had aligned so I had met you 'ere this last winter ...

(MACLAREN *dazzles her with his smile as he takes her hand. IONA meets his gaze with a smile of her own.*)

IONA: Then you would have married a peasant? Truly?

(IONA *teases with an undercurrent of disgust for the class system that binds her.* MACLAREN *is amused by her presumption.*)

MACLAREN: One never knows does one? And would you marry a humble man, not worthy of your grace, but of a high station, thus given the chance?

(IONA *holds up her other hand, displaying her wedding band.*)

IONA: One never knows, does one? 'Ere I met you before summer last–?

(MACLAREN *drops her hand as her husband,* RORY LACHLAN, *enters.*)

RORY: Hello? What's this? Oh, my apologies, My Lord!

MACLAREN: And with whom do I have the pleasure of conversing, good sir?

RORY: Rory Lachlan, proprietor of this humble shop, your Lordship. I see you have met my lovely wife.

MACLAREN: Yes, she is lovely.

RORY: Yes, she is.

Patrick takes a step toward Sean, and places a casual, but intentional, hand on Sean's upper arm and squeezes hard.

RORY: And she is *mine*, you know.

Patrick just went off script, Nicholas realized. *What's he doing? Things were going quite smoothly up to this point.*
Then he noticed the sudden change in the air, a static charge that raised the hairs on his arms and the back of his neck, like the precursor to a thunderstorm.
A faint keening wail began from backstage.
What in the world? Is someone strangling a cat? He wondered, but he didn't have time to think about it before all hell broke loose.

On stage Patrick and Sean had moved within inches of each other; a nearly insane tension between them.
"You can't have her," Patrick said, his voice low and throaty.
"You don't deserve her," Sean warned.
Fiona, although confused, couldn't help sense the danger brewing. Backstage, the eerie wailing grew louder and more frightening.

"You always try to take what's not yours!" Sean screamed as he shoved Patrick hard. Patrick stumbled back across the stage, nearly losing his footing.

His eyes raged, but his voice was calm as he called back at Sean.

"You never had her, *brother.*"

Patrick's cool demeanor infuriated Sean more than if he had screamed the words into his ear. He tried to restrain his fury. He lowered his voice both in pitch as well as volume.

"A little more than kin and less than kind."

"Cruel only to be kind," Patrick replied as he sauntered toward his brother.

"Don't try to match wits with me, *brother.* You always knew *what* to say, but not how to *act.*"

Sean stood his ground, waiting for his brother to come to him. He glanced over at Fiona who was covering her ears from the awful wailing sound growing louder. *What is that?* He had to shout to be heard over the cacophony.

"Oh Patrick, the great stealer of lovers, who can lead poor, sweet Fee on, but doesn't even have the decency to properly bed her!"

Patrick, enraged, was at him in an instant, shoving him.

"Don't you dare speak to me of Fiona!"

Sean staggered back, trying to regain his balance, when Patrick was at him again.

"You have no right to speak of her!" he shoved him again, harder this time. Sean fell. He looked up into Patrick's glare.

"And what of Bethany? Do I not have a right to speak of her?" Sean's eyes flashed both pain and anger. He rose up on shaking legs.

"You could never see it, could you?" came Patrick's suddenly calm reply. "She was a whore. All I had to do was smile." Patrick's mouth twisted into a devilish smirk.

Years of pent up, buried emotions and resentments rushed to the surface. Sean charged him, screaming incoherently, knocking Patrick crashing hard into a stage pillar. Patrick had the wind knocked out of him momentarily, but regained his senses quickly and soon both brothers were tumbling across the stage, throwing punches, wrestling, and growling like two mad dogs.

Andrew and Nicholas, who had sat stunned through the exchange, leapt onto the stage and attempted to break the brothers apart.

Abigail rushed in from backstage wearing the white dress she had been altering for the party.

"What the bloody 'ells going on?" she shouted over the now near deafening wail, looking for Andrew, who was no longer in his seat. Carlisle sat alone. His eyes fixed upon the fight onstage, an amused twinkle in his eye. Patrick and Sean were scrapping for all they were worth, with Andrew and Nicholas caught up in the fray.

"Oy! What this about?" She glanced over to Fiona for an explanation but was startled to see her standing perfectly still, staring at the brothers, both hands covering her ears.

"What's wrong with everyone?" Abigail wailed.

Samuel stepped out onto the stage costumed in a long blonde wig and white diaphanous gown of a banshee, mangling the bagpipes for all he was worth.

Nicholas managed to grab hold of Patrick and pull him off Sean, who was bleeding from several cuts, but Andrew, being of lesser build, was having a difficult time keeping Sean from Patrick. Both brothers seemed possessed as they struggled and screamed.

Samuel finally finished his song and looked up proudly expecting applause but instead saw the melee.

"Shite!" he cried, and dropped his bagpipes—which groaned and bleated like a sick and dying sheep as they fell to the floor—and raced over to help Andrew with Sean, who had been forced back into the curtains by Patrick.

Jeppsen suddenly appeared from backstage and beat Samuel to the rescue. He managed to grab Sean and pull him away, just as Abigail screamed: "LOOK OUT!" her hand raised to her mouth to stifle her terror.

Jeppsen, who had no idea to whom she was screaming, or what about, nonetheless had the fortunate sense to look up in time to see the heavy sandbag counterweight for the curtain crashing down toward him. Jeppsen's quick reflexes allowed him to move aside, but not quite far enough or fast enough, as the sandbag crashed down, grazing his head, knocking him unconscious. The bag hit the stage with a muted *splat!* and split open, spilling sand across the stage.

From the far side of the stage Gavin appeared.

"I thought I heard shouting? Is everyone okay? Or was that just part of the play?"

No one answered him. Everything stopped. Patrick and Sean, both cut, bruised and bleeding, ceased fighting. Fiona started to move to them, but was uncertain which brother to go to. Abigail's hand was frozen to her mouth in a stifled scream.

The fallen bagpipes let out a final gasp, as the remaining air bleated out, and then fell still.

Carlisle gasped out, "Someone help the poor man!" which finally galvanized everyone into movement. Samuel rushed to Jeppsen's side and placed his hand to his throat to check for a pulse. Fiona, dilemma decided, went to Jeppsen as well.

Abigail was shaking as she called out in a weak voice, "Is 'e dead?"

"No lass," Samuel reassured her. "Just had the wits knocked out of him. Could some of you lads give me a hand? I think it would be best to move him to the couch in the dressing room."

Nicholas, who still had a hold of Patrick, glared back and forth between Sean and Patrick.

"Are you two done?" he asked, his voice ringing with anger.

"Aye," Sean replied while Patrick merely nodded.

"Fantastic. Now I'm going to help Samuel get Jeppsen to that couch and then I would like to have a word with the both of you in the lobby."

He released his hold on Patrick and walked over to where Samuel, Andrew, and Gavin were helping lift Jeppsen. They gently carried him off the stage.

Sean and Patrick both looked at Fiona.

"Fiona ... " Patrick began, painfully dabbing a cut lip.

"Not now. Either of you," she shook her head at the two bleeding brothers in disgust. She noticed the very distressed looking Carlisle sitting alone and frightened in the front row. She left the stage to go to his side.

"He is going to be fine Mr. Thornbury. I promise."

"I never knew they didn't like him," he whispered, "or I would have insisted he stay away from the stage ... "

"Who didn't like him?" she asked.

"The spirits," he said.

Fiona felt a shiver go up her spine. She took the old man's hand. "I'd bet when he comes to, the first thing he will want is a nice cup of tea. Would you like to come and help me fetch some?"

Carlisle shook his head to clear it. "What's that? Tea you say? Yes, a very fine idea. A nice spot of tea always makes things better, eh? I could fancy one myself."

The two of them disappeared into the wings.

"THE LOBBY NOW!" bellowed Nicholas to the brothers who were still nursing their wounds. He stormed off to the lobby.

Patrick stood on unsure legs. "I think our director wishes a word with us."

Sean, silent and brooding, left for the lobby.

"This ought to be interesting," Patrick mused, as he followed at a safe distance.

"I will not have this! Not in my theater!" Nicholas roared, stomping back and forth across the lobby. "You two are the reason we are stuck here and I will not allow my troupe or myself to be disrespected in such a fashion!"

Sean and Patrick gazed at the floor, not wishing to make eye contact with Nicholas or one another.

"If I don't start hearing the two of you promising me that this will never happen again, God help me, I will pull the troupe from this damned town and we will hike, bike, or skip out of here, or die trying. And I will gladly leave the two of you behind to fight amongst yourselves, the devil with the fortunes lost! Do I make myself clear?"

"Quite," Sean replied. "It won't happen again. You have my word."

"Aye, mine as well," agreed Patrick.

Nicholas stopped pacing and stared the both of them down. "Good, and I pray that the two of you are being honest. Now if you will excuse me, I have to go and check on Jeppsen, who was injured trying to help the likes of you two. Heaven knows why he should care–and then go and drink myself into yesterday."

He stalked off with regal excellence.

"Did you mean that? About it not happening again?" Patrick asked frankly.

"Can't say for sure, but that row felt bloody fantastic after all these years," Sean grinned, rubbing his bruised chin. He turned and left his brother standing alone.

"Aye," smirked Patrick. "That it did."

Sean was lost in his thoughts as he made his way through the theater. That much needed fight may have finally cleared the air between him and Patrick, but it also may have caused Fiona to run straight into Patrick's arms. She was the kind who lived to tend to damaged bodies and souls.

What was it about Fiona? She's just a woman that I've barely met and know even less. There were always women for the taking–that was the one thing he knew he would never be short of. *Still*…

"Sean?" came Fiona's voice.

Sean turned to find Fiona walking toward him.

"I never asked if you were okay?" she asked, with real concern.

"I'm fine, it's Patrick that will need to be babied. I'm surprised you are not with him now," he instantly regretted his sharpness.

"He's helping take Jeppsen back to the castle. What happened back there?" she asked, ignoring his tone.

"We fought."

"Yes, I know, both of your faces will tell that story for awhile."

"Are you implying that we 'Berenger Boys' aren't much to look at now?" he quipped, gingerly touching his eye.

"No, I just hope you got that out of your system. Listen Sean, I have a small favor to ask you."

Sean shifted his weight and cocked his head, curious. "And what might that be?"

"I was wondering if I could possibly have a bottle of port from your family's wine cellar for the party?"

"*Don't let her drink!*" Samuel's warning echoed through his mind. He didn't even know why he took those words to heart, but he did.

"Sorry, lass, but the answer is no."

Fiona stopped, completely surprised by his answer. She had been prepared to go into how much Nicholas loved port and how much it would mean to him, but he didn't even appear to be joking.

"Well, how much then? I'll buy it from you."

"You have your answer." He began to walk away without any explanation.

"But why?" she pleaded.

He said nothing.

"Is it because I'll be with Patrick? You were invited too, you know! You chose to decline!" she yelled, although not sure why she was so upset.

Sean turned suddenly and strode up to her, stopping when his face was dangerously close to hers.

"A girl like you has better things to do than try and get a man drunk to show his affection."

"What! What are you talking about? It's not even for me!" she screamed, holding her ground.

"I know, it's for you *and* Patrick," he said quietly. "He's toying with your affections, and you know it. He's completely the wrong man for you."

"You misguided idiot! Patrick told me not to believe anything you said!"

"And what if I were to say that you should not believe anything he says?" he countered.

"Then I would say that the two of you are more like brothers than you know," she snapped. With that, she spun around and stalked off.

"Enjoy your party!" he yelled out after her retreating figure.

"I shall! Immensely!" she called back, not bothering to turn around.

* * *

Fiona was furious! She stormed into the costume room and began tearing her clothes off, startling Abigail in the process.

"So, how did it go?" Abigail asked cautiously.

"That bastard!" Fiona cried, ripping her skirt off and throwing it into a corner. She began spouting out the whole story of what had just happened but she didn't stop there. She complained about the rehearsal and the fight and how strangely Patrick had acted earlier and how Sean had twisted the rehearsal she had with him, making Nicholas scold her and praise him.

She pulled off her top and crossed the room almost fully naked, not caring about modesty at all, and snatched her red corset like a misbehaving child, flinging it from side to side. Abigail stood in silence, dumbfounded.

Fiona turned sharply to Abigail. "Well, lace me up! We have a party to go to!"

Abigail moved timidly behind Fiona, grabbing the silk ribbon, not really sure what to say. She pulled the ribbon through once and took a small breath.

"Patrick did seem very affectionate with you today," she whispered, trying to calm the heavy breathing Fiona.

"That he did!" she snapped back. "For all the good it does me!"

Abigail pulled the ribbon through again. "I am sure Sean was just mad about the fight. It was wrong of him to take out his anger on you. I am sure Nicholas will love the glass with or without a bottle of port. He will just be happy to forget about today's rehearsal, the fight, the bagpipes, and Jeppsen."

Fiona said nothing. She was trying desperately to dispel her anger. *What has come over me? This is not me.*

"Fiona, I need you to breathe in, this is where it is going to get tight."

Fiona sucked in air and held her breath. She made up her mind in that moment that tonight she would sleep with Patrick. And if she was going to seduce him tonight she needed the corset as tight as possible.

Abigail continued lacing and pulling. "It appears that Jeppsen will be just fine. Thank God for that. He was a little shaken up but glad that he got to be a hero for a day. He saved Sean's life, and that's for sure. Not that *he'd* ever thank him!"

Fiona, who was still holding her breath, nodded. She was beginning to wonder if she would be able to breathe at all. Abigail was pulling really hard.

She still couldn't believe Sean had said no to her request, and not even that, he had scolded her like a small child, and she in return had acted like one.

"Okay, Fee, it's done. The fun part is getting out of it," she teased.

Fiona felt suddenly very tall and as she reached for her dress she felt herself become stiff and awkward.

"Here," Abigail grinned. "Let me get it. You haven't worn one of these for awhile have you?"

"It's been a long time," Fiona replied with a slight laugh. She felt the silky fabric of the dress pass her head and slide tightly down her body. Abigail began buttoning the dress as Fiona looked at her reflection in a mirror. She caught her breath. She looked beautiful. The dress hugged all the right curves, and Abigail had been right about the corset; she had more than just a promise of cleavage. She was certain it was something that would finally light a fire in Patrick. She could picture his gaze traveling downward before sweeping back up to smile at her.

Abigail finished buttoning and came up to stand next to the mirror.

"You look so lovely! I wish my breasts looked that way in a corset; mine always look like they are about to fly out, which isn't necessarily a bad thing. I bet you Patrick will be pleased!"

"I guess it is a good thing that I can't really breathe now; it's good practice as I am sure it will be much harder for me later," Fiona said.

"What if you swooned and collapsed on the floor and Patrick had to save you by ripping the corset from you!" Abigail laughed. "He would be *your* hero!"

"Your imagination!" Fiona exclaimed. "You should write a bawdy romance novel!"

She giggled at the thought. Fiona was definitely feeling a little light-headed. *How tight is this corset?*

"Does Andrew know what costume you'll be wearing tonight, Abby?" Fiona asked.

"No. He said he'd be waiting for me," she grinned, feeling like she was sitting in the catbird seat. "Won't he be surprised! He's in for the night of his life, that lad is!"

Fiona believed her, and she only hoped she could promise the same for Patrick. The anticipation was building as she thought about the night ahead. *It will be prefect! It has to be!*

"Oh, if only we had that bottle of port for Nicholas."

A sudden thought came to her. It wasn't just Sean's family's cellar; it was also Patrick's. Surely Patrick would have no problem, especially if she told him that Sean had said no. Or, she could just go and take a bottle and tell Patrick later at the party.

Besides, she was not about to let Sean tell her what to do!

* * *

Sean winced as he touched the warm cloth to the cut above his left eye. It came back soaked in blood. He straightened up from the sink and he felt his sore muscles protesting. He had his shirt off and he examined his cuts and bruises. He was a mess; there was no doubt about that. He knew from experience that it looked worse than it was, but there were no two ways about it, he was not looking a pretty sight.

It's been a while since I scrapped like that, especially with Patrick. I used to be able to whip the piss out of him, but I must admit, he put up quite a tussle. I wonder how Patrick looks? I guess Fiona will find out.

That thought made him wince even more.

Fiona. What gall she had to ask me to get her liquor so she could seduce Patrick! The last place I'd want to be is in the same room as those two!

Sean finished dressing his wounds as his thoughts replayed the day's events. In a strange way he felt better about his relationship with his brother, but for the life of him he couldn't figure out why. This entire adventure was staggeringly confusing, and his mind and body were too sore to dwell any further on it now. What he really needed was a good bottle of scotch, an engaging novel and a warm bed to forget this day ever happened.

He retrieved a copy of the latest F. Scott Fitzgerald's novel, peeking out from beneath a pile of clothes that he had thrown on the floor.

He glanced at the cover: 'The Beautiful and the Damned', this certainly sounds appropriate."

He tossed it down onto his still broken bed, gave the bed a second glance and shrugged.

"That seems appropriate as well. Now I just need something to burn the night away." He checked all the cupboards and even under the bed. He found plenty of empties, but no booze.

"Damn it."

And to make matters worse, the lights suddenly flickered and died. He found himself in near darkness. Only the light from the rising moon seeping through the window allowed him to see enough to stumble around and find a candle and some matches.

"So much for reading. I don't have the strength to start up that damn generator. But I still need a pain-killer to get drunk by."

Downstairs was dark and quiet and Sean seemed to have the theater to himself. He passed the ghost light and thought about lighting it but didn't bother.

"Have at it you tormented souls!" he called out. "Just keep it down so I can sleep tonight!"

He hobbled his way toward the cellar, occasionally wincing in pain. He unlocked the padlock, carefully made his way down the steep stairs, grabbed the first bottle of scotch he could find and climbed his way back. He locked the brass lock and tucked the key down inside his pants pocket.

He patted the ghost light as if it were an old friend as he passed by. Soon he was upstairs, dissolving himself into a drunken sleep.

Sean awoke with a pounding headache.

He noticed that the candle had burned down to a nub and he was desperately thirsty. He reached for the bottle of scotch beside him, tipped it to his mouth, and found it empty.

"How's that?" he muttered. There was no way he could have drunk an entire bottle, he wasn't even particularly pissed. He sat up in his slanted bed and rubbed his aching head. *Do I have any aspirin? I don't remember ever seeing any.*

He looked around the dark room. The moon was only slightly higher up in the sky, so he knew he must have only slept a few hours at most.

Then he heard it. A soft voice, singing that strange song that seemed to constantly haunt him.

"*Oh sorrow, sing sorrow ...* "

He rose up out of bed. He placed his ear to the floor. The voice was louder; it drifted up from the theater below.

"*And no one knows she loved him but herself and God ...* "

He had fallen asleep in his clothes, so he had no need to dress. He snatched the nub of a candle and crept down the stairs, following the siren's song.

The ghost light was still out. Standing beside it, shimmering in her own light, stood the woman in a dark blue dress he and Samuel had seen before, once again singing the same, haunting tune. Her face seemed a little less blurred this time, but he still couldn't make out her features.

"Who are you?" Sean approached cautiously. "What do you want?"

She offered no reply. Instead, she drifted towards the back of the stage, still singing. He followed her, as she led him across the stage, through the back rooms to the wine cellar entrance.

He was surprised to find the door wide open. He checked his pockets. The key was gone.

She drifted down the dark stairs.

He hesitated, wavering in the doorway. His candle was nearly burnt out, his head was pounding, he could barely think straight.

Am I actually going to follow a ghost down into a dark cellar?

All reason and justifications aside, Sean simply felt compelled, his mind made up for him by the siren song.

He descended the stone steps. The singing continued, unabated by his presence.

"She smiled and she spoke, but he paid no heed ... "

He reached the landing. He could just make out the woman in the deep blue dress standing in the center of the cellar before the small tasting table looking at a bottle of wine in her hands. Although her back was to him, he could hear her humming the haunting tune. An equally dwindling candle on the table, only served to cast her features in shadows.

He crept forward slowly. She seemed unaware of his presence. He reached out to touch her ... his hand shaking in fear ... he reached ... and touched *real* flesh and bone!

The startled woman leapt at the hand she felt upon her shoulder, the bottle dropped from her hand, exploding in a crash of glass and sea of blood red wine.

"Patrick?" she cried out, as she turned to peer at him unsure in the near darkness.

"No, Fiona. It's Sean," he sighed in mixed relief, as both candles sputtered out simultaneously, followed by the cellar door above them slamming shut and the padlock clicking into place.

* * *

Patrick rounded the corner leading to his room. He carried an ancient shield–a cross of red blazoned upon a yellow field– some chain mail, a *bascinet* (a silver armored helmet) and of course a lance, all of which he 'borrowed' from some of the suits of armor Carlisle had on guard about his castle.

He had coerced Abigail into revealing that Fiona was going to the party costumed as *The Lady of Shalott*, one of her favorite tragic literary figures.

In the Lord Alfred Tennyson poem, a beautiful, but cursed maiden on the island of Shalott, sits alone in her cottage along the road to Camelot, compelled to watch the world pass by only as reflected in her mirror, or be forever cursed. She immortalizes the images and imagined lives of those passing peasant men, women, merchants, and lovers in a tapestry that she continually weaves. One day, Sir Lancelot, armored and majestic, rides past upon his stallion and so taken is she that she dares to sneak a look directly at him. Her mirror cracks and the deadly curse is inflicted upon her. Knowing that she will soon die, she sets herself adrift in a boat she calls *The Lady of Shalott* towards Camelot. When the horrified townsfolk of Camelot discover her dead body, only Lancelot is unmoved. 'She has a lovely face; God in his mercy lend her grace, The Lady of Shalott.'

Patrick had decided to go to the party as Lancelot, thinking that he could be Fiona's knight in shining armor. But reflecting upon the meaning of the poem, he was having second thoughts about what message he might be sending. Lancelot was far from a noble Knight, having slept with King Arthur's wife among other sundry deeds.

Oh well, no time to change costumes now.

The fight with Sean had awakened several desires in him, not all as noble as they might first seem. He had always desired Fiona, he knew that, but now her honor (and his, he could not lie) was at stake. He knew it was going to come down to Sean or him, and he was not prepared to lose Fiona. He knew what Sean was capable of, but Patrick was now ready to claim Fiona and he hoped, despite all his delays, that she was ready for him as well.

"What comes around goes around, but not for you. You lose again, brother," he smirked aloud, and then winced. His mouth was still sore. Sean had really laid into him, but then again, he had hit back equally as hard. The row had been like old times, taking on his older brother despite the odds, which was somehow comforting to him in a strange way.

Yet ...

Could Fiona actually fall under Sean's spell? The thought shuddered him.

He opened the door to his room. He dumped his costume bits clumsily to the bed where they clanked and clashed and some fell unnoticed to the floor. Although his mind was still preoccupied with Fiona and Sean, his first need was to change. He pulled off his shirt, feeling the sharp pangs from his bruised body. He glanced in the mirror at the black and yellowed marks and swellings, not realizing before just how damaged he was, when a folded piece of paper wedged into the mirror's frame caught his eye.

He pulled it out.

I know who murdered your mother. Meet me at the train at seven o'clock tonight. Come alone. Be prompt.

Patrick held his breath and read it again. Once he was sure he had not missed anything he rose slowly and put his shirt back on. The party and Fiona were going to have to wait. He grabbed his coat and ran from the room and out into a very cold night.

* * *

Nicholas nodded in the dreary gloom of his room, nearly napping in his chair, the script in his hand long forgotten. The fireplace held nothing more than dying embers, casting ghostly shadows across the floor.

Slightly drunk, he pondered weak and weary the day's events when suddenly there came a tapping, as if someone were gently rapping, rapping at his chamber door.

Startled he glanced at the door. "Who is it?" he called out.

"'Tis some visitor,'" came the voice, "'tapping at your chamber door – only this, and nothing more.'"

"What the–?" Nicholas sat up straighter. "Come in then!"

The rapping continued.

"I said come in!" but the stranger at the door refused to enter, instead continued rapping.

Rising in anger, Nicholas strode over to the door. He opened it wide, and darkness there, and nothing more.

From around the corner, stepped Andrew in full costume. His hair and eyebrows were darkened black and his unruly hair combed to the side. He sported a bushy, black mustache accenting the dour look upon his face. He wore a dark jacket and white scarf, wound tight around his neck, emulating a photo he had found. His arms were crossed as he waited for Nicholas to recognize him.

Nicholas stared.

"'And his eyes have all the seeming of a demon's that is dreaming, and the lamp-light o'er him streaming throws his shadow on the floor; and my soul from out that shadow that lies floating on the floor shall be lifted'–Happy Birthday!" Andrew grinned, somewhat ruining the effect.

"Are you insane?" Nicholas asked.

"Perhaps. Name me and you shall be rewarded with a prize," Andrew proclaimed.

"Edgar Allan Poe?" Nicholas ventured.

"Correct!" Andrew exclaimed.

"Poe! You are one of my favorites! Do come in, good sir!" Nicholas invited, happily.

Andrew pulled a flask out of his vest pocket and offered it to Nicholas. "Your prize."

"Ah, scotch!" He took a drink. "But why the costume?"

"Come! Others await," Andrew dragged Nicholas by the sleeve out the door towards the parlor.

"Wait. 'On this home by horror haunted–tell me truly, I implore ... '" Nicholas quoted, getting into the spirit of the night. "Where the hell are we going?"

"To your birthday bash, Lenore!" Andrew laughed.

* * *

Sean searched desperately in the dark for the generator. All he had been able to find was empty air. Confused and rattled, he felt he couldn't properly analyze the situation until he could at least see. He finally found the generator by banging his head into the cold metal frame, intensifying his headache even more.

"Fooking shite!" he cried, as he reached for the starter cord. He yanked for all he was worth and the welcoming sound of the sputtering, noisy generator finally fired up.

Suddenly the cellar was lit, revealing Fiona staring at him, still in the same place she was before the candles had gone out. She looked angry, beautiful, and getting more beautiful as she grew angrier, but Sean decided it best to say nothing until he got the two of them out of the cellar.

He stumbled up the stairs and tried the door. It was definitely locked. He pulled at the door with what strength he had left but the lock held fast. He then began pounding and throwing his badly bruised body at the door. After several attempts he knew all too well that he was not going to be able to break through.

He slumped forward, leaned against the door and closed his eyes, trying to ease his throbbing head.

"What the hell just happened?" demanded Fiona from the bottom of the stairs. "Did someone lock the door?"

Sean opened his eyes halfway. "That seems to be the case, yes."

"There must be another way out," she insisted, stalking the room liked a caged animal, looking for another exit. She refused to accept that she could possibly be trapped in *here*, with *him*. "I'm going to miss the party!"

Sean finally opened his eyes fully, rose and slowly moved down the stairs. "Aye, that would be an awful shame. But no, no other way out that I know of."

He made his way to the scotch section, examined a dusty bottle, nodded, and then sat on the floor. He took a drink.

Fiona fumed as she stood over him.

"That's it? You're giving up?" she asked, incredulous.

"No, I'm getting pissed, just as I had planned for the evening. As good here as in me broken bed." Sean took another drink. "You can keep ranting, if you like, or ... " he patted the space beside him, "you can join me."

Sean finally noticed what she was wearing and caught his breath. He stared blatantly at her very exposed chest. "That's a lovely dress, by the way."

"Never mind the dress! You have to get me out of here!" she wailed.

Sean flinched. Her yelling was not helping his headache or his mood. Thankfully the scotch would.

"Sorry lass, I bet you're regretting trying to steal that bottle now, aren't you?"

"What?!?" Fiona was beside herself in anger. She clenched her raised fists in frustration. "I wasn't stealing it! And besides it's not just yours, you know! I'm sure *Patrick* would have said yes."

"Did you ask him?"

Fiona stopped suddenly. She said nothing. Sean started to chuckle.

"Of course you didn't, why surprise someone with port from his own cellar?"

"It wasn't for him, you idiot!" she screamed, shaking her fists again at him. "I told you that! It was for Nicholas, he loves port!"

Nicholas? Sean blinked back surprise. He leaned his head against the wall. *So, Fiona hadn't wanted that port for a cozy night's snockering with Patrick after all. Doesn't matter, I would have still said no.*

He took another drink and met her seething glare. *My God, she's beautiful right before she strikes ...*

Then she kicked him.

Fiona *was* fuming mad! She was trapped in a cellar with a drunken leech who refused to help her. Not thinking, she pulled her foot back and kicked Sean hard in his leg, causing him to wince in pain and nearly drop his scotch.

"What the hell was that for?" he cried rubbing the spot she had kicked.

"It's all your fault I'm down here! Had you just given me the port ... " she burst into tears. This night meant so much to her and now it was ruined.

Sean rose, clinging to his bottle for support. He reached out a hand, awkwardly to her, not sure if he would receive another kick. He stroked her shoulder.

"Easy there, lass," he said.

She looked at him through green, red brimmed eyes. "Who would do this to me?" she cried. "It ruins everything!"

Sean was surprised to admit that he felt otherwise. Whoever had locked the door had done him a great favor. He was relieved to know that she was not going to be with Patrick tonight.

He continued patting her in broad, awkward strokes. "Easy Fiona. I do fear it is my fault. If they wanted to lock you in, they could have before I got here."

Fiona stared at him in disbelief. *If he thinks his pathetic attempt at appeasing me by accepting the blame will work, he is sorely mistaken!*

Sean, thinking his words were succeeding in having a calming effect on her, took another swig. He moved his arm to hug her.

"Stop touching me!" she yelled, shoving him away. "You're right! This is all your fault!" Her eyes were fiery again. She advanced toward him as he continued to back away. "If you had behaved like a normal person and not been such an ass, you wouldn't have gotten us locked in here in the first place! Or was that your plan all along?"

Fantastic, she is beautiful and crazy!

"My plan? You're the one who stole my key and drank me bloody whiskey then caterwauled loud enough to wake the dead, leading me down here to trap me here for God knows what reason! Although I can bloody well gue–"

Fiona cut him off with a hard slap to his face. "I did no such thing!"

Sean rubbed his face. This was definitely the day for bruises.

"Oh really? Who else would want to steal my key? No one else asked me for a bottle of wine, and you knew I kept this place locked. Oh wait! Maybe one of Abigail's fairies–excuse me, *wee folks*–was just playing a little trick on me for being such a pompous, bearded ass!"

Fiona's eyes widened with realization. "You were the one following us when Abigail and I went to the castle!"

"Aye, that I was."

Fiona shoved him again, causing Sean to hit the wall hard with a loud thud. "You bastard, you had no right to listen in on us!"

Sean smiled back through a grimace of pain.

"Sorry about that. I did shave my beard, although I retained the attitude. Seeing as how you're so attracted to Patrick, I knew you must actually like pompous asses!"

Fiona glared down at him. She was speechless for the first time since he had met her, so he continued.

"Oh, and speaking of my dear brother, I am sorry to hear that Patrick has not yet had his way with you. That is quite unlike him. You must be doing something wrong."

"How dare you talk to me like that ... you ... savage!"

She reached out to slap him again, but instead wrenched the bottle of scotch from his hands. She swallowed a mouthful, turned sharply and stormed over to the far wall and plopped angrily onto the stone floor. She held the bottle tightly as she fought back tears.

Sean looked across at her morosely. *I shouldn't have said that.*

"Oh and by the way," she called out, as she took another drink, "if I *had* stolen your key, how could I have locked the door?"

Sean had not thought of that.

* * *

Andrew led Nicholas into the parlor where he was greeted by a rousing chorus of "Happy birthday!" by his gathered friends, already well into their cups.

Abigail rushed up and hugged him. She wore the white bridal dress from the play, modified to be low-cut and quite revealing. Her face and hands were pancaked white, her eyes rimmed in black giving her a ghastly, albeit beautiful, visage. She looked to be a sexy, ghost bride.

"'Ah, broken is the golden bowl, the spirit flown forever ... '" she whispered into Nicholas' ear. Her drunken breath tickled.

Andrew looked on, mesmerized.

"Who am I?" she demanded.

Nicholas smiled. "And what's my prize for guessing this one?" he countered.

She pressed her bosom against him as she clung to his arm and gave him a very seductive smile. "How about a wee kiss?"

"Can I guess?" Andrew interrupted.

She flashed him a coy wink. "Later. It's the birthday boy's chance now. Well, Nicky?"

"Definitely a much better prize than Poe here offered," Nicholas grinned obviously enjoying all this attention. He pretended to be racking his brain, milking the moment. Abigail could indeed be quite the seductress when she wished.

"Let me see ... a bride, that much is obvious. And a lovely one at that, might I add."

"Thank you, kind sir," Abigail curtsied.

"The pale countenance implies a certain abhorrence to sunlight perhaps a vampire? No. Not a vampire. A spirit. The spirit of a dead bride?"

"You're getting warm," Abigail encouraged, rubbing up against him.

"Down right hot, actually," Nicholas quipped. "A famous dead bride from literature? Can't be Frankenstein's monster's bride, she was ghastly ... "

"Oh, come on, you know you know!" Andrew burst out impatiently. Abigail was driving him crazy.

"Quiet. I'm trying to think!" Nicholas furled his brow.

"Time's almost up. Do you surrender?" Abigail asked, ignoring Andrew's childish outburst, but enjoying it nonetheless.

"Surrender my prize? Never! I wasn't aware that there was a time limit. Wait! I think I got it!" Nicholas recited several lines of Poe's *Lenore* in a deep baritone.

"'*The life upon her yellow hair but not within her eyes — The life still there, upon her hair–the death upon her eyes.*' You must be Lenore, Poe's"–indicating Andrew–"beloved.*"

Abigail clapped happily.

"Yes!" She gave him a sloppy kiss on the cheek. "Many happy returns!" She handed him her present. "From Fiona and me."

"Thank you, my dear," Nicholas bowed. "Now I must see to my other guests, and perhaps more prizes. If you two forlorn 'lovers' will allow my leave."

He left to join the rest to the party.

"Oh, we're not lovers," Abigail corrected his departing form. "Yet," she added quietly. Andrew grabbed Abigail and spun her around to face him. She saw the desperate wanting in his eyes. Obviously she had chosen the right costume.

"What an amazing coincidence! How did you pick Lenore? Did you know I was to be Poe? I never told you."

"It must be destiny," she answered, not bothering to reveal that Fiona had slipped her that little bit of insight after she noticed Andrew looking for hair dye and a waistcoat in the costume room. She had also caught a glimpse of the folded picture of Poe in his hand, before he slipped it into his pocket.

"I hope this party ends early, my beloved husband," she whispered, taking his hand as she led him into the foray. "This dress is starting to 'itch' me something fierce."

Andrew allowed himself to be led. At this point he would have allowed himself to be led into the 'night's Plutonian shore' and gladly forge the River Styx to remain beside his beloved 'Lenore'.

* * *

Fiona had been staring the floor very angrily for the better part of an hour. Although she was purposely ignoring him, every now and then she would clang the scotch bottle, take a loud drink, and then slosh it noisily around to remind Sean that she was still mad. She was convinced that this was entirely his fault, despite the fact that she had been down here 'borrowing' a bottle of port without his permission. Every time he shifted and groaned in discomfort, just made her that much angrier.

And where the Hell was Patrick?

For a while Fiona had held out hope that Patrick would realize that she was missing from the party and would come looking and rescue her. But as time passed, she found that hope dissolving into a deep resentment.

Why hasn't he come yet? Isn't he even worried about me?

She shook that thought off, but had trouble battling her feeling of being forgotten and uncared for. She felt incredibly alone. She could understand the others not coming; they were probably drunk and still thinking that she was going to appear at any moment.

But where was Patrick?

She tried to forget what Sean had yelled at her, but those words still flowed through her veins like poison. Nothing she could think of could hide their sting. Her eyes began to fill with tears and some of the tears broke free, trailing down her face.

Sean had been staring at Fiona for a while now, trying to think of a way to erase what he had said to her, but seeing her start to cry again, he knew the damage had been done.

Bloody brilliant, Sean! Make the girl cry! He had to fix this, but he didn't know where to start. He cleared his throat to warn Fiona that he was about to speak.

"And so what is your costume then?" he asked.

Fiona continued to stare at the floor as tears rolled off her face and onto the ground. She no longer cared what she wore or whom she wore it for, it was all just a giant waste of time.

"It doesn't matter anymore," she said, her voice quavering, her posture echoing the bleakness she felt.

"Sure it matters," said Sean. "Let me see ... Lady Macbeth? No wait, you have no spots. Uh, Ophelia then? No, you have no imaginary flowers."

Fiona smirked through her tears. "And how can you tell that I have no *imaginary* flowers?"

"Ah!" he said with drunken logic. "So you only imagine you have no imaginary flowers, ergo you must have some. Thus, you are in fact Ophelia."

She shook her head, confused. "No, I did not choose Shakespeare."

"Haven't you any clues that might help me out here?" He looked at her as if his life depended on figuring this out. "Anything?"

"I have a broken compact mirror and a tapestry in the corner over there," she sighed and pointed.

Sean glanced to the corner. Indeed, both props were sitting there. He rose awkwardly and walked over. He picked up the mirror, opened it and was surprised to see his beaten face staring back at him. He had forgotten about the fight and the headache. *Scotch really does work miracles!* He picked up the tapestry next.

Nothing. No clue from this. Then he found a book hidden beneath the tapestry. It was a book of poems by Tennyson. One page was marked with a ribbon. *The Lady of Shalott?* He had never heard of it. There was painting of The Lady looking sorrowful in a boat, beside the poem. He quickly perused the poem, keeping his back to Fiona.

"Give up?" Fiona asked, not really caring any longer.

He put the book back down, and with a sly smile, made a show of looking at her through the reflection of her cracked mirror as he spoke.

"No. Just watching the world pass by."

Fiona looked up in interest.

Sean continued. "I am afraid that there is something you are lacking in your disguise."

"And what is that?"

"Well, you have your mirror cracked, your tapestry, your lovely, although haunted face, but unfortunately you're lacking a boat to pass away in."

"You know me then?" she asked, pleased.

"Aye," replied Sean, still looking at her through the mirror. "You are Sweet Fee, but you are dressed as the cursed Lady of Shalott."

She clapped. "Excellent. If you were Nicholas I would give you a bottle of port and a kiss right now!"

"Well, no need, for as you know," Sean said gaily as he waved his arms to indicate the walls filled with bottles of wine and scotch, "I can have my pick."

He made his way over to Fiona and handed her the tapestry. "You might want this. It is a bit chilly."

Fiona shyly reached and took it. "Thanks."

"Although, I do regret missing out on that kiss," he said.

She watched Sean make his way back to where he was sitting.

"Well, that's what you get for holding out on me."

"Ahh ... another regret," he confessed.

"I too have a regret," she confessed after a moment. "I'm sorry I hit you, I am normally not a violent person."

"Quite alright, I asked for it really, and emotions have been overly charged today. I don't normally break out into fist fights either," he smiled weakly. "One more bruise more or less–"

"Why *didn't* you let me have the port?" she interrupted.

Sean shifted uncomfortably. He wasn't about to tell her about the ghost and her words of warning, she wouldn't believe him. In fact he wasn't even doing such a good job not letting her drink, but seeing as he had been drinking from the same bottle as her, he figured it was fine.

"Maybe I really like port."

"Or maybe you thought it was for Patrick," she countered.

"Aye, maybe I did."

Fiona stared at him, startled by his frank reply. He really was a wreck. Not only that, he was still bleeding. She guessed he had opened the wound above his eye again from where he had banged his head into the generator. She stood suddenly, taking the scotch and her tapestry and walked over to sit down next to him.

"Look at me," she ordered.

Sean turned his face towards her and she met his blue eyes with hers. She took his face in her hands and drew it closer.

"This cut looks pretty deep," she said examining his wound. She brought a corner of her tapestry up, poured a bit of scotch on it to sterilize it, and prepared to dab at the wound. "You'll probably want to have Abigail sew it up when we get out of here."

Sean stared at her chest as it rose and fell as she tended to his cuts. Her compassion, mixed with the sensation of her gentle touch on his face stirred up unexpected feelings of desire. Had she been any other woman, he would have reached for her, fondled her, and pulled her into his lap. Any other lady would have allowed him. But Fiona was not just any other woman, she would punch or kick him ... but still her touch sent waves of desire through.

You need her, want her, NOW!

The intensity of his thoughts shocked him. Where had this sudden sensation come from? Perhaps it's the circumstance of being trapped here with her alone?

"Ouch! Shite! What the hell was that?" Sean cried. His face felt like it was on fire.

"I need to disinfect it," Fiona replied with a laugh, pulling the whiskey soaked cloth away from his face. "I thought you said Patrick was the baby of the family."

"Yes, but to waste good single malt like that," he grabbed the bottle from her and took a drink. "I'm beginning to wonder why they call you 'Sweet Fee'. A little warning would have helped me out there."

"All done." Fiona dropped her hand from his face and leaned against the wall. She waited a moment before asking, "So, what was the fight about today?"

Sean was tenderly touching his face, still fantasizing about her soft touch when her question brought him back to reality.

"What? Oh. Just something we both needed to get out in the open."

"That wouldn't be Bethany would it?" she asked. Her eyes searched his.

He hadn't really talked about Bethany since it had happened, but suddenly he felt the need to.

"What do you know about her?" he asked.

"Nothing really, her name and some tidbits of gossip," Fiona moved to sit beside him, making herself as comfortable as she could. "Tell me."

Sean hesitated. *Where to start?*

"I was twenty-four. Bethany was my fiancé. We were engaged for about six months. The wedding was only a month away when everything started to fall apart." Sean fell silent.

"What happened?"

"I began hearing whispered rumors of her going out at night. She had a very flirtatious way, but I thought it harmless. She was always smiling and laughing at blokes, but I thought nothing of it; she was mine. Never thought anything of the way she acted around Patrick either."

Fiona braced herself for the next part, already gathering where the story was heading, but instead Sean asked her a question.

"Have you ever been in what you thought was love, Fiona?"

Fiona was surprised at the sudden change of subject but allowed her thoughts to turn to her past. "Aye, that I have."

"I'm not talking about Patrick. Whatever he is doing with you is not love."

"I am not talking about Patrick either!" she said sharply. "I had someone I cared very much about once. Fancied marrying him for awhile even."

"Another actor?" Sean asked, suddenly curious over the bloke that once had her heart.

"No. A farm boy, poor but prefect, with eyes like the sea after a storm ... " she replied with a distant look in her eyes.

Sean couldn't contain himself, he burst out in laughter. "That's rich! You were going to marry a farmer! And do what? Milk his bloody cows?"

Fiona, although she should have been mad, smiled. "I would have done that or anything for him. If only he could have understood my desire to act."

"How did it end?"

"Sadly, very sadly in fact. I left him. He tried to understand my need to act and sing, but in the end he just really wanted me to live on his farm and be content. I couldn't do that to him, you understand? To be with him in body but have my heart and soul be somewhere else? So I fear I am the monster of that story. David wanted nothing but me, and yet I wanted something else. I broke his heart and left. I did see him again after my father died. He was living alone and pleaded with me to stay. I felt terrible for him. Maybe if I hadn't led him on he would have found someone, had someone, and started that family he always talked about. He was broken and I made him that way."

She allowed herself to sink into that sad reflection. She had thrown away everything that could have made her happy for a lifetime, and yet she would have been bitter towards him until the end. Now she had her theater but had yet to be loved. For the first time in her life she was regretting her decision.

"Not your fault at all. Maybe at first, but him being alone when you went back, now that is his own fault. He should have embraced what you loved in the beginning. A man unwilling to do that does not deserve you," Sean stated matter-of-factly.

Fiona nodded. It had felt good to talk about David, maybe that part of her had been healing for sometime, but it was nice to finally get it out.

"And so what became of your Bethany?" she asked. "You've heard my tragic tale, now finish yours."

"I would, but you took my scotch," Sean protested. "It's a sobering enough tale as it is."

"Here, have some of mine," offered Fiona.

He took the bottle and swigged some. "Are you sure you want to hear the rest? Patrick plays the bastard big time."

Fiona nodded. "I think I can handle it."

Sean took a deep breath. "On the eve of my wedding I caught Patrick with Bethany."

Fiona gasped. "What were they doing?"

"What do you think they were doing?"

Fiona didn't answer, instead she grabbed her tapestry and wrapped herself tightly in it.

"Patrick and I had a row to end all rows. The next day she was gone and so was Patrick. I was faced with explaining to my mother and father what had happened. So instead, I left," he said, still holding his gaze away from her.

"I hadn't laid eyes on Patrick until you all arrived. That was some five years ago. I have since learned he wasn't even the only one she was with while we were engaged. She was a bloody tramp, she was. I know that now. I *had* thought all my anger had burned out."

He rubbed his bruised chin tenderly.

"My mother vanished a few days after I left. I didn't find that out until much later. I'm not sure if it had something to do with the shame we brought to the family. I know I accomplished that much, if nothing else," he said bitterly.

"I have never really forgiven myself for leaving her like that, alone with *him*. I don't think Patrick has either. I should have known something was wrong, but I was so caught up with Patrick and Bethany, I missed it completely. She ran. I ran. Patrick ran. I guess it's a family trait."

"Where did you go?" Fiona asked. She couldn't believe it, but she was actually beginning to feel sorry for him. *No wonder he treats Patrick the way he does.*

"Nowhere, anywhere, I got jobs working the ships for awhile, but that didn't work out, so I was working on drinking myself to death in as many pubs as I could get thrown out of when I got word of my mother's disappearance. I saw no reason to return. We were both lost. So what could I do? Then some years later a tall bloke with a summons found me in a pub in Sterling. I was too drunk and worn out to refuse a free train ride and a chance to maybe see my father and kill him."

Now it was Fiona's turn to laugh.

Sean turned to stare at her sharply. "What's so funny?"

"*You* worked on *ships?* With all that you drink how did manage not to fall overboard all the time?"

He smiled. "I managed, but it wasn't easy. They kept sinking."

They sat in silence for a while, passing the bottle. A quiet understanding was passing through them that neither really understood, but yet the mood seemed to be lifting. At least for now.

"Sorry for what I said earlier," Sean said suddenly.

Fiona just nodded and finished drinking the rest of the scotch. "Another dead soldier," she said suddenly, and tossed the empty bottle where it crashed against the wall, shattering.

Sean stared at her in admiration.

"Fancy some wine?" he asked standing up looking through the racks. "We are in a wine cellar, after all."

* * *

Patrick raced through the frigid night air, scarcely feeling the cold. Snow fell in large, quiet flakes, illuminated by the brilliant full sky of stars.

He passed the darkened church.

Murder! I knew it! Her disappearance was kept so mysterious, but someone knew the truth all along!

He played over the events in his mind, searching for clues, as he ran.

After the Bethany incident, Patrick had fled Scotland without a word to anyone. All he knew was theater, and so he made a meager living playing in small theaters moving from town to town.

He had just finished performing a very physically exhaustive play in a small theater in Manchester when a solemn solicitor in black appeared in the wings. Patrick was still wiping the sweat from his brow when the man handed him an envelope that read simply: *Return home. Your mother is missing.*

How his whereabouts had been discovered, he never learned.

The note was so succinct and devoid of emotion that he suspected that it was from his father. He also wondered if Sean had been summoned in the same manner.

Patrick didn't go. He was afraid of confronting Sean and his father; he was not so cowardly to admit that much, at least to himself. He sent word, asked around, even hired a private investigator to look into the matter, but he came up blank. No trace of his mother anywhere. It seemed she had simply vanished.

Patrick did learn from the detective's report that it wasn't his father who sent the note. His father had no idea who would send a note like that, and had denied that there was anything untoward going on. Apparently, according to his father, Delia had suddenly taken ill during a performance at their theater and went off to seek asylum and rest at some clinic in Switzerland or Sweden. She was not to be disturbed by anyone. She would return when she was well and not before. The detective found his father's story vague and unbelievable.

He also learned through the investigation agency that not only was Sean not there, no one knew of his current whereabouts. He was rumored to have been on board the *Lusitania,* but his trail had gone cold after it sank. The detective asked Patrick if he should look for him, but Patrick declined.

Patrick was passing the theater and thought about the night of his mother's final performance. That was the last time anyone other than his father had seen her alive.

She had just finished a scene where she had drank prop wine. She turned to confront her co-star (Patrick had never been able to track him down) when she suddenly staggered back, clutched her throat, fainted and fell against the table. The bottle crashed to the floor, spilling wine across the stage and splashing some of the audience in the front row.

Then pandemonium erupted. Some people rushed to her side, including his father. She was breathing, but faintly. His father whisked her to his chambers. A doctor was called. She was weak, but recovering. The doctor prescribed bed rest.

She was never seen again.

Patrick ran on.

His breath came harder now as he passed the cemetery walls. It was nearly completely dark, which seemed to add an additional chill to the air. Spikes of pain were beginning to stab at his lungs and thighs, but he didn't slow down. In fact he pushed on harder, trying to pass the cemetery faster.

His father had insisted on keeping the theater running after she left. It wasn't for the glory of theater that he was so compulsive about keeping the theater going, there was an ancient codicil to the deed, dating back to Thornbury the First, that provided his family a large stipend, providing the theater remained open and run by the Berenger family–with at least one play performed per year. Delia or no Delia, Angus managed to perform at least one play a year.

Patrick was nearing the train car. Through the veil of snowfall, he could make out a light on in one of the cabins. *Someone was there!*

His whole body screamed for him to stop and catch a breath. He stopped; gulping in great lungs full of frigid air. He checked his pocket watch. It was only six-fifty. Good, he had made it in time. As he captured ragged breath after ragged breath he tried to clear his mind and focus. He realized he had no idea who he might be meeting or what they intended to do. He had best approach with caution.

* * *

"Who do you think locked the door?" Fiona asked.

"I'm sorry, what?" Sean asked. Then he held up a bottle of wine he had just found, already opened. "Did you open this?"

"*Who* do you think locked the door?" Fiona repeated. Sean shrugged off the mystery of the open bottle. He could barely concentrate on one thing at a time.

"I wouldn't put it past me loving brother. Not likely he'd want to see my face at the party."

"He wouldn't do something like that," Fiona shook her head at him, annoyed. "Besides, you said you weren't going."

"Aye, couldn't stomach the sight of the two of you cavorting like a couple of cats in heat," Sean replied.

"That's sweet," Fiona sneered, sarcastically.

Sean ignored her response. He examined the label on the wine. Although he was having trouble focusing, he believed it looked like a good vintage.

"Maybe was Gavin," Fiona slurred. "That spectacle you made at the audition didn't help, you know. And I had finally gotten him calmed down."

"Please," Sean said, gesturing with wine, "that chap has the raging eyes for you. Trust me. He is not calmed down."

"Maybe," she agreed. "But then why lock me down here with the likes of *you*?"

"I never thought he did. It was you that suggested him," Sean reminded her, as he brought the wine over.

"Wh-what if the door locked on its own? A draft of something?"

"Have to be a strong draft to shut the door *and* snap shut the padlock," Sean replied with a grin. "But let's not eliminate the wee folks. I may have pissed them off good and well enough by now."

"They are a vengeful bunch," Fiona giggled.

"Then there's the *ghost*," Sean suggested cautiously. He was curious to see if Fiona had seen her too.

"Which ghost might that be?" she smiled.

"Oh, none in particular." He showed her the wine label for her approval. She nodded consent without even looking at it.

"Why are you so mean to me at times?" he asked, as he stared at her.

"Am I?" she countered, looking away.

His head swam for a moment, the bottle in his hands forgotten, as he stared at her exposed chest and tiny waist.

"I'm sorry I couldn't hold on," he mumbled. He suddenly longed to feel her in his arms, to cradle her as she whispered *his* name and not Patrick's. She had such a teeming, suppressed passion inside her. He wanted that passion!

"Aren't you going to give it to me?" she asked impatiently.

"What?" He was startled back to reality. "Now?"

"Yes," she looked at him with unabashed frankness. "I need a drink."

Sean hesitated. It seemed he knew that she was going to say before she said it. *Why? How could I know?*

Without thinking, she pressed up closer to Sean, reaching for the bottle. She felt his body react to her touch.

"Get me a drink," she sang as if from a distant place. "Now."

Sean held the bottle away from her, not sure why.

"Please?" she asked.

He took a deep breath, his head cleared, and he managed a smile. "Of course. And to what, my lady, shall we drink?"

"To forgetting," she replied simply, albeit somewhat quixotically.

"We have no golden goblets ... " he apologized, as he offered her the wine. Her scent wafted up to Sean–a sweet, almost bitter almond smell.

Why did he think she would smell of jasmine?

"To those things that nearly slipped through your fingers," she whispered.

Her scent was mesmerizing. She was so close. Only inches separated them.

It would be so easy to pull her to me. To unravel her from her dress.

Fiona raised the wine to her lips, just like in his dream.

"After all, wine is bottled poetry ... "

His dream!

The realization hit and Sean didn't hesitate. He slapped the bottle out of her hands, sending it crashing to the floor.

He seized her and shook her roughly.

"Did you drink it?" he cried.

Fiona twisted, trying to loosen his painful grip.

"Did you drink that?" he demanded again, continually shaking her.

"Sean, stop it! You're hurting me!" she pleaded, her fear growing.

Sean swung her around and without thinking, ran her back against the cold wall with such force that it knocked the breath out of her.

"God damn it, Fiona! Did you drink that?"

"NO!" she screamed. "I didn't drink a bloody drop! Let go of me!" she demanded.

Sean instantly eased his grip on her arms, but did not let go. He exhaled. "I thought I almost lost you there."

Fiona was at a loss of words.

"What?" she managed to stammer.

"My dream," he replied, trying desperately to make her understand. "I had this dream. You were dressed entirely in black ribbons that were falling about you and then I dropped you and you were naked and so angry with me. You asked for a drink and when I gave you one you screamed that I had killed you and then you tried to kill me. Samuel had warned me not to let you drink and to forget about Patrick, 'cause *you* needed looking after. Of course, that was before I almost killed him and he broke me bed– Samuel, not Patrick, that is. Oh, and he saw the ghost too, but I don't see how she fits in to any of this."

"What *ghost?*" Fiona asked, staring at him with enormous eyes.

He was losing her. He leaned in closer, desperately. He needed to make her understand.

"Forget the ghost! You're still alive! Don't you see? I didn't at first. I thought it was *you* that smelled so sweet and inviting– almost bitter–and then I realized, that it wasn't you at all. *The wine, Fiona!* I knew that smell; they fumigated the boats with it. The bitter almond smell! It was cyanide!"

"*Cyanide?*" Fiona whispered, disbelief on her lips. "What about cyanide?"

"The wine. It was poisoned with cyanide."

Fiona tried to free herself from his grip.

"Sean, please let me go."

Sean knew there was no way she would understand what he had just said, let alone believe that he had just saved her life. He needed her to know that he wasn't crazy.

"Can't you smell that, Fiona?"

Fiona nodded her head yes, although all she could smell was the scotch on Sean's breath.

"Who wants to hurt you Fiona?" he asked, still holding her in place.

"No one. You said it yourself, you thought someone locked *you* in here."

Sean stopped, she was right. It wasn't meant for her at all. He stared at her pale face. She shivered in his arms, cold, scared, and vulnerable. He had almost gotten her killed, yet, the only thing he could think of was holding her tighter, unraveling her further, stealing more of her heat. Instead of releasing her, he moved in closer.

"Sweet Fee, are you cold?"

"No," she lied. She couldn't stop her hands from shaking.

"You're trembling," he whispered.

"I'm fine."

She watched as he released one of her hands and brought it to his lips, kissing it lightly.

"Does that help?"

"Sean," she whispered, "I need you to let me go."

"Believe me, Fiona, the last thought on my mind is letting you go." He moved closer, forcing her hard up against the wall. "You've been denying the truth far too long, haven't you?"

He didn't wait for her answer. Without thinking he pulled her tight to him, finding her lips. Shocked, she didn't resist when he opened his mouth to her, but instead responded hungrily, eagerly.

He paused, breaking the kiss.

"Do you want me to let you go?"

"No."

Sean pulled her to him again, now finally certain that she wanted him as well.

* * *

"Where's Fiona?" a deep voice asked from behind Abigail's back, just as she was fixing a drink. Her mind was humming along about Andrew and the night ahead, so when she turned her sentence ended in a shriek of fright.

"I haven't seen–CHRIST!"

He was dressed in a white tie, black tuxedo, complete with top hat and cane. What made Abigail shriek was that his face was done up in white grease paint–a frightening ghostly effect–with his startling, piercing icy blue eyes peering out from behind the simple black mask.

"Bloody 'ell! Who is that? *Gavin?*" She leaned in closer to have a look. He shook his head, 'no'. Instead he quoted: "'Go and marry the boy when ever you wish. I know you love him.'"

"Oh, I'm supposed to guess! Very clever, let me think ... not from Dickens's are we?"

He shook his head then gave her another clue. "I am the angel of music. I can teach you to sing the heaven's music, if you grant me a kiss."

"Every bloke wants a kiss from me tonight. This dress must be working. Oh alright, since I 'aven't a clue."

Abigail gave him a kiss on the cheek. He smiled a ghastly smile. "I am Erik! Le Fantome de l'Opera!"

Then he stepped back and disappeared into the darkness.

"Strange lad, that Gavin." Abigail murmured to herself. "But now that he mentioned it, I wonder where Fiona has gone off to?"

Then a sudden realization hit. *Ah, Patrick's not here either.* She grinned a wicked grin as Andrew stepped up behind her and placed his hands over her eyes.

"Guess who?" he asked.

"I don't care. Just kiss me before the night wears on any longer!" Abigail giggled as she turned and took Andrew's face in her hands, kissing him deeply.

From across the room, Nicholas and Samuel smoked cigars as they watched the two of them. "They seem to be hitting it off, eh?" Nicholas stated.

"Aye, it's been a long time coming," Samuel agreed. He scratched incessantly at his legs incased in the itchy wool pants he was wearing. He was dressed in a proper suit, and carried a prop medical bag with the initials JHW, along with Gavin's 'borrowed' Webley Mk VI .455 calibre service revolver and a hand-held magnifying glass.

"This is the first time I seen you not wearing a kilt off stage," Nicholas observed.

"And the last! It would have been worth it if you would have guessed my disguise."

Nicholas nodded. "Sorry about that. I'm surprised you went with Dr. Watson over Sherlock Holmes. He's generally considered the more famous of the two."

"But he's not Scottish, now is he?" Samuel countered.

"No, I suppose you're right. By the way what was my prize going to be if I guessed correctly?"

"You're smoking it," Samuel replied.

"Excellent," Nicholas stated. He was having a grand time. "And a very fine one at that. Ah, I see a new guest has arrived. And what a brilliant costume! Let me go see if I can deduce this clever subterfuge, eh Watson?"

Nicholas staggered off toward the newcomer.

"It's quite an elementary disguise, my dear Holmes," Samuel said with a grin as he puffed out a large cloud of smoke. "More fool you."

The new guest was a rather tall, angular man dressed in simple black clerics, including the reversed white collar. His one distinguishing feature was an enormous bushy, black beard and mustache. He sat alone, drinking sherry when Nicholas, now more drunk than sober, sauntered up to him.

"Don't tell me, let me guess! I got it! Claude Frollo, the Archdeacon of Notre Dame! No, that can't be it, you're severely underdressed." Nicholas tugged on the man's simple garments. "Although you are a drinker, eh? Perhaps Jehan?"

"Pardon me, but have we met?" the man asked, a bit taken aback by this belligerent stranger's manner.

"Is that a clue? A stranger, am I, eh? I'm at a loss, but the beard is marvelous!" He tugged at it hard. It didn't pull off.

The stranger rose up angrily, knocking Nicholas's hands away. "Let go of my beard you insolent, Yankee fool! Don't you know who I am?"

"Jeppsen?" he asked, cautiously. Just then Carlisle came up and placed an arm around both men's shoulders.

"Father McLeary! So glad you could come. And I see you have met the Birthday Boy!"

"Fa-Father?" Nicholas sputtered. He looked over at the Cheshire grinning Samuel who had been watching the entire incident. He toasted Nicholas with a raised glass and a wink.

"Actually, Thornbury, we haven't been properly introduced," Father McLeary said a bit gruffly, but calming considerably.

"Well then, now you shall." Carlisle replied. "Nicholas Ashbury, may I introduce our local clergy, Father Ian McLeary. Nicholas, here, is the director of the play."

"Please to meet you. Sorry about the beard," Nicholas mumbled, shaking the Father's hand.

Father McLeary finally grinned. "Aye, not to worry, it can handle a stout tugging now and again. Actually thinking of shaving it off. The director, eh? That's marvelous. What's you drinking dere lad? You seemed to be down in your cups!"

McLeary led Nicholas to the bar, informing him of his past performances in several local productions over the years.

The party continued on.

* * *

Fiona was lost in Sean's kiss.

She felt as if she had split in two. Part of her floated above, hovering, looking down at her and Sean holding each other tightly, as if more than a kiss they were breathing for each other, sustaining their souls. And part of her was entwined with him, in the very *real* moment, *feeling* the kiss and his hands on her back, slowly moving lower, every touch electric and sustained.

The suspended Fiona watched as Sean whispered, "You are so beautiful," through their kiss. He was pulling at the top of her dress, pulling it down to expose her breasts.

What is happening? What am I doing? This is not right.

Fiona pulled away, her hands shaking. "This is not right. I want–"

She tried to take some deep breaths, but her tight corset was proving to her that it was impossible.

Sean was equally incapacitated. He couldn't speak, could barely stand. He tried a nod, but it came out as a pathetic, spastic twitch. They stood inches apart, silent, bodies raging.

"I can't do this," Fiona finally managed to squeak. She adjusted her dress where it had been pulled off her shoulder.

Sean stared at her, still trying to catch his breath and remain upright.

"It's because of Patrick," he stated simply.

"Of course it's because of Patrick! *He* was the one I was suppose to be with tonight," she screamed, shocked at her outburst. She seemed to constantly be on the verge of losing herself since she entered the cellar. *What was it about this place?*

She glanced into the dark recesses around them and shivered, then she looked to Sean. He was staring at her, waiting for her to make the next move. *He looks so much like Patrick.* His blue eyes had almost gone black with lust. She wanted him terribly and that terrified her.

"I just want out of this God dammed place!" She raced up to the cellar door and pounded on it with all her might. "Let me out of here! Somebody please! Anyone? Please!"

"Someone will come. Believe me. It'll be alright," Sean said softly.

She came back down the stairs, defeated.

"Do you want me because of Bethany?"

Sean didn't hesitate. "No. I just want you."

She looked into his eyes and saw a pure passion that he was incapable of hiding.

He looked into her eyes and saw surrender.

This time Sean knew he would not stop. He reached out and pulled her to him, reuniting her with his mouth. Slowly he worked his hands around and lifted her into his arms, carrying her to where her tapestry lay on the ground.

Fiona did not fight or resist, she was caught in the sudden desire of being with someone who wanted her and that she wanted as well. Her ache for intimacy needed to be extinguished.

She allowed him to undo the buttons down the back of her dress, which he did with the slow precise attention of a painter. Her dress slid from her. She stood before him in her new red corset, with black ribbons and matching underwear.

Sean stopped.

"My God!" he said. "You are ravishing."

He lifted her again, causing Fiona to wrap her legs around his waist as he began to pull at the ribbons of her corset. She sucked at his neck, causing Sean to stumble and nearly to fall. Sean set her back on the ground, still pulling at her corset, the black ribbons like maddening snakes in his fumbling fingers.

Fiona instantly missed the feeling of her legs wrapped around him. She pulled at his waist until he was free of his pants and then pulled his shirt over his head, tossing it to the floor.

She stopped when she noticed the bruises all over his body. Patches of purple and black. In that moment Fiona understood the pain and loss he had endured. She leaned forward, kissing one bruise lightly on his chest.

"I'm so sorry," she whispered, before she moved to the next bruise and gently kissed it. She began to work her way down his lean chest, kissing each bruise with just a whisper of her lips. He was on fire, pulling at the constricting corset. The need he had for her was blinding.

She lowered to her knees as she worked her way down, then paused just a second before advancing further. She had never behaved in this intimate fashion before, not even with David. She heard Sean catch his breath and issue a stifled moan of expectation, which urged her to go further.

She took him in her mouth.

Sean's attempt at undoing her frustrating corset ceased at her sudden intimacy; he no longer had any idea who was in control.

After a few minutes she gently pulled away. Her corset ribbons still entangled in his hands finally came apart. She leaned back, removed her panties and lay back on her tapestry, completely nude now, and waited for him.

Sean flung the damned corset as far away as he could, then lowered to her, arms propped on either side of her head. He kept his body lifted, skin barely touching skin. He looked down at her. She was perfect: silky white skin, soft, curly brown hair sensually framing her face, partially concealing her pleading, emerald green eyes. When she breathed, their bodies locked and he gave in, sliding into her with a sudden wanton thrust. Her hips rose to meet him in an embrace that tightened with each thrust.

Fiona had never had sex like this before. It was neither gentle nor rough, but somehow both. Like riding a huge wave, caught safe in the foam, then suddenly being pulled into the undertow, tumbling beneath the sea. Each time she would try to catch her breath, Sean would move differently, exciting her all over again. She reached for him, clawed at him, pleaded with him to make her feel even more new sensations. Suddenly she was being pounded harder by the waves, by his longing for her. She wrapped her arms and legs as tight as she could around him. She gasped an incoherent torrent of yearnings, moans and cries of ecstasy into his ear. She left her mark in long scratches down his back. She opened her eyes to find his, to connect completely.

Sean had never experienced anything like this before. He felt every inch of Fiona's skin where they touched. He was no longer sure where he was. The room had vanished around him and only Fiona's radiant body remained. He moved to the rhythmic sounds of Fiona's beautiful cries of longing that filled the air. Then he pulled her closer and her cries softened into whispered moans of pleasure into his ear, that tickled and excited him into a faster, harder pace. He was not sure if he could hold out a moment longer, when he felt her nails on his back and arched back. Then she opened her loving eyes and looked into his. He knew he had to have her forever. He surrendered.

The generator sputtered and went out. The lights flickered and went pitch black. Sean and Fiona continued in the darkness.

Sean's lips slid to her right nipple as she gasped for air. He kissed it, twice, before trailing up her breast, along her neck and finally again tasting her lips. He lingered there, kissing her again and again.

She wrapped her hands in his hair and pulled him down to her breast again. Somewhere inside Fiona knew that she would regret everything in the morning, that she would blame Sean and the alcohol, but for now she just wanted to surrender to the night. She would face tomorrow, tomorrow.

He moved his head past her breasts, past her stomach until he found where she longed him to be. She spread her legs wider, tantalizing in the perfect blackness, allowing him deeper access.

Sean brought her to a point of ultimate desperation then pulled away.

"Please, don't stop," she pleaded, between gasps.

"Wasn't planning to," he whispered and continued until she found release.

When she ceased shuddering, he moved back up her body.

He kissed her neck and lips. His hands roved and caressed her, allowing her little relief. He teased her with light touches followed by swift, fast strokes. One hand found her breast and grasped it as his other slid inside her.

She moved and pushed her hips to his movement before the urge consumed him and he entered her full again. She latched onto him with such force that Sean was sure they were joined in a way that could never be undone. Fiona cried out his name and he could hold out no longer.

He lost himself inside her and collapsed into darkness.

$$* * *$$

Patrick approached the train car cautiously from around the back. He was shaking uncontrollably from the frigid air. He tried to walk as quietly as possible, but the crunching snow beneath his feet shattered the stillness.

He noticed a candle in the last stateroom window, so he made his way toward it. He put his face against the frigid glass, and cupping his hands around his eyes, tried to peer inside, but it was so frosted over he couldn't see much. A dark shadow passed in front of the candlelight.

Someone was definitely in there, waiting for him.

The distant whinnying of a horse not too far away startled Patrick.

"What the fook?" he exclaimed, almost losing his footing on the rocky incline, sending some loose gravel tumbling. He was afraid he had made enough noise to wake the dead. He peered again into the window. A dark blurry face peered back; too indistinct to make out who or what it was. Patrick leapt back in surprise, his heart pounding like a sledgehammer. Suddenly the candle went out. The face pulled away.

"Damn!" Patrick hissed.

He didn't have the luxury of time to ponder what to make of any of this. It was nearly seven o'clock. He had better just deal with this head on. He decided to forgo the back door and sneak around to the front hopefully to have some element of surprise over whoever was waiting inside.

As he pulled the railroad car door opened a crack, the frozen hinges protested loudly. Patrick froze. He peered into the darkness, nerves on edge. He listened for any signs of life. Nothing. He took a tentative step inside. He knew he had lost the element of surprise, so he decided to call out. "I got your note. It's nearly seven."

He entered the dark car. "Hello?"

He tried the first stateroom door. It was unlocked. He pushed it open, not knowing what to expect. He peered inside. It was empty.

"There's no need to hide. I'm alone," he tried.

He knew the light and the shadow he had seen was in the last stateroom at the end of the hall, but Patrick was suspicious by nature. This could very well be some kind of trap, to what end he had no clue. There could be more than one person, or they could have moved on in the darkness, setting him up. Satisfied that the room was empty, he moved on to the next room. He placed his hand on the doorknob and his ear to the door and listened.

Silence.

He turned the knob and again pushed the door open.

He peered inside. Empty. He moved on.

The next two staterooms were also empty, leaving just the last one, the one with the candle and the shadowy form.

He grabbed the knob, took a deep breath, and slowly turned it. Suddenly it was yanked forward and he along with it. Patrick fell to the floor and was just lifting his head when something hard, cold and heavy crashed down on him and he slipped into darkness.

Jeppsen wandered about the castle aimlessly. He had a thick white bandage on his head that did little to ease the pounding headache and dizziness he felt. He couldn't quite remember why he had gotten up from bed, or where he was going. He occasionally heard bursts of laughter and the tinkling of glasses and murmurs of spirited conversations, but he put it all down to aural hallucinations from the blow on his head.

"Perhaps ye ghosts are up and about?" he pondered aloud. "It's been some time since you've made your presence so conspicuously known. Perhaps I should inform someone?"

Jeppsen just so happened to be passing Patrick's room and the door was open so he went inside. The room was empty and he was puzzled by the odds and ends of armor scattered on the bed and floor.

"It looks like a proper jousting has taken place here," he remarked. He picked up the helmet. The bascinet's faceplate creaked stubbornly as Jeppsen tried to raise it. It was rusted shut. "Pity the poor fool who was wearing these tin cans. No wonder he lost."

He tossed it down noisily to the floor. It landed beside the note, left by Patrick in his haste.

"What's this?" Jeppsen wondered. He picked it up and read it.

I know who murdered your mother. Meet me at the train at seven o'clock tonight. Come alone. Be prompt.

Jeppsen stared at the note. He rubbed his aching head.

"My mother? But she's not even dead. Surely this must be some kind of ill-conceived joke. I will search out the scoundrel of this jape this very instant!"

Jeppsen stormed out of the room, shoving the note into his pocket. He looked first right, then left, and then stood in a quandary as to which direction to begin. He suddenly felt dizzy. He leaned against the wall in the hallway.

"What was I looking for?" He tried to scratch his head, but the bandages prevented it. Then he remembered.

"Ah, yes. Some fresh air."

Jeppsen made his way to one of the tall, crumbling towers. The cold didn't bother him much. As a matter of fact, the fresh air did him a world of good. He was glad to see so many stars glittering in the night sky, now that the constant storming had finally taken a brief respite.

From up here one could see all of Loglinmooth: from the church steeple to the sea, to the train tracks looking like twin silver snail trails leading off to much happier places.

The Aurora Borealis had sparked up, setting the heavens on fire in a curtain of luminous arches of light. Jeppsen watched them, mesmerized. The whole sky seemed aflame. Even the distant ground was lit up, as if on fire. He had never seen the

Borealis so low in the sky before. The distant train car almost looked as if it were ablaze.

"Bleeding 'ell!" he exclaimed. "I must be radgie. It looks as if that train car *is* on fire."

He watched it for a moment, studying the thick cloud of rising black smoke. Something bothered him. He remembered the note in his pocket, took it out and read it again.

"Mother!"

He raced down the stairs, taking the back staircase to the stable where the automobile was carefully stowed alongside several of Thornbury's horses.

He didn't notice that one of the stabled horses was in a lather, breathing heavy and sweating as if from a hard ride. He was too busy preparing the automobile.

In record time, he had the choke out, the crank attached and the motor sputtering. He pulled open the barn doors and raced out at eight miles an hour toward the burning train.

The train car was indeed burning as Jeppsen pulled up.

"Mother!" he cried, as he raced inside the rear door of the train car, ignoring the flames. Coughing and teary-eyed from the smoke he frantically searched around. He noticed the crumbled form of a body on the floor and dragged it outside.

By now it was snowing again. Jeppsen laid the body carefully in the backseat of the car. He was about to drive off, when exhaustion and a severe bout of dizziness struck him. He fell asleep at the wheel as snow fell like a soft white blanket upon him and his passenger. The train car burned on.

* * *

The lights in the parlor suddenly went out. They were a few cries of good-natured startled exclamations before Miss McStargle entered with a lit candle atop a steaming crock of homemade meatloaf.

The guests all laughed and joined in a rousing chorus of 'for he's a jolly good fellow!' with Gavin singing the loudest, as McStargle presented the meatloaf to Nicholas.

"Homemade meatloaf, Yankee style, with peas and catsup, just the way your good 'ol mum used to make it!" McStargle proclaimed proudly.

"McStargle, *Lucy*. You shouldn't have!" Nicholas was very touched by the gesture, despite the fact it looked like no meatloaf he had ever seen before. The top was covered in a layer of crispy peas soaked in HP sauce. He was unsure what lay beneath.

He was about to accept it when she pulled it back.

"Aye, not yet, birthday boy. You know the rules," McStargle teased. "You must guess who I am before you get your treat."

McStargle had made her own costume and she was quite proud of it. It was a form-fitting American flag dress, with red and white broad stripes and thirteen stars in a low-cut circle across her rather ample breasts. As she normally dressed rather plainly, Nicholas was delighted to see for the first time that she was indeed quite an attractive lady when she decided to be. And it appeared she chose to be so tonight for him. He was so distracted that he forgot that he was supposed to guess her character.

"Well ... " she insisted, growing a bit impatient. Surely it was not this unobvious!

Abigail, noticing Nicholas' befuddlement, decided to help him.

"Oh, he's just putting you on, Miss McStargle!" Abigail laughed as she climbed onto the chair's arm beside Nicholas. "He put me through the same ringer, playing me like a fool, didn't you love!"

She kissed him playfully on the cheek, and secretly whispered: "Betsy Ross, you silly git!" then leapt off the chair.

"Now guess you old fool!" she scolded Nicholas. "Don't you dare keep Miss McStargle waiting any longer!"

Nicholas sat up straighter in his chair.

"Do I get a kiss, as well as the meat loaf, if I guess it in one go?" he asked McStargle.

McStargle blushed. "I don't know; it's so bloody obvious, but okay. Give it your best shot!"

Nicholas studied her costume with the discerning eye of a detective, especially her nearly exposed breasts. He had her turn around, which she did, but quickly and obviously embarrassed.

"That's enough of that! Now make your guess. Your meatloaf's getting cold."

"Ah, but your kisses will be getting hotter, eh, *Betsy Ross?*"

McStargle glanced suspiciously at Abigail, who looked back at her with feigned innocence.

"Aye. You're spot on! Now 'ere's your Yank dish and your Scottish one as well." With a laugh she plopped onto his lap and gave him a resounding kiss. This time it was Nicholas who blushed while the others clapped and hooted.

Gavin pulled Abigail aside. His manner was anxious and concerned.

"Where's Fiona? She's missing all the fun."

"Oh, I'm sure she's not missing any fun," Abigail laughed.

"Why? Where is she?" Gavin demanded, grabbing Abigail by the shoulders. Abigail, drunken and bemused, stared back at him. "Don't get your knickers in a bunch. She's with Patrick."

"What?"

"Oh come now. Surely you've seen the way they dance together on stage. She's been planning this evening's dance for some time now."

From behind his pale mask, Gavin's face grew even whiter. He let loose of Abigail and fled from the room.

Andrew came up from behind Abigail, his arms encircling her waist.

"What's up with him?"

Abigail turned in his arms, pressing her body up against his.

"I don't know and I don't care." She kissed him deeply. "I'd rather find out what's *up* with you," she cooed.

* * *

Snow was still falling. The biting cold finally woke Patrick with its razor teeth. He sat up and shook the snow off. The blood from his gaping head wound had frozen to his face. He had trouble opening one eye, so caked over with frozen blood that the lids resisted parting. He rubbed it gently, blowing on his hands to warm them and transferring the heat to his eye. Finally it opened. He looked around, trying to remember where he was.

It was dark; that early morning darkness so complete it seemed endless. Patrick first noticed the glowing embers of the burnt railroad car. Then the car he was sitting in the backseat of, then Jeppsen, lying face down in the front against the steering wheel, covered in snow.

He crawled over the seat and shook him. "Jeppsen! Jeppsen! Wake up!"

Jeppsen stirred. He looked around.

"What's that? Where am I?" Jeppsen stared at the burnt railroad car with no comprehension. "What happened here?"

"That's what I'd like to know," Patrick said through chattering teeth, "but first we've got to get to a warm fire. Can you start the motor car up?"

Jeppsen stretched his creaking muscles. They popped angrily as he rose and stumbled to the front of the car. He tried to crank the turning wheel in the front, but it was frozen stiff.

"She's frozen, poor old gal. She'll not be going anywhere," he said, sadly.

Patrick climbed out of the car. "Let me try."

Together they tried to turn the crank, using all their combined strength, but it was useless. Exhausted, they stood in the falling snow, looking down the dark, lonely road leading to Loglinmooth. It looked to be a long, cold walk.

* * *

The party had wound down in the wee hours of the morning. Gavin had never returned, not that anyone had noticed. Carlisle, Father McLeary, and Samuel had all retired to Carlisle's chamber for some quiet, cognac, cigars and the telling of tales.

Nicholas, with Miss McStargle still in his lap, murmured soft words before the dying fire. They were set for the night.

Abigail and Andrew lay under the covers in Andrew's room, spent. She had finally had the night she had longed for, and she held tight to Andrew, refusing to let him go lest it all dissolve into some sort of wonderful dream. She reached down and stroked him again. She was not nearly through with this night.

In the wine cellar, Fiona and Sean lay together in the pitch dark.

Gavin had searched everywhere for Fiona. He found Patrick's room empty. He found her room empty. He found Sean's loft empty. Heartbroken and despondent, he wandered the castle like a forlorn ghost until he found himself by Angus Berenger's coffin. Exhausted he lay his head against the cold wooden box.

"Where is she?" he breathed aloud. The night felt endless.

Approaching the church, Patrick noticed that for the first time since he had arrived back in Loglinmooth, a light was on inside and smoke was pouring from the chimney. The Father must have been away visiting some other town. Thankfully he was now back. Between the cold, the blows to their heads and the long walk, he and Jeppsen were nearly done for.

He walked right up to the thick, wooden door. It was unlocked. He urged Jeppsen to follow him in. They entered the peaceful church, warmly lit by numerous tapers. They made their way down the aisle splitting the silent empty pews. Jeppsen paused to make the sign of the cross before the altar.

"Thank you," he whispered.

They continued onto the modest back quarters where Father Ian McLeary lived. He had set a roaring fire before he had left for the party–planning on returning to a cozy, warm bed and a snifter of brandy before retiring. The fire was now waning, but the small room retained its warmth.

Jeppsen and Patrick welcomed his foresight and collapsed on his bed, the brandy left untasted.

* * *

Sometime later, Sean awoke with the feeling that a shadow had passed over him. The hairs on his arm rose, tingling.

Is someone here?

He rose up, and peered into the darkness.

Nothing.

Suddenly, Fiona began thrashing in her sleep and mumbling incoherently. She lay beside him, twisting feverously. Her voice seemed confused.

"The wine ... don't drink ... "

He reached over, calming her movements, as he softly pulled her to his chest and stroked her hair. "Don't worry, you didn't."

"Yes. I did," she whispered.

He reached his arm around her and pulled her closer to him. "Shhh ... lass. No, you didn't."

She relaxed into his chest.

"Wine ... Sean," she whispered before returning to a calm sleep, wrapped in his warm embrace.

"There is a way out." She said suddenly, as she abruptly sat up. She looked around with the empty eyes of a sleepwalker. She looked right past him, not seeing him.

"I am here. Don't let her drink."

Sean was quite unnerved.

Just as suddenly, she folded back into his arms and closed her eyes. She lovingly whispered, "Sean," as she fell into sleep.

He waited a moment, making sure that she had indeed returned to a deep slumber, hoping her nightmares had finally ended, before carefully pulling the tapestry over the both of them.

He held her, underneath the warmth of the tapestry, confused by the ramifications of the night's actions but charmed by the sweet sound of his name on her lips. They had burned like fuel thrown upon fire, but now he was satisfied simply to hold onto the embers.

He was certain that when she awoke fully she was going to hate him, but for right now all was perfect. She was still his in this moment.

His. Sean paused at that thought, not sure of what to make of it.

He felt her soft breath slow and constant on his chest and it arose in him a feeling he could not even attempt to describe. She was a little thing, frail and powerful all at once and so magnetic yet somehow so alone in this world. It didn't make sense. How could Patrick resist her? How could anyone? And how could she remain so desirous of one who did not reciprocate her wants, needs, and desires?

Patrick was a fool, he decided. And so was he, considering the childish way he had been treating her since they first met. Perhaps tonight would change everything; erase the past, start fresh. Could she forgive him? Would she forsake Patrick for him?

He moved his hand though her hair and down her back, stroking the slumbering beauty. She moved a little, repositioning herself before settling back into his chest.

After tonight he was certain he wasn't going to let her go. He couldn't. She had awakened something in him. And this time he wasn't about to run away.

ACT III

'But the gnawing at my heart ... he does not hear.'

– Edna St. Vincent Millay

Fiona awoke slowly, hoping and praying that it was just a dream: that the entire night had been one long, crazy, sexy, incredible dream.

Not real. Please, don't let it have been real.

There was no way it could have happened the way she thought she remembered, but her own body betrayed her hopes. Her skin held on to the memories of the passionate entanglements in a hundred different ways: scrapes, bruises, and scents. Her still naked body was a playbill of the evening's wild, sexual escapades–some positions that she never even knew existed, much less that she initiated.

And to make matters worse–much, much worse–the naked, sleeping man whose arm's were now holding her ... was NOT Patrick!

Holding her breath, she slid out from his embrace. Sean never stirred.

A dim oil lantern burned in a far corner, although for the life of her she couldn't recall who had found it, or who had lit it, or when.

"Shite. Shite. Shite ... " was all she could muster. She looked around for her clothes, desperate to be dressed before Sean awoke. She found her underwear and slipped them on. Her dress was balled up in a corner. She crawled quietly over to it, held it up and examined it. The front was torn–she didn't remember how–

but if she tried to wear it the way it was, it would expose her bare chest.

"Shite. Shite. Shite ... "

She had been wearing a corset, *that,* she remembered clearly. She paused for a moment thinking of how Sean had slowly unbound her, then shook the thought free.

Where is it?

She grabbed the lantern and searched the dark cellar, trying hard to be quiet. Finally, she spotted her corset far across the room, looking like a puddle of fresh blood against the dark floor. As she picked it up she realized that Sean must have flung it there. A smile rose to her lips, despite her morbid feeling of betrayal. He had been so flustered by the ribbon that cinched it to her! Once he had finally gotten it free, he must have flung it as far away from her as he could.

She pulled on the corset. It hung limply to her, useless without the ribbon to cinch it up.

Now, where's that damn ribbon?

She looked around.

"Are you looking for this?" Sean called out, startling her. She whipped her head around to where he was now sitting up. He held the black ribbon in his hand, teasingly. He made no effort to hide his nudity, which made her even more aware of her own state of undress.

"Give me that!" she cried, stomping over and grabbing it.

"My, you are fiery in the morning," he grinned. "I like that. I thought I had you figured out, but last night you–"

"I want out of here now!" Fiona hissed in frustration, as she tried to attach the ribbon to her corset herself, to no avail.

"You're either going to have to take that off to lace it or let me help you," Sean suggested.

"I'm not taking this off!" she glared.

"You want me to take it off for you?"

"No!"

"Here, then let me help you lace it."

As he rose she turned away quickly, keeping her back to him.

"Put some clothes on. Have you no modesty?" she scolded.

Sean grinned as he stared at her scantily clad rear end. "None that I know of. I apologize, but this is how you left me." Sean found his pants and pulled them on. "All decent. You can turn around now."

She cautiously turned to make sure he wasn't lying. She found his grin to be insufferable, but held her tongue.

"So, may I help tie you up?" he asked again.

She nodded. "Make it quick!"

He moved very close behind her, pressing his body needlessly against hers. She could feel his warm breath on her neck as his hands softly grabbed her waist, touching her soft skin just below the silky fabric ...

She quickly pulled away. "You don't have to stand so close!"

"Yes, as a matter of fact, I do. And I have to touch you to tie it properly."

She glared at him, but she knew he was right. She allowed him to move back up close against her. She grit her teeth, biting off her anger as she felt his fingers caress her waist, as he slowly laced and tightened the corset. She knew he was deliberately taking his time and touching her as much as possible.

As he moved up her back, she had a harder and harder time holding onto her anger. She felt his breath slowly falling on her neck now as he pulled and laced the corset tighter. She found herself leaning back into him, her breath becoming shallow as his fingers continually pulled, tightened, and caressed. Her willpower weakening, she felt herself grow flush, hot, and excited.

When his lips found her neck, she exhaled slowly as his hands left the corset and moved to her waist, trying to gently nudge her to turn around to him.

"No!" She pulled away. "That's good enough. Thank you!" She finished adjusting the corset herself. She couldn't meet his startled stare. She pulled her dress on. It couldn't be helped, but she realized that she only achieved a more enticing ensemble, with the exposed corset under the torn dress.

"Stop staring at me and find us a way out of here!"

Sean continued to stare. "There is no way. Not until someone comes and let's us out."

"I can't be found down here, like *this* ... with *you!*"

"Can't be helped," he shrugged.

Fiona paced the room angrily. She needed to see Patrick. She didn't know how she could explain last night to him, she wasn't even clear why she behaved the way she did.

"You tricked me!" she screamed at Sean, who sat on the floor watching her.

"What? How?" he replied, astonished.

"The port you wouldn't let me have! The scotch! The poisoned wine! You waited until I was drunk and then ... you ... had your way with me!" She moved farther away from him.

"I would never force myself on a drunken lass," he said softly, sensing that she was about to explode.

"Oh, really?" She stopped to glare at him. "Are you saying that *you* didn't seduce *me* last night?"

"Wait just a second there, lassie." He rose and took a step towards her. "You were the one that was all over me like a woman possessed."

"*Me?* Look at this!" She held out her torn dress. "You couldn't wait to get your hands all over me!"

He stopped. He knew he couldn't win this one. For the life of him he really couldn't say what came over him *or* her last night. He had never acted that way before, and from her reaction this morning he was sure that the same was true for her. And it apparently frightened her. The best he could ask for was a draw.

"Fine. You win. I got you drunk and forced you to lay with me numerous times." He held his hands up to her in a fake surrender. "Oh, I should add, ignoring your very vocal and repeated objections."

He went back to the tapestry to lie down and wait this one out. His supplication only angered her more.

"You insufferable ... " She couldn't think of a suitable word to describe him, so she huffed loudly instead and stormed off, moving as far away from him as her prison would allow, all the way to a far wall where she spied a pile of broken chairs behind a wine rack. She froze.

Her dream. A woman? Wasn't there a way out?

She hurried behind the wine rack and tossed the broken chairs away. They crashed to the floor, splintering.

"What are you doing now?" Sean called out, a little concerned for his safety. If she was going to start tossing chairs at him, he wasn't sure what he would do.

"Get over here!" she commanded.

He rose warily and walked over to the wine rack. He found her staring at the rough-hewn wall, her fingers gently caressing the surface, as if feeling for something.

"What are you doing?" he asked again.

"I'm looking for the way out." She was suddenly, eerily calm. "She said there was a way out. She indicated that it was here someplace."

"Who did?" Sean asked, confused.

"The woman. Wait! Right here!" She grabbed his hand and held his fingers to the wall. "Can you feel it?"

"Feel what?" Sean found himself suddenly pressed up against her, his hand in hers, her eyes pleading for him to understand what she was doing. He had to control the sudden urge to grab her in his arms again and take her right there.

What is wrong with me?

"I don't feel anything," he lied.

Then he felt it. A cool breeze blew through a small crack in the stone. He met her expectant gaze.

"There's something beyond this wall," he agreed.

She nodded, excitedly. "I told you."

They searched the wine cellar for something to dig away the mortar.

"How about this?" She offered up a jagged piece of wood from the broken chair. "Too soft. We need to find something metal."

They dug around in the semi-darkness until Sean discovered the remnants of an oak wine cask rotting away under a pile of discarded wood. Around the barrel was a broken steel hoop. He pulled on it until it wrenched away. It had a jagged edge and was long enough to get a solid grip on. He held it up, triumphantly.

"You can stop looking. I found it!"

Sean chipped away at the mortar holding the rock wall in place. He had never noticed it before, but while the rest of the cellar was carved out from natural stone, this wall was stone and mortar, obviously built separately and much more recently, relatively, from the rest of the cellar.

"I don't remember seeing this when I was a boy," he explained to Fiona as he dug. "And it's hard to tell when it was built, because the stones are so old—"

"Just dig!" she insisted.

He shut up and dug. Once the first stone was out, the rest came easier. Whoever had built this wall was not an experienced mason, as the mortaring was inferior and the stones quickly fell away. Soon they had a passage big enough for both of them to crawl through.

Fiona peered into the darkness beyond. "I wonder where it leads?"

"There's only one way to find out," Sean replied, grabbing the lantern. There was very little oil left. The idea of being plunged into total darkness in a mysterious tunnel was not an appealing one to him.

"You wanted out of here. Let's get going."

Sean took the lead with Fiona holding onto his shirttails in fear they might get separated.

It was a natural rock tunnel, nearly six feet tall, and four feet across. It slanted slightly upward. Sean could feel an icy draft against his face, which he hoped meant it led outside.

"What is this place?" Fiona whispered.

"I have no idea," Sean replied. "There seems to be a bend up ahead. Do you see it?"

Fiona nodded, shivering in the cold. The draft felt stronger and icier.

"Hopefully that's the way out," Sean added, as much for himself as for her.

They turned the corner and stopped. Fiona gasped. A casket was in the middle of the tunnel, and lying against it, snoring slightly was Gavin still wearing his hideous mask.

"Who is that?" Fiona whispered, frightened.

"I'm pretty sure it's my dearly departed father," Sean said touching the coffin.

"Not the coffin," she hissed. "Him!" she pointed at Gavin.

Sean leaned in very close, careful not to wake him as he examined his face.

"I believe it's *Garvin*."

"*Gavin*," she corrected, with a hiss of annoyance. "What's he doing here? With that thing?" She shuddered, looking at the coffin.

Sean shook his head and held his finger to his lips. He whispered into her ear, "I have no idea, but let's not wake him to ask. This must definitely be the way out."

Fiona nodded.

They had to squeeze against the freezing wall to get past Gavin and Angus. Fiona slipped on the slippery stone floor and had to brace herself against the coffin to keep from falling. An instant feeling of dread swept through her as she felt the cold, polished wood. She shuddered, involuntarily. Sean was at her side immediately. He steadied her and led her off.

Sean and Fiona came to the fork in the tunnel. It had widened considerably. The left fork was the origin of the breeze, the other a steeper climb.

"Which way?" Sean asked her.

Fiona indicated the left. "I'm through exploring. I just want out." Sean nodded in agreement.

They followed the tunnel up and soon found themselves in the garage/stables. Fiona sighed in relief. It was still dark outside, but a faint lightening to the east indicated an imminent sunrise.

They stood shivering in the stable unsure of what to say or do. They felt both the coldness and the exhaustion from their night's antics in their bones and aching joints.

One of the horses sensed them and grumbled for food.

"Well ... " Sean began.

"Yes." Fiona nodded. She kissed him, unexpectedly, on the cheek. "Thanks for getting me out of there."

"You're welcome. Thanks for trapping me down there. I shan't forget it."

A flare of anger burned in her eyes.

I probably shouldn't have said that, thought Sean, mentally kicking himself.

"We have to talk," she said briskly. "Later." She strode off, leaving Sean totally unsure of where he stood with her.

He decided the best thing was to just go home and wait for the next storm to hit. He gave her enough distance before shuffling off after her, longing for a warm jacket, a hot toddy, and his broken bed.

* * *

Fiona managed to hold herself together until she reached the privacy and warmth of her room. She swayed for a moment, leaning against the door, trying not to think of what she had done, but then caught sight of her ripped dress in the mirror. She broke into angry tears and tore at her dress viciously as she struggled to get out of it.

"What have I done?" she cried, finally free from the garment. She hated the feel of it, she hated the smell of Sean on it. She flung it into the fire.

"How could I have been so stupid?" she sobbed at the flames.

She fell in front of the fire, reaching behind her for the ribbon that would release her from her corset. She pulled desperately before it finally separated, twisting free in her hands. She gazed at the red and black fabric through her tears. The corset was stained with the memory of who had tied it last and who had ripped it off as she made the biggest mistake of her life.

"That was not me," she whispered. The corset hung limp in her hands, a reminder of her betrayal to Patrick.

She tossed the corset into the fire, taking small joy in watching it burn, wanting to believe that whatever strange hold Sean had had on her was now burning away.

Slowly she rose, walked to her closet, and pulled out a dress. She slipped it over her head. She had hoped that having something on that held no memory of the night before would be calming, but her body ached in every movement she made, reminding her of the evening before.

She realized, as she collapsed onto her bed, breaking into a flood of tears, that there was no way she could not think about last night, no way she could erase it from her memory like some dissipating nightmare. She cried for her shame, cried for the man she felt she no longer deserved. She had no idea how to continue.

She had so long wanted Patrick and now she had betrayed him in the worst way conceivable. She had thrown it all away for one night with his brother.

She sobbed knowing there was no recovering from her actions. She would never be the same. Of that she was certain.

Exhaustion overtook her and she fell into a troubled sleep.

She awoke hours later to the giddy face of Abigail, shaking her awake. "Fiona, wake up! You just have to!" she exclaimed.

"What?" Fiona asked, groggy and confused, not even bothering to hide her irritation. "What do you want now?"

Abigail's smile seemed to vanish for only a second before it found its way back to her face again.

"He loves me!" she cried. She leapt up and began dancing around the room. "He told me this morning that there was no way in this whole, vast world he could ever want anyone else!"

Abigail caught sight of a remnant of Fiona's blue dress, the one she had worked so hard on, sticking out among the ashes of the fireplace. She stopped cold, keeping her back to Fiona.

"And how was your night, Fee?" she asked cautiously.

Fiona sat up. She couldn't tell Abigail. Telling her would make it real

"I will never rid myself of it," was all she could manage. She rose from the bed and straightened her dress. She caught a glimpse of herself in the mirror. Her hair was a mess, her eyes puffy and red from crying, she had scrapes and scratches on her arms and bare shoulder's. She looked like hell.

Abigail's eyes widened. *Patrick must have done something despicable.* She could not even conceive of what must have occurred for Fiona to burn the clothes she had worn especially for him. She started to ask what had happened, but was cut short by the sound of the door closing behind her.

Fiona needed to get out of that room, away from the ever-gleeful Abigail. She needed to feel her remorse, not disguise it, dance around it or even worse, talk it all out with Abigail.

No, now was not the time. She wasn't ready. She would come back to Abigail when she felt like herself again, then she would know what to say. Although she knew she had just offended her good friend, she was sure Abigail would understand once she was told the truth.

She wondered if Patrick could look past what she had done? If he could forgive her? But somewhere in her mind she feared he would never look at her again with his soft brown eyes and cunning smile.

One thing was certain; she would have to tell him herself. She had to make sure that Sean did not tell him first; it would surely ruin Patrick to hear it coming from his brother. If she could just find the right words, the right moment, Patrick might understand. He just had to!

Fiona needed to get to Sean immediately and make sure that he would keep his silence. She would beg; he was sure to listen.

She raced across the street, but in an instant her hopes were dashed. She had just enough time to catch a glimpse of Patrick walking into the theater. He had reached Sean before her!

Sean had climbed into his broken bed and fallen fast asleep.

He had gone over the night's confusion–as he had decided to refer to it–over and over on his lonely walk home. He had come to no reasonable conclusions, other than he was pretty certain he had fallen in love with Fiona, and that she hated him, that Patrick was sure to want to kill him, and that he couldn't really blame either of them.

By the time he made it to his loft, his frozen feet were dragging, his bleary eyes barely open, and his bed was the only thought remaining in his head.

His sleep was sound and deep, no dreams, no thoughts, so it was a bit of a miracle that he even woke from such slumber to the sound of heavy footsteps climbing up his ladder.

He opened one weary eye to see his brother standing over him.

"Sean, we have to talk."

Sean opened the other eye. "What time is it?"

"Time to talk," Patrick repeated. "Do you have any coffee in this dump?"

"Yeah," Sean groaned, sitting up, his entire body protesting every movement. "By the sink."

Patrick went about fixing a pot of coffee as Sean stared at him. Patrick was tensed and disturbed, but he wasn't angry, Sean noted, relieved. *Perhaps I'll live through this day after all.*

"Last night someone tried to kill me," Patrick stated matter-of-factly as he brought a cup of coffee over to Sean.

"Wh-What?" Sean stammered, nearly spilling the hot coffee in his lap. "How? Who?"

Patrick sipped his coffee, watching Sean carefully. "Where were you last night?"

"You don't think I had anything to do with it? I hate you, but I wouldn't try to kill you." Sean's attempt at levity fell flat.

Patrick waited for his answer.

Sean took a sip of the scalding hot coffee, trying to buy some time. What was going on here? Was Patrick speaking literally, or did he mean that someone was killing him emotionally? Sean had a definite alibi for the first, which would also convict him on the latter. Sean decided he needed more information, so he told the truth ... *sort of.*

"I was here drinking. Alone." Then he noticed the caked blood on the back of his brother's head. "Where were you?" he added, somewhat cautiously. "And how did you get that nasty gash?"

"Have you ever given much thought to mother's disappearance?" Patrick asked instead, his gaze distant.

Now Sean was completely confused. He noticed Patrick's clothes were disheveled and torn, and that he had a lingering smell of smoke about him.

"What *happened* to you?" Sean asked.

Patrick's gaze returned to the present.

"I found a note in my room. It said that someone wanted to talk to me about mother's murder and I was to meet him at the abandoned train car at seven PM. When I got there, someone knocked me out then set the train on fire. Luckily Jeppsen came along and rescued me. We spent the rest of the night in the church, sleeping out the storm."

"Wait ... " Sean shook his head trying to clear it. "Did you say *murder?*"

"Yes, murder. It's all in the note," Patrick checked his pockets for it as he explained. "I think that the falling sandbag in the theater was meant for me. Someone doesn't want me to find out about mother's murder." His pockets came up empty. "I don't know what happened to the note."

"Hold on!" Sean cried, trying to keep Patrick on track. "What murder? She vanished. No one thinks she was murdered."

Patrick stared at him.

"What? You think she's dead?"

"And you don't?"

Sean was taken back by the question. He knew a part of him thought she might be, but he never wanted to confront that possibility.

"She was on stage," Patrick continued. "She was murdered in front of an entire audience of witnesses and yet no one saw it."

"What? You've lost me there, brother," Sean drank another sip of coffee. It tasted especially bitter.

"She drank poisoned wine," Patrick explained with calm certainty.

All the color drained from Sean's face.

"She drank poison wine?"

"Don't you see? It's the only thing that makes sense. Someone poisoned her and had an entire audience for an alibi! And that person is still around. And now that we're back in town, they're afraid we'll discover who it is. They've tried to kill me twice. And they'll probably try to kill you as well."

"Wait." Sean was still trying to process this information. "Who would want to kill mother?"

"I don't know." Patrick rose. "I'm still trying to figure that out myself. I just wanted to warn you to watch your back. You're in danger and I may not be able to help you."

"Where are you going?"

"I'm going to question everyone, discreetly, about where they were last night," Patrick said, preparing to descend the ladder.

"Wait!" Sean tried to stall him. "Wasn't there some kind of party last night? Surely everyone was there?"

"Yes. But I wasn't there, and neither, apparently, were you," Patrick said as he continued down the ladder.

"Great," murmured Sean, "what else can go wrong with this day?"

Sean had just settled into the scalding tub when he heard a feminine voice calling up to him from downstairs. "Sean? Sean are you up there?"

"For Christ sakes! Who the fook is it now?" he swore.

He had hoped to soak away some of the pain and confusion in his body and mind by immersing himself in the hottest water he could tolerate. Patrick's visit had shaken him on several fronts. For the first time since they had arrived he had felt the walls around them begin to crumble. They were brothers again, and he wanted to unite them on this common front against whatever mysterious enemy had allegedly killed their mother and was now apparently trying to kill them.

Or could it be that his brother was just suffering some delusion from the crack on his head? He hadn't been able to produce the note he said was left for him. Could he even prove that he hadn't just slipped and cracked his head at the train, rather than being the victim of some fiendish plot? And while it was odd that the train had caught fire, if it indeed had, maybe there was some logical explanation.

But, then again someone had apparently locked him in the cellar and left a bottle of poisoned wine. Maybe someone was trying to kill them both.

Sean didn't really know what to think of any of this.

What a fooking mess!

And now there was someone calling for him to come downstairs, and he wasn't about to have any of that.

"Come the fook up if you want to speak to me!" he yelled down.

Abigail climbed the stairs leading up to Sean's loft. She had never been up here before and she was quite surprised by it. It had the potential to be quite cozy, if it were cleaned up a bit. She noticed the broken, disheveled bed and her mind leapt to all kinds of sordid thoughts. Sean was nowhere to be seen.

"Sean?"

"In here!" he replied, sounding irritated.

She followed the sound of his voice and was startled to find him in a cramped bathroom, unabashedly immersed in a steaming bathtub.

"Pardon me if I don't get up," Sean smiled at Abigail's blushing face.

"I was just looking for Fiona."

Sean made a show of looking around the room, and even in the tub. "Nope. Not here."

Abigail noticed the scratches and bruises on his body, as far as she dared look. She could only assume, *imagine*, he had them all *over*.

"Why are you looking for her?' Sean asked, pulling her out of her reverie.

"What? It's just that she left in a hurry. I felt I must have offended her. She seemed to have had a rough night."

"Really?" Sean sat up a little higher in the tub. "What did she say?"

Abigail had to fight to keep her eyes and mind from roaming over Sean's body. *He is definitely well built. I'm surprised Fiona wasn't attracted to him.*

"*What* did she say?" Sean repeated.

"What? Oh, nothing really. That's the whole thing. She usually tells me everything and this morning she was silent as a church mouse. And when I saw the dress and corset burnt in the fireplace, I just knew something horrible must have happened between her and Patrick."

"The dress and corset ... " Sean began, his eyes wide.

Abigail nodded. "She wore them especially for Patrick. I helped her into the corset. It was red silk. You should have seen her; she looked so incredibly–" she cut herself off. She shouldn't be telling Sean this, especially as he was right there, naked, just inches in front of her.

"I'd better be going. She's obviously not here." Abigail backed away. She felt flushed and hot and her need to speak to Fiona had suddenly become overwhelming.

Sean stared at the doorway long after Abigail made her hasty departure.

The long soak had done little to ease Sean's aches. He felt completely lost as to where to go and whom to see. He wanted desperately to see Fiona, but he knew that now was definitely not the time. She needed time to sort things out, if that was even possible. It felt like any move he might make would only make matters immeasurably worse. So he sat at his table, nursed another coffee, this time with a wee bit of scotch in it, and let the world come to him. Which it did.

He heard heavy footsteps climbing the stairs, slow, careful, and deliberate.

Gavin's head appeared and stared at him impassively. "May I come up?" he asked.

"Looks like you already have," Sean replied, softening it with a grin.

Gavin didn't return it as he entered. He scanned the room meticulously as he spoke. "Missed you at the party last night," Gavin said, unconvincingly.

"Really? That's sweet. I never knew you cared. I hope you had a swell time without me."

Gavin shot him a hard look. "Where were you all night?"

"Right here."

"Alone?" Gavin came closer.

"Just me and the ghosties getting pissed. What's this all about? You're beginning to nerve me a bit, Gavin." Sean rose to face him.

They stared at each other, neither flinching.

"Just looking for Fiona. Have you seen her?" Gavin asked softly, a faint threat in his voice.

"No," Sean replied. "So maybe you should go look someplace else."

Gavin held his gaze a moment longer before turning to leave.

"Maybe try the train car. She often goes out there to be alone," Sean called out to the retreating figure.

Gavin froze for a moment. Then finally, without turning around, "Thanks. Maybe I will." He descended the ladder.

"That was odd," Sean said, once he was sure Gavin had departed.

Almost immediately more footsteps could be heard ascending the ladder.

"What is this, Victoria bleeding Station?" Sean peered down the opening to see Samuel's red-eyed, grinning face peering up at him. He was about a third of the way up the ladder. He held on with one hand, swaying a bit, while in the other he gripped a bottle of scotch.

"Thought you might like some company, seeing as you missed a bloody great bash last night," Samuel offered up the bottle of scotch.

"Normally, I would," Sean called down. "But I'm nursing a bit of a sick headache, mate. But you could leave the scotch. For medicinal purposes only, mind you."

"Aye. I've got a bit of a pounder myself," Samuel admitted, handing up the bottle. "I think sleep might be just the thing, after all. I'll come around when I'm more me self."

Samuel looked relieved to make it all the way down the ladder without falling. He staggered off, presumably to bed.

* * *

Fiona's footsteps resonated loudly inside the church as she walked. She had been walking aimlessly for an hour, trying to find peace of mind when she had passed the chapel and, for some unknown reason, felt immediately drawn to it. Perhaps it was the promise of solitude. She opened the wooden doors and walked inside.

The chapel was rather small, but Fiona liked its traditionalism. She admired the stained glass windows, the many candles illuminating the chapel, the large cross that hung over the altar, the little wooden pews that were poised as if silently waiting for a crowd of fifty. Even the small kneelers had different religious decorations sewn into them. She walked past the first two pews then bowed and crossed herself, and took a seat.

Fiona immediately felt calm. It was always in churches that she felt closest to her father. As a teenager she and her dad would make a weekly trip to their church for mass and to light a candle in memory of her mother. Fiona now had to light two candles.

"They are never really gone, they are just unseen," she whispered.

Fiona took a deep breath. She was almost certain that Sean was in the middle of telling Patrick about their night in the cellar. Even more so, Sean was probably bragging about the whole thing. She could see Patrick's face dropping in disbelief. Now that Patrick knew, she was certain she would lose him. Her eyes burned again and Fiona fought back tears. There was nothing left to do or try to hide. She would have to go to him and plead for forgiveness. If he would not, she would lose the one thing she wanted more than anything else in the world.

Tears finally ran down her cheeks. She turned her eyes to the ceiling as she pleaded to God for Patrick to show some kindness and forgive her. *If I could only find a way out of this, please.*

Tears continued to spill from her eyes as she gazed above, hoping God would take notice of her. She rarely ever asked Him for anything. She hated the way she felt and yet she would not want to feel any other way after what she had done. She had such distain for her actions.

"I should have become a nun," she said aloud.

"Now, why would a pretty thing like you say something like that"

Fiona whirled around to find a priest sitting behind her. He was a tall man with an unruly black mustache, but a clean-shaven chin. She had no idea where he had come from or how he had managed to sit behind her without making a sound.

He smiled at her. "I am Father McLeary. You must be one of that troupe that's here, although I didn't really remember seeing you last night at the costume party?"

It was the last thing Fiona had wanted to hear. She began to cry all over again.

"Easy there, lass. Whatever it is, the Lord God will help you through it," he said sweetly.

"I ... I feel as if my heart is broken in two, and it cannot ever be fixed," Fiona cried.

McLeary rose, came around the pew and sat beside her.

"It's alright. You have come to the right place to be fixed, I can promise you that."

"I am such a horrible person," she wailed, leaning forward and laying her sobbing head on the pew in front of her. The father moved his hand to her head and brought her face up to his.

"Ssshhhh. There is no such thing as a horrible person, only a lost one," he replied.

"No, I am wicked, Father. I have lost the man I loved," she said between gasps.

"Are you talking about that Berenger lad?" he asked suddenly. Fiona's stare was enough to answer his question. "Bless your heart, he is fine, safe and sound. A little shaken up but he'll live."

Fiona tears stopped. "What are you talking about?"

"Jeppsen and the Berenger lad. They were both here this morning. Actually, I discovered them in my bed."

"What?"

"Seems there was a fire at that train car and they had tried to put it out and their car wouldn't start after, so they walked back last night through the nasty weather and only made it as far as here."

Fiona was stunned silent. Patrick must have been looking for her throughout the night and his search for her had led him directly into harm's way.

"They are okay?"

"Yes, dandy. We had breakfast this morning before they went on their merry way. I would have joined them, but your director last night convinced me it was time to shave my beard," he added, stroking his bare chin.

Fiona only nodded. She had to get to Patrick, had to apologize, had to make sure he was okay. She rose and turned back to the priest.

"Thank you, Father, but I must go."

She started to head back to the theater and the two brothers that she didn't want to face when she was stopped by the voice of the priest.

"Peace be with you my child."

Fiona only nodded and crossed out the door. Peace was getting harder and harder to find.

* * *

Sean drank about a third of the scotch. His pounding headache finally pounded into submission. He fell asleep, only to be awakened by someone shaking his shoulder, roughly.

"Sean. Sean. Wake-up."

He opened his eyes to find Fiona staring down at him. He sat up.

"Fiona?"

"Glad to see you haven't forgotten me," she replied sarcastically.

"I can't think of a prettier sight to awaken to twice in one day." He reached out for her hands. She pulled them back out of his reach,

"No, I need to talk, you need to listen. Does Patrick know?"

"What?" Sean shook his head. "No. He doesn't suspect a thing."

"Are you sure? I saw him coming over here earlier."

"That was something else. He thinks someone murdered our mother and was trying to kill him, us actually. I think he's delusional. He bumped his head ... "

Fiona stopped listening. She stalked across the room, as Sean rambled on, relief flooding through her. She came up here expecting the worse; now she realized, she still had a chance.

She cut Sean off in mid-sentence.

"Okay. Fine. Listen, I don't want to be seen up here with you so I'll make it quick. What happened last night, *never* happened. Do you understand? You can't tell anyone. And, not on your life–and I say this with all the threat that it implies–never, EVER mention it to Patrick. Do you understand?" she implored.

Sean nodded.

"You were here all night. I was in my room. We were both alone. Do you understand?"

Again, Sean nodded.

"Good."

He thought he saw a slight softening in her eyes and for the briefest moment hope flickered in his. She lingered for a moment, wrestling with the desire to say more, but decided that this was for the best. She turned and left, not seeing the utter devastation she left behind.

* * *

Patrick sat on the burned out chassis of the railroad car. The snow was falling softly. He often came here to be alone and to think during the weeks since *that* night.

A lot had changed, and something had changed within nearly everyone, it seemed. While the play was proceeding with surprising smoothness, he found himself completely detached from it and really uncaring about anything other than finding out why he was brought here.

He had become preoccupied with discovering the alleged murder of his mother, and the attempted murder of him and Sean. He had discretely questioned everyone, and while he had the distinct feeling several people were saying less than they knew, he couldn't pin any of them down. So far his investigation had come up with very little result, and more questions than answers. He thought his father's death was tied in, but how? Every angle he approached came up tenuous at best.

He knew he would have to confront Carlisle again. He was an odd duck, always talking in circles. Patrick would have to question him again soon, perhaps insist that he recount the entire event of his mother's collapse in detail, as he suspected he was most likely there that fateful night in the theater. And Patrick still didn't know the details of his father's death. Could there be some link between the two?

Patrick rose and shook his head to try and rattle some sense into it.

He entered the burnt out train car. It was still a mess. He gingerly stepped through what was left of the charred car. He wasn't looking for anything, just wandering, lost in thought.

They were certainly not leaving town on this wreck of a car. He wondered briefly what had happened to the rest of the train. He had never heard. No trains were moving in the Highlands this time of year so it really didn't matter. But he did wonder how they were going to leave once the play was done. His paranoid mind leapt to a dark thought. *Or was someone going to make sure they didn't?*

He brushed that thought away, returning to the one persistent question that hounded him.

Why?

Why would anyone want to kill his mother, his father, Sean, and him?

The charred remains of the train car offered no clues or insight. Then he came to his berth. He paused at the doorway, staring at what was left of the bunk and with it the memories of that night with Fiona. It seemed like so many years ago.

Fiona, too, had changed. She had become much more attached to him, making it very clear she was there for him in any way he wished, yet allowing him the time and distance he needed to pursue this obsession of his. She didn't question him, didn't even seem to resent his lack of affection, she simply waited. She seemed to be working through some issues of her own, and even with the amount of time they spent together, neither one seemed truly willing to open up. They were closer, yet strangely further apart. He blamed himself for that. He knew he was so incredibly fortunate to have found a woman who loved him so absolutely, and he only hoped he would soon be able to return that love.

Perhaps once this damn play was over, and this mystery solved, he and she could get the hell out of this town.

He glanced at his watch. There was a late rehearsal scheduled, and there were some things he needed to do while it was going on. Patrick took one last glance at the burned out room, then left.

* * *

"I am expecting your child!" cried Fiona.

No, that was too histrionic. She should be happy, if somewhat fearful, that her husband might somehow discover the real father of her child. She tried saying it in a different, more controlled way.

"I am expecting your child?"

No. No. Now it sounded more like a question.

Where the hell was Sean? I need to get this over with!

The last few weeks had been a nightmare for Fiona. She had desperately tried to cut a wide swath of distance from Sean while weaving a closer knit with Patrick. Neither attempt had been very successful. The harder she pushed Sean away, the closer he seemed to hover with his caddish remarks. And Patrick ... if she didn't know better, she'd think that he knew. But she knew he didn't. Abigail had confirmed it in her sly, beguiling way. No, Patrick was obsessing over the other strange events of *that* night, convinced that somehow, someone was trying to kill him, the same person who had apparently 'killed' his mother.

Fiona feared he was losing his grip on reality. Why should anyone want to kill him or his mother? She had tried on several occasions to be alone with him and talk to him about it, but he always politely rebuffed her. She could see the pain in his eyes, but she knew it wasn't because of anything she had done; it was the idea that someone had deliberately killed his beloved mother. If he knew about her betrayal on top of all his misery, it would surely devastate him. And now, here in this play, the irony was that she was deceiving him again.

"I am expecting your child," she said sincerely. Better, she thought, but still not right. *Thank God this wasn't true!* She shuddered at the thought. There was a time in the recent past that she had envisioned having a baby and settling down with Patrick, but how horrible it would be to live with that lie, living with the one you love but secretly raising his brother's child. A reversal of the play's storyline, for in the play she had the child of her lover and was forced to raise it with the husband she detested.

Where was Sean?

He was over an hour late! Nicholas will be furious! Well, at least it gave Andrew time to re-write this scene. She glanced across the stage to where Andrew was scribbling furiously, scratching out lines that he wrote, considered, re-considered then scratched out again. Abigail sat beside Andrew, enrapt with his every pen stroke.

It had taken a lot of pestering by Abigail, and countless promises, heart crossings, 'word of honors', and 'swearing on her mother's grave' for Fiona to finally tell her what happened that night—at least most of it. She had left out one minor detail: she never mentioned that they had been intimate.

In truth, thinking back, it had all seemed like some kind of hazy dream, and she had managed to almost convince herself that it had happened the way she told Abigail it had. They had become somewhat amorous, loosened by alcohol and darkness and the overall situation ... but surely if it had been such an incredible night of passion as she had initially remembered, she would not now be loathing Sean's very presence and desiring Patrick stronger than ever.

Wasn't she?

The weeks had dulled some of the intensity. And by the time she had told Abigail, she had almost convinced herself that they had been merely locked away in near darkness for several hours before discovering a secret passage and a way out. Sure, they drank a lot, they were in a wine cellar after all—she admitted to Abigail—and yes, she was sorely missing Patrick. And, yes, they had passed out under her tapestry together, but only because it was cold and the lights had gone out, and they feared stumbling over each other or worse in the cluttered wine cellar. But once they had sobered up and took stock of the situation, they discovered a way out. They felt everyone would surely misconstrue the innocence of the situation, so she made Sean promise to speak to no one of this. And she was only telling her this because she was her best friend and trusted ally, and she need to unburden her guilt to someone.

She remembered the look on Abigail's face. It was astonishment, colored with disbelief, but she swore she believed Fiona. She promised she'd never tell a soul, including Andrew— but in exchange she was finally allowed to reveal to Fiona in intimate, uncomfortable detail, the night that she had spent with Andrew. Fiona didn't really want to know, as it just reminded her of the missed opportunity with Patrick, and her regrettable night with Sean, but it was the price she had to pay for Abigail's fidelity.

As far as she knew, Abigail had been true to her word. She had not ever whispered a hint about that night. If Patrick ever found out, she was sure it wouldn't be from Abigail. Which meant, of course, that sooner or later it would be up to Fiona to tell him the truth.

That was something she dreaded.

She tried to concentrate on the script, but couldn't focus. She glanced again across the empty stage where she saw a pensive Nicholas pacing the aisles, as he had done for the last forty-five minutes, now working on his second cigar and probably wondering the same thing.

Where in the hell was Sean?

"Hello everyone!" Sean cried out from the theater entrance. "I hope you went ahead and started without me?"

Fiona didn't know why her heart seemed to stop when Sean entered the theater, but the image of him brought a smile and a small release of breath. If she didn't know better, she would have thought she had been worried about him. No, she convinced herself, it was merely relief that he had finally showed and they could start the rehearsal at long last. She dropped her smile and changed to annoyance and distaste.

"Sorry. Lost track of time," he announced unconcerned.

He walked down the aisle to where Andrew and Abigail sat.

"Do you have today's script?" Sean asked. Andrew handed it to him without a word. Fiona glanced over to Nicholas, who was finally standing still, glaring at Sean. *He's going to lose it.*

"I am not going to yell at you for being late," Nicholas finally broke the silence. "No, to do that would mean I actually expected something different from you, that you were as serious about this play as I and the rest of us are, and you have been quite clear that you are not. Instead, I am just going to ask the rest of the cast to stay late and make up the time you lost us."

Nicholas's words cut through the theater like a thrown knife.

Sean met Nicholas's stare head-on, not with defiance, but with contriteness.

"Again, my apologies," he said with seeming sincerity. "It shan't happen again."

He nodded to Andrew and Abigail, then turned and leapt up to the stage. He approached Fiona. She stiffened, not knowing what to expect. Sean lowered his eyes and repeated his apology directly to her, adding a slight, formal bow.

For a moment, it appeared to Fiona that Nicholas' words had really affected him. But before she could allow that thought to become a belief, Sean shifted his gaze back up to Fiona's eyes and smiled a crooked smile.

"I love that angry look in your eyes," he whispered. She smelled the whiskey on his breath.

Fiona's angry expression grew deeper as Sean's smirk grew. He held up his script in defense. "Please, I don't have time for one of your flirtations, I must read my script."

Sean walked back and forth across the stage reading his script. Every now and then Fiona could catch a slight twitch of his lips, as if he was trying to figure out how he was going to deliver one of his lines.

He looks tired.

His hair seemed especially unruly and Fiona could tell that he had not shaved in at least two days, although the slight hint of a beard was really becoming on him, more so than a full beard. Then another thought rose, unwelcomed and disturbing. Sean had originally shaved his beard for her and now he was growing it back again.

"Are you finished?" Nicholas asked, leaning forward in his chair. It was quite obvious that he did not want to wait on Sean anymore.

Sean looked up from his pages and nodded. "I hope so."

He crossed to center stage and faced Fiona for the second time tonight. He bowed. "Whenever you are ready, My Lady."

Fiona shot him a dirty look, took a deep breath then became Iona.

* * *

Patrick couldn't help but feel he was being the worst kind of sneak, the kind who snuck into a friends' room while they were at rehearsal, but that was exactly what he was doing. He realized after that night that he was unsure whom he could trust. He didn't really know these people. Yes, he traveled with them and did performances with them, but they were all actors–they were trained to submerge their identities, to wear masks and fabricate lives they never lived. No, he couldn't really be sure who any of them were. *Not even Fiona.*

No. Fiona, he could trust.

He was shuffling through Andrew's things, looking for God knew what, when he found something very strange. It was Carlisle's odd journal crammed with scraps of this and that from which the script was supposed to evolve. Patrick had never looked at it before, so he picked it up and flipped through the pages of drawings, scribbled notes, scraps of paper ... and then he felt the blood drain from his body as he came across a familiar face staring at him. It was his mother's face on a scrap of newspaper.

It took Patrick several deep breaths to calm down enough to read the article.

It was a historic piece from a local newspaper now long defunct looking back a century, to a forgotten town called Isyeless. The article described the town's horrific demise, instigated by a strange woman's arrival and the cholera epidemic she spread.

The church bells tolled out to warn everyone to stay away, while in the town panic and horror ensued, as the healthy killed the sick and even the suspected sick, before the sick finally fought back, and soon it was a near complete massacre. Because of the horror, the town was shunned by all who lived nearby, its name never spoken, its isolated location on a virtual island no longer visited.

Now in ruins, it rots away in a shroud of desolate fog.

And Patrick's mother, Delia, according to the newspaper article, seemed to be the only known surviving relation of any of the original families.

Unfortunately, the reporter noted, she too had disappeared.

A range of emotions swept through Patrick. How much did he even know about his mother? Or his father? He had never given much thought to his heritage, and upon reflection he realized that every time the subject had been brought up as a child it was always deflected or ignored by both parents.

He stared at her image in the paper, then thought of all the painted reproductions and wondered. *Was this a clue? Was Thornbury trying to tell him something? What if she wasn't dead after all? What if she was hiding out there, in the forbidden town, and all he had to do was go and get her?*

Patrick knew where this town was.

He had never told anyone, not even Sean, about his secret boyhood adventures sneaking into this castle in the dead of night while everyone slept. He would climb to the north tower and survey the moon-bathed landscape towards the sea. He remembered, on one particularly clear night, he spotted a single light on a bump of land just barely off the coast where no village ought to be. He stared at the light, feeling its mysterious pull, a secret escape should he ever need one.

He had never ventured out there. His family had no vehicles or horses, and it would have been too many days walk.

Even today, there was no road leading that direction, only desolate moors that no automobile could maneuver, but a horse could make it in several hours. Thornbury owned horses.

The sun was setting low at his back, casting long shadows over the landscape as Patrick pulled the heavily panting horse to a halt at the sea's edge.

He patted the horse's neck and whispered some comforting words. He knew he had ridden him hard trying to beat the sunset, and now they were here.

The horse—*Shadow*—seemed both equally exhausted and wary. He snuffled, stomped his hooves, and stared wide-eyed at the village ruin across the shallow water.

Patrick knew just how Shadow felt. The village was anything but inviting. It lay just off shore, an island sometimes, due to the massive tidal currents. It was completely surrounded by water at high tide, but at low tide, especially very low tides like right now, the water was so shallow one could walk to it barely getting his feet wet.

A full moon was rising like a bad omen.

Patrick was not familiar with the tidal schedule to know just how much time he would have before he and Shadow would be trapped there. He did know that a full moon meant severe tidal fluctuations, which meant he was looking at both the lowest tide and the highest tonight. It would be the easiest crossing, possibly the only crossing this month, but also the most impossible return.

Could his mother really be hiding out there?

It seemed unlikely that anyone could live there, although he could make out some standing stone structures. What insane person decided that this would be a good place to build a village?

Shadow whinnied his impatience. Patrick had to make a decision. They go now, sweep through the town and hurry back, or they wait until the next full moon?

Patrick had to know. He urged Shadow on.

As Shadow loped across the shallow water, Patrick couldn't help but feel uneasy. It was as if he were being led on some strange manipulated journey to get him to this dead village.

Why?

Shadow reached the outskirts of Isyeless and refused to go any further. He planted his hoofs in the sand and dared Patrick to make him move on, stomping and tossing his head.

Patrick patted his neck reassuringly as he dismounted.

"It's okay. Wait here, boy. I'll just be a few minutes."

It wasn't much of a town: a church, a few stone homes, a store or two ... all in disrepair, all empty, desolate. Patrick didn't have a light, but the full moon showed him all he needed to know. There was no one living here.

He returned to Shadow.

"She's not here," he said with resignation.

Shadow shook his head in agreement, and, anxious to leave, didn't wait for the command but galloped across the rising sea, as fast as he could, away from Isyeless.

Act 2
Scene 4

IONA'S clothing shop. IONA and MACLAREN.

IONA: I never wanted it to happen this way. I wanted ... I dared to dream ... that the two of us ...

(MACLAREN *wraps his arms around her.*)

MACLAREN: Shhh! A child! That is all that matters. We are blessed.

IONA: We'll be found out. Of this I am certain.

MACLAREN: I can't believe that. Nothing has altered; nothing has changed. I am still here. I will always be here.

IONA: But so is my husband! I have done such a terrible thing, and I fear that no good can come from this. I am not worthy of either of you.

(*IONA breaks away from MACLAREN and walks downstage.*)

MACLAREN: Nonsense! It is he who is not worthy of you!

IONA: How can I let him raise a child I know not to be his? And the child will never know his true father.

MACLAREN: Our child will know me. I will be present in his life, even if he never knows I am his father. He will be well taken care of, even if it must be clandestine.

IONA: No. You don't understand. I can't see you anymore. It would be too dangerous. Our baby deserves a life without deception. And I can't live in the constant fear of the truth somehow unraveling with a slip of my tongue, or a longing look in your presence. I am not as iron-willed as you. You must remain distanced.

(MACLAREN *is staggered.*)

MACLAREN: Are you saying that I can never hold our child? Can never kiss his cheeks or feel his tiny fingers grasp my hand?

(IONA *cries.*)

IONA: I will love him for the both of us. He will know your love through me. I came here because you needed to hear the truth and let me go. If you love me as much as you say, you will let me go and know that I will always love you.

(IONA *crosses to leave.* MACLAREN *stops her with a heart-wrenching plea.*)

MACLAREN: Wait! Iona, I can't just let you go.

IONA: I am expecting your child. You are a Lord and married. I have no choice.

(MACLAREN *grabs her arms, forces her to look into his eyes.*)

MACLAREN: What am I to do? I can't be without you!

IONA: I am afraid you have no choice as well.

(IONA *finally breaks his hold.*)

IONA: My *Lord.*

(IONA *curtsies.*)

MACLAREN: *My* Lady

(MACLAREN *bows.*)

(End Scene)

Sean reached for Fiona as she turned and walked off stage.

* * *

Patrick felt desolated as he dropped a blanket over Shadow. They were back in the stables. It was late and he had just finished brushing, feeding, and thanking the horse for the hard ride when he saw a whitish shadow moving through the stables.

"Don't blame me," it mumbled.

Then it was gone.

Patrick gave Shadow one final pat, and then hurried after the figure. He saw the figure disappear around a corner, heading towards the kitchen. He ran after it.

He soon caught up to it. It was Carlisle Thornbury!

"Carlisle? Are you okay, there?" Patrick asked, keeping step beside the old man. Carlisle either didn't hear or didn't want to answer. He kept on walking, mumbling apologies and broken phrases. He appeared to be in a sleep daze.

"Sleeping walking, eh?" Patrick realized. "Is that it?"

"Can't blame me," he muttered, eerily. "Not my fault."

"What's not your fault?" Patrick tried.

"It wasn't meant for her."

"What? What wasn't meant for her?" Patrick insisted. "For who? Whom are you talking about?"

Carlisle became silent as he made his way through the kitchen. Patrick thought that maybe Carlisle was simply hungry, and he would make himself a sandwich then head back to bed, his hunger satiated, the cause for this mysterious sleep strolling solved by a full stomach. But no, Carlisle didn't even hesitate by the cupboards, but instead made his way into the large walk-in dry goods pantry and squeezed past a well-stocked shelf to a closed door, apparently set into the castle's stone wall.

Intrigued, Patrick followed him as he entered the dark passage.

The way was narrow, but Carlisle seemed to have no trouble finding his way in the dark tunnel. Patrick kept close beside him, holding tight to his dressing gown. Thankfully he had a pack of matches in his pocket, along with a forgotten, crumpled cigar, that Samuel had given him some time ago. He decided not to light one yet, although the darkness was claustrophobic, Carlisle lead the way unerringly.

The passage was completely quiet, as well as dark, so when Carlisle stopped suddenly and cried out, Patrick practically leapt out of his skin.

"Stop haunting me! I beg you!" Carlisle screamed. His anger dissolved into a muted pleading. Not able to bear the darkness and confusion any longer, Patrick struck a match. In the puddle of thin light, before the match burned his fingers, he saw that Carlisle lay across his father's dark coffin, sobbing.

Patrick remained in the dark for some time listening to the soft moans and pleas of the old man, until they finally dissolved into silence. He waited until he heard the soft shuffling of

Carlisle's slippered footsteps fading away before he struck another match.

His father's dark shiny coffin reflected the match back eerily. He had wondered where his father had gone; yet he never thought to ask. Now he knew. *A fitting repose,* he smirked.

He didn't know what to make of Thornbury's somnolent shuffle. He listened for signs of any kind of movement, but by now even Thornbury's soft footsteps had receded beyond hearing. That was when he noticed the tunnel continued on in the opposite way in which he came. *What was down there? It must go way below the castle, because we definitely walked beyond the perimeter of the castle walls, on a slight decline the entire time.*

He peered ahead, but could see nothing but an empty passage leading on before the match went out. *This castle is full of secrets,* he thought as he lit another match. *I may as well find them out.*

He proceeded down the tunnel.

He heard a distant rumbling coming from further down. He had no idea what it could be. Undaunted, he headed on.

Several matches later he came to a broken wall. The rumbling sound was louder there. There was a hole big enough for him to crawl through, admitting a dim bit of light from the other side. He crawled through it.

He was surprised to find himself in a place he recognized from his childhood: the wine cellar beneath the theater. He never knew there was a passage leading from the theater to the castle.

The rumbling sound was coming from the generator, providing light for the dim, bare bulb in the cellar as well as the theater lights above. *They must be doing a full lighting and stage rehearsal,* he assumed.

He spotted what looked like a discarded tapestry, but paid it no mind. He crunched across some broken glass. The place was a mess. Sean always had been a bit of a slob, he recalled. Now, that he thought of it, this would be a very good time to check out Sean's room while they were all deep into rehearsal. He had no idea what he might find. He grabbed a bottle of wine as he headed up the stairs, just in case Sean happened to catch him. He could always claim he was dropping by for a drink. Sean would probably find that suspicious, but he never turned down a free drink.

The door was open, and the broken padlock lay on the ground. He heard faint voices drifting from above.

Patrick stood in the shadows of the theater entrance, watching for a moment.

> MACLAREN: Shhh! A child! That is all that matters. We are blessed.
>
> IONA: We'll be found out. Of this I am certain.
>
> MACLAREN: I can't believe that. Nothing has altered; nothing has changed. I am still here. I will always be here.
>
> IONA: But so is my husband! I have done such a terrible thing, and I fear that no good can come from this. I am not worthy of either of you.

Sean and Fiona seem so natural together. Patrick turned and nearly collided into Gavin standing in the wings, also watching.

"They play the betrayers very well, don't you think?" Gavin asked quietly.

"How do you mean?" Patrick asked, taken aback.

Gavin turned away from the stage to meet Patrick head on.

"In this scene. Fiona must choose who to lie to and who to ultimately lie down with," Gavin stated.

"Yes. I know. I've read the script," Patrick said bluntly, as he started to push past Gavin and the strange, obtuse insinuations he seemed to be making.

"My job is to cast light upon the whole thing," Gavin said, darkly.

"How do you mean?" Patrick said, suddenly turning back. He grabbed Gavin roughly by the shoulders. "What are you trying to say?"

Gavin stared at him unflinching for a long moment. "Just that I have a lighting cue coming up," he stated, finally.

"Then you better get to it," Patrick said releasing him gruffly.

As Patrick left, Gavin whispered, too low for him to hear. "Maybe *you* should ask Fiona where she was the night of the party ..."

As Patrick stalked away he reflected briefly about his encounter with Gavin. *That guy has become very strange since he was denied a part in the play.*

But he quickly shook his attention away from Gavin and concentrated on the job at hand. He took a mental note of who was present in the theater: *Sean, Fiona, Abigail, Andrew, Nicholas, and, of course Gavin. So that just leaves Samuel, who could be anywhere, and Jeppsen, who also could be anywhere.*

Neither one of them were much of a concern, although he had not officially crossed either off his mental lists of suspects yet. Patrick left the doorway and made his way to the drop ladder leading up to Sean's room when he ran into Samuel coming into the lobby from outside, his arms filled with books on Scotland.

"Say, Patty boy. What are you doing here?" Samuel asked, good-naturedly.

"Uh ... " he stalled. *At least now I know where Samuel is.* Then he remembered the cigar in his pocket and the wine in his hand. "Looking for you," he finished, withdrawing his cigar. "Thought maybe you'd like to join me outside for a smoke and a drink."

"Sounds like grand idea," Samuel said with a smile as he dumped his books in the lobby. He pulled out his flask. "Although I don't much care for wine. I hope ya don't mind if I brought me own?"

"Not at all," Patrick said, opening the front door.

Outside Samuel and Patrick sparked up cigars. Patrick realized that he didn't have a corkscrew, so he skipped the wine.

"Nice night," Samuel said. It was bitterly cold, icy with a fine sleet falling. He took a sip from his flask, and offered it to Patrick. Patrick, despite the cold, declined.

"Yeah," Patrick agreed, gritting his teeth against the cold. "So, Samuel, I wanted to ask you–"

"I think, I know what you're going to ask," Samuel interrupted. "So you've seen her too?"

"Seen who?" Patrick asked, confused.

"Was she singing?"

"Who? Fiona?"

"Fiona?" Samuel was incredulous. "Nay, are you daft? Fiona's the one that she warned about." Samuel took a deep drag on his cigar.

Patrick simply stared at Samuel.

"I know you probably don't believe in haunts, I dinna, either, but Sean's seen her and so have I, twice."

"Are you saying you've seen a ghost?"

"Aye"

"Here? In the theater?"

"Aye. Haven't you?"

"No."

Samuel stared at Patrick suspiciously. "Then why did you ask me about her?"

Patrick shook his confused head. "What? I didn't. I was just going to ask you about the sandbag that fell on Jeppsen."

"What about it?" Samuel asked.

"Did you think it was an accident?"

"Aye. What else might it have been?"

"Nothing. I don't know."

A sudden realization came to Samuel. "Oh, so you think the *ghost* may have done it?"

"No. That's not what–"

"I think you're on the wrong track there. She's not–"

"Nice chatting with you," Patrick shook his arms and legs, trying to warm them up, as he rose. He tossed his cigar into the snow. "I must go."

Samuel nodded. "Aye, likewise." He finished the contents of his flask. "All dry here. Would ya join me at the Piper?"

"No, thanks," Patrick said, "perhaps later."

"Aye. Have a nice night, then," Samuel took off toward the Broken Piper, trailing a fine smoke cloud. Patrick waited until he was a good distance away, before he re-entered the theater and climbed the ladder to Sean's loft.

"Still a dump!" Patrick exclaimed. The broken bed had never been fixed. Discarded clothes, dishes and empty bottles littered the floor. He went to the sink, found a wine opener and opened the bottle he had carried up from the cellar. He deserved a drink, he thought. He drank deep from the bottle and looked around.

The room brought back a flood of memories. As kids, he and Sean would often escape his dad's wrath by sneaking up here and hiding. Sometimes they would play draughts or cards. Or when the wind was up and the moon glowering, they would tell ghost stories well into the night, trying to see who could out scare the other.

How their dad didn't know about this place, he never figured out. Unless he did, the sudden thought occurred to him. What if he knew all along, but allowed them this one place of sanctuary? He didn't know what to make of that; if true, it shattered some of the dark visions he clung to about his father.

"Fook the bastard," he said softly.

Time was running out. He began to search Sean's room, not even sure what he was looking for. Patrick found very little personal possessions of Sean's to indicate any conspiracy, or even offer a clue as to where he'd been, or what he had been doing before he got here. He certainly travels light, he mused, like a shadow.

He never really suspected Sean of anything other than being in the wrong place at the wrong time, but he had thought that perhaps he might find some inkling as to why he was being pegged for murder.

He was about to leave when he noticed a book that looked familiar. It lay beside the broken bed, its gilt-edged pages catching the dim light.

He went and picked it up. It was a handsome, hand bound edition of poems by Lord Alfred Tennyson. He turned to the page held by the red cloth sewn in bookmark. It was *The Lady of Shalott.*

"The Lady of Shalott?" He flipped through the book until he came to the title page and found an inscription:

Dearest Fiona,

Don't let the world pass you by, like your beloved Lady. Instead, sing joys like the lark, tirra lira, tirra lira … all along this birthday day !
Your loving, Father.

Patrick sat down hard on the broken bed stunned. It groaned under his weight. What was Fiona's book doing here beside Sean's bed?

He laid back, not sure what think or do.

Later, as Patrick descended the ladder, he could hear murmured voices coming from the stage, so he knew the rehearsal was still going on. He left the theater and headed towards the Broken Piper.

Still carrying his bottle of wine, Patrick entered the pub and discovered Samuel passed out and snoring at one of the far tables, his hand clutching a nearly empty pint of beer. Patrick ignored him and climbed the stairs.

He was in a grave mood as he let himself in Fiona and Abigail's room. He sat back on Fiona's bed and waited for her to return. He sipped his wine. He would wait all night if he had to. He had but a single question to ask her.

Abigail and Fiona entered the room, laughing and in high spirits. The rehearsal had lasted longer than they had anticipated, but in the end it turned out well. Sean had settled into his part and had played off Fiona's character with emotional brilliance. Despite all the troubles and conflicts, Fiona was riding the momentary high of coming off stage from a staggeringly good performance.

"I just need to grab a few things before I head up—Oh!" Abigail's sentence was choked off in surprise as she noticed Patrick sitting on the bed.

"Patrick!" Fiona exclaimed. "What are you doing here?"

"Waiting for you," he said simply. He finished off his bottle, and placed it on the nightstand.

"Maybe I should leave," Abigail suggested, backing out the doorway.

"No need," Patrick said, standing and walking over to Fiona. "I'll just be a moment. I need to ask Fiona a question."

Fiona met his gaze.

"Of course, Patrick," she said. "You can always ask me anything."

Patrick held her gaze for an uncomfortably long time. Then he asked with unnerving calm, "Fiona, where were you the night of the party?"

Her heart stopped. She wavered, feeling as if she might faint. She glanced over at Abigail, who also looked pale and unsteady. A thousand thoughts raced through her mind, a thousand possible answers, including the truth. She looked into Patrick's eyes. There was no clue to betray any emotion.

Fiona made a decision.

"I was right here waiting for you. I fell asleep and missed the party. Why?"

"No reason," he said, emotionless. "Goodnight ladies."

Patrick started to leave, when he stopped in the doorway and turned.

"Oh, and by the way, I found your book."

Then he left the room, not waiting for a response. They could hear his footsteps, heavy and even, as he descended the stairs. The pub door closed. Fiona finally turned to Abigail.

"What was that about?" her voice cracked.

Abigail shook her head. She had no idea.

"What was that about a book?"

Then Fiona noticed the book of poems her father had given her on her bedside table beside the empty bottle of wine. She had forgotten all about the book, not even sure what had become of it. The last time she remembered having it was in the wine cellar ... *The wine cellar!* Patrick must have found it down there. But that didn't mean anything. She could have left it down there at any time.

No, it had to be something else ...

She sat down heavily on her bed.

* * *

(IONA *enters stage left coming up behind* RORY *as he drinks at the kitchen table.* RORY *is slightly intoxicated and troubled.*)

IONA: Rory. I have been looking for you for an hour. I went to the pub and our store–

RORY: Odd that you didn't think I would be here, in *our* home.

IONA: I know I have been distant for sometime now. I have been seeking the right words to speak to you about–

RORY: I KNOW! DAMN IT! How did you think I would not suspect that you were seeking another man's arms? I who have always loved you! I who never wanted anything more than–

IONA: I am with child.

(RORY *is shocked.*)

IONA: *Your* child.

(IONA *cries.*)

IONA: I have been trying to find the right words to tell you. How am I supposed to tell you that I am afraid of you? With all that you drink, and your constant, unfounded, suspicions when you do. I wanted to run away, Rory. From you, for the sake of our child, but I realize now I owe you a choice.

(RORY *rises: a beer in one hand, his other a fist.*)

RORY: And what choice is that?

IONA: First, I need to know if you still love me?

(*Uncomfortable silence.* RORY *sets down his beer and crosses to* IONA. *He takes her in his arms.*)

RORY: Of course I love you! It is I who should ask if you could love a miserable, drunken sod like me. I have been aching and desolate these past few months. I feared I was losing you. I couldn't deal with that thought, Iona. I tried to drink it away. But I couldn't ... I didn't mean it when–

(IONA *kisses him.*)

IONA: It is I who was foolish to think that you no longer cared. I see my error now, I am so sorry.

RORY: But you still love me?

IONA: I do.

RORY: The child is mine?

IONA: Yes, of course.

RORY: And the other man?

IONA: There never was.

(RORY *smiles at last.*)

RORY: I will be a father! Iona it's a way to start again, don't you see?

(RORY *laughs in joy. Then stops suddenly, as another thought troubles him.*)

RORY: What was the choice you wanted me to make?

IONA: It matters not now. I choose you, I always will.

(RORY wraps his arms around her and kisses her)

The curtain falls.

Fiona felt sick the moment the curtain fell. This scene almost seemed too close to what she was going through. Sean had been in the audience, watching intently. She made up her mind in that instant that she would tell Patrick everything, right now.

But the minute the curtain closed, Patrick immediately turned away from her as if touching her for even a second longer would be the worst torture in the world. And, to make matters worse, he wiped her kiss off his mouth in one cruel gesture as he began to walk away.

"Patrick, wait," she cried, stopping him in his tracks.

Patrick did not turn to face her. He stood with his back to her waiting to hear what she had to say.

"I have ... I need to talk to you!"

He turned slowly. The lack of emotion on his face startled Fiona even more then the words that followed.

"Is there really anything left to discuss?"

"Yes. There is. The truth," she squeaked. She searched his eyes to find a trace of kindness and understanding, but all she saw was bleak emptiness.

"What truth might that be?" he asked quietly.

She had brought this all on herself, she decided, she deserved what happened next.

"The truth about the night of the party. See, I went to get a bottle of–"

"*Sweet Fee*, you have nothing to say about that night that I wish to hear," he whispered. Then he turned and disappeared into the wings.

Fiona suddenly needed air. She rushed through the curtain immediately blinded by the lights on the other side of the stage.

Nicholas was talking to Andrew in the front row of the theater, but stopped the minute Fiona broke through the curtain.

"Well done you two!" he roared. "It gives me such joy to see my two favorite actors carry out a scene like that! Now that's the kind of Christmas gift a director loves to receive."

Fiona stood dumbfounded in the lights. Only then did she notice that Sean, too, had left.

* * *

Sean assumed Fiona was by now behind the curtain in Patrick's arms. The sight of Patrick touching her, if only on stage, was so infuriating, that he decided it was better that he return to his loft, in search of a good strong drink and a definite plan to get Fiona back into *his* arms.

He fantasized about rushing backstage, punching Patrick and sweeping Fiona up in a loving embrace and carrying her off– but soon dismissed the thought. It smacked too much of romance novel heroics. That was not really his style, although, another row with Patrick might relieve some tension. No, better he remain up here for the rest of the day, the ladder pulled up, shut off from the world.

"Bloody Christmas Eve," he mumbled. He had forgotten how miserable the holidays could be when one was alone. He groaned with the thought of the Christmas dinner tomorrow, having to sit across the table from Fiona and Patrick. He considered if he should even bother going. Of course he could slough through the festivities fortified by drink hoping that he would awake the following morning with all memory erased. Or, he could just remain here, alone, while his imagination tortured him endlessly with far more hurtful scenarios than reality could inflict. Sighing, he took another drink. Either way, he couldn't bloody win.

He heard the drawing down of the ladder and the ascending footsteps, and the next thing he knew Fiona was standing in front of him, hands on hips, breathing hard, her beautiful green eyes like emeralds aflame.

He swallowed. "Fiona. What brings you calling?"

Fiona continued to stare.

Sean swallowed again, not trusting his voice. "Would you like to sit down?" He indicated the chair across from him with a shaky hand.

Fiona waited for a long moment before sitting. She faced him, her stare boring into him. He shifted nervously, wishing she'd say something, anything. He offered her the bottle of scotch. She stared back even harder. He took that as a no. Whatever was coming was not going to be pleasant. He'd better put more armor on, so he poured himself another. He didn't have to wait long.

"You told Patrick?" she hissed.

"Told Patrick what?"

"About us! About the night in the cellar!" she screamed.

"No. I did not!"

Fiona stopped, confused. She had not expected him to deny it.

"When I give my word, I give my word. Why would you think I had?"

"He found my book down there and he asked me where I was the night of the party. And then Patrick was so mean today at rehearsal—"

"Your book? What book?"

"The book of Tennyson poems my father gave me for my birthday. *The Lady of Shalott* was in it. I must have left it in the wine cellar, you know, *that* night. He found it and I guess he must be jumping to conclusions."

"Yes, I imagined he probably is," Sean stole a look at his bed. The book was gone! When did Patrick sneak up here?

"You never talked to him about that night with me?"

"Believe me, I *wanted* to shout it to the world."

Fiona was confused. It didn't make any sense. Just finding a book in the wine cellar shouldn't make him that suspicious. There had to be something else. All she knew was that she just couldn't go on like this any more.

"This has to end," she said suddenly, shattering the silence as unexpectedly as a gun retort. She snatched the drink from his hand and leaned in very close to his face, demanding his full attention.

"What? The drinking?" he asked.

"NO! THIS! US! YOU! ME!

"What? I mean ... *what?*" Sean was confused by both her sudden intensity and the fact that her lips were so inviting, so close, and so damn kissable.

"Stop it! Stop your strange, delusional flirting, and your wanting looks. You don't want me!"

"Don't I?"

"No." She leaned in even closer, her intimacy almost frightening. "And I don't want you," her voice cut like a blade. "So stop. Stop it right now."

"Okay," he agreed.

"Okay?" she sat back suddenly. Again, this was not the answer she expected.

"Yes." He raised his eyes to meet hers. He saw the flame in them waning, being replaced by confusion and a hint of sadness. "You're right. I can never have you–I mean besides that one time–but you and Patrick belong together. You deserve to be with the one that makes you happiest. I am sorry."

She stared in disbelief as he rambled on.

"I was ready to fight for your love, but I see I am only battling windmills. There is no enemy to conquer. The war was over before it even began." Then he added with a smile of remembrance. "We had one fine skirmish. For that, I shall always be grateful."

Fiona stared at him, scrutinizing, her mind filled with mixed emotions.

"So you're fine with this?" she asked, softly. "You will leave me be?"

"Absolutely." He took his glass back. "To you and Patrick. Cheers!" He downed it. There was more in his glass than he had anticipated. Either that or his throat had somehow tightened. He began to choke a little, trying to swallow it all. He was drowning while Fiona watched, not moving to help. He finally managed to swallow it all down. He drew a deep breath followed by a long sigh.

She was still staring at him.

"Was there something else?" he asked politely.

She shook her head, no. She started to rise.

"Uh ... there is one more thing that I'd like to say," he said. There was something in his soft tone that made her sit back down. He leaned in close to her. This time it was his turn to keep her silently waiting. His stare was intense. Fiona felt conflicting emotions flooding through her: confusion, sadness, wanting, anger, passion, longing, frustration ... If he didn't say something quickly she was either going to slap him or kiss him. And what baffled her most was she really didn't know which would have been the more satisfying.

"I can, and will, do whatever you ask ... " he began. "I can tell you that I do not love you, that I can cheerfully watch you walk away arm-in-arm with Patrick, and tell you with absolute certainty that I will find another woman, fall in love, and be bloody well fine for the rest of me days. "

He breathed out, struggling to finish his thought.

"Ah ... but there is one wee thing ... "

"What?" she whispered so softly she was not even sure she had spoken it aloud.

"I'm such a liar."

He looked at her, shields down, armor tossed away and she saw it all in his eyes.

And looking back on that moment, as she often would, she was not certain who moved forward first, or if they moved together, but they were suddenly in each others' awkward arms, the wooden table an intrusive wedge between them, as they collided into a deeply passionate kiss.

For Fiona, the room spun, all the elements of that night in the cellar flooded back. Her blood rushed hotly to every inch of her body. Her arms reached hungrily across the table, clutched at him, tried to bring him in as close as she could, hold him as tight as possible, as if this were the last embrace, the last kiss of her life.

For Sean, it was a long held breath finally exhaled, an intense release, the abating of a dark tension that had gripped him ever since that night. Sean felt Fiona's hands grasping for him, and took them in his and roughly pulled Fiona toward him atop the table, then crawled up, meeting her half way. He moved her onto her back, as he rolled atop her, kissing, touching, pressing their bodies together, yearning to be as close as he possibly could.

It seemed to last forever, or an instant, then–

CRACK!

The wooden table had given way, and they tumbled apart on the hard floor.

Surprised, embarrassed, confused–they lay there for a moment.

Sean started to laugh, but choked it off. He stood and offered Fiona a hand up.

She took it, reluctantly, refusing to meet his gaze as she gathered her senses, dusted off, and straightened her clothing.

Sean sat down heavily in his chair, one of only two pieces of furniture still intact, feeling as if all his bones had dissolved.

This changes nothing, Fiona tried to convince herself as she grabbed the ladder leading down. *This ... changes ... nothing!*

"Fiona," Sean called out.

She froze but did not turn.

"I love you," he said.

She climbed down the ladder, not looking back, not daring to look back.

"She'll be back," Sean said, as he grabbed his drink and waited for her return.

* * *

Carlisle Thornbury was in his room, at his desk, frantically scribbling on a sheet of paper when Patrick knocked.

"Go away!" he called out.

Patrick opened the door. "Did you say come in?"

"No! Oh! Patrick, my boy! Of course come in! Come in!"

Patrick entered. He took a seat beside the desk.

"I thought you were that nuisance writer fellow. He's been asking me so many questions–"

"How's the script coming?" Patrick asked, as he tried to read what Carlisle was writing.

"Fine. Fine. Should be done soon," Carlisle quickly collected the scribbled pages and shoved them into his top desk drawer. He locked it with a key on a chain around his neck. "A real surprise ending. Can't show you, of course. You do know the old superstition about the cast not seeing the last line of dialogue until opening night?"

"Yes, of course. Into superstitions are you?" Patrick asked.

"We are theater folk, are we not?"

"Oh, are *we*?" Patrick asked, coyly. "Were *you* ever an actor Mister Thornbury?"

The question seemed to take Carlisle by surprise. He quickly turned away, and went to the drink trolley. "Would you care for a brandy? It suits the holiday season so well, don't you think?"

"Indeed," Patrick answered. Carlisle poured brandy into two tumblers then returned. He handed one to Patrick.

"Thank you. You never answered my question."

"Oh, yes ... " Carlisle nodded, taking a gulp. "No, not an actor as such."

"Meaning?"

"I do have a great interest in the theater."

"Much like my father?"

Carlisle swallowed with difficulty. He finally nodded.

"Or perhaps, more than just the theater?" Patrick continued. "Perhaps in actors? Maybe just one actress in particular."

Carlisle stared defiantly at Patrick. "Is this what you came to talk about? Because I am a busy man."

"No. Something else entirely." Patrick noticed Carlisle's age was showing through: his wrinkles seemed deeper; his pallor grayer, his movements shakier. "I came to talk about ghosts."

Carlisle stared at him for a long moment then broke into raucous laughter. "Ghosts? The perfect subject for a Christmas Eve."

He rose still laughing. He went to the fireplace and added a small log to the dying fire.

"I'm nearly one myself."

"So, you know a lot about ghosts, do you?" Patrick asked.

Carlisle shrugged. "Charles Dickens said: 'An idea like a ghost, must be spoken to little before it will explain itself.'"

"Are you saying you've spoken to some?"

"Aye. A few." Carlisle nodded, returning to his chair. His gaze distant.

"The one some say haunts the theater? The singing lady? Have you spoken to her?" Patrick prodded. "Or perhaps my father's spirit?"

"Your father does speak, yes." He answered enigmatically, then added sadly, "But you don't believe in ghosts, do you lad?"

"No." Patrick brushed the question off. Instead he prodded further. "What does he say to you? Is he concerned that he is not in his final resting place? Is that why you sleepwalk down to see him? To reassure him? Or is it something else?"

"Reassure whom?" Carlisle asked, suddenly back to the present. "What are you talking about?"

Patrick sighed in exasperation. "My father's coffin is in a tunnel beneath this castle. I followed you there one night when you were sleepwalking."

"I sleepwalk? I've never heard such nonsense!" Carlisle was indignant.

"Regardless. There is a coffin below the castle. Is there not?"

"Oh, yes," Carlisle replied, nonplussed. "Probably more than one, I should think. When one dies in the winter months, we keep them down there until the ground softens. We tend to forget about them when spring finally rolls around. I'll have Jeppsen take an inventory. Now what else did you have on your mind?"

"Nothing." He was getting nowhere, as usual. He finished his drink then rose to leave. "I should be going. Good night."

"Sleep well, my boy," Carlisle called out. "And do try not to sleep walk. Could be troublesome with all these slippery steps and rotting floorboards, don't you know."

Patrick nodded. "I'll try my best."

He exited, his head feeling thick, a feeling he often associated with after an extended conversation with Thornbury.

* * *

"Are you here to complain about your part? You want more lines? More kissing? More killing?" Andrew grumbled to Patrick who stood just outside his door, having just knocked.

"Not as such," Patrick replied calmly then added, "May I come in?"

Andrew ran his tired hands through his already disheveled hair, biting back his reply. He looked as if he hadn't slept in days (he hadn't). This play was killing him and it showed.

"Is something wrong?" asked Patrick as he invited himself in. He took the chair across from the desk Andrew was sitting at— a desk strewn with scribbled notes and crumpled papers, heavily stained ink blotters and that old journal that Patrick had glanced at.

Andrew looked up at him, his eyes bleary and strained. "Is something wrong? *Wrong*? Well, let me see ... It seems like every time we have a rehearsal one or more of you *actors* insists on suddenly changing a line here or there, or maybe even an entire scene with new dialogue that makes no sense to the story, yet that insane old man, Lord Thornbury, claps his hands like a slow-witted child and insists that I rewrite the script to include that new thread of storyline—which, by the way, did I mention makes no BLOODY sense? And then, there's Nicholas, our esteemed director, who has but one bit of direction for me —when he's not shagging the innkeeper, of course—which is: 'When is the goddamn play going to be finished? We have a performance in a few days and that steaming pile of manure is nowhere near done!' And ever since the party Abigail will not leave me alone for a single bloody minute to write. I'm surprised she's not here now. Where is she? It's been ... let's see ... " He checks his pocket watch. "Oh my God, over forty minutes since she left! How ever do I manage? OH! And let's not forget the Scottish mountain of a man who pops in every day or so with some bleeding ridiculous suggestion for how he should play 'Scotland' for Christ's sake. I mean it's a bloody country not a person. How the hell am I supposed to write a part for a bleeding country? And then there's that creepy Gavin always lurking around, looking through my papers, re-arranging my pens, offering suggestions for props and story lines, lurking backstage, lurking side-stage, always lurking some bloody where when he's not turning lights on-and-off willy-nilly! What the bloody hell's up with him anyways? He's supposed to be drawing the curtains not be telling me who should kill who!"

Andrew paused for a breath. He glared defiantly at Patrick, who stared calmly back.

"Now," Andrew said, as he straightened some papers on his desk, a bit more composed, "what was it that *you* wanted?"

Patrick waited for as long as he could, allowing Andrew as much time as possible to calm down. He knew the question he was going to ask would not sit well, especially after Andrew's tirade, but he had to ask it.

"Well?" Andrew prodded.

"I was just wondering if you had any idea how the play was going to end?" Patrick asked with as much casualness as he could muster. He expected an exploded stream of profanities ending with a finger pointed to the door along with a window shattering shout of: 'GET OUT! NOW!' Instead, he got Andrew's blank stare, ending with a will-dissolving thud as his head smacked the desktop in resignation.

"No," he mumbled, his lips crammed into the polished hardwood desktop. "And it's killing me."

"Maybe I can help?" Patrick offered. "What do you have so far?"

Andrew kept his head pressed to the desktop as he slid the ancient journal across blindly to Patrick.

"It's all in there. The 'whole' story: the mystery, the mastery, ghosts and recipes and some diabolically simple conclusion somewhere. According to the old man, it's a *fait accompli*. Feel free to decipher it, I sure as bloody hell can't. I'm just going to sit here and rest. "

Patrick took the journal and thumbed through it again, this time with much more interest. Andrew began to snore.

* * *

Fiona arrived at the Broken Piper still very much aware of Sean's taste on her lips, the razor burn of his rough beard on her cheeks and his lingering smell.

What have I done?

She had gone to Sean to tell him to leave her alone, to tell him that she only had eyes for Patrick but ended up in his arms again and even worse, he claimed he loved her! What reason had he to love her? She treated him badly, she constantly berated him, and she threw herself at Patrick every chance she got.

Could he be misconstruing my lust as love? Did he actually really feel something for me beyond his moment of conquering?

No, she decided, *he doesn't love me! He doesn't even know me! How could he love me?*

She sat down on the nearest barstool. She did not want to think about what had just happened.

She was caught by the smell of fresh cut pine. Instantly, intense, pleasant childhood memories came forth. Fiona grinned like a schoolgirl when she saw the reflection in the mirror behind the bar, realizing that Christmas had arrived at The Broken Piper.

Miss McStargle had erected and completely decked out a Yule tree.

The air wafted with the smell of roasted nuts as Miss McStargle, dressed in a lovely red dress, burst in from the kitchen, holding a steaming tray of chestnuts.

"Ah, Fiona! Merry Christmas and grab yourself a nut while they're still hot."

Fiona laughed. "Merry Christmas!" She grabbed a very hot nut and had to toss it from hand to hand, trying to cool enough to eat.

"I love the tree!" Fiona exclaimed.

"Aye," McStargle agreed, glancing at it. "That dear Nicholas wandered out heaven knows where with axe in hand and came back with that beauty. He also brought me some of this." McStargle pulled out a sprig of mistletoe.

"Mistletoe?" Fiona asked.

"And I have some extra I could spare if you fancy a kiss from someone?" she winked.

Kissing was the last thing Fiona wanted to think about.

"No. Thanks," she replied sadly. "There's no one. You keep it."

Miss McStargle's face clouded.

"That's a shame surely. This is not the season to be alone. I wanted to get you good and kissed." She pushed some mistletoe into Fiona's hand. "Why not hold on to it just in case. I've got plenty."

Fiona accepted it, deciding to change the melancholy mood she seemed to have inspired.

"Thank you. How about I buy us a round of bitters to cheer in the evening?"

"Certainly!" McStargle brightened. "Two pints coming right up." She rushed over to pull the draughts.

Fiona remembered the finally cooled nut in her hand and popped it into her mouth.

"To absent friends! May this be the best Christmas ever!" McStargle toasted.

"To absent friends!" Fiona toasted back. They both took deep drinks from the cold pints.

"Oh my word!" McStargle announced suddenly, running towards the kitchen. "I have more nuts roasting!"

Fiona was happy to be alone with her thoughts, if even for a few minutes. She couldn't dismiss that tiny voice in the back of her mind telling her that everything *had* in fact changed and that she would have to deal with it sooner or later. *Sean loves you,* insisted the tiny undying voice. *But what about Patrick?*

And the answer that came both frightened and saddened her.

"He has never said he loved me," she whispered under her breath.

"Who has never said he loved you?" came a familiar voice from behind her.

Fiona turned and found Gavin standing behind her. He looked more confused and misplaced than usual.

"No one, just running lines," she lied, forcing a smile. "Join me? Miss McStargle and I were just toasting to absent friends."

"Sure. But, come now, Fiona," he insisted taking the seat next to her, "rehearsal is over for the day. Let it rest, after all we have the whole day off tomorrow."

Fiona nodded and grabbed her drink. Company with Gavin was the last thing she had wanted, but it appeared now that she was going to be stuck with him.

McStargle arrived from the back with more steaming nuts. She brightened, seeing Gavin. "Merry Christmas, Gavin! Fancy a nut and a wee pint?"

"Merry Christmas, Miss McStargle. Yes, please."

Behind Gavin's view, as she drew the pint, Miss McStargle slyly held up the mistletoe to Fiona and nodded toward Gavin. The horrified look on Fiona's face was all she needed to hurriedly put it back down and bring the beer to Gavin unaccompanied.

They drank in silence, all lost within their own thoughts.

Gavin broke the silence by ordering another round. He waited for McStargle to leave to get the drinks before he slid his stool closer to Fiona.

"So tell me, Fiona. What do you think of the new show?" he asked.

"It's fine," she replied noncommittally.

"From my perspective, it all seems very realistic. It's almost as if you and Sean and Patrick were really involved in some kind of a ... " He let his thought fade, too embarrassed to finish what he was implying.

Fiona, on the other hand, was not about to let him get away with that. She turned a steely gaze at him and asked, "Some kind of what?"

Gavin fidgeted a little, before replying. "Intense relationship. You know, like your characters. It's quite a story going on between the three of you."

"Four," Fiona corrected. "If you count Abigail."

"Right." Gavin conceded. "Actually it's just been a long time since I watched you onstage, from an audience point of view. Usually we are acting together. This is a unique perspective for me. You are very convincing and enchanting. I can see why the audience always falls in love with you," he finished, his eyes sweeping over hers, looking for answers to all his unasked questions.

"Thank you," Fiona replied, staring into her glass, avoiding his scrutiny.

Gavin studied her for a moment. He reached for her hand.

"Come now, Fiona, we are friends and old ones at that. Let's face it. You haven't been yourself lately. I can't ever remember seeing you in a pub drinking by yourself. What's wrong? You can tell me."

"It's nothing Gavin, just doing a little soul searching is all." She slid her hand out from his.

"Does this soul searching have something to do with Patrick? I've noticed he hasn't been around much lately. Must be hard for you."

Fiona blinked back her surprise.

"I am sorry Gavin, but I am not really in the mood for company right now."

She rose to leave.

"Fiona?" Gavin pleaded.

"I'll be okay. I really just need to be alone," Fiona replied as she rushed up the stairs.

Fiona arrived to her room hoping that Abigail would be there. Disappointedly, she wasn't. The room was cold, dark, and empty. She fell onto her bed, her mind reeling in despair. She took a few deep breaths but her mind wouldn't quiet down.

Sean. Sean. Sean.

Why couldn't she get Sean out of her head? What kind of hold did he have on her? She loved Patrick. She wanted Patrick. Or did she? Why was she still clinging to Patrick despite the way he was treating her? Once again she felt the overwhelming need to talk to Abigail.

Please, please come home, she silently begged. After a long moment she forced herself to sit up. *If I will it, perhaps Abigail will appear.*

She told herself not to think of anything else until her friend arrived. Abigail would know what to do.

Fiona rose and lit a fire in the fireplace. She glanced at the door expectantly. She listened hard for footsteps dancing up the creaking steps, as Abigail so often danced up them after a tryst with Andrew.

Everything was still. She sighed. She changed into her silk chemise and crawled into bed, still watching the door.

Christmas, it was almost Christmas day.

The feeling of Christmas was all around her and yet Fiona realized she would have to face this Christmas alone. Abigail would surely be spending the day with Andrew and it was quite obvious Patrick was not in the holiday spirit. At least she had a Christmas dinner to look forward to. Her troupe was her family now, she sighed, and it's not every year that you get to spend Christmas in a castle with your loved ones. Then, she thought of Sean. After what just happened she didn't even know if she could face him again. Maybe he won't show up, she hoped. It would be just like him to ruin Christmas.

Still, she missed the feeling of love at Christmas. She missed her mom and dad. She longed to spend one more Christmas Day with them in front of the fire telling stories. Her father spun funny, ridiculous, thinly disguised tales about a young mythical girl named *Fina* who was constantly wandering into trouble and mischief by not being polite or disobeying her parents, all the while Fiona would listen raptly, drinking her cocoa, as the smell of her mother's pies baking in the oven somehow wove their way into the tales, and Fina's reward would ultimately be a steaming fresh slice of apple or mince pie. She could almost smell the pie and hear her mother's lilting voice singing Christmas carols from the kitchen. She missed them all the time, but she deeply ached for them at this time of year.

Tonight, she thought again of her childhood friend, David. Ever since they were ten, they had made a pact that they would always share a sweet little kiss on Christmas Eve.

One particular Christmas Eve, many years ago, a huge snowstorm hit her parent's farm and Fiona sat in vigil at the frosted window, thinking sadly that this year David could not possibly show up. Although his parents' farm was the next one over, it was still almost five miles away. He would freeze to death before he got halfway there. Still, she hoped and waited, her nose resting on the cold glass. She wiped the mist from the window even as her warm breath instantly misted it back up.

Suddenly a figure had appeared in the snow.

Wearing a silly red hat and giant heavy coat of his dad's, David had walked all the way through the snow. She rushed to the front door to greet him. He kissed her cheek and she kissed his. He wished her a 'Merry Christmas!' then turned around and headed back into the snowstorm for the long walk home.

Fiona smiled at the memory. She hardly dared admit it, but more and more times lately she really missed David. *Had I not left* ...

She could not pursue that thought.

Fiona knew what she wanted to do. She rose, wrapped herself in her coat and raced downstairs.

The pub was empty. Fiona was relieved that Gavin must have gone to bed but she had hoped McStargle would still be up. Then she heard soft murmuring coming from the dimly lit dining area. She followed the sound to discover Miss McStargle and a slightly intoxicated and disheveled Nicholas, who wore a sprig of mistletoe on his head, sitting near the Christmas tree.

They glanced up when they noticed Fiona.

"I'm sorry to interrupt," Fiona apologized. She started to back away.

"Nonsense, dearie," Miss McStargle insisted. "It's Christmastime, the more the merrier. As a matter of fact I was just about to put the kettle on. Would you join us in a spot of tea?"

"Are you sure?" Fiona asked, hesitantly.

"Of course!" Nicholas bellowed. "By all means, join us!"

"Thank you," Fiona said as she went to sit besides Nicholas. "Some tea would be very nice."

"Can I get you anything else?" Miss McStargle asked, as she headed toward the kitchen.

"Actually, I was wondering if you had some bread I could have?" Fiona asked.

"Getting a late night hankering are you?"

"No, I want to leave it out in my room. My parents and I always left bread out for the nativity walk. I just thought it would be nice."

McStargle smiled. "Of course. There are some candles you can use, if you'd like. Unfortunately the mistletoe is occupied," she winked at Nicholas.

Fiona beamed. "I would love to light some candles, you can keep your mistletoe."

"I'll go fetch them." She disappeared in the back.

"You always are so sentimental, I find that charming, Fiona," Nicholas remarked. Fiona glanced at Nicholas. *He looks so happy, almost like he does on opening night.*

"Yes, I suppose I am. You should light one with me. Perhaps make it a new tradition. I'd rather like that."

"Why not?" Nicholas agreed, just as McStargle arrived back with the candles, tea and bread, "I'd be honored. Although I am not entirely sure what I am doing."

"You light a candle and leave it in the window so Mary and Joseph will see it as sign of welcome on their way to the Nativity. It's a lovely sentiment," McStargle replied, as she served the tea.

"What about the bread?" he asked, reaching for a slice of bread. McStargle playfully slapped his hand, forcing him to drop it back onto the plate.

"That's not for you!" she exclaimed.

"You leave bread out as a gift for Mary and Joseph, or even a passing wanderer," Fiona replied.

"Sounds wonderful," Nicholas agreed, rubbing his hand. "And what a perfect night to invite strangers into your home."

"Is it so different from the traditions you have in the States?" Fiona asked as she sipped her tea. Then added slyly over her cup. "I heard your lot liked to throw our tea in the ocean."

"Not my lot," Nicholas laughed. "And that was only the one time, and for tax reasons. But funny you should mention tea, because there is a rather obscure connection. Did you know the reason Jesus was born in Bethlehem was because Mary and Joseph had to pay their taxes to Caesar Augustus in the town of his lineage? Otherwise, Jesus probably would be have been born in Nazareth."

"I'm impressed," Fiona replied. "Tea parties aside, how else do you celebrate Christmas?

"Well the traditional *tannebaum* and caroling of course. And let me see ... we would leave out fresh baked cookies for Santa Claus–or Father Christmas, as I gather you call the old gent here–and some veggies for his reindeer, of course. And we'd hang stockings by the fire hoping for toys, but generally only found nuts and fruit. Oh, and we'd have a special night where we'd all get together to trim the tree with ornaments and tinsel, candles, and strings made out of popcorn and cranberries that we'd wind around and around the tree. I always liked that."

"Popcorn?" McStargle was astonished. "You mean that stuff you eat?"

"Of course! And believe me, my strands were always a bit lackluster after I'd eaten most of the popcorn off them," he chuckled. "My favorite part was waking up early Christmas morning and discovering all the presents left by Santa under the tree. My mother used to let me open one present on Christmas Eve–I never did figure out how Santa managed to drop off one present in advance–but it was always a pair of wool stockings to wear that night. My dad's favorite tradition was that he'd regard the socks with mock seriousness and say that we had been too naughty all year and that socks were all we'd be likely to get and should expect nothing the next morning, unless we went straight to bed and behaved like perfect children all night long. Which made my sister break down into tears as she ran off to bed, but the next day it always seemed like we had more toys than the year before."

"Sounds like a cruel man," McStargle joked. "No wonder he named you Nicholas."

"Cruel, but fair," Nicholas laughed.

"What no food for Mary and Joseph?" Fiona asked.

"Not that I'm aware of. But some people did put up miniatures of the Nativity in their house and sometimes in their yard."

"Savages! Popcorn on strings, cruel fathers, and a tiny Nativity?" McStargle laughed. "You call that Christmastime? Bah! Come!" she grabbed Nicholas by the hand and pulled him up to his feet. "We'll show you a proper holiday."

In a few minutes they had three candles lit in the windows and Fiona realized she had just spent Christmas Eve with a very fine makeshift family.

She wished them both a Merry Christmas with hugs and then went back to her room. Once in her room, she lit one more candle and placed the bread on the mantel above the fireplace. She stared at the flame as it bounced from side to side. She was reminded of her father again. Every night before she went to bed, he would lean over her candle and whisper, "It goes out so fast, even though love burns slow, when the candle goes out, there is still evidence of a glow."

She leaned over to blow out the candle and made a wish–actually more of a prayer–to always remember her family, be with her friends, and love, always love.

Then she blew out the candle.

* * *

Abigail entered Andrew's room unannounced, unbuttoning her blouse as she spoke, "Andy boy, it's Christmas Eve and I thought–what are *you* doing here?"

She was startled to see Patrick sitting at Andrew's desk. He looked up at her with a slight grin. "Put those away, Abby. Your lad's dead," he said.

She glanced over at Andrew face down on his desk, fast asleep.

"I don't know what you've done to the poor lad, but he's bloody well exhausted," Patrick added. "You'll kill him, you know. If you keep that up."

"Aye, but he hasn't been complaining none, 'as he?" Abigail asked embarrassed, as she buttoned her blouse.

"No, not as such, but he does have a play to finish, and he's not go'na finish it if you keep distracting him."

There was a slight edge in his tone that Abigail couldn't miss.

"Since when do you care about Andrew so much?" she asked, hesitating in the doorway. She had thoughts of ignoring Patrick and waking Andrew, or in the very least climbing into bed with him for the night–after all it was Christmas Eve–but something in Patrick's voice made her doubt if either was a wise choice.

"Actually, I don't," Patrick replied. "'The play's the thing', to quote a wise old gentleman. Don't you have someplace else to sleep? Your own bed perhaps?"

Abigail hesitated. She was tired, and the thought of the long, cold walk down to the pub did not appeal to her.

"I–I just don't wanna be making that long walk back in the cold ... " she pouted, hoping he would change his mind and wake Andrew.

Patrick tossed her his heavy coat. "Here, this should keep the chill off."

Abigail caught it, staggering back under the weight. She shrugged it on. She was dwarfed by the size and weight, but it was warm and it carried Patrick's musky odor. She glanced again at Andrew's sleeping form and wished that he would wake up and take her in his arms. He snored loudly once and rolled over, turning his back to her.

Some Christmas Eve this was turning out to be.

"Merry Christmas," Patrick insisted. "I'll let Andrew know you stopped by. I'm sure he'll be very glad to see you in the morning."

Abigail smiled chastely, and then turned to leave.

* * *

Fiona awoke with a peculiar tickling feeling that she was being watched. She turned her head towards the fire to let her eyes adjust. She discovered that she was, indeed, not alone.

Sean leaned against the fireplace mantel, clutching a bottle while chomping on the slice of bread Fiona had left out. He stared at her silently. Fiona let out a startled gasp and reached for the comforter that had slipped down.

Sean watched bemused, but did not move.

"Sean! What in God's name are you doing here?"

Sean was dressed in a slept-in looking shirt, wrinkled pants, and bare feet, although, Fiona noted, he was surprisingly clean-shaven since she last left him. He brought the bottle up to his lips and took a deep drink, washing down the stale bread before replying.

"You ... " he more breathed than spoke, as he pointed at her. "Never came back."

Fiona sat up higher in bed and prayed that he was not drunk.

God was not listening.

"I should hate you!" he blurted out, gesturing so wildly that some liquor flew out from the bottle and splashed into the fire causing a small flare-up that seemed to accentuate his anguish.

"Sean, it's probably best if you go home and sleep this off. We can talk tomorrow–"

"Do you *know* why I should hate you?" he slurred as he tried to take a step forward, then decided that he was better off with the wall's support. He fell back against it, hitting it with a loud thud. For some reason he found this funny. He chuckled for a moment. "I *should* hate you because that's exactly what you *want* me to do. It would give you reason to hate *me*, but I won't give you the sat-satis-satisfaction." He nodded, profoundly.

He tried walking again. This time he managed to take two steps towards her. He stood in the center of the room, swaying.

"You ... you make me bloody insane! I say 'I love you' and you leave. I wait for you to come back ... you know, you know ... and you never do. I even shaved my bloody beard off again."

He paused to stare at her, rubbing his bare chin thoughtfully.

"And you wonder why *I* drink so bleeding much?"

"Sean ... " Fiona began.

"No. You listen! I *caught* you as you sang some bleeding song to that horse's arse *Garvin*. Then *you* kissed *me*. Fine."

"Sean ... " Fiona tried again. He halted her with a raised hand. He wasn't done.

"As you well know, we did much more than kiss in the cellar ... "

The fire popped loudly, and he turned, bleary-eyed and confused, to look at the flames.

"Why did you burn your clothes? Because I touched them?" he asked, bitingly.

"Aye, the dress was ripped because of you," Fiona answered. "I didn't want to explain it."

"I liked that dress!" Sean said, turning back toward her. "You looked ... "

"Please Sean, just leave," she pleaded.

"No!" He shouted. "I will *not* go back to my bloody empty room with its bloody broken bed and table to wait for you to not come back again."

Sean moved closer on unsteady feet. His voice was now a confused, babbled whisper.

"Maybe if? What if I was more like Paddy? I could try, try to be a wee bit more of a bastard. Keep you close, but stay out of your bed?"

He towered over Fiona, who was huddled against the headboard of her bed. He leaned his face in very close to hers.

"Or do ya really think Patrick will even want to touch you now, once he knows I have already had me way with his sweet–?"

He was cut off with a sudden, hard slap to his face. Fiona's anger had flared and she had moved her hand so quick that her action caught them both by surprise. Sean lost his grip on the bottle. It fell and broke on the hard wooden floor.

"Stop it!" she shoved him back roughly, pleading.

Sean took a few awkward steps backwards. A shard of glass sliced into his bare sole, instantly drawing blood.

"Ouch! What the fook?" He pulled the imbedded glass out while balancing on one foot. He lost his balance and fell heavily onto the bed just as Fiona scrambled off it, her comforter now forgotten.

"You make it sound as if I planned all of this!" she screamed down at his confused face. "I didn't! You deciding that you love me changes nothing!"

Sean sat dumbfounded not able to take his eyes off of her. In her haste, Fiona had flung her covers aside and was standing in front of him in nothing but a thin night chemise. The fire behind her outlined her body. Sean's gaze changed to a look of drunken lust.

"Aye. So you say, but I don't believe you," came Sean's reply. He reached out to grab her arms, trying to pull her close to him on the bed.

"Let go of me!" Fiona protested, struggling.

Sean was so distracted by the feel of her struggling body and her heat rising through the silk, that he could barely think straight.

"I close my eyes and you're there. I open my eyes and you're *not* there. You feel the same way."

"No!" Fiona screamed, pushing him back onto the bed. "You've ruined everything! I was so happy before you!"

"*Happy*?" he bellowed, as he rose painfully on his bleeding foot. "With *Patrick*? Nah. You were in love with the bloody idea of a man, not a real man!"

Fiona raised her hand to slap him again, but this time he caught it and held it tight in his.

"Tell me you love him. Lie to me like you've been lying to yourself," he dared.

Sean stared hard at her, waiting. Fiona's breasts heaved as she stared back, the words trying to form on her lips.

"Well?"

Fiona wavered. She stared deep into Sean's eyes, taking a moment before she finally spoke.

"Why did you come here, Sean?"

"I told you, I love you."

"And I heard you," Fiona snapped back.

"But you never answered! I wanted ... I needed ... " he tried desperately to find the right words but his eyes kept going back to Fiona in the firelight. "God damn it, Fiona! Why do you have to be wearing that! I can't think straight!"

"Maybe you shouldn't drink so much, then you would be able to think straight enough not barge into a woman's bedroom in the middle of the night!"

"Aye, and maybe you should lock your door!"

Awareness grew in his eyes. He hadn't come here to scold her. He let his temper calm.

"That night. Did it mean nothing to you?"

"More than you can ever know," she admitted. "It means that I doubt I can ever lie with another man and not think of you. Is that the answer you wanted to hear?"

"No," he grabbed her a little more roughly than he intended. "I don't want to ever think of you with another man."

"Let go of me!" she cried, twisting, trying to break free from his now very tight grip.

"No," he answered. "I can't."

She pushed again and somehow managed to free herself. She turned to move, but Sean caught her from behind and held her with one arm draped across her chest and the other wrapped around her waist. She felt his heart racing against her back, very much aware of the strength of his body locked against hers.

Slowly, gently, his lips found her neck, brushing it lightly.

"He never deserved you," he whispered.

"And you do?"

"Nah. Not me. Never." His cheek brushed hers, as he moved to whisper in her ear. "How I ache for you."

Fiona leaned back in his arms touched by what he said, but she was unable to think clearly beyond that. It was as if her mind had drifted to blissful static. There was a low, wonderful humming all around her and she didn't dare speak.

"Fiona," he beckoned. His hands were moving now; one tightened its hold across her chest while the other began a slow glide up her leg. The brilliant hum was growing, wiping out the world surrounding them. She closed her eyes to try and find her bearings, to have a moment of lucid thought.

"Forgive me," she whispered.

"What?" he turned her around, to try and better read her. "Forgive you?"

"Forgive me for acting like I would rather have anyone else but you."

Sean stared at her stupidly, the weight of her words having trouble sinking to a depth of proper understanding.

"You don't want me?"

"No, I do. I always have; I was just too foolish to admit it."

"And Patrick?"

She leaned forward, her lips biting into his once, before gently kissing him. He returned it with a deep, passionate kiss that quite literally took her breath away, as he backed her up against the bed.

Fiona felt her knees buckle as they pressed up against the mattress. She was having trouble breathing, her thoughts once again swimming. His hands drifted over her body in gentle caresses felt through the thin, shifting silk of her chemise. She needed to break the kiss just to catch her breath but didn't dare.

Finally he pulled away and she surfaced with deep gasps of air. As if in slow motion, she felt herself floating backwards against the downy soft bed. She found herself completely naked, looking up at Sean holding the thin chemise in his hands.

"No bloody ribbons this time," he grinned. He tossed the chemise away as he began unbuttoning his shirt, his eyes sweeping over her.

"Come to me," she whispered.

And he did.

Exhausted and covered in the sheen of sweat, they lay side-by-side in silence. Only the occasional popping of a bursting knot of wood in the dying fire broke the stillness.

Sean rolled to his side to stare at Fiona. The flickering firelight illuminated her. She looked like an elegant portrait, like a golden painting one might see in a museum and be content to stand and admire all day long, but never touch. But he *had* touched her. And she had touched him.

"Okay, go ahead, I'm ready," Sean said, breaking the silence.

"What?" she turned her head to gaze back at him.

"Isn't this the part where you start yelling, kicking, and biting me?"

"Do you want me to yell, kick and ... hey! When did I ever bite you?"

"Well, never. But you did do—"

"Shhh!" she laughed, placing her finger on his lips.

"Aye," Sean complied and he pulled her into his arms.

Fiona wrapped herself in his embrace and tried to relax. This was a moment she wanted to savor and remember. But she couldn't totally relax as she was unable to stop her mind from wandering to the last time she had spooned with a different Berenger boy.

With a sigh, she admitted her thoughts.

"We can't tell him," she whispered. "Not yet."

"After the show," Sean agreed.

Fiona nodded and nestled in closer to him, hoping for all their sakes that he was right. She realized she had no idea how Patrick would react, but if things went badly and she never saw him again, she was surprised to note that she didn't feel the great sadness she had expected.

"You were right, you know," she murmured, sleepily.

"Was I now?" Sean replied with a hint of playfulness. "About what?"

"About me being in love with an idea. I was afraid for so long that if I let go of that idea, that image of what I thought I wanted, I would realize just how much of a fool I was and how really alone I am ... *was*," she corrected, as she yawned.

"I have no idea what you just said," he confessed, as he leaned in to kiss her forehead.

Fiona sighed. The warmth of his body, the sound of his breathing, and the crackling fireplace lulled her to sleep.

* * *

Abigail headed up the stairs, cold and tired. Fiona would most likely be sound asleep, and any questions about why she wasn't spending the night with Andrew on Christmas Eve as planned, she could deal with in the morning.

She turned the knob to their room.

She had no response prepared as she entered their room and discovered a nude Fiona sleeping beside an also very nude Sean Berenger.

A smile crossed her face as she stood frozen in the doorway. She had always assumed more had happened that night in the cellar than Fiona had let on, but never this much. However, she was no fool, she noticed the way they had looked at each other since, like small children who made a point of avoiding each other as they attempted to keep a secret.

She was happy for her friend. Finally Fiona had found someone who would actually love her back, but now was not the time to tell her. Now was the time to find a way out of the situation she had just inadvertently walked into.

Stifling a giggle, Abigail stepped further into the room and slammed the door with such a force that it shook the walls. *That ought to do it,* she thought.

Fiona's eyes popped opened suddenly with sound of the slamming door. Her first thought was that Sean had for some reason left in a huff. She was relieved to see Sean sprawled next to her, still asleep. Then she heard giggling.

Blinking her eyes in the gloomy light, Fiona could just make out a small figure in a large coat. It was Abigail. She giggled again.

"Sorry, I didn't mean to ... I'll just go out in the hallway for a couple of minutes and then I'll come back in, okay?"

Abigail left without waiting for an answer.

"Well, we've been found out," Sean said, surprising Fiona that he was awake.

"She'll be fine," Fiona replied, sitting up. "She can hold her tongue. I suppose you'd best go though, before the whole town knows."

"Aye, probably a wise idea." He rose and went to where his pants lay on the floor. He paused, hopefully, halfway in the act of pulling them on. "Although I'd rather stay, you do look amazing."

Fiona blushed. She knew she didn't, still she smiled at him. "It's probably the dim light. I'm sure I look a horror."

Sean shook his head in mock disgust. He pulled his pants all the way up then reached for his shirt and put it on without paying any mind to his buttons as he crossed the room to find Fiona's night chemise. Once found, he tossed it to her.

Fiona put the chemise on and slid out of bed to him. She reached out to stop his fumbling fingers and finished buttoning his shirt for him.

Then she kissed his cheek.

"Merry Christmas," she said.

"Aye, that it is," he grinned, his eyes twinkling. He pulled her into a full kiss that left echoes of warmth throughout her body.

"Until later," he whispered. Without another word he limped out, leaving Fiona wanting.

Gavin's eyes popped open as the sound of the slamming door resonated through his room. He was on his feet in no time, scrambling for his clothes, ready to aid Fiona in whatever trouble she was in.

Samuel mumbled in his sleep, apparently deeply invested in a dream. Gavin didn't bother to wake him.

Gavin rushed into the hallway just in time to see Sean standing in front of Fiona's closing door. Through the small gap he saw Abigail's face disappearing behind the door with a wry grin, apparently meant for Sean who was trying to peer past her into the room as she shut the door.

"What the hell are you doing here?" Gavin demanded.

Sean turned slowly to gaze at Gavin. A look of immediate distaste came over him.

"Bloody caroling," he replied, as he pushed past him towards the stairs. Sean began to sing, in a raspy voice: "Good King Wenceslas looked out on the feast of Stephen when the snow lay round about deep and crisp and even. Brightly shone the moon that night though the frost was cruel ... "

Gavin caught the heavy scent of whiskey on Sean's breath and noticed that his clothing was in disarray. Assuming that Sean had just arrived, drunk as usual, and tried to force himself on the girls, he became instantly furious. He grabbed Sean roughly by the shoulder and twisted him around.

"You stay away from them, you sodden bastard! You hear? I know all about–"

"You don't know shite," Sean replied calmly as he stiff-armed Gavin hard against the wall. Gavin crumbled to the floor.

Sean casually continued on his way singing: "When a poor man came in sight, Gath'ring winter fuel ... "

His voice faded down the stairs.

Samuel, groggy and rubbing his eyes, appeared beside Gavin. His massive form looked ridiculously boyish in a long nightshirt and cap.

"What's all this noise, eh?" he muttered.

"Bloody carolers," Gavin spat, as he rose. He pushed past Samuel and headed back to his room, chagrined.

"What? At this time of night?" Samuel mused.

Gavin paused just outside Fiona's room. He could hear the frantic voices of Abigail and Fiona whispering to one another. He tried to make out what they were saying but couldn't. He heard Abigail squeal with ribald laughter, then Fiona's honey-coated response, just a sensuous mumble, but it made him mad with desire for her. Gavin fumed in impotence.

Samuel, enchanted by the unexpected, late-night caroler, softly continued it: "Sire, the night is darker now, and the wind blows stronger, fails my heart, I know not how, I can go no longer ... "

Gavin couldn't believe his ears.

Everyone's insane! He thought, as he slammed the door to his room.

Christmas morning arrived quietly on a blanket of steadily falling snow and stilled wind. There was to be no rehearsal today, a free morning for all, with a gala Christmas feast to be attended by any who wished at Thornbury Castle beginning at three in the afternoon.

This was one of very few days the troupe had been off since the rehearsals started. Fiona slept in late, and as she awoke, the memories of last night swept in like some wonderful dream. So unbelievable was last night that she planned on blissfully storing it to memory for a later review. Then she noticed Abigail's lascivious grin and sparkling eyes staring at her and she realized she would have to talk about it now.

"Merry Christmas," Abigail said innocently. "*Sleep* well?"

Fiona blushed. "It did happen, didn't it?" Fiona asked, hesitantly.

"Well, I wasn't there for the whole event, but if I had to use my imagination based on the amount of skin I saw—"

"Stop!" Fiona laughed, embarrassed, throwing a pillow at Abigail to shut her up. "I remember. I remember."

Abigail grinned. "I should hope so! Now, should we pop down for a ploughman's breakfast while you give me all the juicy details?"

She threw the pillow back at Fiona.

"You must be famished after all that ploughing!"

Andrew raised his head from the desk. The blotter left a large crease imprinted on his cheek where he had pressed against it. He was surprised to find Patrick in his room staring at a sheaf of papers in his hands.

"Patrick?"

Patrick looked over at the sleepy youth. He grinned. "Awake at last?"

Andrew sat up stiffly. His bones popped as he stretched.

"Yeah. I suppose. So what are you doing here?"

"Merry Christmas," Patrick said, tossing the papers to Andrew. "I finished your script for you."

Andrew clumsily caught the thrown papers. "You did what?"

"Now you can spend the whole day with your lass. She popped in earlier, by the way."

"Abigail was here?" Andrew asked, paging through the script with interest. "And you didn't wake me?"

Patrick rose, equally stiff and weary. "You seemed so shagged, we both thought it be best if you took a long kip."

"That was kind of you both," Andrew said distractedly, his nose buried in the pages.

"Are you leaving?" he asked, finally looking up.

Patrick was already gone.

Sean awoke to find Samuel bent over his stove noisily intent on making coffee. Thankfully his kilt was long enough to not expose any more than it did.

Sean's head felt like it was in a vise, and the clanging of pots, swearing, and slamming down of the coffee can did not help. He peered at Samuel with unfocused eyes nearly glued shut with sleep. Sean tried to speak, but all that came out of his dry and swollen mouth was: "Aghhh ... "

Sean tried to rise from his severely canted bed, but couldn't find the strength. All he could muster was to feebly raise and wave his arm, in the hopes that Samuel might notice. Eventually Samuel did, but not until he had the stove burning at full flame under the battered coffee pot.

"Sean!" Samuel beamed. Snow still caked his thick beard, his cheeks ruddy from the chill outside. "Good morning to ya!"

Sean nodded with what he hoped was enough of a rejoinder.

"Seems someone was up too late caroling. Coffee be ready in a wee second. I brought my tools!" Samuel shouted, causing Sean to wince visibly.

"That's good ... wait? What?" Sean managed to croak.

"I'm Father Christmas!" Samuel laughed. He poured out two cups of coffee.

"Well you do have the beard," Sean said more to himself than to Samuel, who had strode over and handed him a burning mug of black coffee.

"Aye, that I do," Samuel agreed, taking a deep gulp, the scalding coffee having no seeming effect on his throat.

Sean gingerly lifted the mug to his lips, about to allow a mere trickle to burn his throat, when Samuel plopped heavily down onto the bed beside him. The bed creaked dangerously and the mug slopped burning coffee down Sean's chest and lap.

"Holy Mother of God!" Sean screamed as he tried to brush the searing liquid off him.

"Is it too hot?" Samuel asked.

"Bloody hell! Yes it's too hot! What are you trying to do, fookin' kill me?"

"What, on Christmas? Don't be daft. I came here to give you your present."

Sean stopped wiping away at the coffee. He looked up at the grinning giant. *"Present?"*

"Aye. That's why I brought me tools. I'm a gonna fix your bed, once you get your lazy arse out of it." Then Samuel noticed the collapsed table for the first time. "And I suppose your table as well. You sure be rough on the furniture."

"Aye," Sean said. "And thank you. Merry Christmas, old bean."

Samuel smiled a huge Father Christmas grin.

"Merry Christmas."

* * *

"Christmas brings us all good things. God give us grace to see the New Year, and if we do not increase in numbers may we at all events not decrease."

"Here! Here!" they cheered Father McLeary's toast. They were gathered in the library, back where it all began just a few scant months ago, although this gathering included a few additional faces, namely Father McLeary, McStargle, and Jeppsen, minus one conspicuous corpse.

Christmas dinner was sumptuous and masterfully prepared by McStargle. Served at three-thirty just as full darkness was setting in, it was a traditional feast beginning with cock-a-leekie soup followed by *bubbly jock,* explained to Nicholas as Scottish for roast turkey, and heaping plates of roast potatoes, oat and sage stuffing, neeps (turnips) carrots, and a thick gravy to drown it all. Dessert was Christmas pudding, Clootie dumpling, and an assortment of fruits and cheeses. Wine, champagne, whiskey, and cider flowed freely.

Explosions of laughter and paper stringers filled the air and covered the guests as 'crackers' were popped open and the multi-colored crowns hidden within were examined, traded, or playfully coveted. Naturally everyone wore his or her brightly colored paper crowns, especially Carlisle, who found the only golden crown, which he bore upon his snowy head with majestic dignity.

Now, completely satiated, they sat before a roaring fire as tea, coffee, brandy, and cakes were served. Some smoked, some mused, some shared glances with secrets in their eyes. After the obligatory murmured compliments and reminiscences of the feast, all fell silent into their private worlds.

Suddenly, Carlisle broke out with a complete non sequitur recitation.

"'The story had held us, round the fire, sufficiently breathless, but except the obvious remark that it was gruesome, as, on Christmas Eve in an old house, a strange tale should essentially be, I remember no comment uttered till somebody happened to say that it was the only case he had met in which such a visitation had fallen on a child. The case, I may mention, was that of an apparition in just such an old house as had gathered us for the occasion–an appearance, of a dreadful kind, to a little boy sleeping in the room with his mother and waking her up in the terror of it; waking her not to dissipate his dread and soothe him to sleep again, but to encounter also, her, before she had succeeded in doing so, the same sight that had shaken him'. I'm sorry, that's all I can remember."

"That's from the 'Turn of the Screw' by Henry James. Right?" Andrew proclaimed proudly.

"Spot on, laddie!" Carlisle beamed. "It's the perfect Christmas ghost story, it is. One of my favorites, I've read it so often it feels real to me."

"And here's your prize!" Abigail shouted, holding the mistletoe over Andrew's head as she plopped into his lap and gave him a big, noisy kiss. Abigail had been making judicious use of the mistletoe all evening, having 'stolen' kisses from all the men including a very chaste peck on the cheek to Father McLeary.

"And this is another Scot's Christmas tradition, I take it?" Nicholas asked, puffing on his cigar. "Telling spooky stories by firelight?"

"Aye," Miss McStargle agreed. "It goes way back. Not sure why, but a lovely tradition it is."

"Lovely," laughed Nicholas. "Must be that the very long nights need filling."

"Aye, but we have other ways to fill them," McStargle cooed.

Nicholas blushed.

"Perhaps someone should impart another tale," Father McLeary suggested.

"I know one," Gavin announced. "A true one."

Everyone turned to regard him.

He had been rather quiet all evening, silently studying each guest as if they were insects under a microscope. Several times Fiona attempted to bring him into the congenial conversational flow swirling around the table, only to have him politely respond with a monosyllabic grunt or nod. Eventually, she simply shrugged him off, assuming he was perhaps waxing nostalgic about absent friends or family.

It had been a most interesting evening for Fiona. She was seated between Patrick and Sean, a choice that made her very nervous at first, but miraculously there were no fireworks. Sean was surprisingly civil all evening, keeping their new-found romance so discrete, that if it weren't for the thrilling feel of his hand sliding up her thigh during the pudding course, she might have thought he had forgotten last night's escapade.

Patrick, on the other hand, seemed totally his old self: laughing, telling stories, and toasting. At one point when Patrick turned to deliver the punch line of a bawdy joke to Fiona their eyes met, and his hand rested on her knee, briefly. Fiona felt a momentary twang of sadness and regret. He now seemed so open, trusting, and vulnerable. She felt a certain sadness realizing that her relationship with Patrick could never be the same, that even their friendship could be jeopardized by the news that was coming. It was the only dark cloud hovering near an otherwise joyous evening.

"Do tell it!" boomed Jeppsen encouragingly to Gavin, bringing Fiona back to the present. "I love a good shivery tale!"

Fiona wasn't sure if it had something to do with the bandages wrapped around his head, or some desire not to be neglected now that he was included in the 'inner circle' as it were, but she noticed that ever since Jeppsen's accident he seemed to bellow out all his words. Or perhaps it was all the drinking she had done this evening that was making her ears ring a bit. No bother. She too, was up for a 'good shivery tale.'

Gavin required little encouragement. "If you insist," his voice lowered to a spooky whisper, "but I must warn you, it is a strange and frightening tale."

"Oh no!" squealed Abigail. "I hate ghost stories."

"Then you are most definitely in the wrong castle," Gavin whispered, ghoulishly.

Abigail climbed into Andrew's lap, while chairs were scooted in and everyone's attention was turned to Gavin.

"This is a story I heard as a wee lad. It's about a haunted town, and place where evil liked to lurk. It was said to have happened very near here," he began. "The town's name has been lost, erased from maps, refused to be even spoken by any that care to remember it even existed."

"What's the name of it?" asked Abigail, as she snuggled deeper into Andrew's lap.

"Shhh!" Andrew insisted. "I want to hear this. Go on, Gavin."

"This town wasn't always evil. There was a time when the residences were happy, the children laughed and played, the church bells rang every Christmas Eve ... until one Christmas Eve when *she* arrived.

"The church bells had just started to ring for midnight mass when she suddenly appeared in the doorway.

"She was as devastatingly beautiful as she was dark and wispy. They say she had tombstone eyes and lips so pale they were nearly blue. No one knows from which direction the evil wind blew her in from, or why she chose this town, but she did ... "

As Gavin's story spun on, Fiona tuned him out as she reflected on all that had happened since they first received the summons to come here. Everyone's life had changed in some way, either subtly or majorly. And who knew what lay in the days ahead? They still had a play to perform, and she had a major confrontation to deal with. And after that, what? What additional changes were to come? Would they part and all go their separate ways? Would this be the last week she spent with all of them together? That thought brought a deep sadness to her.

Then she caught Carlisle's stare. He smiled knowingly at her, something in his soft eyes seem to say, 'dinna worry Lass, I know what's ahead and it will be beautiful'. She smiled back at him just as Gavin's story was coming to an end.

" ... And in the same manner as she arrived, she left. The church bells tolled their final mass, but there was no one left to hear them and no one left to ring them."

Gavin let the last words settle like falling snow.

The room was silent.

Outside, above the whistling wind, the church bell began to ring the midnight hour.

Abigail shrieked. "The bells!"

Father McLeary looked concerned. "I wonder who's ringing them?"

"He's making it all up!" accused Jeppsen. "He's not even from around here!"

"He *is* making it up, right?" Abigail asked Andrew with a shudder as the bell kept ringing.

"I don't know," whispered Andrew, holding her tighter.

Once again the room became silent, unsettled, as they listened to the church bells ringing, not sure what to think. Gavin relished the uneasiness he had created. He had told the story well, complete with unique voices for each character and appropriate dramatic rise and fall. Abigail had squeaked in fright during several particularly spooky moments and, best of all, he now had Fiona's complete attention.

"Jolly good!" bellowed Nicholas suddenly, as he rose to get a drink. "Make a hell of a children's play." His jovial outburst broke the tension in the room.

Gavin was stunned. *A children's play?*

Sean checked his watch. "Bell's are running a bit early aren't they Father? I have eleven fifty-one."

Father McLeary stammered, clearly confused. "But they shouldn't be ringing at all. There is no one there to ring them."

"I don't understand," Abigail said, pale as a ghost. "Was he talking about our town?"

"No," Andrew whispered back without much conviction. "It's just a story."

"Yes, a ripping good yarn!" exclaimed Patrick jollily, rising. "I'm sure it's just the wind blowing the bells about. A bit of good luck there, quite a capper!"

He slapped Gavin heartily on the back. "Good job. And not to spoil the swell, creepy mood but I do believe Andrew has an announcement that he's been waiting all evening to make."

"I do?" Andrew asked, startled.

"Yes. You do." Patrick asserted. "Don't be so modest."

"What is it, Andy?" asked Abigail.

Now all attention was diverted from Gavin to Andrew. Gavin had enjoyed his momentary basking in attention, especially Fiona's, but now Patrick had gone and ruined it.

Damn him! He fumed. *Damn them all!*

"Well," Andrew began, he really had no idea what Patrick was talking about, then it hit him. *The play!* The play was finished. But he hadn't finished it, Patrick had. Andrew hadn't even finished reading it. What was he supposed to say?

Patrick came to his rescue.

"Andrew's too modest. Not a clever trait in an up-and-coming writer, but we'll forgive him that, as it is Christmas. Anyway," continued Patrick as he raised his glass indicating a toast, "the fact of the matter is that not only has Andrew finished the play, but I have had the honor of being the first to read it and may I say that it is simply brilliant! Here! Here!"

"Here! Here! Author!" the others chimed in, glasses raised. "Congratulations! Good job. Well done!"

They surrounded a blushing Andrew, asking questions and congratulating him.

Only Jeppsen noticed Gavin slink out of the room.

A howling came, followed by a room-startling rattle of the thick paned window. Samuel glanced outside. The storm had worsened.

"It's neither a fit night for man nor beast out there," he remarked, as he returned to the bar to pour a refill from the glass decanter of scotch.

"I heard on the wireless this morning that a fierce Nor'easter was expected." Carlisle called out. "The storm of the Century they predict. I took the liberty of having Jeppsen prepare rooms in the castle for all of you, in anticipation."

"That's very kind of you," Fiona said. The others agreed.

Carlisle adjusted his crown nervously. "I did have an ulterior motive, I must admit."

"And what might that be?" Sean asked, somewhat suspicious, as he joined Samuel at the bar.

"To have my family," he threw out his arms to include them all, "surround me on this Christmas evening."

"And a merry one at that," Sean replied, as he toasted. "To our fine host. A gentleman, a scholar, and a royal sneak."

They laughed as they shared the toast.

The night passed with more drinks, more stories, more longing looks between couples. Fiona felt her inhibitions slipping away with the night. For the first time in a very long time, she felt at home.

The guests began leaving two by two. First to leave were Abigail and Andrew. Andrew had had enough of Abigail racing around with her mistletoe and stealing kisses from other men. He snatched it from her hand as she taunted him with it, pulled her into his lap and kissed her fiercely. He tossed the mistletoe onto a nearby table and stood up with her in his arms.

"Good night, and a Merry Christmas to all!"

Jeppsen rose to escort them out, but Andrew waved him down. "No need Jeppsen, I believe I can find my own room."

"And the young lady's?" Jeppsen sputtered.

"She can find my room as well!" Andrew grinned.

The others called out farewells as Andrew bowed, and with Abigail still giggling in his arms, he turned and swept out of the room. There was a moment of silence before everyone broke out into rowdy laughter.

"And I always thought writers were meant to be taciturn and unromantic," Nicholas laughed.

"It's always the quiet ones you must watch out for," Miss McStargle stated with saucy nuance.

"Well!" announced Nicholas, "then I say we make a quiet departure. Silent Night and all that." He rose and offered Miss McStargle his hand. "My lady?"

"How charming." She said, lasciviously, as she grabbed his hand and was led out the door. A drunken, off-key chorus of 'Deck the Halls' could be heard down the hall.

"Blind eyes! I am turning a blind eye," Father McLeary grinned, as he rose. "You lot remind me of a life I could have led." He crossed himself dramatically. "I expect to see you all in confession, but not too early," he warned as he refreshed his drink. He then rejoined Samuel in their continuing conversation of Scotland's history and the current worries of the church.

Carlisle yawned, then rose on legs shaky with age and drink.

"Well, this has been a most wonderful evening. One I shall cherish forever, although sadly these old bones must rest. But please, I beg you all to stay and freely partake from all my wine and stores. Jeppsen, if you'd be so kind to escort me back to my room I will bid adieu to these fine folks."

The others thanked him and wished him a fine sleep. Jeppsen took his hand and slowly the bandaged servant and the crowned host slipped away.

A fine silence settled over Patrick, Fiona and Sean as they sat in a semi-circle around the fire, lost in their own thoughts. Only the soft conversation of Samuel and Father McLeary and the occasional popping of dry wood in the fire filled the air. The wind howled again, rattling the windowpane and breaking into their thoughts.

"Father Christmas will have had a terrible time delivering gifts tonight," Fiona joked.

"Aye, probably be blown across the channel to Ireland and just give up on us Scots," Patrick agreed.

"Actually, I believe he stops in Ireland first, us being more deserving and all," Fiona stated with a wicked grin.

Patrick retorted, in his heaviest Scot's accent, "And how would that be, then Missy?"

"Well, you are a thieving, conniving lot of trouble boys, aren't you? I should expect the great Santy Claus would have little, if anything, left for the Berenger boys," she said, not daring to look Patrick in the eye for fear of laughing.

Patrick rose in feigned indignation. "Why, I will not have you slander my brother's name like that!"

"She may have a point there, brother," Sean said, pulling him back down. "Although I believe she was referring to you."

He turned confidingly to Fiona, "Paddy here always hid near the chimney on Christmas night, hoping to jump out and surprise Santa into dropping his bag."

"Why I have never heard of anything so vile!" she exclaimed in mock shock.

"Oh, don't you sell me so rotten, *Seany*." He grabbed Fiona's arm to get her attention away from him. "Sean here always hid my presents, telling me I received nothing because I was a bleeding wanker and Santy knew it."

"And how you would cry, Paddy!"

"I didn't cry!" he protested.

"Waaaa! Why does Santy hate me so?" Sean cried, imitating Patrick's small child wail.

"I never! You're making that up!" whined Patrick, instantly transported back to the days of being the younger brother and always picked on.

"Am I?" Sean replied, smirking. "Then how come you're doing it right now?"

For the first time, Fiona could see how they must have been as little boys.

She placed her hand on Patrick's arm. "I am sure if you cried, it was his fault. He never should have hidden your gifts."

"Thank you, Fee." Patrick replied, placing his hand on her leg. "It's nice to have someone stand up for me. Where were you when I was five?"

"In Ireland. Rolling in all the gifts Santa left me for being such a good little girl," she smirked.

Sean laughed. "Aye, she would have never been seen with the likes of us back then. A little lady, she was, tea parties and dolls and gentleman callers."

"I did not have tea parties!"

"Cotillions, then. Either way we were never invited," Patrick said, acting hurt. Sean nodded in sympathy. This was a game they knew how to play, and play well.

"But I didn't even know you then," she wailed. "And I only had *one* doll, Sally!"

"Only one doll eh? I thought you said Santa brought you loads of gifts," Sean retorted.

"No. I mean yes, of course I had other gifts, but Sally was my best—"

"So, you are saying that Sally, a mere potato-headed doll, was held to a higher esteem than us Berenger's? That she was invited to your myriad soirees, but not my dear brother *Patrick*?"

"Nor even *Sean*?" added Patrick, in mock outrage.

"What? No! I never invited Sally to ... as a matter of fact I never even had a single soiree or cotill—"

"That is so like you to drag poor Sally into this, Sean!" Patrick exclaimed suddenly taking Fiona's side, confusing her even more.

"And she didn't have a potato head, she was porcelain and ... and ... " she noticed their barely suppressed grins and realized she had been played. "And you two are incorrigible!" she tried to play mad, but couldn't maintain it.

The two bullying brothers laughed.

"Aye, little miss sweet Fee," Sean said sweetly, "you did ask for it."

Patrick agreed.

With the ice broken, they passed another hour filled with stories of childhood.

Eventually, Fiona rose to leave, staggering a bit as she wished the brothers a Merry Christmas. Awkwardly, they both rose simultaneously to escort her but she waved them back down.

"No. You two stay and enjoy the evening. I can find my room."

Reluctantly, both brothers sat back down.

Fiona crossed to Samuel and Father McLeary and gave them both kisses on the cheek and wished them goodnight. She was halfway across the room before Patrick stopped her.

"Fee, hold up one minute."

Fiona turned to face the fast approaching Patrick.

"I just wanted to wish you one more Merry Christmas."

"Thank you, Patrick, you as well." She turned to leave but was suddenly caught by Patrick and pulled into his arms.

"One more thing," he whispered, his dark eyes twinkling. He held Abigail's mistletoe above her head. "Sorry, but it's a tradition that cannot be ignored."

Before she could respond he pulled her to his mouth. Her mind fled to wondering what Sean must be thinking. But as he kissed her, she found it was no longer filled with the same heat. Now it only tasted of sadness. This evening, he had seemed so close to the Patrick she had once fancied herself in love with. It quietly broke her heart. She did not want to cause him any pain, but she knew she that fantasy was over.

The kiss suddenly deepened and she came to her senses and pulled abruptly out of it.

Patrick was stunned. He didn't realize it yet, but he sensed that he had somehow lost her. A look of dread crossed his face, matching the look on hers.

"Fee, I'm so sorry, I assumed you'd ... it was wrong of me."

He turned without another word and was gone.

She remained where she was. She owed Sean an explanation, but when she turned to speak to him, he too was gone.

Fiona staggered drunkenly down the hallway of the west tower, scanning every room she passed. She wanted to talk to Sean. She needed to reassure him that nothing had changed. When she saw that he had gone, believing immediately that he had run off because of Patrick's kiss, a sickening fear settled in her stomach like a stone, followed quickly by panic. She had excused herself from the few remaining guests at the party and hurried out the door.

Not now! she pleaded silently, as she wove her way along. *After all we've been through, don't let him just walk away!* She had no idea which room he was staying in, or hers for that matter, all she cared about now was finding him.

Fiona tried a few doors, knocking tentatively, but received no response. Finally she came to a door that, after knocking, a muttered grunt was uttered.

"Who the hell is it?"

Sean!

"It's me, Fiona. Please open the door."

There was no response from the other side of the door for several long moments. She waited, trying to figure out the words she would say to him, but she couldn't think of anything that didn't sound pathetic. She hoped that this was one of those situations where the right words would just come, although she barely trusted herself to speak. She just wanted to make sure that she was not going to lose him. She had finally admitted to herself that she was indeed falling in love with him.

No, she corrected herself harshly. *Not falling, already fallen.*

If she would have allowed herself to be completely honest and not blinded by the fantasy of Patrick, she already would have admitted that she had been taken with Sean since that first night she fell into his arms.

Sean flung open the door and stared hard at her. His eyes flashed in the firelight coming from his room.

"Sean ... I," was all she got out. He pulled her inside and slammed the door shut. She was pressed up against the closed door and he was upon her. His lips found hers; his hands rubbed her curves and his heart raced.

She relaxed into the door and kissed him back deeply. She needed this, needed him to touch her, needed to feel him.

Sean pulled back abruptly.

"What in God's name are you doing here?"

"I had to see you."

"You foolish, lovely girl." He kissed her again. "Tonight was complete torture for me. Then to watch Patrick kiss you, I almost bloody punched him."

Fiona smiled in relief, as Sean ran his hands through her hair. Sean had not left because he feared losing her; he had left out of jealousy of watching someone else flirt with her. It was actually quite charming.

"It's only six more days." she assured. "Then the play is over and we no longer have to carry our secret."

"May as well be a decade," he whispered. "I'll do it, but I'll hate every minute of it."

They stood together, holding each other, each understanding they could not do this again until after the show.

"You should go," Sean said.

"I know," she replied, but didn't move. "I love you, Sean. I'm not sure when it happened or how."

"I know. You should go," he repeated, "very soon the true cad that I am won't be able to let you go."

"Don't tease me Sean ... " she whispered, nibbling his ear.

"Be gone with ye, temptress," he smiled, pulling away. He opened the door and urged her through the threshold.

"I have yet begun to–" Fiona started to walk back inside

"Woman, go to bed," Sean pleaded as he closed the door in her face.

Fiona turned and crumpled against it, sliding down to the floor. She leaned against the door, smiling like a lovesick fool, which indeed she was. She did not want to move, she wanted to stay as close to Sean as she could. She wondered if Sean was sitting against the door behind her, feeling everything that she was?

After a moment, she rose, unsteadily. She kissed the door then turned, staggering off in an uncertain direction, not concerned with where she was going. She was not going to be able to sleep tonight, she was certain of that. Maybe she would just roam these stone passages all night, like some happy ghost. Or, if she did find her room, she would probably lie in bed and replay her moments with Sean again and again until daylight drifted in through her window.

She began to hum, 'You made me love you.' Now, more than ever, the song made sense in a way it never had before. Had Gavin not dropped her, she never would have fallen for Sean ... She giggled at her word play.

Fiona was startled out of her thoughts by a sudden howling of a wind gust that blew past her and down the dark hallway.

She had never been in this part of the castle before. She stopped humming, finding the echo a bit spooky. She had no idea where she was. Now, she really wished she knew where her room was and that she was there right now.

The night seemed darker, the walls were closing in, and every noise became some unknown evil lurking toward her. She wished she had not drunk so much, wished she had not listened to the ghost stories at dinner, and wished she wasn't suddenly so frightened.

Then she heard footsteps.

She froze.

She remembered a nightmare she had growing up, and now she feared, irrationally, that it was about to come true. In her dream she came face-to-face with a very dead, empty apparition of herself drifting towards her from blackness. She knew, instinctively, that if she allowed herself to see her reflection in its dead eyes, that her soul would be abandoned, instantly transferred into this soulless husk, to be lost forever, roaming the earth, never to be recognized again. And still, she would not look away.

She shook off the memory. *Damn, what am I? Six years old? And how much did I drink?"*

Someone or *something* was coming, and giving into her irrational fear, she scrambled into a corner and hunched down, hoping it would pass her by. She shivered, as she heard it come nearer.

Gavin rounded the corner holding a candle. He was whispering to himself, but he stopped when he caught sight of Fiona huddled in a dark corner.

"Fiona?"

Fiona jumped to her feet and ran towards him. She wrapped her arms around him in relief. He held her as she regained her breath.

"What are you doing out here? You should be in bed."

"I know! But, I got lost, and I thought you were me, I mean my spirit coming for me, for my soul," she babbled.

"Alright, now lass, someone has had a bit too much to drink."

"No! Well, maybe, but it's all true. It is!"

"Aye, I believe ye," Gavin consoled with a slight smile. "Come." He led her away, down the hall, his arm still protectively around her shoulder. "This way. I'll take you to your room; it's near mine."

Fiona finally began to regain her senses and allowed Gavin to escort her.

"You must think me such a silly fool," she said.

"Nonsense," Gavin replied, only too happy to be able to rescue her. "I've roamed all through this castle, and I've got to admit, it's frightened me more than once."

"I'm glad to know I'm not the only one."

"Believe me, you're not," Gavin assured her. As if on cue, the wind picked up outside and its eerie wail echoed down the corridor.

Fiona shivered. Gavin squeezed her a bit tighter.

They turned a corner down a familiar hallway. Her heart nearly flew out of her chest as they passed Sean's door. She took a deep breath, hoping Sean wouldn't hear them passing and come out.

Once the danger passed, and they turned another corner, she again relaxed. She started to hum.

"You are in a merry mood for someone who was nearly killed by the spirit of herself," Gavin joked.

"Aye, but now they're Christmas Spirits, the merriest spirits of the year!" She tripped on the uneven floor, nearly falling.

Gavin caught her just in time. "I think you've had way too many spirits for one night, me lady."

She laughed in agreement and rested her slightly spinning head against his shoulder as they continued to walk down the corridor. He seemed to know his way around quite well.

"I have a question," she said.

"And what's that?" Gavin asked.

"The story. The ghost town and all that?"

"Yes?"

"Did you make that all up?"

Gavin took a long time in answering.

"Yes," he finally replied.

"I thought so," Fiona nodded.

They walked again in silence for a time. Then Fiona spoke again.

"Thank you, Gavin," she said.

"For what?"

"If you hadn't found me, I might have been lost for all of eternity."

"Lucky I found you then."

"Aye, it's a blessing to have a friend that has traveled beside me for so long. You are a vision of home, Gavin."

Gavin looked quite pleased. They walked in silence a bit further before Gavin stopped in front of a door.

"This would be yours," he gestured. "Mine is two down should you need anything."

"Thank you again for saving me, Gavin. I am forever in your debt." She hugged him briefly then moved to her door.

"Fiona," he called, with a crack in his voice. Fiona turned. He held up something green, smashed into pulp in his hand.

"Mistletoe," he explained, shyly.

He moved to hold it tentatively above her head. His look was a silent beg for a kiss.

Fiona was torn. This was the man who had spouted out his desire for her in anger, while on the other hand he was also an old friend. Why not give him a wee kiss? It was innocent enough.

Gavin's eyes glistened as she leaned into him, her lips brushing his softly.

It was a quick kiss. A chaste one, not at all what Gavin had desired, but sweet nonetheless.

"Goodnight," she said joyfully, then again turned to her door, this time entering her room.

ACT IV

'Love is like war: easy to begin but hard to stop.'

–*H.L. Menck*

TROMPERIE
An original tragedy

Written by: Andrew Wakeman

Directed by: Nicholas Ashbury

ONE NIGHT ONLY!
December 31st. 1924
8 o'clock sharp

CAST OF PLAYERS
Patrick Berenger
Sean Berenger
Samuel McDermott
Fiona Corrigan
Abigail McGauligh

In celebration of Hogmanay a complimentary dram of whiskey to all who attend! *(Immediately following the performance)*

FREE FOR ALL!

The errant torn flyer blew across the frozen moors, tumbling in the breeze as it caught reflections of the moonlight. Like a broken-winged bird it took short hopeful flights in the updrafts before tumbling back down to the ground, before the wind carried it off and out of sight.

Adverts had been pasted up in the Broken Piper, the church bulletin board, and Wade and Karin's store. It was assumed that most of the locals would have heard about the play long ago, but if not, they would more than likely frequent one of these locales. It was Carlisle's idea to offer a free dram of scotch to all attending, in hopes of increasing attendance, although it was Nicholas who suggested that it would be better to give it to them after the play rather than before or during intermission as an incentive to stay to the end. Not that he didn't think the play was going to be entertaining–surprisingly, given the bizarre circumstances, it was actually rather good–it was more his concern that this was a small town and probably not much of a theatrical crowd anymore, that made him worry that anyone would show up at all. That and the fact they were competing with Hogmanay, the most popular celebration of the year. Fortunately too, the weather had recently improved. If luck would have it, it would be one of those freakish Scottish days where smack dab in the dead of winter, the skies suddenly cleared, the sun rose into the brilliant, blue sky, and the landscape would glitter with sparkling, crystal snow diamonds. They never lasted long; but hopefully just long enough to ensure that there would be no weather excuses for the villagers to miss the play that evening.

Right now it was morning, still dark and icy cold. The sun wouldn't be up for hours.

From the darkness a woman's voice softly called out.

"Yet you will be hanged for being so long absent, or to be turned away—is not that as good as a hanging to you?"

Sean had no idea who spoke that line. He had just become aware that he was alone on stage, dressed as Clown in Shakespeare's *Twelfth Night*.

"Many a good hanging prevents a bad marriage; and, for turning away, let summer bear it out," Sean replied, automatically.

His words echoed throughout the nearly empty theater. He couldn't remember his next line. He vaguely realized that someone, *Maria*, was supposed to be on stage here with him. He looked aside for help.

In the wings, the troupe members glared at him impatiently, waiting for him to proceed. They were of no help.

He stared into the audience.

There were only two people, sitting, front row dead center– his mother and his father.

His mother rose from the chair to feed him his line.

"You are resolute, then?" she whispered to him.

Before Sean could reply, his father, anger burning in his eyes, grabbed his mother and threw her back into her seat.

He stood defiant between Sean and Delia, a pistol appeared suddenly in his hand.

"No!" Fiona screamed, rushing from side stage into Sean's arms.

"You do not belong here!" Angus screamed, aiming the gun at Fiona, spittle running down his quivering lips. "You should have died long ago! Leave us alone!"

He pulled the trigger.

BLAM!

Fiona was hit in the heart, she crumbled, a rose of red forming on her bosom. "Sean ... " she moaned.

Angus, grinning, raised his gun at Sean.

"Now it's your turn."

BLAM!

Sean was awakened from the chilling nightmare by the sound of a crash downstairs. He looked around his room disorientated. He tried to put the snippets of dream fragments back together when another loud crash came from down below.

BLAM!

Some large bit of the stage props must have fallen over downstairs. He heard cursing, stomping feet, dragging, and hammering, all the sounds of frantic last minute preparations before opening night.

"Shite! Keep it down would you," Sean yelled.

This last week of final rehearsals had often run very late, and he was suffering from exhaustion and a lack of sleep. His nightmare now forgotten, he supposed he'd better get up and see what he could do to help.

Upon entering the theater proper, he found Samuel and Gavin arguing on stage over a broken wooden set piece while Nicholas and Andrew stood by trying to help.

Nicholas noticed Sean standing there sleepy-eyed and bewildered.

"What are you doing here? Get over to the Broken Piper to get your costumes."

"The pub?" Sean asked, confused.

"Miss McStargle won't enter the theater," Andrew answered. "She still thinks it's haunted."

"It is," Sean replied nonchalantly, scratching his night growth of beard. "Does that mean she won't watch the play tonight?"

"Never mind!" Nicholas growled. It was obviously a sore subject. "Just get over there and get fitted. Then come right back."

"Aye." Sean saluted. He sauntered off to the pub.

The Broken Piper was a beehive of activity. Miss McStargle had closed it to the public for the day—naturally it would be open later for Hogmanay—but for now it was a makeshift wardrobe fitting room. She had hung blankets across the pub dining room dividing it in two, one for the women and one for the men to change in. She was busy scurrying back and forth between the curtains, mouth filled with pins, a cloth measuring tape draped around her neck and bits of wardrobe accessories in her arms. Somehow she was managing to simultaneously berate and compliment the actors as needed to get them all adjusted into their costumes.

Sean entered the pub just as McStargle was passing through the women's curtain. He inadvertently caught a glimpse of Fiona wearing only the flimsiest of slips, bending down to pick up a dress. Her provocative state sent an intense wave of desire through him. This last week of being so near yet unable to touch her had been torture. He froze, unable to look away, and just as Fiona's eyes met his the curtain fell back into place, blocking his view.

Fiona noticed Sean's desire through the curtain opening. She didn't blush, nor attempt to cover herself like she would have done not so very long ago.

"Fiona!" McStargle commanded. "Hurry up and get that costume on. I have to hem it up. I don't understand that fool Nicholas making last minute costume changes. What does he think I am? A magician?"

Fiona slipped on the dress as McStargle fussed with the hem.

"We do all appreciate your hard work Miss McStargle," Fiona tried to appease.

"Humph!" McStargle grunted, but it was clear that she was pleased with the compliment.

"Are you sure you can't come watch the play toni–OUCH!" Fiona cried out as a straight pin 'inadvertently' stabbed her calf.

"Sorry. You must remain still. These pins are so difficult. Now, what were you saying, dearie?" McStargle asked coolly.

"Nothing," Fiona replied, wisely.

"Aye. I thought so," McStargle agreed.

Abigail, who had been fixing her hair in a large mirror, appeared beside them. She spun around, parading her wedding dress costume for Fiona.

"What do you think? Isn't it lovely?"

"Yes. It's stunning. You've never looked so elegant!"

"I can't wait for the play to start. I'm so excited!" Abigail ran off.

"I can't wait for it to be over," Fiona mused, dreamily.

"What was that, dearie?" McStargle asked.

"Nothing," Fiona replied.

In Carlisle's study, behind a locked dark glass cabinet, lay six dusty bottles of vintage red wine, *Chateau St. Vermillion 1873*, in a specially built rack fitted for eight bottles. Two spots were vacant. The lock was simple enough to pick with a two-penny nail and a bit of fiddling. Which is what had just happened. A hand reached in and withdrew one of the bottles. And then there were five.

Whether it was due to curiosity, boredom, or the offer of a free dram of scotch was unclear, but by seven-thirty the theater was nearly full. Townspeople who had seemed to have been in hiding for most of the winter had all come out of hibernation. The theater was alive with the humming of murmured conversation in anticipation of the play and a chance to glimpse these strange invaders to their sleepy little town. Not to mention the return of the infamous 'Berenger Boys'.

Wade Hannah and his beautiful, ginger-haired wife Karin sat in the front row beside the empty seat reserved for Carlisle Thornbury.

"Seems all of Loglinmooth is here tonight," Wade said to his wife, turning around in his chair to note the audience streaming in. "Didn't realize they're were so many play-acting aficionados here."

"Because there aren't," Karin said. "Haven't you been listening to the gossip?" She punched his arm. "Now, turn around and behave. "

"No, I ain't heard any gossip," Wade said grumpily, rubbing his arm. "I ain't a woman now, am I?" After a pause he added, "So, what's the gossip then?"

Karin lowered her voice. "There hasn't been a play since the last time when ... you know."

"When what?" he asked, loudly.

"Lower your voice," she hissed

"Why I thought you said everyone already knew," he replied, confused.

"Not *everyone!*" she hissed again. "Do you want to know or not?"

"Yes, get on with it."

Karin rolled her eyes in exasperation. "Forget it."

"What?" Wade exclaimed. "How can I forget it? You haven't told me anything yet."

Karin noticed that Carlisle Thornbury was making his way toward them. She knew she had better speak quickly.

"Okay. There hasn't been a play here since the Berenger boys' mother mysteriously disappeared. Some believe she was murdered and still haunts the theater."

"That's bloody nonsense! Who believes–?"

"Shhh!" Karin hushed. "Don't say a word in front of the old man!"

Carlisle was nearly besides them.

"Why?"

"Oh, good evening Mister Thornbury!" Karin said a bit too over-exuberantly as Carlisle approached his seat. "We are so looking forward to this evening's performance."

"Yes. It is a marvelous play to be sure," Carlisle nodded pleasantly to Karin and Wade as he took his seat. He was dressed very formally in a black tux and a bright red paper crown. "It has quite the ending," he added. "Quite the ending indeed."

The house lights flickered on and off. The play was about to begin. The last minute arrivers and lobby loiterers hurried to their seats.

Just as the lights dimmed and the curtain was about to rise, McStargle slipped into a seat in the back row, eyes darting nervously about.

So far, no devils.

She crossed herself and held on tight to her rosary.

From the moment the curtains rose until intermission, McStargle forgot where she was–she seemingly held her breath for the entire time, so taken was she with the play and performances.

She gasped in delight during the masquerade scene as Sean glided across the stage, dancing with Abigail. She grew confused at times in separating the story and characters from the real people she had grown so attached. She allowed herself a small smile of satisfaction when she noticed the little alterations she had done to the costumes, a couple stitches here, a mending there. Everything looked so perfect. A swell of pure pride rose up in her heart the moment Fiona entered wearing the green ball gown McStargle had designed and made from scratch. She had chosen the dark green color to match her eyes. She knew Fiona would be wearing a black mask, so she had wanted her eyes to radiate out from the moment she arrived onstage.

As the play went on, McStargle became totally engrossed in the story. She no longer paid any attention to her work on the costumes or that it was her friends on stage—now it was Sir Keir Maclaren, Lady Lilais and Rory and Iona Lachlan that mesmerized her.

The audience, too, watched enrapt as Maclaren and Iona danced. Maclaren drew Iona closer, begging her to reveal her identity, then finally kissing her.

McStargle's anxiety matched Iona's each time Rory would drink and rage or become rough with her. She silently hoped Keir and Iona would run away together to start a new life somewhere in the most exotic place she could imagine.

She had not expected that Keir would actually go through with his wedding, but as a man of honor she realized he had no other choice. But the sight of Iona watching from the shadows had her on the verge of sobbing along with her.

She was shocked back into reality when the first act suddenly ended, the curtain fell, and the blinding house lights came up.

McStargle remained in her seat, vigorously rubbing her eyes. She did not want anyone to see that she was foolishly crying at a make-believe play, especially not Nicholas. She had intended to join the audience as they moved outside into the lobby, yearned to talk about what she had just seen, but she caught sight of

Nicholas sneaking into the wings and she decided she would rather sit and let the tension of the last act dissipate. If the second act was anything like the first, she was afraid she might faint!

This was a masterpiece, she decided, and she had the heart of the director of a masterpiece. Her mind drifted to thoughts of Nicholas and his calming demeanor. She couldn't imagine what her life had been before him. She lost herself in memories of the nights she had spent with him, his sense of humor, the way he cared for his troupe, and her. She was caught off guard as the lights dimmed for the curtain to rise once again.

The story continued–with scenes of hidden love, deceit, betrayal, rage and even a surprise pregnancy–all the while Miss McStargle hung on every word, gesture, and emotion.

Fiona walked out on the stage for her final scene, adrenaline pounding in her chest. After this scene was over, the only one that remained was the Rory and Lord Maclaren scene toasting Iona's new baby. She had a sudden, sad realization that this would almost certainly be the last time they would all act on the same stage together. She quickly choked down that thought and concentrated on her performance.

Patrick sat on stage at a table with his back to her, clutching a bottle of wine, and drinking whiskey from a pint glass. She approached him and spoke.

> IONA: I have been looking for you for over an hour. I went to the pub and our store ...

> Patrick (RORY) held the bottle up to the light and regarded the swirling red liquid.

> RORY: Odd that you didn't think to look here, in our home.

From the darkness of the first row Carlisle caught sight of the label on the wine bottle. "No, it can't be," he uttered, but his whisper went unheard.

Fiona was confused for an instant. She couldn't remember a wine bottle having been introduced into this scene. It was too late now to do anything about it. Probably someone had left it on the table during the last scene change. Not only that, but Patrick didn't turn to look at her as he had done before in every rehearsal. Undaunted, she continued.

> IONA: I know I have been distant for sometime now. I have been seeking the right words to speak to you about–

Patrick suddenly stood and slammed the bottle down on the table. He turned to face her, fire in his eyes.

> RORY: I KNOW! DAMN IT! I KNOW!

Fiona stared up at him, frightened by his sudden intensity. Patrick hadn't delivered his lines with this much passion during rehearsals. He grabbed her roughly by the arms and shook her.

> RORY: Did you not think I would suspect that you were seeking another man's arms? I, who have always loved you? I, who never wanted anything more than you? I, who should have had you? I–I do not take loss well. I should warn you!"

Fiona tensed. He was improvising lines and she had no idea where he was going with his babbling. She had to cut him off and try to get the play back on track.

> IONA: I'm with child!

A few gasps could be heard from the audience.

Patrick suddenly let go of her and staggered back a few steps, as if from a physical blow. She stammered out her next line.

IONA: *Your* child. I have been trying to find the right words to tell you. How am I supposed to tell you that I am afraid of you? With all that you drink, and your constant, unfounded suspicions when you do. I wanted to run away, Rory. From you, for the sake of our child, but I realize now I owe you a choice.

Patrick slowly inhaled before hissing out his next line.

RORY: And what choice is that?

Patrick's intensity caused Fiona to pause. He waited, as if he had all the time in the world. Fiona stood rigid, trepidation thick in her voice.

IONA: First, I need to know if you still love me?

Patrick stared at her for what seemed like hours, before whispering.

RORY: *Love?* You ask me if I *love* you?"

Patrick rushed to her and took her face in his hands

RORY: OF COURSE I LOVE YOU! It is I who should ask if you could love a miserable drunken sod like me? I have been aching and desolate these past few months. I feared, I thought, I was losing you. I couldn't deal with that thought, Iona. I tried to drink it away, but I couldn't. I didn't mean it when I didn't take you, when I dismissed you ... when I left you alone so many nights. How I wanted you then. How I wish I could have you now! I wish you could have known. I wish I had told you. I have always–

Fiona kissed him then, not for what he was saying, although guilt was sweeping in around her, but because it was in her blocking to do so and she couldn't bear to hear anymore. She remembered the many nights on stage when a kiss like this from

Patrick would have sent thrills through her, back when he was all she longed for in her world. Sadly, she realized, this kiss on stage, most probably their last, was her final goodbye. Bitter and sweet as it was, she knew she needed to break it to keep the scene moving.

> IONA: It is I who was foolish to think that you no longer cared. I see my error now; I am so sorry.

> RORY: But, you still love me?

Patrick was pleading now, his hands trailing down her back, intimately and she knew she did, but not in the way she once had. She glanced away, trying to escape his prying eyes. She couldn't bear to deliver the next line while looking at him.

> IONA: I do.

Patrick lifted her face back to his eyes. He smiled, a smile she knew all too well.

> RORY: The child is mine?

> IONA: Yes, of course.

Fiona could hear sniffles coming from the audience, especially those who wanted Iona to be with Keir, her true love, but this was not what this play was about. This play was about choices.

> RORY: And the other man?

Fiona paused, perhaps too long, summing up courage. Silently, she cursed him for pushing the scene, adding new lines, and making it all too real.

> IONA: There never was.

She had whispered the line, then, she remembered the audience and repeated it louder so they could hear.

IONA: There never was.

RORY: I will be a father! Iona, it's a way to start again, don't you see?

Patrick laughed and swung her around in a mad circle and Fiona found herself in a whirl, spinning and spinning. Her head began to swim and then all to sudden he stopped and looked deep in her eyes.

RORY: Sweet Fee, we should celebrate.

Fiona tried to look to him but she couldn't focus, her head still dizzy. She tried to walk towards the chair Patrick had been sitting in earlier, just to regain her senses, to figure out if she was forgetting a line. She thought she heard him say 'Sweet Fee', and that only confused her more.

RORY: What do you say to a celebration?

Patrick moved her more center stage, and blindly she followed.

IONA: I think that's a lovely idea.

She was stammering and she nearly lost her footing. Patrick caught her and held her close.

RORY: I can see you're giddy with excitement. Stay, I will fetch the wine. I know you never drink it, but tonight I feel we can make one exception.

He went to the table and poured a glass of wine. Her senses were slowly returning, enough to let her know that this was no longer the script. Movement caught her eye and she turned to the wings and caught sight of Sean gesturing madly.

RORY: To life!

Patrick brought her the glass of wine.

RORY: To a renewal of the soul, to a new life as a family!

He thrust the glass into her hand. She stared at it, dumbfounded. She could hear the audience whispering. This all somehow seemed familiar. Her head spun again as she tried to decipher what was happening. Again she looked to the wings for guidance and this time she saw a strange woman in a blue dress standing there, pale and shimmering. She appeared to be the same woman from her dream that freed her from the cellar. Although her faced was still veiled, she looked to be very agitated.

Fiona turned as Patrick announced:

RORY: Cheers!

Patrick held up his pint glass.

IONA: To you ...

Fiona held the glass to the light for the whole audience to see. It's almost over, she told herself, soon this wayward scene would be over, the curtain would fall and she could escape this dream-like world she had somehow found herself trapped in.

IONA: To our life together!

RORY: Yes. To our *long* life together.

Fiona raised the glass to her lips. The bitter, almond scent of the wine seemed oddly familiar.

"NO! FIONA! STOP!"

Hearing her name shouted caused Fiona to turn and see Sean rushing towards her onstage. He slapped the wine glass out of her hand. It crashed across the stage, a bloody red smear.

"I can't hide this any longer!"

Sean pulled Fiona to his chest. Hushed gasps of delight could be heard from the audience, including McStargle, who was ready for a fight to ensue between the Lord and the commoner. She wouldn't admit it, but she was a sucker for love stories and was thrilled with this twist that she had not seen coming. She perched on the edge of her seat, holding her breath, not daring to miss a minute.

On stage Sean shook Fiona. "I almost lost you there. If you would have drunk that wine ... "

He leaned in and whispered, "The cellar, Fee, that almond smell? Cyanide? Remember?"

Fiona's eyes grew large with sudden realization. She swayed in his arms. He held her tight. In a fury, he yelled to Patrick.

"You tried to poison her!"

Patrick remained oddly calm. He smirked, as he answered in Rory's voice. "Poison? Why would I poison my wife, my Lord?"

"Because you knew! Christmas night, when you kissed her and she broke off the kiss, you knew then that I had already won her. I know you, brother!"

Cries of disbelief were heard throughout the audience as they sat stunned by this newfound information. McStargle couldn't contain her shock.

"So that's why they look so much alike!" she cried out loud, forgetting that they actually were brothers.

Patrick looked Sean in the eye.

"Aye, that I did," he replied nonchalantly. "I had my suspicions but that kiss was indeed the defining moment."

"And for that you tried to kill her?" Sean roared.

"Why would I kill the woman we both love, even if she loves you? I thought you knew me better."

"I don't know who you are!" Sean countered.

Patrick took those words as a blow. Rather than confront Sean, he turned instead to Fiona, his voice breaking with pain.

"I never deserved your affection. I've mistreated you. It was all my fault, I will have to live with that." He turned back to Sean. "I would never poison her."

"Then why the wine?" Sean asked incredulous, pulling Fiona protectively closer. "You could have killed her!"

"I was trying to discover what happened to our mother. To expose her killer."

"*Mother?* Killer? Are you insane?"

"No. She was poisoned on stage, but this is not poisoned," Patrick insisted, striding to the table and picking up the bottle. He regarded the label.

"Odd, this is not the bottle I chose," he mused, as he raised it tentatively to his mouth.

"STOP!"

The words flew out of Carlisle's mouth.

"Don't drink it!"

Patrick froze as the old man struggled out of his seat and climbed awkwardly onto the stage. His paper crown fell off, unnoticed. Panting heavily with exertion, he snagged the bottle of wine from Patrick.

The audience gasped. Some were confused, thinking this was still part of the play, others were just plain lost, but all were riveted to their seats.

Carlisle staggered away from the cast and stood alone center stage. He addressed the audience and the troupe, turning awkwardly between them as he spoke. His words came out in a desperate jumble of explanation as he held the bottle of wine out before him. He screeched at it, as though it were a living thing.

"Who? Who brought this here? It was locked! This *cursed* wine, these bottles, they haunt me, taunt me ... no more. Never. NEVER AGAIN!"

His words echoed throughout the silent auditorium. Then he became more coherent and his voice dropped to a whisper.

No longer addressing the bottle, he spun in place trying to get the audience and the troupe to understand.

"My fault, don't you see? If any one deserves to die, it is I."

He staggered to the very foot of the stage. He blinked into the footlights as he addressed the blurry shadows seated before him.

"I loved a woman once. She sang like an angel and was an actress, by very definition of ignoble stock as far as most in my circle were concerned, and so she could never be mine. I sat in a high castle on the hill, but never looked down upon her. She married within her class, a brute of a man, who ran the theater, this very theater.

"Truth be told, this story parallels one many, many years before. This theater was built for love and secret rendezvous. A passage runs from beneath this very stage to my home. I knew this. She knew this. So she came to visit often, clandestine meetings in the dead of night. She bore me two secret sons."

Carlisle turned to meet Sean and Patrick's eyes.

"You were raised by the vicious hand of a father who believed you were his. I had to stand and watch, impotent to help. I shall never forgive myself for that."

Carlisle turned back to the audience, tears now streaming down his face.

"One day *he* found out."

Carlisle let the words sink like stones. It appeared for a moment that he wasn't going to be able to continue. Somehow he found the strength.

"He came to me. He didn't threaten; he needn't. He just put it simply. I was to pay him a handsome sum for the rest of his days. I also had to invest in ways to keep his beloved theater thriving. I was never to see his wife or my sons again.

"I agreed and kept my word. I restored the crumbling theater to its former glory. I paid to have the ancient train tracks put back into working order so that a special express run could be made to this remote location. I begged royalty, friends, and any members of the upper crust I could contact to make the long journey out here to attend his plays.

"All the while I stayed hidden in my castle until the time seemed right."

Carlisle sat down on the edge of the stage, his old legs hanging over like withered sticks. He noticed his fallen paper crown and placed it back on his head. It was bent and tilted badly, but somehow it appeared majestic.

"Time passed. I had one trusted servant and spy who kept me informed of all the activities going on below.

"He told me that the boys had grown old enough to realize they'd had enough of the beatings and abuse. They knew they'd break their mother's heart, but they either had to kill him or leave. They were, and still are, of higher moral fiber than I. There was also some trouble with a girl. Everything was falling apart. They left. That was a pitch black day for me."

Again another long silence. Someone in the audience coughed. It echoed like a rifle shot through the stony silent theater. It was the impetus that jarred Carlisle into continuing.

"Shortly after the boys left a new play was announced. Written by Angus and to be performed by he and her, among others. My spy got me a copy of the script. I read it and an idea began to form.

"*In Vino Veritas.* 'In wine there is truth'. There were two things I knew and one thing he didn't. He most assuredly knew, as did I, that my Delia was repulsed by the grape, although he was lousy for the taste of it. He drank it every chance he could, even on stage. And his play, without re-telling the drivel that it was, relied significantly around its character's toast with wine. Perhaps you see where this is going?"

Carlisle held the wine bottle up to the audience to make his point.

"The second thing I knew, but the one he didn't, was about the secret passage. It was a simple task of stealth through his wine cellar, to the stage, replacing the bottle. Then with a theater full of alibi's, have him drink himself to death ... "

His hands shook as he raised the bottle to his lips.

"It was not meant for her, don't you see? It was meant for him. He convinced her to drink instead. Somehow he must have known. You understand now? You see, don't you?"

His words were cut off by a soft, lilting song that suddenly drifted into the theater.

"*Oh sorrow, sing sorrow ...* "

The audience murmured as they looked about, turning in their seats, craning their necks for the origin. It seemed to be coming from everywhere at once.

"*Now she sleeps in the valley where the wild flowers nod ...* "

Carlisle knew the voice and the song. His attention was diverted to the wings where *she* shimmered into being, oscillating between substantial mist and memory. She stood in the shadows of the wing, pale white wearing paler blue, as she sang to him.

"I loved you," he cried to her in apology. "Please believe me. Please, I never meant to hurt you. I still love you."

She stopped singing. She held her arms out to him in acceptance and forgiveness.

"Thank you," he whispered. The flood of despair, guilt, and misery seemed to leave him all at once. His eyes were shiny with an inner light long since dimmed. He raised the bottle to his trembling lips.

"No!" Fiona cried. "Don't let him drink!"

Sean and Patrick immediately raced toward the old man. A trickle of wine poured down his throat before Sean could grab the wine out of his hands. Patrick caught Carlisle in his arms just as he collapsed. Fiona was soon beside them.

"How much did he drink?" Fiona asked.

"I don't know," Patrick replied, anxiously. "Sean got to him pretty quickly."

"We'd better take him up to my room," Sean insisted.

Jeppsen, worry and concern creasing his angular face, and Samuel who was waiting in the wings to deliver the play's epilogue, both came hurrying out to help. Abigail hovered further back on stage, hands wringing, uncertain what to do. She looked expectantly to Andrew in the front row. Andrew, who like most of the audience, had sat stunned throughout the monologue, was finally nudged out of his shock.

"We'd better help," he said to Nicholas, as he rose from of his seat.

"Yes. Yes of course."

They made their way onto the stage.

Only Gavin remained in the wings, in shock. He stared across to the stage left wing where the apparition of the woman in blue regarded him solemnly before fading back into the shadows.

Abigail flung herself into Andrew's arms as soon as he made it up to the stage. Nicholas joined the others gathered around Carlisle.

"How is he?" Nicholas asked.

"He needs a doctor," Patrick replied.

Carlisle appeared to be losing consciousness. Sean sprang up and shouted out to the audience. "Is anyone in the theater a doctor? This man just drank poison!"

A concerned murmur trickled through the crowd. Finally in the back row Miss McStargle stood up and called out.

"I was a nurse during the war. I have some ipecac at the pub. Will that help?"

"Yes! Please hurry!" Sean called. "Bring it up to my room!"

Jeppsen hoisted the old man easily in his arms. Fiona watched, trembling, as he followed Sean to his loft. Abigail and Andrew went off stage in each other's arms. Samuel started to follow Sean and Jeppsen, when Nicholas, who stood off to the side of the stage, stopped him.

"Stay with me. You may be needed."

Samuel nodded. "Aye, sorry didn't mean to run out. I still have my bit to perform. The play must go on as they say, eh?"

Patrick had started to follow Sean and the others when he noticed Fiona standing in the wings, looking waif-like and vulnerable. He went to comfort her.

"Don't worry, Carlisle will be all right," Patrick assured. "Sean's with him. Then he'll be back for you."

Fiona crushed her face into his shoulder, letting her tears flow.

"I love him, Patrick. I am so sorry."

"Shhh," he pulled her closer. "That is nothing to be sorry for."

"You should go. You need to be with your fa–father just in case ... " Fiona insisted.

Patrick's voice faltered with emotion.

"I'm not sure who he really is. But, I don't think you should be alone. I'll stay with you until Sean returns."

Seeing as all the action now appeared to be over, a few confused people in the audience clapped hesitantly.

"Was that it then?" someone protested grumpily.

"Is it over?" a concerned voice called out. "Is the old man okay?"

Nicholas stepped to the foot of the stage ready to address the concerns of the audience with Samuel in step beside him. He overheard Wade and Karin in the front row in disagreement about what they had just seen.

"It was all part of the play," Wade insisted.

"No, it was real. He really drank poison. Why else would they call for a doctor?" Karin argued.

"Yes they *did* appear to call for a doctor, but that woman was Miss McStargle. She and the director are, to put it delicately, in intimate ways. I'm sure it was all rehearsed."

Wade knew he had Karin there. Surely that bit of gossip had long since reached her.

"Oh yes, I *had* heard about those two," Karin agreed. "And Mister Thornbury has always been a bit of a character. So it would be easy enough to entice him–"

"Exactly," Wade cut her off.

"What an odd play. But very clever," Karin nodded. "Very clever indeed. But what about the ghost?"

"What ghost?" Wade asked. He hadn't seen a ghost.

Nicholas couldn't believe what he was hearing. He realized that some honestly thought that it was all just a very unorthodox play they had witnessed. He decided to keep the illusion going, if only to reduce the anxiety. But before he could say anything, someone in the audience stood up and demanded: "What about the whiskey?"

More than a few murmured in agreement: "You promised us whiskey! Aye, a wee dram the paper said! We stayed until the end!"

Nicholas was about to say something when he noticed Samuel standing by patiently. He took his cue and addressed the crowd.

"Ladies and gentlemen. There is a brief epilogue before the conclusion of the play. I hope you enjoy it. Afterwards, if you'd all congregate into the lobby, we will be serving whiskey and cakes as promised. Thank you all for attending." Nicholas signaled to Samuel. "You're on," he whispered.

Samuel nodded solemnly and strode to center stage where he stood alone.

"Ah, what's this now?" someone near the front complained. "I want me whiskey!"

"Scotland was in turmoil!" Samuel bellowed out, startling the audience to silence. He drew his sword threateningly. "The Royals were in danger, aye, it was a bleak time o'er the moors. Poison was in the air."

As Samuel continued his somewhat aberrant discourse on the history of Scotland, Nicholas gathered with Patrick and Fiona in the wings.

"I could use some help serving the whiskey and cakes to the hoi polloi out there before they grow any uglier. This is the first time since I've been here that I wished the Prohibition had made its way across the pond."

Fiona laughed as she pulled away from Patrick. She wiped her eyes, embarrassed by her tears. "Yes, of course. Patrick, perhaps you can look in on Mister Thornbury and see if Miss McStargle needs anything?"

"Will do. If you're sure you don't need my help?" he turned to Nicholas.

"No, thanks. Fiona and I can manage. However, if you see Andrew and Abigail, send them our way," Nicholas added, as he took Fiona by the hand and led her off.

"So it became customary for those of high privilege to have a wee set of special bottles of wine, pre-laced with cyanide, at their disposal to toast with should their situation became so horrible that they had no other choice. It was considered a most honorable method of death. The wine of choice, although the reason for the vintner and vintage remains clouded in mystery, was always *Chateau St. Vermillion 1873* ... "

Whether Samuel was truly finished or not was not clear; however the curtain came down with finality and the audience applauded perfunctorily before hurrying off to the lobby.

"I'm avoiding the wine," one woman was overheard to have said.

"Aye, good idea that," her husband agreed.

Upstairs in Sean's bed, Carlisle was pale and fading, but still breathing. Miss McStargle had brought some ipecac and had induced the old man to expel most of the poison. He lay weak and disorientated. It was unclear if he would pull through. Father McLeary had been summoned and was standing by to perform the last rites if they seemed necessary. Patrick had joined Sean and McStargle at Carlisle's side.

"Did you hear her?" Carlisle mumbled, his eyes staring upward, unfocused. "She still sings like an angel."

McStargle mopped his feverish brow with a cold cloth. "Yes, I did. Now try and relax. We don't want to lose you."

Patrick turned to Sean, "Do you really think this old man is our father?"

"Yes. Yes, I do."

Patrick snapped. "Are you serious? He's done nothing but lie to us since he got here!"

"He spoke you the truth," Jeppsen stated, solemnly. "Every word of it."

"Aye, and how would you know?" Patrick demanded.

"Because I was the one who snuck into the theater that night and I placed the poisoned bottle on the stage."

"Then you killed my mother!" Patrick cried, as he lurched forward, trying to wring Jeppsen's throat. Sean intercepted him, tackled him by the waist and spun him away. Jeppsen never moved.

"Yes. I killed your mother," the regret in his voice was unmistakable. "Your father was a man of his word. He would not leave the castle. I willingly did his bidding, as I still do."

Patrick wrenched himself free of Sean's grasp, but he didn't make a move toward Jeppsen.

"Then it was still his fault!" he exclaimed, pointing at Carlisle. "He ordered it done, he–she–she didn't have to die." The enormity of pain, hate, and regret swelled up and overwhelmed him.

Sean went to comfort his brother, his pain equal.

"We didn't know. We had to get out."

Patrick shook his head. "No. I forced you to leave. You would have stayed here with Bethany if I hadn't–"

"No, that's not true. We were going to leave anyway." Sean said. "I don't blame you."

Patrick looked up. He saw in his eyes that Sean spoke the truth. He released ten years of pain in those few words.

"Thank you."

After a moment, Patrick added, "You've made out much better with Fiona. You know that, don't you? "

"Aye," Sean's agreed. "That I know."

"Then *you* should be the one thanking *me*, you shite!" Patrick cried, putting his brother in a headlock.

"Aye! Okay! Thank you for not stealing me other gal ya thieving bastard!" Sean laughed, his words muffled by Patrick's hold. Patrick released him with a laugh.

"Aye, that's better."

They clasped hands, shook and exchanged a nod. Sins forgotten.

* * *

By the time the whiskey and cakes had run out, there was already a massive Hogmanay *céilidh* taking place in a field just beyond the theater. A local band of traditional musicians played jigs and reels as the townsfolk danced around the massive bonfire flames, singing, calling out in laughter, snogging, and of course drinking in the New Year with a heavy thirst.

Fiona sighed with relief as she watched the last straggler leave the theater. She had worked in a rush serving drinks and cakes never having had time for unwinding from the revelations and emotions of the plays events.

For the moment, she was alone in the lobby. There was still a wee bit of scotch left in the bottom of the last bottle, so she took what she considered to be a well-deserved drink. She still hadn't seen Sean or Patrick or heard any news about Carlisle, but she had seen Father McLeary climb the ladder to Sean's loft–not a good sign. She realized that the best thing she could do right now was to leave them all alone. If Carlisle were at death's door, he probably would have some personal words to impart to them, words she needn't be present for. Besides, Patrick had told her that he would send Sean down to her as soon as he could.

Glancing through the window at the roaring flames and dancing crowds, she knew that she was in no mood for a celebration. She was exhausted, confused, and couldn't believe that most people had passed off tonight's events as part of the play. It was probably easier for them, she conceded, to believe in make-believe rather than to believe that they had just witnessed an old, wretched man try to commit suicide and that the shimmering woman in the wings was merely a trick of light and shadows and not a real ghost.

Or was she?

Fiona wasn't certain of anything that had happened tonight. She was fairly certain that she heard a phantom voice singing and later saw a shade of a woman in blue in the wings. And she was also fairly certain that she was not the only one who saw or heard her. Still ...

Fiona examined the empty scotch bottle. "Another dead soldier!" she proclaimed loudly, just as her dad always announced when a bottle was finished. She was about to toss it when she heard a crash coming from inside the theater. Startled, she ran inside, thinking someone had fallen and was possibly hurt.

Gavin was alone on stage, striking the set, quite literally, with a sledgehammer. Pieces of the set, props, and backdrop lay in smashed bits all around the stage. He was demolishing a small end table into several large chunks when Fiona called out.

"Gavin? What are you doing?"

He stopped swinging the massive hammer. Sweat caked his hair and ran down his face.

"The play is over. It's never going to be performed again, so I'm striking the set."

Fiona didn't know if it was the violent way he was attacking the set or the tone of his voice, but something about him disturbed her.

"Can't it wait until morning? Why don't you go out and join the celebration?"

"Aye, I will," he grinned, wiping his brow. "I just thought they could use some more wood for the bonfire. Are you going? Shall we go together?" Suddenly, he seemed his old self again.

Fiona never got a chance to answer, as Nicholas entered the theater and interrupted them.

"Fiona, there you are. I just spoke to Miss McStargle, Carlisle is resting comfortably with Patrick and Sean at his side."

"Thank God!" Fiona said, as she hugged him. She allowed Nicholas to escort her back out into the lobby as they talked.

"It was quite a performance," he said, with some difficulty. "I'm sorry, dear, I realize that I should have brought that damn curtain down the minute Patrick started going off book."

Fiona squeezed him tighter. "It's alright. I'm fine. Everyone is fine."

Gavin watched them vanish into the lobby.

Nicholas felt he had let the whole cast down with this debacle, but at least Fiona seemed to be okay. He was about to say something to that effect when the sound of thick wood splintering crashed out from the stage.

Gavin's hammer came down again and again.

Nicholas laughed. "Perhaps I better cast the lad in my next play, before he comes swinging that at me!"

Fiona agreed with a grin. "He does seem to have theater in his blood. He can never get enough."

"Right! Now, go get the hell out of this dreary place. It's either back to your room with you or go and join the céilidh. I'm sure Gavin will stop chopping wood long enough to keep you company out there until Sean can slip away."

"And what about you?" Fiona asked.

"No *Hog many*, or whatever you call it, for me. I'm planning on ringing in the New Year alone with a bottle of champagne and then falling into Morpheus's sweet arms. Unless of course, Miss McStargle decides to join me," he added with a wink.

"Sounds like you're going my way. I'm completely shagged. It's just Morpheus for me too, I'm afraid," Fiona said, not unhappily, as she grabbed his arm and they headed outside.

Not even the sudden snap of freezing cold air or the sights and sounds of the dancing revelers could stifle the yawn escaping from Fiona's exhausted lips.

"I feel I could sleep for a week." She yawned again, then, arm in arm with Nicholas, headed back to the pub.

* * *

Miss McStargle had been listening to Jeppsen's story in stony silence. Something about it was nagging at her, so she finally spoke up.

"If you don't mind me asking? There's one thing I cannot understand. I saw the original play. I saw Delia become ailing and leave the show. But then it all became very mysterious. Why did she supposedly disappear? Why not just say she was dead?"

"Aye, that was Mister Berenger's doing. He was afraid if Master Thornbury knew she was dead, he would have nothing to hold against him. So he concocted a story that she drank a wee bit of poison and was sent away to convalesce and recover. He *claimed* to have told her that my master had tried to poison her. He *claimed* she now feared for her life and would not return until Master Thornbury was dead."

"The bloody bastard!" Father McLeary swore, startling everyone. "Well, he truly was. I know the orphanage he was kicked out from," he added.

"Aye, he was indeed," Jeppsen concurred. "As I was saying, Master Thornbury didn't know what to believe at the time, and I could discover no proof either way. He was in a bad way thinking he may have accidentally killed his one true love. It was easier for him to believe that she was still alive and hating him than to accept her death."

Patrick rose to face Jeppsen.

There was no fight left in him. "Then what happened to her?" he asked. "Where is my mother?"

"No one knows for certain," Jeppsen said with a deep breath, "but I think we saw her tonight."

Sean's eyes grew wide. "The singing ghost? You think that–?"

Jeppsen nodded. "She wore a blue dress the night she was poisoned."

"But that means ... " Sean realized.

Patrick, agitated, paced back and forth. This was too much.

"No. No. I don't believe it. I *don't* believe in bloody ghosts," Patrick stated defiantly.

He paced some more, muttering. Then asked, "Did your master kill our so-called *father* as well?" Patrick spat the 'f' word out venomously.

"Nay! Of course not!" Jeppsen was taken aback by the accusation. "Master Thornbury learned his lesson and re-swallowed that bitter pill every moment he thought of your mother, which was very often, I'm sad to say. These days he would not so much as hurt a wee gnat. No, that awful deed Mister Berenger performed on himself. He was in the house behind the theater when it caught fire. Mister Berenger was drunk and fell asleep with a cigar, they supposed. I saw the smoke from the castle and pulled him out before he burned up, but I was too late, he weren't breathing."

"You tried to save him?" Sean asked quietly. "After all he had done?"

"Aye. That I did," Jeppsen nodded. "No one deserves to die like that."

Sean and Patrick stood silent. They exchanged a look that spoke volumes. They were no longer sure what to think about any of this.

But Jeppsen wasn't quite done. "That was when my master knew it was time to tell you both the truth, too many secrets had been held for too many years. Once that Mister Berenger was dead, my master had me seek you out and compel you to return home. He arranged for the train to abandon you outside our town so you couldn't possibly leave. He wished for one last performance in tribute to your mother. Then he was planning to tell you the truth and bequeath all that is rightfully yours, including his land and your titles, my *Lords*."

"I don't know about you, but after all this I need a bloody drink," Patrick exclaimed. Several hours had passed, the fire was low, and Carlisle was now resting comfortably. They were all nearly as spent as the evening.

Patrick rummaged through Sean's cupboard. "Don't you have any whiskey?"

"A *Lord* out of whiskey? Don't mock me," Sean was appalled. He reached behind him, without even bothering to look, and grabbed a nearly full bottle and tossed it to his brother. Patrick caught it neatly.

"Sorry, your Lordship. Would anyone else like some?" Patrick asked.

"I could use a wee dram," Father McLeary called out.

"Aye. Sounds well and good," McStargle agreed.

"So long as everyone else is," Sean acquiesced.

"Jeppsen?" Patrick asked.

"Aye, me Lord, if you'd please," Jeppsen replied with a slight bow.

"Don't *you* start," Patrick warned. Jeppsen grinned.

Patrick poured the whiskies and served them all around. Jeppsen checked Carlisle's pulse as Patrick handed him his glass.

"How is he?" Patrick asked.

"Stronger," Jeppsen said, pleased, as he took the glass.

"He'll probably out live the lot of us," Patrick grinned. He straightened the crumpled crown that Carlisle had insisted on wearing. "A toast!" he announced.

They raised their glasses in toast.

"To cabbages and kings ... " Patrick began.

"And new Lords on the wing," finished McStargle.

"To new Lords on the wing!" They toasted to their father, their friend, an honorable man or their master, whomever it fit best.

After they drank, Patrick went to fetch the bottle.

"By the way, brother," he said as he refilled their glasses. "I believe your young lady friend may be expecting a visit from you, to catch her up on the events of the evening."

"Surely I couldn't visit at this late hour?" Sean grinned.

"My fault there. I promised her you'd come by earlier. I'm sure she's still waiting. You probably shouldn't dawdle any longer."

"Then I shan't," Sean said, as he grabbed a scarf and coat. "Goodnight all!"

* * *

Fiona awoke to feel Sean lying beside her in her bed. She hadn't heard him enter her room, but his comforting weight on the mattress, and his body pressed up tight against her back made her feel warm and safe. The fire had died out, the room was black and still, but she could tell from his breathing that he was still awake.

"Why didn't you wake me? I've been waiting for you."

He didn't answer. Instead he slid his arm around her, brushing almost casually against her breast as he pulled her tighter against him. A tingle of heat surged through her as she succumbed to his deeper embrace. His breathing picked up pace as he began to slowly trail his hand up and down her side, so softly it nearly tickled her.

Earlier, before falling asleep, Fiona had been anxious for him to arrive so she could ask him about Carlisle and how he and Patrick were handling the truth about their father and mother. She also wanted to express her still lingering fear about how close to death they all came tonight—but that was all forgotten as he worked his hand lower down her side, along her upper thigh then across her stomach until his fingers finally found her.

Her breath escaped in a sudden gasp, and she arched her back to press tighter against his awakening body, her movements urging him to quicken his pace.

She moaned.

She was losing herself to his touch, all the fear and confusion from the enormity of the evening was surrendered in a simple wave of ecstasy from being alive at this very moment with the man she loved.

One hand sought her own breast as her other hand blindly reached behind her.

"Sean," she whispered, searching for him, but his hand caught hers, grabbing it a little too roughly as he suddenly stopped all his ministrations.

He joined her other hand in his and raising them both, he held them above her head.

She half fought his firm grip, not accustomed to being held helpless, wanting instead to pull *him* into her, onto her. Obviously he had other plans.

"How I love you," she sighed in surrender.

She felt him lean forward to kiss her, but when she tried to turn her head to meet him, his grip tightened again on her hands, jerking her back into a painful position. He was starting to hurt her, and she was about to say something, when he brushed her lips with his, then turned instead and kissed her on her cheek, whispering in her ear.

"Whore."

Fiona eyes opened in horrified realization.

"Oh my God, no!"

She rolled onto her back, trying frantically to throw him off, but his other free hand slammed hard into her stomach knocking the air out of her.

"I wouldn't move again. I might not be so gentle next time," Gavin whispered.

Fiona couldn't believe what was happening. She turned her face to scream, hoping someone would hear her. Just as she opened her mouth, a strongly scented rag suffocated her face. She could barely make out what Gavin was saying as she slipped into unconsciousness.

"My Fiona, it will all be over soon."

* * *

Fiona's door was ajar. Sean creaked it open and called softly: "Fiona? Are you still awake?"

The room was dark and had the instinctual feeling of emptiness. An unfamiliar feeling of dread seeped into him.

"Fiona!" he called out louder. No answer. He fumbled for the gas lantern and matches she kept on the dresser by the door and with shaking fingers he got the wick lit and the lantern blazed on.

He swung it around the room taking in the tossed up bed sheet, scattered clothing and absence of any soul, live or dead. He didn't know what he expected, but he breathed a sigh of relief in not discovering her lifeless form. His relief was short lived, however, when he noticed a note placed carefully on her pillow. He snatched it up and read it.

O' thou invisible spirit of wine, if thou hast no name to be known by, let us call thee devil.

What the bloody hell? It was written in a feminine, spidery hand, he assumed was Fiona's, but what did it mean? He reread it. It sounded like Shakespeare, but he couldn't identify the play. Even if it was, he still didn't get it.

Was she being playful? Coy? Enticing? No. None of that made sense for her or for this time of night. She really wasn't the mysterious type. So where was she?

He stood transfixed in the middle of her bedroom, studying the bed and the room for clues. None of Abigail's scattered clothes were lying about, so she obviously never made it to bed. Could she have come up and dragged Fiona off to celebrate? That was possible but then why the vague, mysterious note? And, although his mind was avoiding it, he did have to add that it was also somewhat sinister.

Still, Abigail was the best hope he had. He took one last look around and left the room.

* * *

Thunka. Thunka. Thunka.

The sound woke her up. The first thing Fiona realized, before opening her eyes, was the feel of a familiar thin cloth beneath her, barely cushioning a cold stone floor. She opened her eyes and tried to adjust to the near darkness.

Where am I?

She could barely sense someone moving restlessly in the dark around her.

Thunka. Thunka. Thunka.

Fiona took in the damp smell and dank air, the pounding *thunka thunka thunka* sound and suddenly she knew exactly where she was.

The noise was the generator thumping.

She was in the wine cellar, lying on her side on her tapestry, her hands tied painfully behind her back.

But why?

Then she remembered everything with a sickening sting of clarity. She gasped aloud.

Gavin was suddenly squatting beside her.

"You have returned to me," Gavin said, as he stared intently at her, like someone inspecting a particularly interesting insect.

"Gavin, what are you doing? Why are we here?"

"Waiting, my love, we are waiting."

He grabbed her suddenly. Fiona tried not to groan in pain as he yanked her up to a sitting position. His face was very close to hers, swollen and moonlike, his eyes brimmed with madness.

"I want you to see it happen with your own eyes; it is the only way."

Uncertain of his plan, she tried to remain calm and hold on to an edge of reason. She willed herself not to quiver in fear; she didn't want to give him the satisfaction, but she couldn't help it, she shuddered uncontrollably.

Gavin did indeed notice her shaking, but he did not think it was from fear. His hands intentionally lingered along her body as he reached down for the tapestry. He pulled it up and draped it around Fiona.

"That day in the Model T, huddled beneath that blanket, you remember?" he whispered into her ear.

Fiona nodded, swallowing the sick feeling his closeness caused.

"I think about that day all the time. You held my hand as we drove, laughing at Jeppsen's horrible singing. Then, after being frightened by the raccoon, you ran into my arms. That was the day I knew you finally felt the same love for me as I do for you."

"Gavin ... " Fiona said softly.

His eyes shifted to a far away place as he continued talking.

"I had waited for you for so long Fiona, so long. Then that day Jeppsen dropped us off, and you kissed me, we both knew how badly you wanted me."

His features hardened and his eyes burned with a sudden hatred.

"Then that bastard showed up and ruined it! Just like his son-of-a-bitch brother had ruined it so many times before!"

"Gavin, you're not remembering it right."

"I REMEMBER IT FINE!"

He took a deep breath.

"You wanted me that day, and he ruined it. I tried to kill him, he is such a drunk I figured he would drink anything."

He stared at the broken bottle on the cellar floor.

"I guess that was my first mistake. Never trust a *fooking* drunk to do the right thing."

He kicked the shattered bottle, scattering glass across the floor.

"My second mistake was leaving Patrick in the burning train car. I would have shot him, but Samuel borrowed my gun for that stupid party, so I had to improvise."

Fiona couldn't believe what she was hearing.

"And the sandbag?" she asked.

"A half-hearted attempt. My aim has always been terrible," he smiled at her. "Not tonight, though." He pulled out his revolver from his pocket and flashed it at Fiona.

Her blood ran cold.

"Gavin, why are doing this?"

"You are supposed to be *mine!*" he roared as he rose to his feet. "The moment you came into my town I knew you had come just for me. You looked down into the audience and smiled at me. Even you knew even then, although you needed time to fully realize it. But that was fine. True love is worth waiting for and I was prepared to wait.

"You silently begged me to join your troupe, so I did. You wanted me to be near you night after night and I was only too happy to comply.

"Aye, you sure do like to tease, Fiona, but I saw through your charade, as you withheld your love only to draw me nearer. When you pretended to be interested in Patrick, flirting with a man who obviously showed no interest back, that was to test my love, was it not?"

"But, Sean ... " He suddenly grabbed her by the jaw, forcing her to stare into his eyes. "That was not funny!"

He flung her backwards. Fiona knocked her head hard against the floor of the cellar. Stars danced before her eyes. She struggled to remain conscious. As she tried to force herself up to a sitting position, she felt a round piece of metal beneath her hands. She instinctively grasped it, running her fingers over its shape trying to determine what it was.

Gavin raged on.

"I hated him more each and every time he touched you! Every time he held you onstage, each time he ... *kissed you!*" he spat the words out.

He rushed over and grabbed her by the shoulders, shaking her.

"What were you trying to prove, Fiona? Don't you know you went too far? Don't you know that? *WHORE!*"

As much as she wanted to look away she kept her eyes fixed on Gavin.

"I–I don't know," she finally whispered.

Gavin let her go. "I think you do," he said in an ominously soft voice. He moved away from her, leaving the lantern by her as he flowed into the recessed darkness of the cellar, lost in some thought. She had no idea what his mind might invent, or what he might do in the shadows.

She turned the curved piece of metal in her hand, over and over. *What the hell is it?* She needed to keep him talking, if only to buy some time, besides, anything was better than his brooding silence.

"The poison wine tonight, did you have something to do with that?"

She heard Gavin freeze. He spoke from somewhere in the darkness.

"Aye, I brought it in for the last scene, the one where they were supposed to toast each other. Kill two birds with one stone, eh?"

He entered into the pool of light, his eyes flashing her with unmistakable madness.

"My stone missed. Instead, of two little dead birds, I have two fook'in live Lords to deal with. But, that's okay, I have another stone," he grinned.

"Gavin, you said we were waiting, what are waiting for?" she dared ask.

"Oh, didn't I tell you? We're waiting for Sean. He should be here any minute. You left him a clever note inviting him here."

"What?" she gasped.

"I should make you more presentable for our guest," he roughly stood her up on her feet. He yanked her chemise down, ripping it, exposing one bare shoulder. He ran his hand tenderly down her cheek.

"It's a new year, a new start for us both. Tonight you will be given a choice and if you chose correctly, God will smile down upon us both."

Fiona was barely listening. She suddenly realized why the object in her hand felt so familiar. She was holding the cracked mirror. A plan began to form in her mind.

"With Sean out of the way there will be no illusionary distractions, none of his evil charms mesmerizing you. You will desire me without hesitation, like you desired me earlier tonight when you welcomed me into your bed."

She half listened to his prattle as she desperately tried to get the latch open on the mirror. If she could get it open she might be able to grab a piece of the broken glass and slice through her ties. With free hands she could–Wait. If she could force him to throw her down to the floor again, and she held the mirror just right, the impact might force it open.

She knew what she had to do and what to say. It was a small chance, but she had no other. Of course she realized with a fear unlike she had ever experienced, that she had no idea how he might react. He could kill her on the spot. And he might regardless, but if she did nothing, Sean was sure to die.

She took a deep breath.

"Don't fool yourself, Gavin, I thought you were Sean. Although I should have known; his touch in bed is far superior to yours–"

His fist met her face with a sickening thud. Tears of pain filled her eyes as she flew back, but she made sure she landed on her back, concealing her hands. The compact hit the concrete, hard. It popped open!

"WHORE! DON'T YOU LIE TO ME! I KNOW YOU'RE LYING!"

Fiona swam through a moment of near unconsciousness as she grasped the open compact in her hands.

Gavin stood above her, hand raised to strike again, seething in anger.

She locked eyes with him, attempting to keep him at a distance through sheer will power, while behind her back she pulled a small shard of the broken glass out and sawed it against the rope.

"You want to know something ironic, Gavin," she grinned, as she sawed away, "that night you locked Sean in the basement, you also locked me in here with him. We spent that entire night together. Your little plan backfired, because that was the first time I discovered his touch and he mine ... "

She cut through the rope!

"But, believe me, that was not the only time we've lain together, and I have you to thank for that."

Gavin, enraged, lunged at her, but Fiona was able to dodge out of the way. She rolled away and scrambled to the wine rack just as Gavin was turning for her. Desperately, she grabbed the nearest bottle she could find and threw it with all her might at the generator.

Gavin raced toward her just as everything went black.

Blindly, she dodged him again, scrambling halfway across the cellar on her hands and knees. She heard Gavin crash into a wine rack. She would have to move fast to get to the tunnel. Silently she prayed that he wasn't aware of the tunnel and would instead head for the door and wait for her there.

She ran smack into the wall, stunned for the moment, but just for a moment. She regained her senses and ran her hands along the wall, searching for the breeze she had felt that night before. After a moment she found the opening.

She started for it, her heart racing, just as Gavin's arms closed around her waist.

She screamed for all she was worth, clawing and kicking at him as much as she could, but Gavin was too strong, his hold too overpowering. He dragged her across the cellar in the dark until he felt the generator with his foot. He viciously flung Fiona into the generator. She crashed into it, her head smashed into the metal and she crumbled to the floor, losing consciousness.

The sky had been clouding all night, and now a new storm was threatening. The flames from the enormous bonfire licked the sky, hissing the early snowflakes into steam as they fell. Sean noticed none of that. He was singularly focused on finding Abigail, or more importantly, Fiona.

Surprisingly, Abigail and Andrew were easy enough to spot in the crowd of couples in the céilidh dance. They were by far the rowdiest and most energetic. Sean gathered more than a handful of baleful looks when he burst into the circle of dancers and yanked Abigail out.

"Hey! Find your own lass!" Andrew protested, jokingly, as Sean drew Abigail further from all the noise and music.

Abigail was drunk. She stared up at Sean happily confused.

"Wanna dance?" she slurred. "I'm sure Drewy won't mind, and I know I won't." She batted her eyes in an attempt to be coquettish.

"Maybe later," Sean shook his head. He had no time for her silly games. "Have you seen Fiona? I'm trying to find her."

Abigail stared off into space trying hard to remember. By this time Andrew, who had grown tired of dancing alone, joined them.

"You looking for Fiona?" he asked.

"Yes! Have you seen her?" Sean nearly pounced on him.

Andrew took a couple of steps back.

"No. Not since she left the theater with Nicholas. They were walking toward the Piper. I assumed she was going to bed. Why? What's wrong?"

Before Sean could reply, Abigail interjected.

"Yes! She was going to bed! I tried to get her to come dance with me, it's New Years for goodness sakes, so I—"

"Was that the last time you saw her?" Sean interrupted.

The two of them nodded. They both looked uncertain if they should be worried.

"It's okay, nothing to worry about," Sean assured them. "You go rejoin the céilidh."

Sean noticed all the lights in the theater across the street suddenly go out. *The generator is down again,* he frowned. *I'll have to go down to the wine cellar and start it up, again. I don't have time for that—*

The lines from the note suddenly went through his mind.

'*O thou invisible spirit of wine, if thou hast no name to be known by, let us call thee devil.*'

The wine cellar? Is she waiting for me down there?

Sean took off in a sprint toward the dark theater.

As Fiona came to, she could hear Gavin pulling the starter cord on the generator, trying to start it. She could taste blood in her mouth, her blood. She was pretty certain that when the lights returned, he would kill her. She knew she would never see Sean again or any of her friends. She fought back her tears as she silently pleaded to God to stop Sean from coming to the cellar.

The generator began to sputter to life. She recognized the familiar gasping sound it made before it cranked up. Gavin was only a couple of pulls away.

Then she heard the cellar door start to creak open.

"No!" she cried, struggling to her feet. "Sean, run!"

Gavin was on her in an instant, as one hand brought her in close and the other slapped across her mouth, brutally silencing her.

The door creaked open further. She watched in horror as a blinding flash of bullets fired out of Gavin's gun. There was a briefest moment of silence before she heard the sickening thud of a body tumbling down the stairs.

She screamed through Gavin's hand, attempting to bite it in her rage, but he continued to hold her tight. He dragged her closer to the generator. With his free hand, Gavin yanked the starter cord one more time and the lights sputtered back to life.

Fiona gasped in surprise.

It wasn't Sean, but Patrick, who lain sprawled out at the bottom of the stairs, a pool of blood already starting to form.

"*Sweet Fee*, look what you made me do," Gavin said, not at all displeased. "Oh well. That's one bird down. One to go."

Sean raced through the theater doors into the pitch dark of the lobby. Damn! He should have brought a candle. Surely there was one around in the lobby, but where?

As he stood, momentarily paralyzed with indecision, he felt a chill in the air that raised the hackles on his neck.

The apparition in blue, pale and shimmering from her own light, appeared before him.

"Sean," she said softly. "Listen to me."

Sean was dumbstruck. The way she called his name. Her voice suddenly so familiar.

"*Mum?*" he managed to ask.

"Sean. Pay attention. Something bad is about to happen—" She suddenly dissipated, as from deep in the cellar, a shot rang out.

"Fiona!" he raced blindly toward the wine cellar, but he only got a couple of feet before he smashed into an unseen chair and tumbled to the floor. As he struggled back up to his feet, he heard the familiar ghostly voice.

"Wait!" she commanded.

He turned to find her hovering in front of him, just out of reach. Her hands were held out before her, barring him from going forward.

"What? Tell me what to do!" he cried, desperate to get moving. "She needs me!"

"It's not too late, but if you wish to save her. You must go the other way."

"What other way?" he pleaded, not understanding.

He felt a cold, soft hand on his cheek. "The passage, son."

Then the lights sputtered back on and Sean stood alone in the lobby.

The snow was falling heavier as he raced up the steep hill to the backside of the castle. He was near the crest, when he slipped on an icy patch and skidded part way down the frozen slope, scrapping his hands, and bashing his knee painfully against a stone.

"Damn it!" he cried, as he grabbed a tuft of scrubby brush and pulled himself to his feet. He limped back up the hill as fast as he could; his labored breath bursts of swear clouds in the icy air.

Finally, he made it up to the stables. He searched frantically for a lantern, not wishing to waste any more time, but knew he could navigate the dark passages that much faster with a light. He found one near Shadow's bench of tackle, and fortunately, there was a pack of matches alongside. It took five matches to get the lantern lit. He rushed toward the entrance to the secret passage.

Gavin kept his pistol trained on Patrick, who laid on his stomach in a silent, crumbled heap. He wasn't sure if Patrick was dead as *he* hadn't moved or made a sound since he was shot. He should be, he could have hardly miss at this range, Gavin reasoned, as he tried to decide what to do next. Should he waste another bullet just to be certain? Or should he save them for Sean? Hopefully Sean had found the note and was still coming. Patrick's interference was no big loss–he was planning on killing him no matter what–this was just not the way he had it planned. No matter, he was always good at improvisation. But where the fook was Sean? Surely, he wouldn't have sent Patrick instead?

"Uhhh ... " Patrick groaned, causing Gavin's trigger finger to tighten involuntarily in surprise, although not quite enough to fire.

"He's still alive!" Fiona exclaimed.

"Shut up!" Gavin snarled. He cautiously dragged her closer to Patrick, never wavering his deadly aim. He kicked Patrick, who groaned again.

"Please. Let me help him," Fiona pleaded.

"No. He'll be dead soon enough."

Gavin pulled her back a few feet away from Patrick, his eyes keeping watch of the doorway, expecting Sean, or anyone, to appear at any minute. Surely someone must have heard the shot.

"You said you'd give me a choice? Remember," Fiona interrupted his thoughts. "I'm ready to give you my answer."

"Which is?" he demanded, as he roughly grabbed her face with his gun hand and forced her to look at him. The hard steel barrel bruised her cheek as he searched her eyes for sincerity. She stared back at him in total frankness.

"You let me tend to Patrick and I will leave with you willingly tonight. I assume that is what you want, isn't it?" her voice laced with her bitter challenge.

Gavin's mind whirled. Was she acting or had she finally seen the light? He sensed a deceit, but at the same time he knew, he knew for certain, that deep inside she loved him as much as he loved her.

"Take care of him," he said releasing his grip on her. "Then we leave, my love."

As she dropped to her knees beside Patrick, she asked, "And Sean?"

"I'll take care of Sean."

Fiona didn't like the sound of that but she knew she had at least bought five minutes. She tried to think of some way out of this as she gently turned Patrick over, revealing a small, bloody gash in his right shoulder. It wasn't as bad as it first looked; the bullet had just grazed it, although it was bleeding quite a lot. His head had a huge lump from where it hit the stone floor, but fortunately that wasn't bleeding. Hopefully he didn't have a concussion, although he was definitely in for a hell of a headache tomorrow, if, she reminded herself with a gulp, any of them managed to survive this horrible night.

She had no intention of going anywhere with Gavin; she would rather he kill her; that much she knew resolutely.

She tore a small strip from her chemise for a bandage. She could *feel* Gavin's probing eyes staring intently at her exposed thigh. She made a crude bandage, but she didn't have enough material to make a proper compression bandage. Instead she pressed hard on the wound hoping to stem the flow of blood. Her thoughts flickered desperately to Sean.

Please don't come!

Patrick slowly regained consciousness. He stared up at Fiona's pale face with confused, fuzzy vision. "Mum?"

"Shhhh ... "

"What happened?"

"You've been shot," Gavin inserted, matter-of-factly, as he squatted down, face-to-face with Patrick, but at a careful distance. "By me," he added proudly. His eyes continued to dart towards the cellar entrance.

"Gavin?" Patrick asked, trying to focus on the blurry face in front of him.

"Yes. Me. Gavin. The one you snubbed as an actor and stole Fiona from. But now you are the one bleeding to death, and I am the one about to walk out of here with Fiona, who has confessed *her* love for *me*, and there's nothing you or anyone can do about it."

Patrick was having difficulty following this conversation. His head was swimming and he felt near to fainting with every breath.

"Where's my mum? She pushed me out of the way ... "

"Shhh ... " Fiona wiped his fevered brow with her cool hand, calming him.

"Your five minutes are up," Gavin announced, rising to his feet. "Looks like your boyfriend doesn't care enough about you. Pity. I was looking forward to saying a final goodbye to him."

Fiona stared up at him. "What about Patrick?"

"You've done all you can. He's on his own. Perhaps someone will find him before he bleeds to death."

"Just a few more minutes," Fiona pleaded. "The bleeding has almost stopped."

"NO!" Gavin screamed. "If you prefer to not let him take his chances I could put him out of his misery," he cocked the gun and aimed it at Patrick's temple.

Something moved at the top of the stairs. Gavin spun his gun around in an instant and blindly fired. There was nothing there.

"Seeing ghosts, Gavin?" Sean asked, stepping out from behind a wine rack, holding a dusty bottle in each hand.

Gavin, startled, turned to fire just as Sean flung one of the bottles at him. The bottle caught Gavin in the chest, knocking him back and deflecting his aim. The gun fired wildly into the wall.

Sean smashed the other bottle against the wine rack. He held the jagged bottleneck out like a makeshift knife. He rushed Gavin before he could regain his senses.

Gavin managed to pull the gun up just as Sean rammed into him, but it was knocked loose from his hand before he could pull the trigger, vanishing into a dark corner of the cellar.

Sean and Gavin grappled, punching and gouging at each other, before stumbling back and crashing into a wine rack, toppling it over. Wine and glass crashed all around them.

Fiona and Patrick watched helplessly.

Sean and Gavin continued to wrestle in the sticky sea of wine. Sean managed to slash Gavin across the cheek with his broken bottle, drawing blood from the huge gash. Gavin appeared not to notice as he punched Sean relentlessly in the face and shoulders.

A strange stream of blue light suddenly streaked out from the bullet hole in the wall, illuminating the fallen gun.

Fiona noticed it, and without pause, scrambled for the gun.

Gavin managed to find a broken plank from the shattered wine rack to deliver a nasty, bone-crunching blow to the side of Sean's head.

Sean stumbled back, reeling from the blow, the broken bottle falling free from his hand. He slipped on the spilled wine and crashed hard on his back. Gavin crawled over to him and raised the plank high above his head, a protruding fang-like nail gleaming in the pale light of the cellar.

"You fooking bastard! Dying is too good for you!" Gavin screamed. Spit flew from his frothing mouth, as he leaned back and with all his strength, swung his weapon down toward Sean's head.

BLAM!

A shot rang out, hitting Gavin in the back, the momentum of his swing offset by the impact of the bullet. He spun in place, the plank flying out of his hands, thudding against a far wall.

He faced Fiona with a look of total disbelief.

"Fiona? But I thought—"

"No!" BLAM! "No!" BLAM! "NO!" BLAM! Click. Click. Click.

Fiona's gun clicked empty. Gavin twisted in place, each shot jerking him like a manic marionette, until he fell grotesquely, and slammed to the floor, face-first, with a sickening splat.

Fiona held the empty gun firmly in both shaking hands, a look of shock frozen upon her pale face. Finally, she dropped the gun as if it were a red-hot poker.

"Nice shooting," Sean said, as he rose and went to her, limping painfully, his face and body streaked with blood and wine. She sank into his arms, sobbing uncontrollably.

"It's all over now, Fiona," he murmured as he held her tight. "It's all over."

The pale blue light from the wall caught his eye as he held her.

What is that light?

And as if reading his thoughts, it faded out until it was just a pinprick in the wall. Then was gone.

"Aye. A bit of mess down here."

It was Samuel, who had appeared at the top of the stairs and was taking in the whole confusing scene with the practiced eye of a seasoned soldier. McStargle and Nicholas were crowded behind him. They pushed past his hulking form to see what was going on.

"I thought I heard gunshot—oh my lord," Nicholas cried. "Patrick's been shot!" He and Miss McStargle hurried down to Patrick.

The next few minutes were chaos. Gavin's body was also noticed. He was pronounced dead by Samuel, who covered his body with the tapestry.

The others listened as Patrick, Sean and Fiona tried to explain what had happened, piecing it together as best they could.

None could understand what drove Gavin's tortured, misguided love to inflict such a tragedy.

As Patrick was helped away by Nicholas and McStargle, and Samuel was preparing to move Gavin's body, Sean remembered the mysterious light.

He went over to the wall and discovered the spot where it leaked from, a bullet hole. He poked his finger inside. There was some kind of hollow opening behind the rock wall.

"Sean, what are you doing?" Fiona asked, exhausted. "Please, can we just leave? I want out of this awful place." She looked down at the shroud-covered body of Gavin and shuddered.

"I saw some kind of strange light coming from this wall." Sean said, as he chipped away at the crumbling hole. "Come look. See here? There's a space behind this wall."

Fiona reluctantly came and stood behind him, unimpressed. "Yes, I see. It's a hole in the wall. Can we please go?"

"Let me see," Samuel insisted, striding over to where Sean had managed to enlarge the hole by a couple of inches. Samuel pulled Sean's hand away and held a lantern up to the hole in the wall. He touched it lightly with his fingers then suddenly yanked back his massive right fist and punched the wall. A large section crumbled away.

"He's right!" Samuel held the light to the hole so that they could all see inside.

Inside the wall, still clad in the blue costume dress she wore the night of the play, a drape of black cloth veiling her face, were the skeletal remains of Delia Berenger.

Fiona screamed, then fainted.

Epilogue

Fiona followed Sean toward the newly finished cottage behind the theater. She had pleaded with him for months to allow her a peek inside but had been turned down repeatedly.

"No one gets to see it before the bride and groom," he insisted firmly, as he and Samuel worked feverishly to complete it in time.

"But if it's meant to be a wedding gift from me as well, shouldn't I do something to help in some way?" Fiona had tried to reason with him.

Sean shook his head. "You'll only be in the way. Besides, I doubt you'd be able to keep it a secret."

Fiona stomped her feet in frustration, infuriated at his stubbornness and insults of her character, but she grudgingly admired his dedication and hard work—all to give her best friend the nicest gift ever.

Yet contrary to his allegation and despite all the opportunities she had, she had *not* blown the secret to Abigail. When Abigail asked her what Sean and Samuel were building, she had kept to the cover story that they were rebuilding their old family cottage in memory of their mother. While all this was going on, Patrick, Jeppsen, Nicholas, and Andrew were busy working on renovating the castle as a place for the others.

Fiona was very pleased that they had all decided to stay on. Carlisle, after he had recovered from that terrible night, had offered the troupe money to last a lifetime and lodging for as long they wanted it, making the choice to stay and run the theater a very easy one. Fiona was also thrilled to not have to choose again between being with someone she loved or following her muse. For now they all would remain.

And finally, on this sunny day before Abigail and Andrew's wedding, she was going to have a sneak peek at the wedding cottage. Everyone else was up at the castle attending to the last minute decorations and preparations for the wedding. It was going to be simply breathtaking, an elaborate wedding in a castle. She was so happy for Abigail and Andrew. And, she had to admit, a bit jealous, but she pushed that aside, so excited was she to see inside their new home.

Sean had finally consented to allow her to see inside, only, he insisted, because he thought that she might be able to offer some additional feminine touches and point out anything he may have left out. She had agreed, and despite his annoying, secretive behavior, wore a huge grin all the whole way up to the front door.

"It's not much, but it should do," he said, suddenly modest, as he opened the door.

Fiona rushed inside and caught her breath.

The first thing she saw was the living room with an overly stuffed sofa sitting before a blazing fire. She took in everything at once, impressed that Sean and Samuel had seen to almost every detail, from the reading nook off to one side, muted peach colored walls, lace curtains and an arched entrance leading into a lovely and quaint kitchen.

"Well?" Sean asked.

Fiona said nothing as she walked into the kitchen.

The sink had a window just above it that gave it morning sun and a wide view to a plot of land that she thought would make a perfect vegetable garden. She pulled open one drawer and was shocked to see a complete set of sterling silverware inside it. She held up an elaborately carved steak knife. It caught the light brilliantly. She recognized the Thornbury family crest imbedded on it. A stab of jealousy shot through her.

"You didn't have to fill the entire kitchen for them," she stated flatly, replacing the knife.

Sean shrugged his reply, missing her tone completely.

"I am a Lord now."

"Yes you are," she said as she none-to-gently pushed past him to explore the master bedroom.

It was just next to the living room and she wasn't surprised to see it fully stocked with satin sheets and lush blankets. The choice of fabric made the room seem to glow. She ran her hands across the bed, having no other choice but to touch it.

She walked past him again to the stairs to the second level attic where there were two more fully furnished bedrooms. From the size of the furniture and the small chest of drawers, they were obviously meant for children. She traced her hand along the fine carved wood railing as she came back down the stairs.

Sean waited at the bottom of the stairs, watching her expectantly.

"Well, what did I miss?"

She started to say something churlish, but at that moment she realized that her jealousy was childish. Here was a man who loved her madly and had done all this for her best friend. How could she be so petty?

"You don't need my help at all. It's all so lovely." She hugged him. "Abigail will be absolutely thrilled."

She noticed the small rug near the fireplace and smiled.

"Can't you just see a wee one playing in front of the fire?"

"Aye, that I can."

"And I bet Christmas morning's will be a stunning sight, with stockings on the mantel and holly and a tree. The smell of roasted turkey and Christmas pudding from the kitchen ... "

"I can smell it already," he replied.

Fiona flopped down on the sofa with a contented sigh. "Did Miss McStargle help you pick all this out?" she asked, running her hand over the quilted blanket that lay across the arm.

"She actually made most of it, and believe me she doesn't come cheap."

Fiona laughed. "I bet she doesn't." She looked around the room appraisingly.

"It's simply perfect," she said, then reclined, long ways on the sofa, soaking in the heat from the fireplace. "You'll have to come over early tomorrow and start another fire, it makes everything so comfortable. It'll be nice for them to come home to."

"Aye, that's a good idea."

"Maybe some flowers in the kitchen to make it feel like home right away. And a wireless over there by the reading nook, for cold late nights, and I didn't see a cradle in the child's room. Samuel can make one and–"

"Slow down, I thought you said it was perfect."

"You can always add to perfection," she smirked, then rose. "And I should take another look at the kitchen. Abigail is brilliant in the kitchen, I want to make sure that she has everything she needs."

"I'm sure everything's there, seeing as she picked it all out."

Fiona stopped in her tracks.

"Sean Berenger-Thornbury, you didn't! You can't surprise someone with something that *they* picked out!"

Sean knew he blew it.

"I know," he faltered. "I simply asked her–"

"No, you don't *know*! I know you; you're the one that can't keep a secret. If you asked her *anything*, then she probably suspects *everything*!"

"Fiona ... "

"I can't believe you! You should have asked me! I mean I *am* her best friend! I would have picked everything out and set it up for–"

He grabbed her suddenly and pulled her tight toward him.

"Then how could I have surprised you?"

Fiona stopped, not sure what she was hearing. "What?"

"It's for you Fiona. I, well we, built this for you. For us."

She gasped. "You mean?"

"I wanted to do this right, Fee. I wanted to give you a place to call home."

He paused, but when she didn't respond he continued.

"I wanted to give you both of your worlds. The theater is in front and you can plant whatever your heart desires in the field behind us. You can have a farm or a garden, or both. If you want milk cows, I'll buy you milk cows. I just want you to live here with me. Forever."

Fiona was stunned. "Wh-where are Abigail and Andrew going to stay?"

"In the castle. Andrew loves the castle. Carlisle is having a room built up special for them."

Fiona couldn't believe her ears. All this had been going on behind her back. What else has she missed?

"How long have Andrew and Abigail known about this?"

"Since their wedding."

"Their *what?*"

Sean threw up his hands in defense.

"Don't go getting mad at me, I just built you a bloody house. Andrew and Abigail got married in a private ceremony a few days after they learned she was pregnant."

"She's pregnant?" her voice rose two pitches higher. "Why didn't she tell me? She got married without me? How could she?"

"It would have blown the surprise, wouldn't it?" Sean smiled lamely. "And seeing as how she was pregnant, they really didn't have a choice ... "

Fiona fumed. This was too much to take in all at once.

"What surprise? What are you talking about?"

"You know, the secret wedding."

"What secret wedding?"

Sean smiled weakly. "Ours."

"*Ours?*" she said in disbelief. "What! Are *you* planning on marrying *me* tomorrow?"

"Er ... yes. Why are you yelling?"

"I'M NOT YELLING!" she yelled.

"Aye, I get it, I should have asked you. You're right there. More fool me," Sean admitted, backing up a few steps.

"Damn right, you should have asked me!" She flung her hands in the air. "Go ahead then!"

"You want me to ask you now?" he asked meekly.

"Yes! Right bloody now!" she insisted.

He bent down timidly on one knee.

"Don't bother doing that now! I know what you're going to ask." She shook her head in exasperation. He straightened, not sure how to proceed.

"Right, then ... so, Fiona—"

"Yes!" she cut him off.

"Is that a yes you will marry me tomorrow, or a yes to get on with it?"

She just glared at him.

"Why don't I ask you after you've calmed down a wee bit?"

She took a deep breath. "I am calm. I just found out that my best friend is pregnant and is secretly married, and I was the only one not invited, and the cottage that was built for her is actually for me, and I am—*surprise!*—the last one to know that *I* am getting married tomorrow. Why wouldn't I be calm?"

Sean paused. "Then you are going to marry me?"

"I didn't say that!"

"Yes you did. You said you were getting married tomorrow."

"I ... " she paused, tears forming. "Of course I am. I love you, you stupid, infuriating, silly man." She waved her arm around to indicate the cottage. "It's beautiful, all of it. Everything here is wonderful. Earlier, as I was walking around wishing it was mine, I was so jealous, and now ... "

She rushed into Sean's arms, tears falling down her face. "It's perfect."

Sean hugged her back tightly, relieved. "Except, of course," he couldn't help but add with a grin, "it needs some flowers, a wireless ... "

"Oh, just kiss me, Sean!"

"Aye. That I can do."

They kissed passionately and then he gathered her in his arms and carried her to the sofa in front of the fireplace. He set her gently into the cushions before moving beside her. She undid his shirt and threw it aside. She moved to kiss his chest when Sean pulled her face back up to his.

"Marry me, Fiona?"

"I already said I would."

"Oh, aye. I must have missed that through all the shouting," he smiled.

She pressed her fingers to his lips and he got the message. He made love to her then—warmly, gently, savoring every moment.

After, as Fiona lay in Sean's arms gazing into the embers, she knew for certain that the fire Sean had kindled inside her heart would never die out.

— Curtain fall —

LeeAnne Hansen was born in Paris, grew up in Oklahoma and now lives in sunny southern California with her husband and cats. She enjoys writing, acting and playing bass guitar. She can be seen gracing the stage in various theaters or even directing. She is a graduate of the American Music and Dramatic Academy in New York City and has studied art and astronomy. She also thoroughly enjoys long walks on the beach and dark and stormy nights.

For more info or to contact me please visit:

LeeAnneHansenbooks.com

* * *

Turn the page for a preview of my novel set in Mississippi in the 1940's. It's chock-filled with spooky happenings, mysteries and romance.

Yonder

A Southern Haunting — Book 1

"The perfect book to make you want to pour a sweet tea and be swept away!" —Elisa Lords

A Series Of Miserable Birthdays

10th Birthday, 1925

Isabel Jones rounded the corner of the foyer and flew into the sitting room. She would only have a couple of seconds to hide. She scrambled for the first hiding place she saw: an over-stuffed pink sofa.

She lay flat to watch for movement from beneath the couch as she waited quietly, listening to the squeals of the other children being found and the steady thumping of their feet as they ran from her brother, Doug, who was 'it'. She heard her best friend Samantha yelling from the hallway, "No fair!"

She smiled. Her brother would never think to look in the sitting room; he was far too dumb! There was also the *tiny* detail that the room was off limits to children, but it was her tenth birthday, and she was sure she could break the rule today. Isabel didn't even understand the rule; it was just a room with a fireplace and a couple of chairs and sofas for receiving guests. No one ever used it. Mama had explained that children ruin nice things, but Isabel didn't see anything particularly nice in the room.

Thump Thump Thump

She heard the sound of approaching footsteps. She took a deep breath and bit her bottom lip in anticipation of flinging herself up and running from her brother's grasp to another hiding place. She wished that it was Charles who was 'it'. Then she wouldn't have minded being caught.

Thump Thump Thump!

He was getting closer now. She was bracing herself for a mad chase when she caught movement in the corner of her eye;

two little shoes stopped still. Sitting up, she peeked around the sofa. A small, pale, frightened boy stood in the middle of the room. He appeared no more than five. Although she did not recognize him, he was wearing party clothes, but he was not hiding, and he would surely give her away!

"Psst!" she whispered, "over here."

The little boy turned to her. His brown hair was all over the place and his light blue eyes were swollen and puffy. He appeared lost and upset. He remained frozen in place.

"Over here. You can hide over here," Isabel whispered again, a plan quickly forming in her mind. If her brother found her, she would simply push the boy into her brother as an obstacle while she raced past to find another hiding place before he could think twice to tag her.

The little boy stared right through her. He broke into a sob, "I can't find my mom!"

"Shhh! You'll give us away. Come, hide with me and I promise I will take you to your mom."

His sobs softened.

"What's your name?"

"E–Eli," he said uncertainly, as if not used to saying his name aloud.

"I'm Isabel," she smiled. "Nice to meet you, Eli."

"It's dark," he whispered.

"No Eli, it not that dark back here. Come here, I will show you."

THUMP THUMP THUMP

The footsteps were heavier now, and Isabel knew her brother or one of his friends was close.

"Eli, you have to hurry and hide. You don't want to be it. He is almost here." She lay back down to better conceal herself.

Eli sniffled and Isabel popped back up to look. He still had not moved. She could see him standing in the middle of the room, looking more frightened than ever. He was definitely going to give her hiding place away and ruin her reign as hide-and-seek champion, the title she had just bestowed upon herself minutes earlier.

"Just be real quiet and stand still and he'll go away," she whispered.

An odd chill filled the room and static, like the air just before lightning, made the hairs on Isabel's arm rise. Part of her wanted to grab Eli's hand and tear out of the room, and the other wanted to stay put and hide deeper from whatever was coming. She couldn't explain it, but an unknown terror had seized her. She had never felt this way before. Shaking violently, she sprang out from behind the couch and made a mad dash toward Eli.

THUMP! THUMP! THUMP!

"Mama!" he cried out over the approaching footsteps.

"Come on!" she yelled, grabbing Eli's hand to pull him towards the door, but Eli remained frozen in place. He stood with a resistance uncommon to someone his age, eyes pleading with a deep agelessness that chilled her.

"Find me." Isabel watched in horror as the child she was holding onto faded in front of her!

She screamed and ran from the room, sobbing for her mama just as Eli had, right into the arms of her brother's best friend, Charles.

14th Birthday, 1929

Isabel Jones watched her foot skim the surface of the lake and imagined once more throwing herself off the swing and sailing free for a few precious moments before plunging into the water that she had been staring angrily at for the last twenty minutes. She pictured herself sinking to the bottom, surrounded by the many folds of her lavender dress sweeping around her like paint gliding off a brush put to water, her long brown hair branching out and pulsating with the movement of the lake. She would hit the bottom and just sit there, breathing in water like air until she was covered in silt and moss.

The story of her short, tragic life would become a tale little girls would whisper to each other late at night: "On her fourteenth birthday she asked for her first kiss and was turned down by the only boy she knew she could ever love, so she went to Jones Lake and cried so hard that she filled the lake with her tears; then she drowned herself in them.

"And to this day, her lonely soul cries from the bottom of the lake, searching for the love that will never come. Her endless tears are a promise that the lake will never again run dry. And that's why you should never swim there unless you want to join her."

Isabel watched the tears that rolled down her face disappear into the water, certain that she would be known forever as 'the girl who was never kissed.' It should be easy enough to throw oneself into the water and drown, she realized. All she had to do was not breathe. Her brother once held his breath in protest to eating Brussels sprouts and passed out, so she could do the same thing. She could simply hold her breath while she swung high over the lake, then, just as she was passing out, leap off the swing and slip down into the murky depths forever. She decided to give it a try.

She inhaled deeply, held her breath and started to swing. Her face was just beginning to turn red when she had a thought. *Mother will kill me if anything happens to this dress.* She exhaled loudly. She would have to remove it, but then she would no longer be the tragic, beautiful lady in the lake: she would be the half-dressed girl found in her unmentionables. She wasn't sure she liked the vision of her spending eternity in her unmentionables. Petulant, she sucked in air again and pulled her legs back with aggression to rise higher into the air. She dared herself not to breathe.

Isabel had dreamt of this birthday for weeks. She had had a crush on Charles Browman even before she fled into his protective arms after what she secretly referred to as the 'Eli event', but it was at that exact moment, when Charles held her as she cried and explained to him what she had seen in the forbidden room, that she truly fell in love. He didn't say she was being foolish or childish; he just did his best to soothe her. Although only two years older, he was so mature and caring.

Charles had been one of her brother's best friends for as long as she could remember, and she had grown up tagging along on all their adventures. Every time Doug would tease her or fight with her, Charles would come to her rescue. His was the voice of reason telling Doug that it did no harm to have his sister follow them around. When Isabel finally decided that fourteen was the age that a woman should have her first kiss, she knew Charles was the one to give it to her. He was cute and nice and she deserved it because, after all, it was her birthday.

After Isabel had blown out her candles, (blushing with her secret wish of her first kiss with Charles) and all the kids had scattered, she sought him out. He was standing alone in the shade of a large willow tree. She slipped between the dangling branches (thrilled at the romantic setting) and surprised Charles. She twirled in place, her birthday dress billowing out around her the way the lady's do it in the picture shows. She asked him what he thought of her purple dress. Charles, looking awkward, laughed and said that she looked like an overstuffed plum from the waist down. She hid her hurt with a small laugh, and then moved in closer and declared that it was her birthday and he was to kiss her. Charles backed away and tripped over a tree root. He hit the ground hard. His blue eyes peered up through disheveled blond hair as his face reddened in embarrassment.

"Adults don't kiss little girls!" he sputtered, then scrambled to his feet and ran off.

That's when Isabel fled to the lake.

As she continued to swing over the lake, she realized that she didn't believe that being sixteen made you an adult. Her own brother certainly didn't act like one, and especially not stupid Benjamin. Charles just simply didn't want to kiss her.

Isabel now knew that life could begin and end in one single day. She had nothing to look forward to but being an old maid for the rest of her life. Instead of drowning in the lake, she would die of loneliness and spend eternity haunting her parents' mansion. She would drift down the halls moaning about lost love, and every spring she would stalk the gardens, destroying any flowers she came across, leaving only broken stems and petals strewn across the lawn like colorful tears.

She finally released her breath with a huge, angry sigh. She couldn't even die properly. Defeated, she continued to swing joylessly over the stagnant lake. Then she had an inspired thought: In a gesture to this loveless world, and to Charles in particular, she would drop the beautiful dragonfly pin Charles' family had given her for her birthday into the water. She pulled the pin from her hair, allowing her curls to tumble free in the slight breeze.

She held the pin and regarded it. It was beautiful. It would be shame to lose it … but she must go through with her grand gesture.

The water here was too shallow. For best effect she needed to go out to the end of the dock and drop it in there so that it would sink into the deepest, coldest part of the lake. She slowed herself until she could hop off the swing onto the small hill beneath the huge oak tree where the swing was tied.

She made her way to the dock through some overgrown weeds. The weight of the Mississippi heat pushed down on her as she moved, and the hiss of the bugs seemed to play her a dirge as she made her solemn procession to the end of the dock. Her reflection revealed that her hair had gone mad. The ever-present humidity had caused her naturally wavy hair to go completely out of control. Regardless, she could never again wear that pin.

Holding the pin over the water, and in an overly dramatic voice, she incanted to her reflection: "To my broken soul that now resides at the bottom of this lake. May your waters, like my tears, never dry." She dropped the pin onto her reflection. She watched as her face dissolved into ripples, echoing away, while the shiny pin caught flashes of sunlight as it sank into darkness.

She gasped when she saw a pale, white face peering up at her from the depths. It was the same small boy she had seen on her tenth birthday. His hands were reaching up to her, beckoning . . .

"I hope your soul is worth it. That looked expensive," came a voice behind her.

Isabel whirled around to find Benjamin Caster, her brother's other best friend and their neighbor, on the dock.

"Dang it, Benjamin! Don't do that!" she cried.

"Do what?" he asked.

"Sneak up on someone like that! I could have fallen in the lake," Isabel shivered from the thought. She peered back down at the water, but it was now void of any ghostly children.

"I didn't sneak. I walked down the dock, plain as day."

"What do you want anyway?"

"Your brother and I have been looking for you for the better part of an hour, Izzy. You shouldn't run away from your own party." His brown eyes scolded, but his wry smile softened the effect.

She was immune to his smile. "Maybe I just want to be alone for my birthday!" she snapped. "It's my birthday and I can do whatever I want!" She plopped down on the dock with a loud and overly dramatic sigh.

"Charles told us what happened."

Isabel could feel her eyes start to well up with tears. "I bet he did."

"He didn't mean it when he said you looked like an overstuffed plum."

"That's not why I ran off!"

Benjamin sat beside her. "What else did Charles do?"

"None of your business!"

"Tell me."

Isabel stared at him. Benjamin normally teased her about everything under the sun; why was he being nice now? It wasn't like him. "My birthday is simply ruined!" She flung her hands into the air. "Completely, forever ruined!"

"Now Izzy, you just need to settle down. You're all riled up over nothing. Your birthday is not ruined. Your mama is gonna be awful mad if you stay away from the party much longer."

Isabel broke into sobs. She hadn't meant to cry in front of Benjamin, but she was finding that being a woman was harder than she had thought.

Benjamin, unsure what to do, patted her gently on the shoulder to calm her. He struggled for something to say, but nothing came out.

"He didn't want to kiss me!" she bawled. "I asked him to, and he said no!"

Benjamin's eyes widened with surprise. "He didn't tell us that part."

"Why should he?" Isabel snapped. "He could care less! He told me '*adults* don't kiss little girls.' And it was even my birthday wish when I blew out the candles!"

"I ... I'm sure he didn't mean it. You're just ... you're Doug's sister. He didn't know what to do," Benjamin tried to explain. "Doug said he would kill us if we ever hurt you, and I don't know if that was what he meant, but–"

"It was just a dumb little kiss!"

Benjamin was wishing that Doug had found his sister. He had no clue how to deal with this. "Your Mama said it was time to open the rest of your gifts, Izz. Don't you want to do that? Why don't you dry your eyes and come back to your party."

Isabel crossed her arms, "No sir! I am just fine right here, thank you very much!" Her eyes filled with tears again. "I can't face Charles now!"

"You don't have to. He went home."

Now the tears really came. Benjamin regarded her helplessly. He especially didn't know how to handle a crying girl.

"If it helps, I don't think you look like an overstuffed plum," he offered.

Isabel's tears slowed as she looked at him in disbelief. Benjamin had been Doug's shadow growing up. Whenever her brother poked fun at her, Benjamin always added onto it. She could never remember Benjamin complimenting her without a backhanded comment to follow.

"It doesn't, but thank you," she replied.

He stood and reached his hand down to her. "Come on, Izz, let's go open your presents." He ran his other hand through his dark brown hair, swiping away a strand that got in his eyes. Benjamin had hoped presents would get her to stop crying. After all, girls liked gifts, at least his mother had always told him, 'The way to a woman's heart is with a lovely gift of value.'

Isabel ignored his hand and went back to staring mournfully into the water.

"Izzy, stop it right now. Come on and get on up."

"No. You go back to the party. At least someone will enjoy my birthday!"

Benjamin came up behind her. He put both his arms around her and yanked her up on her feet. He had had enough of trying to get her to come on her own. "Come on. You are done crying now, you hear me?" He began dragging her away from the end of the dock.

"Benjamin, stop it! Let me go! I want to be alone!" she cried, flinging her arms wildly in all directions, trying to free herself from his grip. "I will not go back there!"

"Your mama is going to be awful mad if you don't come right now!"

Isabel stomped on his foot as hard as she could. She broke free of his hold and ran, but he was right behind her. He caught her again and spun her around.

"Benjamin, no! Let me–"

Benjamin brought her to his mouth in a flash. She was being kissed! Isabel was stunned motionless by the surprise of her first kiss. The touch of his warm, gentle lips on hers made her mind reel. Benjamin Caster was kissing her!

She stood frozen, unsure how to react. She *had* wanted her first kiss to be with Charles, but Benjamin was cute and he *was* the one kissing her now. She was also surprised to learn that what a kiss felt like: a soft meeting of lips on lips. She began to wonder if she should touch his face as she had seen some couples do. She felt awkward, and yet she could feel a blush starting to spread around her face. She wondered if the blush meant that Benjamin was a good kisser; she didn't know how to judge.

Without warning, Benjamin grabbed her wrist and began dragging her down the dock. "Now you can stop crying and come back to your party."

Realization hit, and she dug her heels into the dock. "Stop!"

"What is it now, Izzy?" he whirled around to her. "You gonna cry because you want your hair pin back?"

"Did you kiss me so I would stop crying?" she asked.

"Yes, and you did. So let's get–"

He was cut off by a sharp slap across his face.

"Ouch! Izz, you said you wanted to be kissed," he stammered in surprise. He *had* thought that the kiss had gone rather well. After all, he *had* kissed Eve Lindsey just last year after walking her home from Sunday school, and Eve *had* informed him that he should make a career of kissing her, and he *had* considered Eve's suggestion with great thought and pride, so he was completely confused as to why Isabel was now hitting him. But he didn't have to wait long for the truth to come out.

"By Charles! *Charl*es was supposed to kiss me! You! You have ruined everything! I wanted it to be Charles who gave me my first kiss! My true love!" Tears streamed down her face again.

"Charles? You love Charles? Arrogant rich boy Charles?" He laughed.

Isabel slapped him again, but this time Benjamin responded by pushing her away from him. He hadn't meant to send her off the dock into the water; all he had wanted was for her to stop hitting him. He watched in great horror as Isabel, in her puffy lavender dress, fell backwards into the water, tears and all.

If her birthday had not been ruined already, it was now.

(to be continued)

Made in the USA
San Bernardino, CA
05 October 2016